Secrets
in the
Regency
BALLROOM

Joanna Fulford

Mills & Boon, an imprint of Harlequin (UK) Limited,
Eton House, 18-24 Paradise Road, Richmond, Surrey TW9 1SR

SECRETS IN THE REGENCY BALLROOM
© Harlequin Enterprises II B.V./S.à.r.l 2014

The Wayward Governess © Joanna Fulford 2009
His Counterfeit Condesa © Joanna Fulford 2011

ISBN: 978 0 263 90681 3

052-0314

Harlequin (UK) policy is to use papers that are natural, renewable and recyclable products and made from wood grown in sustainable forests. The logging and manufacturing processes conform to the legal environmental regulations of the country of origin.

Printed and bound
by CPI Group (UK) Ltd, Croydon, CR0 4YY

Joanna Fulford is a compulsive scribbler, with a passion for literature and history, both of which she has studied to postgraduate level. Other countries and cultures have always exerted a fascination and she has traveled widely, living and working abroad for many years. However, her roots are in England and are now firmly established in the Peak District, where she lives with her husband, Brian. When not pressing a hot keyboard she likes to be out on the hills, either walking or on horseback. However, these days equestrian activity is confined to sedate hacking rather than riding at high speed towards solid obstacles.

The Wayward Governess was a finalist in the Romantic Novelists' Association's Pure Passion awards, 2011.

In The Regency Ballroom Collection

Scandal in the Regency Ballroom – Louise Allen
April 2013

Innocent in the Regency Ballroom – Christine Merrill
May 2013

Wicked in the Regency Ballroom – Margaret McPhee
June 2013

Cinderella in the Regency Ballroom – Deb Marlowe
July 2013

Rogue in the Regency Ballroom – Helen Dickson
August 2013

Debutante in the Regency Ballroom – Anne Herries
September 2013

Rumours in the Regency Ballroom – Diane Gaston
October 2013

Rake in the Regency Ballroom – Bronwyn Scott
November 2013

Mistress in the Regency Ballroom – Juliet Landon
December 2013

Courtship in the Regency Ballroom – Annie Burrows
January 2014

Scoundrel in the Regency Ballroom – Marguerite Kaye
February 2014

Secrets in the Regency Ballroom – Joanna Fulford
March 2014

The Wayward Governess

To Vee Leighton for her insight and encouragement
throughout the writing of this book

Chapter One

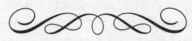

'Gartside! Alight here for Gartside!'

The guard's voice roused Claire from her doze. Feeling startled and disorientated, she looked about her and realised that the coach had stopped. She had no recollection of the last ten miles of the journey to Yorkshire and had no idea what hour it might be. At a guess it was some time in the midafternoon. Her cramped limbs felt as though they had been travelling for ever, though in reality it was three days. For more reasons than one it would be a relief to escape from the lumbering vehicle. Further reflection was denied her as the door opened.

'This is where you get down, miss.'

She nodded and, under the curious eyes of the remaining passengers, retrieved her valise and descended onto the street in front of a small and lowly inn.

'Can you tell me how far it is to Helmshaw?' she asked. 'And in which direction it lies?'

The guard jerked his head toward the far end of the street. 'Five miles. That way.'

'Thank you.'

After a grunted acknowledgement he closed the door of the coach and climbed back onto the box. Then the driver cracked his whip and the coach moved forwards. Watching it depart, Claire swallowed hard, for with it went every connection with her past life. Involuntarily her hand tightened round the handle of her bag. The latter contained all her worldly possessions, or all she had been able to carry when she left, apart from the last few shillings in her reticule. The rest of her small stock of money had been spent on the coach fare and the necessary board and lodging on her journey. Her last meal had been a frugal breakfast at dawn and she was hungry now, but the inn looked dingy and unprepossessing and she felt loath to enter it. Instead she hefted the valise and set off along the street in the direction the guard had indicated earlier.

It soon became clear that Gartside was not much of a place, being essentially a long street with houses on either side, and a few small shops. As she walked she received curious stares from the passers-by but no one spoke. A few ragged children watched from an open doorway. A little way ahead a small group of men loitered outside a tavern. Uncomfortably aware of being a stranger Claire hurried on, wanting to be gone. She hoped that Helmshaw would prove more congenial, but a five-mile walk lay between her and it. Massing clouds threatened rain. Would it hold off until she reached her destination? And when she got there, what would be her welcome? She hadn't set eyes on Ellen Greystoke in seven years, and nor had there been any correspondence between them apart from that one letter, written to her aunt's dictation, not long after Claire had removed there. Seven years. Would her old governess remember her? Would she still be at the same address? What if Miss Greystoke had moved on? Claire shivered, unwilling to contemplate the possibility. She had nowhere else to go, no money and no immediate prospect of earning any. Moreover, there was always the chance that her uncle would discover where she had gone.

For the past three days it had been her constant dread. Each time a faster vehicle had passed the public coach her heart lurched lest it should be he. Every feeling shrank from the scene that must surely follow, for he would not hesitate to compel her return. After that she would be lost. She had no illusions about her ability to resist her uncle's will: those had been beaten out of her long since. His maxim was: *Spare the rod and spoil the child*, a policy he had upheld with the utmost rigour. He would have her submission all right, and would use any means to get it.

At the thought of what that submission meant her stomach churned. Within the week she would become Lady Mortimer, married against her will to a man old enough to be her father, a portly, balding baronet with a lascivious gaze that made her flesh crawl. The memory of his proposal was still horribly vivid. She had been left alone with him, an occurrence that had set warning bells ringing immediately. Her aunt and uncle were usually sticklers for propriety. After a few minutes of stilted conversation Sir Charles had seized her hand, declaring his passion in the most ardent terms. Repelled by the words and the feel of his hot, damp palms she had tried to break free, only to find herself tipped backwards onto the sofa cushions. Claire swallowed hard. Almost she could still feel his paunch pressing her down, could smell the oily sweetness of hair pomade and fetid breath on her face as he tried to kiss her. Somehow she had got a hand free and struck him. Taken aback he had slackened his hold, allowing her to struggle free of that noxious embrace and run, knowing she'd rather be dead than married to such a man. How her refusal had been represented to her uncle afterwards she could only guess, but his anger was plain.

'You stupid, ungrateful girl! Who do you think you are to be refusing such an offer? Do you imagine you will ever get another as good?'

All her protestations had counted for nothing. She could see her uncle's cold and furious face.

'You have until tomorrow morning to change your mind or I'll know the reason why. By the time I've finished with you, my girl, you'll be only too glad to marry Sir Charles, believe me.'

She had believed him, knowing full well it was no idle threat, and so she had run away the same night.

'Now there's a fancy bit of muslin.'

'Aye, I wouldn't mind ten minutes behind the tavern with her.'

The voices jolted Claire from her thoughts and, as their lewd import dawned, she reddened, recognising the group of loafers she had seen before. From their dress they were of the labouring class, but dirtier and more unkempt than was usual. Uncomfortably aware of their close scrutiny Claire kept walking, determined to ignore them, but as she drew nigh the group one of them stepped in front of her blocking the way. When she tried to go round him he sidestepped too, blocking the path again. He looked to be in his early twenties. Taller than her by several inches and sturdily built, he was dressed like the others in a brown drab coat and breeches. A soiled green neckcloth was carelessly tied about his throat. Lank fair hair straggled beneath a greasy cap and framed a narrow unshaven face with a thin-lipped mouth and cold blue eyes. These were now appraising her, missing no detail of her appearance from her straw bonnet to the dark blue pelisse and sprigged muslin frock. Although she had dressed as plainly as she could to avoid attracting attention, there was no mistaking the fine quality and cut of her garments.

'Can you spare a coin, miss?'

'I'm sorry, no.'

'Just a shilling, miss.'

'I have none to spare.'

'I find that hard to believe, a fine young lady like yourself.'

'Believe what you like.'

She made to step round him again, but again he prevented it.

'Suppose I take a look for myself.'

Before she could anticipate it he grabbed her reticule. Claire tried to snatch it back, but he held on. His four companions gathered round, grinning. Seeing herself surrounded she fought panic, knowing instinctively it would be a mistake to show fear. He shook the reticule and heard the chink of coins. Her last few shillings!

'Sounds like money to me,' he remarked with a wink to the general audience.

'Give that back.'

He grinned. 'What if I don't, eh?'

Claire glared at her tormentor. She had not risked so much and come all this way merely to fall victim to another bully. Resentment welled up, fuelling her anger, and without warning she lashed out, dealing him a ringing crack across the cheek.

'Give it back, you oaf!'

In sheer surprise he let go of the reticule while his

companions drew audible breaths and looked on in delighted anticipation. Claire lifted her chin.

'Get out of my way!'

She would have pushed past, but he recovered and seized her arm in a painful grip.

'You'll pay for that, you little bitch.'

Glaring up at him, she forced herself to meet the cold blue eyes.

'Unhand me.'

'High and mighty, aren't we? But I'll take you down a peg or two.'

'Aye, that's it, Jed,' said a voice from the group. 'Show her.'

A chorus of agreement followed and with pounding heart Claire saw them move in closer. Jed smiled, revealing stained and decaying teeth.

'Since you won't give a coin I'll take payment in kind. Perhaps we all will, eh, lads?'

A murmur of agreement followed. Her captor glanced toward the alley that ran alongside the tavern. Claire, following that look, felt her stomach lurch.

'Let go of me.'

She tried to twist free, but his grip only tightened. In desperation she kicked out. The blow connected and she heard him swear, but it was a temporary victory. Moments later she was dragged into the alley and shoved up against the outer wall of the inn. Then his arm was round her waist and his free hand exploring her breast. She could feel his hot breath on her neck. Claire struggled harder.

'Aye, go on, fight me. I like it better that way.'

'Let me go!'

'Not before I've given you what you need, lass.'

'Save some for us, Jed,' said a voice from behind him.

He grinned appreciatively. 'I reckon there's enough here to go round. You'll get your turns when I'm done.'

More laughter greeted this. Claire screamed as Jed's hands fumbled with her skirt.

'Let her go!'

Hearing that hard, cold command, the group fell silent, turning to look at the newcomer who had approached unnoticed. Claire swallowed hard, her heart pounding even as her gaze drank in every detail of her rescuer's appearance. An arresting figure, he was a head taller than any present. His dress proclaimed the working man, but there the similarity ended: if anything his upright bearing smacked more of a military background. The brown serge coat had seen better days but it was clean and neat and covered powerful shoulders; waistcoat, breeches and boots adorned a lean, athletic figure that had not an ounce of fat on it. Dark hair was visible from beneath a low-crowned felt hat. However, it was the face that really held attention, with its strong bone structure and slightly aquiline nose, the chiselled, clean-shaven lines accentuated by a narrow scar that ran down the left side from cheek to jaw. The sculpted mouth was set in a hard, uncompromising line, as uncompromising as the expression in the grey eyes.

For a moment or two there was silence, but the hold on Claire's arm slackened. With pounding heart she glanced up at the newcomer, but he wasn't looking at her. The hawk-like gaze was fixed on her persecutor. The latter sneered.

'This is none of your business, Eden.'

'Then I'll make it my business, Stone.' The quiet voice had the same Yorkshire burr as the others, but it also held an inflexion of steel.

'We were just having a little fun, that's all.'

'The lady doesn't seem to share your idea of amusement.'

'What's it to you?'

The reply was a large clenched fist that connected with Stone's jaw. The force of the blow pitched him backwards and sent him sprawling, stunned, in the mud of the alley. Before he could stir, one of his companions threw a punch at Eden. He blocked it and brought his knee up hard into his attacker's groin. The man doubled over in agony. As he staggered away a third stepped in. Eden ducked under the swinging fist and landed his opponent a savage upper cut that lifted him off his feet and flung him backwards to lie in the mud with Stone. Seeing the fate of their fellows, the remaining two men hesitated, then backed away. Eden threw them one contemptuous glance and then looked at Claire.

'Are you hurt, miss?'

'No. I…I'm all right,' she replied, hoping her voice wouldn't shake.

'Good. Then I'll set you on your way.'

He looked round at the others as though daring them to challenge the words, but no one did. Instead they avoided his eye and moved aside. Seeing her bag lying nearby, Eden picked it up. As he did so, Stone came to, propping himself groggily on one elbow, his other hand massaging the lump on his jaw. Blood trickled from a split lip.

'You'll get yours, Eden, I swear it!'

If the other was in any way perturbed by the threat he gave no sign of it save that the glint in the grey eyes grew a shade harder.

'I'll look forward to that, Stone.'

Then, placing a firm but gentle hand under her elbow, he led Claire away from the scene.

For a few moments they walked in silence and she was grateful for the respite because it allowed her time to regain her self-control. She was trembling now with reaction and the knowledge of how narrow her escape had been. Moreover she was ashamed to the depths of her soul to have been seen in such a situation. Respectable young women did not travel unaccompanied and would never place themselves in circumstances where they might attract the attentions of such brutes as those. Her face reddened. What must he think?

She stole a glance at her protector, but the handsome face gave nothing away. Nor did he venture a comment of any kind. Instead they walked on in silence until they were well clear of the tavern, she all the while aware of the warmth of his hand beneath her elbow. It was a gesture that was both comforting and disturbing at once. Yet the nearness of this man was not threatening as those others had been. How much she owed him. She stole another look at his face.

'Thank you, sir. I am most grateful for what you did back there.'

The grey eyes regarded her steadily a moment.

'I beg you will not regard it, madam.'

Claire knew a moment's surprise for the Yorkshire burr had disappeared to be replaced with the pure modulated diction associated with a very different social rank. However, fearing to seem rude, she did not remark on it.

'Who were those men?' she asked then.

'Scum. They needn't concern you further.' He paused. 'May I ask where you're going?'

'To Helmshaw.'

'Helmshaw. That's a fair walk from here.'

'Yes, I believe so, but the public coach doesn't go there.'

'You came on the coach?'

'Yes.'

'Alone?'

Her cheeks reddened. 'As you see.'

'You have family in Helmshaw perhaps?'

'A friend.'

'But your friend is not expecting you.'

'No, not exactly.'

'Not at all, I'd say, or you would have been met at the coach.'

Not knowing what to say, Claire remained silent. A few moments later they reached the end of the street. There he paused, looking down at her.

'Yonder lies the road to Helmshaw. I'd walk along with you, but I've important business requiring my attention here. However, I think you'll not be troubled again.'

She managed a tremulous smile. 'I'm sure I shan't be. You've been most kind, sir.'

'You're welcome, Miss, er…'

'Claire Davenport.'

He took the offered hand and bowed. For one brief moment she felt the warmth of his touch through her glove. Then he relinquished his hold.

'Farewell, Miss Davenport.'

'Farewell, Mr Eden. And thank you again.'

He handed her the valise and touched his hand to his hat. Then he turned and walked away. Feeling strangely bereft, she watched the tall departing figure with a rueful smile. In all likelihood they would never meet again, though she knew she would never forget him. With a sigh she turned and continued on her way.

As the man Eden had predicted she met with no more trouble on the road, but half an hour later it came on to rain, a thundery summer shower. The open roadway offered no shelter and in a very short time she was soaked through. It was with real relief that she saw the first houses on the edge of the village. An enquiry of a passing carter directed her to a grey stone house set back from the road in a pleasant garden. Claire paused by the gate, feeling her stomach knot in sudden apprehension. What if Miss Greystoke had moved on? It had been seven years after all. What would she do then? Where would she go? Taking a deep breath, she walked up the paved pathway to the front door and rang the bell. A maidservant answered. On seeing Claire's bedraggled and muddied appearance she eyed her askance.

'The doctor's not at home,' she said.

Shivering a little now, Claire stood her ground.

'It is Miss Greystoke I seek, not the doctor.'

Before the girl could answer another voice spoke behind her.

'Who is it, Eliza?'

Claire's heart beat painfully hard. The woman's elegant lavender-coloured gown was different, but everything else was familiar from the light brown hair to the blue eyes now regarding her with shock and concern.

'Claire?' The woman came closer, wonder writ large in her expression, and then a beaming smile lit her face. 'Oh, my dear, it really is you!'

'Miss Greystoke.'

'What a wonderful surprise. But what am I doing talking here on the doorstep? Come inside, do.'

Only too happy to obey, Claire stepped into the hallway and for a moment the two women faced each other in silence. Then Ellen Greystoke opened her arms and drew her visitor into a warm embrace. Knowing herself safe for the first time in days, Claire began to shake.

'Good gracious! How cold you are! We must get you out of those wet clothes at once. Then we shall sit down and have some tea and you can tell me everything.'

Claire was escorted to a pleasant upstairs bedroom, provided with hot water and towels, and then left in privacy. Shivering, she removed her bonnet and then stripped off her wet things. How good it was to be free of them at last and to be able to bathe again and tidy her hair. Having done so, she donned a clean gown. It was one of two that she had been able to bring. Apart from those, a russet spencer, a few necessary personal items and her sketchbook, the valise contained nothing of value. Involuntarily Claire's hand sought the locket she wore around her neck. It was her sole piece of jewellery and it bore the only likeness of her parents that she possessed. She had inherited her mother's dusky curls and hazel eyes and her face had the same fine bone structure. Her father too had been dark haired with rugged good looks. It was not hard to see why her parents had been attracted to each other or why Henry Davenport should fly in the face of his family's disapproval and marry a young woman with only a pretty countenance and a hundred pounds a year to recommend her. Goodness was not a marketable quality in their eyes. Yet, contrary to all predictions, the marriage had been a success. Claire had fond memories of her early years, days filled with sunshine and laughter when she'd been truly happy and carefree. How long ago it all seemed and how like a dream.

An outbreak of typhus changed everything: her father had sickened first and then her mother, the fever carrying them off within three days of each other. At a stroke she was an orphan. Miss Greystoke had taken it upon herself to inform her father's family and in due course Uncle Hector had arrived. Her thirteen-year-old self could see the likeness to her father in the dark hair and grey eyes, but there the similarity ended. The tall, unsmiling man in black was a stranger whose cold expression repelled her. She hadn't wanted to go with him and had sobbed out her grief in Miss Greystoke's arms. In the end though there had been no choice and she had been taken to live at her uncle's house.

From the moment of her arrival she knew Aunt Maud disliked her and resented her presence there. At first she had not understood why, but as time passed and she grew from child to young woman the contrast between her and her much plainer cousins became marked. To be fair her cousins showed no resentment of her good looks, but then they were so timid that they never expressed an opinion on anything. Claire, outgoing and high-spirited, found them dull company. Moreover she found the educational regime in the house stifling.

From the start Miss Greystoke had always encouraged her to think for herself and to read widely and Claire's naturally enquiring mind devoured the books she was given and easily assimilated what she found there. She loved learning for its own sake and enjoyed gaining new skills, whether it was drawing or playing the pianoforte, speaking in French or discussing current affairs. In her uncle's house everything was different. Independent thought was discouraged, and only the most improving works considered suitable reading material. They were taught their lessons under the exacting eye of Miss Hard-castle, a hatchet-faced woman with strict views about what constituted a suitable education for young ladies, and an expectation of instant obedience in all things. In this she was fully supported by Aunt Maud and any infraction of discipline was punished. Claire, loathing the constraints imposed on her, had been openly rebellious at first, but she had soon learned the error of her ways. Remembering it now, she felt resentment rise in a wave. She would never return no matter what.

Some time later she joined Ellen in the parlour where she was plied with hot tea and slices of fruit cake. When she had finished she favoured her friend with an explanation of why she had fled her uncle's house. Ellen listened without interruption, but the blue eyes were bright with anger and indignation. Claire swallowed hard.

'I'm so sorry to impose on you like this, Miss Greystoke, but I didn't know where else to turn.'

'Where else should you turn but to me? And let us dispense with this formality. You must call me Ellen.'

'You don't know how I missed you all these years.'

'And I you. My brightest pupil.'

'Did you receive my letter?'

'Yes, I did.'

'I wanted to write again, but my aunt would not permit it.'

'Then you did not get my other letters?'

Claire stared at her. 'What other letters?'

'I wrote several, but there was never any reply, so in the end I stopped sending them.'

'On my honour I never received them.'

'No, after what you have told me I imagine you did not.'

Anger and indignation welled anew and Claire bit her lip. To think that all that time her aunt had lied to her, if only by omission.

'It was the saddest day of my life when I had to leave you. Your parents' house was such a happy place and they were always so good to me. I felt more like a member of the family than a governess.'

'I feel as though I have been in prison for the past seven years. And then this. I could not do what they wanted, Ellen.'

'Of course not! No woman should ever be compelled to marry a man she does not love and esteem. What your uncle did was shameful.'

'But what if he finds me?'

'He shall not remove you from this house.'

'I wish I were not so afraid of him, Ellen.'

'I am not surprised that you are. The man is a perfect brute.'

'If my aunt read your letters, she will have seen the address and may guess where I am.'

'She probably burnt them without reading them. In any case it was a long time ago. It is most unlikely she kept them.'

'I pray she did not.' Claire's hands clenched. 'If only I might reach my majority and be out of their power for good.'

'That day cannot be so far away now. How old are you?'

'Four months short of my twenty-first birthday.'

'No time at all. It will soon pass and then you will be a free woman.'

'Somehow I must earn my living and I am not afraid to work, provided it is honest employment. I do not wish to be a burden.'

Ellen smiled and squeezed her hand gently. 'You could never be a burden to me.'

'But what will your brother say when he returns?'

'You leave George to me.'

Doctor Greystoke returned some time later. In his early forties, he was a little over the average height and had a strong athletic build, which made him seem younger than his years. His face was pleasant and open rather than handsome and, as yet, relatively unlined save for the creases round the eyes and mouth. Like his sister he had light brown hair, in his case greying a little at the temples and lending him a distinguished air. Claire thought he had a kindly face. Even so there was no way of knowing how he would respond to having his home invaded by a stranger—and a penniless stranger to boot.

She need not have worried. Having been apprised of the situation, he seated himself on the sofa beside his unexpected guest, regarding her keenly.

'My sister has told me everything, Miss Davenport. I confess I am deeply shocked to learn of the reason for your coming here, but can in no way blame you for leaving. To force a young woman into marriage must be in every way repugnant to civilised thinking.' He smiled. 'You are welcome to remain here as long as you wish.'

'Thank you. May I also ask that my reason for being here remains a secret?'

'You may rely on it. Neither my sister nor I will divulge it to a soul.'

Claire's eyes filled with tears and a lump formed in her throat.

'Indeed, sir, you are very good.'

To her horror tears spilled over and ran down her face and she dashed them away with a trembling hand. Seeing it his face registered instant concern.

'Don't cry,' he said. 'You're safe here.'

Claire drew in a shuddering breath and fumbled for a handkerchief. Before she could find it he produced his own.

'Here, try this. I prescribe it for the relief of tears.'

It drew a wan smile and he nodded approvingly.

'That's it. Now dry your eyes and let us have no more of this. I absolutely forbid you to be sad here.'

Ellen rose and rang the bell to summon the maid.

'Shall we have some more tea?'

Her brother looked up and grinned. 'I thought you'd never ask.'

Chapter Two

Gleams of moonlight shone through flying rags of cloud, its pale glow illuminating the moor and the winding road along which the wagon made its steady progress. Drawn by four great draught horses it lumbered on, its load a dark mass concealed beneath a heavy tarpaulin. Apart from the driver and his companion on the box, six others accompanied the wagon, big men chosen for their physical strength. Two walked in front with lighted torches; the others rode on either side of the vehicle. All were armed with clubs and pistols. Conversation was kept to a minimum. The only sounds were the wind and the muffled rumbling of iron-rimmed wheels over the track. For it was more track than road, an ancient drovers' trail that crossed the hills above Helmshaw. As they walked the men kept a sharp look out, their eyes scanning the roadway ahead and the pooled shadows to either side. No other sound or movement revealed any more human presences. The little convoy might have been the last living things upon the face of the earth.

'All quiet so far,' muttered the driver, 'but I'll not be sorry to see journey's end.'

His companion merely grunted assent.

'If it weren't for t'money you'd not catch me out here with this lot,' the other continued. 'I thought long and hard about it I can tell thee. A man should be at his fireside of an evening, not wandering t'moors to be prey to scum.'

Another grunt greeted this. Seeing his companion wasn't in a responsive mood, Jethro Timms gave up the attempt at conversation. From time to time he eyed the other man. A taciturn cove, he thought, and no mistake. However, what he lacked in amiability he made up for in sheer physical presence for he was tall and well made with a lean, athletic figure that had about it something of a military bearing, though nothing about his clothing suggested it. Coat, breeches and boots, though strong and serviceable, had seen better days. Still, the driver reflected, that was not surprising. Since Napoleon went to Elba there were lots of ex-soldiers roaming the land looking for work, though heaven knew it was in short supply. If a man was desperate enough he might volunteer to ride guard on a wagon in the middle of the night.

He gave his companion another sideways glance, but the other seemed unaware of it, his gaze on the way ahead. Dark hair was partly concealed under a hat which shadowed the strong lines of brow and jaw. Down one cheek the faint line of a scar was just visible. It might have been a sabre slash, but the driver didn't care to ask. Something about those steel-grey eyes forbade it. Nevertheless, he thought, Eden was a comforting presence tonight, not least for the blunderbuss he held across his knee and the brace of pistols thrust into his belt.

Timms made no further attempt to break the silence

and the wagon lumbered on. Gradually the scenery began to change, the open heath giving way to more rugged terrain as the track passed through a deep valley. On either hand the dark mass of the hillsides was just visible against the paler cloud above, but to one side the ground fell away in a steep drop to the stream. As it passed through the declivity the track narrowed. Suddenly Eden sat up, his expression intent.

Timms swallowed hard. 'What is it?'

'I thought I heard something. Stones sliding.'

'I can't hear owt.'

For a moment or two they listened, but the only sounds were the wind through the heather and the chuckling water below.

'Tha must have imagined...'

The driver's words were lost as the darkness erupted in a flash of fire and the sharp report of a pistol. A linkman cried out and fell, his torch lying unheeded on the path. As though at a signal a dozen dark shapes rose from the concealing heather and rushed forwards. Cursing, Timms reined in his startled team as a masked attacker reached up to drag him from his seat. Beside him the blunderbuss roared and a man screamed, falling back into the darkness. On the other side of the wagon two others launched themselves at Eden. He swung the blunderbuss hard and felt it connect with bone. His attacker staggered and fell. The other came on. Eden kicked out at the masked face and heard cartilage crunch beneath the sole of his boot. A muffled curse followed and the would-be assailant reeled away, clutching his ruined nose. Eden drew the pistols from his belt as his gaze took in the chaos of struggling shadowy forms in the roadway. As another masked face loomed out of the dark he loosed off a shot. The ball took the man between the eyes and he fell without a sound. Several others swarmed toward the wagon.

Timms, struggling to control the restive horses, cried a warning as hands reached up to drag him from the box. Eden heard it and, turning, fired the second pistol. He heard a yelp of pain and saw a man go down, but almost immediately another shot rang out and Timms swore, clutching his arm. A moment later he was dragged from the box and lost to view. Other hands caught hold of Eden. Instead of resisting them he threw himself forwards, diving off the wagon to land on top of his assailants in the road. Fists and feet connected with flesh amid muffled cries and oaths. Then he was free. Leaping to his feet, he spun round to find himself staring at the mouth of a pistol. Pale moonlight afforded a swift impression of cold eyes glinting above a mask, and below it a soiled green neckcloth. For one split second something stirred in Eden's memory. Then there was a burst of flame and a loud report. Hot lead tore into flesh and he staggered, clutching his shoulder. Blood welled beneath his fingers and then vicious pain exploded in a burst of light behind his eyeballs and he fell.

He lay in the dirt for some moments, aware only of the pain that seemed to have replaced all other sensation. The sounds of fighting receded. With an effort of will he forced back the threatening faintness and became aware of a voice issuing instructions. Moonlight revealed dark figures round the wagon, some unhitching the horses, others loosening the ropes that held the load, flinging back the tarpaulin to reveal the crate beneath. Eden's jaw tightened as the figures swarmed aboard and levered it off the wagon. As in slow motion it crashed onto the road and rolled forwards down the slope, tumbling over and over, gathering momentum until it came to rest, smashed and broken on the rocky streambed below. A ragged cheer went up from the wreckers. At that a man stepped forwards to face the remaining members of the escort. Like his companions his face was covered by a scarf and his hat pulled low.

'Tell Harlston his machines are not wanted here,' he said. 'Any attempt to replace this one will result in more of the same.'

With that he jerked his head towards his companions and the whole group made off into the darkness. Eden tried to rise, but the pain scythed through his shoulder. Crimson bombs exploded behind his eyes and then blackness took him.

He had no idea how long he lay there; it might have been minutes or hours. For some moments he did not move, aware only of cold air on his face and the dull throbbing ache in his shoulder. Instinctively he lifted his hand to the wound and felt the stickiness of blood. Then the details began to return. As he became more aware of his surroundings the first thing that struck him was the eerie silence, a hush broken only by the wind and the stream. The sky was a lighter shade and the stars fading so dawn could not be far off. Experimentally he tried to rise; pain savaged him and he bit back a cry. With an effort of will he dragged himself to a nearby boulder and used it to support his back while he forced himself to a sitting position. The effort brought beads of cold sweat to his forehead and it was some minutes before he could catch his breath. Then he looked around. In the predawn half light he could make out the dark silent shapes that were the bodies of the slain. Grim-faced, he counted half a dozen. Where were the rest? The wreckers were long gone, but surely some of the wagon escort had lived. He could see no sign of the wagon or the horses. Had the surviving members just abandoned their fellows to their fate and saved their own skins?

Anger forced Eden to his knees and thence to his feet, using the rock to steady himself. Agony seared through the injured shoulder. His legs trembled like reeds. Gritting his teeth against the pain, he drew in a few deep breaths. As he did so he glanced over the edge of the hillside. Among the rocks that lined the stream he saw the smashed remains of the power loom and with it the wagon. At the sight his fists clenched, but he understood now why he had been left behind in this place. The survivors had taken the horses for themselves and the injured. He had been mistaken for one of the dead. The thought occurred that if he didn't find help soon he might well be among their number. The nearest town was Helmshaw: Harlston's Mill was located on its edge. It was perhaps two miles distant. Mentally girding himself for the effort and the coming pain, Eden stumbled away down the track.

His progress was pitifully slow because every few minutes he was forced to rest. The sky was much lighter now and the track clear enough, but pain clouded his mind until he could think of nothing else. Moreover, the darkened patch of dried blood on his coat was overlain with a new scarlet wetness that spread past the edges of the original stain. He had tried to stanch the bleeding with a wadded handkerchief, but that too was sodden red. His strength was ebbing fast and only sheer will forced him to put one foot in front of the other. He had gone perhaps half a mile when the level track began to rise at the start of a long steady climb up the next hill. Eden managed another fifty yards before pain and exhaustion overcame his will and he collapsed on the path in a dead faint.

Claire was woken just after dawn by heavy pounding on the front door. Her heart thumped painfully hard and for one dreadful moment she wondered if her uncle had discovered her whereabouts and was come to drag her away. Forcing herself to take a deep breath, she slipped from the bed and threw a shawl about her shoulders. Then she crept to the bedroom door and opened it a crack, listening intently. The pounding on the door increased and was followed by Eliza's indignant tones as she went to answer it. Then a man's voice was heard demanding the doctor. Claire breathed a sigh of relief. Not her uncle, then.

'What's so urgent that the doctor must be dragged from his bed at this hour?' demanded Eliza.

'There's half a dozen injured men at Harlston's Mill,' the man replied. 'Some bad hurt.'

'Good gracious! Not another accident?'

'No accident. They were escorting a consignment of new machinery for t'mill. Seems they were attacked on their way over t'moor. There's been some killed an' all.'

'Heaven preserve us from such wickedness! Wait here! I'll fetch the doctor.'

Within a quarter of an hour Dr Greystoke had left the house. Claire heard the sound of horses' hooves as the men rode away, and in some anxiety digested what she had heard. Her limited knowledge of the machine-breakers' activities had been gleaned from newspaper accounts: here evidently it was far more than just a story of distant industrial unrest. Here the violence was all too real. Could it be true that men had lost their lives? The thought was chilling. What could make men so desperate that they were prepared to kill?

It was a question she put to Ellen when they met in the breakfast parlour some time later.

'When the war with France cut off foreign trade it caused a lot of hardship hereabouts,' her friend replied. 'Even now that Napoleon is exiled the situation is slow to change. The advent of the power looms is seen as yet another threat to men's livelihoods.'

'Then why do mill owners like Harlston antagonise the workforce in that way?'

'They see it as progress and in a way I suppose it is. The new machines are faster and more efficient by far than the old looms. All the same, it is hard to reconcile that knowledge with the sight of children starving.'

Claire pondered the words, for they suggested a world she had no experience of. In spite of recent events her life had been sheltered and comfortable for the most part and although she had lost her parents she had still been clothed and fed and there had always been a roof over her head. Other children were not as fortunate. For so many orphans the only choice was the workhouse. If they survived that, it usually led to a life of drudgery after. For a young and unprotected girl the world was hazardous indeed. Recalling the scene in Gartside, she shuddered.

'Are you all right, Claire? You look awfully pale.'

'Yes, a slight headache is all.'

'No wonder with all you've been through.'

Claire managed a wan smile. She hadn't told Ellen about the incident with Stone and his cronies. She had felt too ashamed; the memory of it made her feel dirty somehow and she wanted nothing more than to forget about it. Yet now it returned with force and with it the recollection of the man who had saved her.

'Why don't you go for a walk this morning?' Ellen continued. 'I'm sure the fresh air would do you good.'

'Yes, perhaps you are right.'

'There is a gate in the garden wall that leads out onto the moor. It is quite a climb, but the views from the top are worth the effort.'

'I could take my sketchbook.'

Ellen smiled. 'You have kept up your drawing, then?'

'Oh, yes. It is one of my greatest pleasures.'

'You were always so gifted that way. I shall look forward to seeing your work later.'

'Will you not come with me?'

'I wish I could, but this morning I have an engagement in town. Never fear, though, we shall take many walks together in future. The countryside hereabouts is very fine.'

Looking out across the sunlit moor an hour later Claire could only agree with her friend's assessment. From her vantage point she could see the town below, and the mill, and then the wide expanse of rolling heath and the hills beyond. Far above her a skylark poured out its soul in song. Listening to it, Claire felt her spirits lift for the first time and suddenly the future seemed less threatening. Smiling, she walked on, revelling in the fresh air and exercise.

She had followed the track for another mile or so when she saw the figure lying on the path. It was a man and he was lying very still. Claire frowned. What on earth was he doing there? How had he got there? She approached with caution but he did not move. Her gaze took in boots, breeches and coat and the dark stain on the shoulder. It was unmistakably blood. Swallowing hard, she drew nearer and then gasped.

'Mr Eden!'

In a moment she was beside him, her fingers seeking his wrist for a pulse. For a moment she couldn't find one and her heart sank. Her fingers moved to his neck and in trembling relief she found it at last, a slow and feeble beat. His face was very pale, the skin waxy where it showed above the stubble of his beard. When she spoke to him again there was no response. Claire gently lifted the edge of his coat and her eyes widened.

'Dear God,' she murmured.

Shirt and waistcoat were soaked, as was the wadded handkerchief thrust between. He had been shot. Shocked to the core, she stared a second or two at the scarlet stain. Who could have done such a thing? Unbidden, the memory of their first meeting returned and she heard Stone's voice: *'You'll get yours, Eden, I swear it.'* Feeling sick and guilty, Claire bit her lip. Was this her fault? Had his earlier action brought this on him? There was no time for further reflection; he needed help and soon. She looked around in desperation, her mind retracing her route and the length of time it would take to get back and wondering if she would find Ellen or her brother returned yet. In the midst of these thoughts her eye detected a movement further down the track. Straightening, she shaded her eyes and strained to see, praying it might be a rider. In fact it was several riders and in their midst a cart. Almost sobbing with relief, she waved frantically.

'Help! Over here!'

It seemed to take an age before they heard her. Then two of the men spurred forwards to investigate. Claire stood on the track and watched them come. They reined in, regarding her with open curiosity. Then they noticed the still form lying at the edge of the path.

'What's happened here, lass?' demanded the first.

'He's badly injured. He needs a doctor and soon.'

'Have no fear. Help is at hand.'

The first rider dismounted and hastened over to the injured man. Then Claire heard a muffled exclamation.

'Merciful heavens, it's Mark Eden.'

'What!' His companion edged his mount closer. 'I heard he was missing, believed dead.'

'He soon will be if we don't get him to a doctor. Help me get him onto my horse.'

Claire eyed the approaching vehicle. 'Would it not be better to put him on the cart?'

The men exchanged glances, then shook their heads.

'Better not, lass.'

'I don't understand.'

They gave no further explanation and she could only watch in helpless bewilderment as they lifted Eden and put him on the horse. Then one mounted behind, holding the inert form so it could not fall. They had no sooner done so than the lumbering wagon drew nigh. Seeing what it contained, Claire went very pale.

'Come away, lass, it's no sight for a woman's eyes.' The man's voice was gruff but kindly. 'I'll take thee up on t'horse behind me.'

'Those men in the cart, are they…?'

'Dead? Aye. Killed last night in the attack on Harlston's machines.'

Claire drew in a deep breath and then glanced at the slumped form on the other horse, praying they had not come too late.

When Eden came round it was to the sound of voices and hurrying footsteps. Through a fog of pain he had an impression of walls and floor and ceiling. He didn't recognise the room. It had a strange and yet familiar smell too, something vaguely chemical that resisted identification and yet one he thought he ought to know. He shifted a little and winced as pain knifed through his shoulder.

'Don't try to move.'

He looked up and saw a face bending over his. His mind registered a girl—no, a young woman. Twenty years old or thereabouts. Dark curls framed a face with high cheekbones and beautiful chiselled mouth. But it was the eyes one noticed most: huge hazel eyes deep enough to drown in. They seemed familiar somehow.

'Where am I?'

'At the doctor's house.'

His brows knit, unable to comprehend how this had occurred, but having to trust the evidence of his eyes. Before he could say more he heard another voice.

'Lift him onto the table. Gently now. That's it.'

He stifled a groan as hands raised him, felt the hard, flat surface under his back. Then he heard the same voice speak again.

'Fetch me hot water, Claire, and clean cloths.'

A swish of skirts announced her obedience to the command. Her quiet voice brought the two erstwhile assistants after her. As their footsteps receded a man's face swam into view, a pleasant clean-shaven face with clear-cut features. It was framed by light brown hair, greying a little at the sides. The eyes were blue and now staring as though they had seen a ghost. The same shock was registered in the grey eyes of the injured man.

'George,' he murmured. 'George Greystoke.'

'Marcus?' The doctor looked closer, taking in every detail of the pale face and resting on the scarred cheek.

'Marcus Edenbridge. By the Lord Harry, it *is* you. But what in the name of—?'

He broke off as a hand closed over his in silent warning.

'No, it's Mark Eden at present.'

For a moment the blue eyes narrowed and then the doctor nodded. Then he took Eden's hand in a warm grip.

'Tell me later. Right now I must get that ball out of your shoulder or the wound will fester.'

Before either of them could say more the girl returned. With her was an older woman who seemed to resemble George. They set down the bowl of water and the cloths and then came to stand by the table. George glanced round.

'Help me get his coat and shirt off, Ellen.'

They were gentle, but nevertheless Eden bit his lip against the pain. Once the task was accomplished George laid out his instruments and, selecting a probe, held it in the flame of a spirit lamp before dousing it in alcohol. He did the same with the forceps. Then he put a thick strip of leather between the patient's jaws.

'Bite down on this.'

Eden obeyed. A moment or two later the probe slid into the wound. Sweat started on his skin. Greystoke frowned in concentration and the silence stretched out. The probe went deeper. Eden's jaw clenched. Then he heard the other speak.

'Ah, here we are. Hand me the forceps, Ellen.'

Eden's fists tightened as the pain intensified until it dominated every part of his being. Then the light in the room narrowed to a single point and winked out.

Claire watched Greystoke extract a wad of bloody cloth from the wound and drop it into a metal bowl. Then he returned for the ball. It dropped into the receptacle with a metallic clink. After that he swabbed the area liberally with alcohol before covering it with a thick pad of gauze and bandaging it securely in place.

'Will he be all right?'

'Time will tell,' replied Greystoke. 'He's lost a lot of blood and is much weakened by it. There is also the chance of fever.' Then, seeing Claire's white face he gave her a gentle smile. 'But he's young and strong and with God's grace and good nursing he may recover.'

Eden was riding down a dusty road. It was hot, very hot. He could feel the burning sun on his skin and the rhythm of the horse beneath him, could hear the hoof beats and the jingling harness of the mounted column behind. The air smelled of dry earth and dung, spice and horse sweat. Above him the sky was a hard metallic blue. Then he heard shouting and the clash of swords, he saw the mêlée in the road ahead and the litter, its curtains a vivid splash of colour in the midst of all. Women screamed. Then his sword was in his hand and the column swept like a tide onto the dacoit raiders and washed them away or drowned them quite. And then there was silence and the curtains of the litter parted and he saw her: Lakshmi. For a moment he was struck dumb, unable to tear his eyes away. He thought he had never seen anything so beautiful in his life, a living dream and lovelier than a fairy-tale princess, though a princess in all truth. Unable to help himself he smiled and she smiled too, though shyly. And he spoke to her in her language and she to him in his and he offered her his protection for the remainder of her journey home. Four days and four nights. Nights of velvet starlit skies and air fragrant with jasmine and frangipani, warm nights of firelight and shadow, cushioned with silk, scented with sandalwood and patchouli; nights made for love. Four nights. That was all. He had prayed that the fourth one might last for ever, but the daylight came anyway and brought with it the end of their road. He could see her face and the sadness written there and then the yawning palace gateway that swallowed her up. He thought his heart would break.

'Lakshmi!'

Later he lay on his hard bed in the sweltering heat of the barracks, too hot even for a sheet, hearing the whine of mosquitoes in the sultry air while the sweat trickled down his skin. When he shut his eyes he saw her face, the wonderful eyes filled with love and longing. Sometimes he dreamed she was there, bending over him, speaking softly and bathing his forehead with cool cloths. But he knew it was a dream because she was lost to him, given in marriage to the rajah of a neighbouring state, a man old enough to be her grandfather.

'Lakshmi.'

And then his brother was there, shaking his head.

'Why the devil didn't you take her away while you had the chance, you fool?'

And he was right. Greville was always right. But the chance was gone now. Why had he not acted? He had broken his promise.

'I'll find a way, my love.'

He had believed it too, then. They could have found a place somewhere; they could have carved out a future together. What matter if others looked askance; what matter if there was a scandal? He was no stranger to it. But the thought of what it might mean for her had stayed him for the news would have swept like fire through the length and breadth of the Indian continent. News travelled fast there. And while he hesitated, she was lost.

'Lakshmi!'

* * *

Claire wrung out the cloth in cool water and laid it on Eden's forehead. His flesh so pale before was now flushed and hot to touch. Though his eyes were open they did not register her presence and when she spoke to him he did not hear her, but tossed in feverish dreams, speaking the names of people and places she had never heard of. Sometimes he spoke in a strange foreign language whose origin she could only guess at. Her own helplessness tormented her. What if he were to die? She owed him so much and yet knew so little about him. How had he come to be involved in that dreadful business on the moors? She had gleaned a little from the men who brought him to the house, but many questions remained unanswered.

From the beginning she had insisted on doing her share of the nursing care, taking turns with Ellen when the doctor was from home dealing with his other patients. It was the least she could do and precious little at that. It was shocking to see so strong a man laid low. Yet half a dozen others had been hurt in this affair and seven killed. Five were Harlston's men, the rest were wreckers. Yet death made no such distinctions. It mattered little whose hand fired the shot. She shivered. She knew it was illogical, but the uneasy feeling persisted that she was somehow to blame.

Lifting the cloth from his brow again, she replaced it with a cooler one and rinsed out the first, using it to wipe the sweat from his face and neck and the hollow above the collarbone. For a brief moment her hand brushed the skin of his breast. Claire drew in a sharp breath. His flesh was fiery to the touch. Hastily she poured more cold water into the basin and rinsed the cloth again. Then she bathed his chest as far as the line of the bandage would permit, her gaze taking in each visible detail of the powerful torso. She had not thought a man's body could be beautiful until now. Beautiful and disturbing, too, for it engendered other thoughts.

She had fled her uncle's house to avoid being married to a lecherous old man, but what of being married to a younger one, a man like this? If her suitor had looked and behaved like Eden, would she have fled? Would the thought of sharing his bed repel her? Her own flesh grew warmer then for it took but a second to know the answer. Yet what mattered most was the freedom to choose. She had always thought that somewhere there existed the man for her, though she had no idea of the circumstances in which she might meet him. What had not occurred to her was the idea that someone else might wish to do the choosing for her. How could one find love through another's eyes? Only the very deepest love would ever tempt her into matrimony, the kind of love her parents had shared. It was that or nothing and on this she knew there could be no compromise.

Shocked by the tenor of her thoughts she tried to dismiss them, but it proved impossible while that powerful physique was before her demanding consideration. Her eyes returned to his breast, her hand travelling thence to his good shoulder, moving with smooth and gentle strokes down his arm. Beneath the fine-veined skin she could see every detail of the curved musculature beneath, the strong bone at elbow and wrist, the dark hair along his forearms, the sinews in his hands. She took his hand in hers and drew the damp cloth down his palm to the fingertips, then turned it over and repeated the process. His hands were big yet finely shaped with long tapering fingers; hands capable of knocking a man down, or supporting a woman in need. The recollection sent a *frisson* along her spine. Disturbed by the memory for all sorts of reasons she forced it to the back of her mind. Mark Eden was a stranger who had once come to her aid. She knew nothing more about him. Perhaps she never would.

The thought was abruptly broken off by a hand closing round hers. Claire's gaze returned at once to her patient's face. His eyes were open now and apparently directed at her, though they shone with a strange inner fire.

'Mr Eden?'

He made no reply save to carry her hand to his lips. Feeling their hot imprint on her skin, she tried to extricate herself from his hold. It tightened instead and pulled her down towards the bed. She fell across him and suddenly his lips were on her neck and cheek, seeking her mouth. Claire turned her head aside, feeling the rasp of stubble and hot breath on her skin.

'Mr Eden, please!'

The words had no effect. His lips sought her ear instead and found it, his tongue exploring its curves. The touch sent a shiver through her whole body, awakening new and unexpected sensations.

'Lakshmi,' he murmured. 'Lakshmi, my love.'

Claire stiffened and pulled away, heart thumping, but Eden was no longer looking at her, his head tossing on the pillow, the grey eyes feverish and unfocussed. She realised then that he had not seen her at all, in all likelihood had no idea of her presence. In his disordered mind he was with a very different woman.

The knowledge hit her with force. It was a timely reminder of how little she knew of this man or the events that had shaped him. Detaching herself from his slackened hold, she walked a little way from the bed and took several deep breaths to try and recover her composure, her thoughts awhirl with what she had heard. It raised

so many questions. Questions she knew she would never
dare to ask nor had any right to. Looking at her patient
now, she thought he was an enigma in every way. She
would swear he was not from the labouring class whatever his dress proclaimed. His speech, his whole manner,
precluded it. And yet the men in Gartside obviously knew
him and he them. However, he was as unlike them as
fine wine was from vinegar. On the other hand many ex-
soldiers, even of the educated officer class, were forced
to look for alternative employment now that hostilities
with France had ceased. No doubt Eden too had had to
adapt to the circumstances in which he had found himself. Those circumstances would remove him from her
sphere soon enough. It was a disagreeable thought, for
she could not forget how his touch had made her feel,
if only for a moment. Yet it was no use to dwell on it;
another woman had his heart. She could only pray that
when he was recovered he would recall nothing of what
had just passed.

Marcus had no idea how long he was unconscious,
but the next time he came round it was still light and
he was lying in a large comfortable bed between clean
white sheets. For a moment his mind was blank. Then
memory began to return. Turning his head, he saw a
familiar figure at the bedside.

'George?'

'Welcome back.'

'How long have I been here?'

'Almost two weeks.'

'Two weeks!' He started up, only to feel a painful
twinge in his shoulder.

'Have a care. It's mending, thanks to the efforts of my
sister and Miss Davenport, but you're not there yet.'

Marcus lowered himself onto the pillows again. His friend was right; the savage pain was gone to be replaced with a dull ache. Clean bandages covered his injured shoulder and breast.

'Could you manage a little broth?' George inquired.

'Yes, I think I could.'

In fact, with his friend's help he managed half a bowlful.

'Excellent. Your appetite is returning. You'll soon be up and about.' The doctor replaced the dish on the side table and smiled.

For a moment neither man spoke. Then Marcus met his friend's eye.

'Thank you for all you've done, George. That's two I owe you now.'

'You owe me nothing.'

'Not so. I only hope I can repay you one day.'

'My hope is that the men responsible for the outrage are found and brought to justice.'

'You're not alone in that.'

'You were lucky, Marcus. It was a bad business. Seven men dead and six others injured. Those are the ones I know about. The wreckers took their wounded with them.'

'They had no choice. Arrest would mean a death sentence.'

'Aye, desperate men will do anything it seems.'

'Including murder.' Marcus's jaw tightened. 'They knew we were coming, George, and they knew our route. They chose a perfect spot for the ambush.'

'So it would seem.'

Seeing the other man's quizzical gaze, Marcus smiled faintly. 'You want to know how the devil I got mixed up in it, but are too polite to ask.'

His friend laughed. 'Is it that obvious?'

'You were never good at hiding your thoughts. But I do owe you an explanation.'

'I admit to curiosity.'

'When I returned from India two months ago I was summoned to Whitehall.'

'Whitehall?'

'Yes. The government is keen to break the Luddite rebellion. That's why the rewards for information are so generous. Intelligence gathering is dangerous, though, so they knew whoever they chose would have to be experienced.' He paused. 'They sent one of their finest operatives up to Yorkshire, a man born and bred in the county who, suitably disguised, would blend in.'

'What happened?'

'He was betrayed and murdered. Shot in the back.'

'Good Lord!' George shook his head in disgust. 'But betrayed by whom?'

'That's what I mean to find out. I am his replacement.'

'You?'

'Who better? I've done this kind of work before, for the Company in India. It seems word of that got back to London.'

'But you could have refused.'

'They knew I wouldn't, though.'

'How so?'

'Because the murdered man was my brother.'

Chapter Three

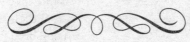

For a moment George stared at him dumbfounded before the implications of the words struck home.

'Greville?'

'Yes.'

'Dear Lord, Marcus, I'm sorry. I had no idea. I read about his death in *The Times*, but the piece said he'd had a riding accident.'

'The matter was hushed up and the story fabricated. The authorities didn't want the truth made public. Greville was a government agent working under the alias of David Gifford.'

'Ye gods.' George sat down while he tried to marshal his scattered wits. 'The news of his death made quite an impact in these parts, what with Netherclough Hall being virtually on the doorstep.'

'I can imagine. It rocked London, too. Greville was well known in diplomatic circles. Besides which he left no male heir, only a young daughter.'

'Then the title and the estate pass to you.'

'Yes. Behold the new Viscount Destermere.' Marcus

accompanied the words with a humourless smile. 'It is a role I never thought to have.'

'But one you will perform well nevertheless.'

'Thank you for that vote of confidence. I'll do my best, though I never wanted to step into my brother's shoes. He was always welcome to them, for it seemed to me that my destiny lay elsewhere.'

'Circumstances have a habit of changing our plans, do they not?' said George.

'As you say.'

'So what now?'

'Officially I'm not back from India yet, but I shall have to put in an appearance soon.'

'And what of your niece?'

'Lucy is now my ward. At present she is being cared for by an elderly aunt in Essex. Hardly a suitable state of affairs. I shall bring the child to live here in Yorkshire. After all, Netherclough is her ancestral home.'

'I see.'

'After that I shall pursue my investigations.' He paused. 'The house is ideally situated for the purpose, being right in the heart of things.'

'You can't be serious. These men are dangerous, Marcus. They've murdered Greville and tried to kill you. I know they had no idea of your true identity but, even so, if they got wind of your real purpose here…'

'Let's hope they don't. But come what may I shall find out who killed my brother. It is a matter of family honour that the culprit be brought to justice. That is the very least I can do for his daughter.' He paused. 'Besides, I owe it to his memory.'

George nodded reluctantly. 'I can't blame you for wanting to discover the truth, but have a care, I beg you.'

'I'll be careful. As soon as I'm able I shall leave for London and Mark Eden can disappear for a while. Give it out that he went back to his family to convalesce.'

'Very well.'

'How much have you told your sister and Miss Davenport?'

'They don't know your real identity. Apart from that I stuck as close to the truth as possible.'

'Good. I regret the necessity for deception.'

'So do I. Ellen and I are very close and I should not like to impose on Miss Davenport.'

'When the time is right they will be informed. I owe them that much at least. In the meantime I take it I can rely on your discretion.'

'Need you ask?'

'I'm sorry.' Marcus sighed. 'That was unpardonably rude after all you've done.'

'Just promise me you won't leave until you're strong enough.'

'You have my word. Besides, at this moment the thought of a journey to London fills me with dread.' He ran a hand over his chin. 'In the meantime I need to bathe and shave. I'm beginning to feel like a pirate.'

Having spent over two weeks abed, Marcus was determined to get up and, as George provided no opposition to the idea, he did so the very next day. Though still weaker than he would have wished, the pain of the wound had almost gone and provided he made no sudden movement it felt almost normal. Somewhat reluctantly he submitted to wearing a sling for a few days, but felt it a small price to pay, all things considered. A message had been sent to his lodgings and his things were duly sent round.

Looking at his reflection in the mirror, Marcus smiled wryly. The best that could be said was that the clothes were clean and serviceable and they fitted. They were hardly in the first stare of fashion. Just for a moment he saw his brother's face in the glass and it wore a pained expression. Almost he could hear his voice:

'*Good Lord! What ragbag did you get those out of, Bro?*'

Marcus grinned. A ragbag indeed, by Greville's standards anyway. His brother had always been both extravagant and elegant in his dress. They hadn't met since Marcus had been packed off to India ten years before. Now they would never meet again, or not in this life anyway. His jaw tightened. If it was the last thing he ever did, he would find the men responsible for that.

He finished dressing and made his way downstairs to the parlour. When he entered he discovered he was not the first there. A girl was sitting by the window, bent over the open sketchbook in her lap. For a moment he checked in surprise, sweeping her with a comprehensive gaze from the dusky curls to the toe of a small slipper peeping from beneath the hem of a primrose yellow morning gown. She looked familiar somehow. Then he remembered.

'Ah, Miss Davenport. Good morning.'

The pencil hovered in mid-air as she looked up. Claire had been so absorbed in her task that she had not heard him come in. For a moment she was rooted to the spot and could only stare. She had forgotten just how imposing a presence he was. In addition to that she was only too aware of the scene that had taken place in the sickroom earlier. Did he remember any of it?

If he was discomposed by her scrutiny it was not evident. Indeed, the cool grey eyes met and held her gaze.

His expression gave nothing away. Recollecting herself quickly, she returned the greeting.

'Mr Eden, I am glad to see you so far recovered.'

'If I am, it is in no small part due to you.'

'I did very little, sir.'

'George tells me you have been a most excellent nurse. An unusual role for a young lady.'

'I…it was the least I could do.'

'It is my profound regret that I have no recollection of it.'

Claire's spirits rose in an instant. 'I'm so glad.' Then, seeing his eyebrow lift, 'I mean, so glad that I was able to help—in some small way.' Knowing herself to be on dangerous ground, and growing warm besides, she changed the subject. 'Please, won't you sit? You should avoid tiring yourself unduly.'

His lips curved in a satirical smile. Ordinarily he would have treated such advice as presumption and responded with a pithy set down, but on this occasion he said nothing. Having taken the suggestion, he watched her resume her seat. As she did so he let his gaze rest on her, quietly appraising. The sprigged muslin gown was a simple and elegant garment, but it revealed her figure to perfection. A most becoming figure, he noted. Moreover the primrose yellow colour suited her, enhancing her warm colouring and dark curls.

'What are you drawing?'

'It's just a sketch that I wanted to finish.'

'May I see it?'

'If you like, but I wouldn't want to excite your antici-pation.'

She rose and handed him the book, watching as he leafed through it, wishing she were not so aware of his

nearness, wishing she could divine the thoughts behind
that impassive expression.

'You are too modest, Miss Davenport. These land-
scapes are very fine. You have a real eye for line and
form.'

'You are kind, sir.'

'I speak as I find.' He glanced up at her. 'Who taught
you to draw?'

'My mother, mostly. She was a talented artist. And
Miss Greystoke taught me a great deal.'

'Miss Greystoke?'

Claire was silent for a moment, conscious of having
given away more than she had intended. Then she upbraided herself silently. It was a trivial detail and could
make no possible difference.

'Yes. She was once my governess.'

'I see.'

Marcus was intrigued, for suddenly another piece
of the puzzle had fallen into place. However, he had
not missed her earlier hesitation either. Why should she
wish to hide the fact? Unwilling to antagonise her, but
not wishing for the conversation to finish just yet, he
continued to leaf casually through the book.

'These are all local views, are they not?'

'That's right. The countryside hereabouts is an artist's
dream. It's so wild and beautiful.'

'And dangerous,' he replied.

Claire's cheeks grew hot as the recollections of their
first encounter returned with force. It angered her that he
should allude to it again for he must know it was painful
in every way. However, it seemed she was wide of the
mark for Eden gestured to the newspaper lying on the
occasional table beside him.

'Another mill has been attacked by a mob and another loom destroyed, and all in the space of a fortnight.'

'Oh, yes.' Recovering her composure, she followed his gaze to the paper. 'Men fear for their livelihoods. So many have been laid off and those who are still in work have seen their wages cut.'

'Does that excuse murder?'

'No, of course not, but it does explain why people are so angry. It is well nigh impossible to feed a family on eight shillings a week.'

'You say that with some authority.'

'I have been with Miss Greystoke to visit several families in the town. She and her brother do what they can to help, but…' The hazel eyes met and held his. 'It is no pleasant thing to see children starving.'

'No, it is not.'

'You must have seen much poverty in India.'

'Yes.'

'Ironic, is it not, that it should exist in England too, a country we think more civilised in every way?'

There could be no mistaking the earnest tone or the sincerity in her face and he was surprised by both. In his experience young ladies of good family were usually preoccupied with balls and pretty dresses, not the problems of the poor. Would she prove to be one of those worthy but tiresome females eternally devoted to good causes?

'True,' he replied, 'but the war with France has been much to blame. Until trade can be resumed at its normal levels the situation is unlikely to change.'

'And in the meantime the mill owners lay off more men. The introduction of the steam looms only exacerbates the situation.'

'Progress cannot be resisted for ever. The wreckers will be brought to a strict accounting eventually.'

She heard the harsh note in his voice and met it with a sympathetic look. After his recent experience it was not surprising that he should be angry.

'Have you any idea who was responsible for shooting you?' she asked.

'No, but I do intend to find out.'

'You will put yourself in great danger.'

'So I apprehend.'

'I wish you would not.'

'Why?'

Again the grey gaze met hers and it was she who looked away first.

'Because I would not see you killed. There has been enough bloodshed of late.'

'I am grateful for your concern, but if bloodshed is to be prevented in future the men responsible must be brought to justice. I mean to see that they are.'

The tone, though quiet, was implacable, and for a moment there was an expression in the grey eyes that sent a shiver along her spine. Then it was gone.

'But these are disagreeable subjects,' he said. 'Let us speak of other things.'

'Such as?'

'Tell me about yourself.'

'It would hardly make for interesting conversation.'

'On the contrary,' he replied. 'I find myself curious.'

Her heart missed a beat. 'About what?'

'About why a young lady like yourself should bury herself in a place like this.'

'I am not buried here.'

'No?'

Ignoring the provocative tone, she lifted her chin.

'Certainly not. I have good friends and am kept busy enough.'

'And what do you do for your own amusement? When you are not about your good works?'

'I sketch, Mr Eden.'

'Touché!'

Claire's cheeks flushed a little, not least because she suspected he was the one in control of this situation. It was too dangerous to let it continue so, before he could question her further, she seized the initiative.

'And what of you, sir?'

In spite of himself he was amused. 'What of me?'

'Doctor Greystoke said that you and he are old friends. From your days in India.'

'That's right.'

He was glad George had told a partial truth even if he could not divulge his friend's real name. It made things easier. Anyway, he didn't want to lie to her.

'He said you were based in the same barracks at Mandrapore.'

'Did he also tell you he saved my life?'

The hazel eyes widened. 'No, he did not.' She paused. 'Won't you tell me how?'

'My men and I were ambushed by bandits and there was a fierce fight. Many of the force were killed and the rest of us left for dead. Fortunately, another contingent of soldiers happened along and took the survivors to the company barracks at Mandrapore. George Greystoke was the doctor in residence. It was thanks to his efforts that I pulled through. While I was convalescing we played a lot of chess and the friendship developed from there.'

'He said only that you and he met as a result of his work.'

'True enough, but also far too modest. Typical of George.'

She smiled. 'Yes, I believe it is. He is a good and kind man in every way. You must have been glad to see him again after so many years.'

'It was a welcome surprise, believe me. I had no idea he was here. Last time we spoke of such things his family was living in Richmond.'

'Miss Greystoke told me that he removed here after their father died.'

'I remember George left India to take care of the family's affairs at that time.'

'He was subsequently offered a position in Helmshaw,' she explained. 'When the previous doctor retired.'

'And you, Miss Davenport?' he asked. 'How came you to be in Yorkshire?'

'I told you, I came to visit Miss Greystoke.'

'Your parents permitted you to travel alone?'

The pink colour deepened in her face, but she forced herself to meet his gaze.

'My parents had no say in the matter since they are both dead.'

'I'm sorry.'

'Yes, so am I.'

He heard the note of bitterness beneath the words and was surprised since it was at variance with her normally cheerful demeanour.

'Then whom do you live with now?'

'With my father's relations.'

'And when do you return to them?'

'I…I have no set plans.'

For a moment there was a heart-thumping silence. She had told as much of the truth as possible and hoped now that he would let the subject drop. Much to her relief he

seemed to accept it and merely nodded. Then he handed
her the sketchbook.

'I look forward to seeing the finished picture, Miss
Davenport.'

She took it thankfully and retired to her seat by the
window to continue the task. For a moment or two he
watched and Claire, conscious of that penetrating gaze,
had to force herself to ignore it. It was with relief that
she heard the rustle of paper as he picked up the news
sheets and began to read.

In fact, Marcus barely scanned the page in front of
him. His mind was otherwise engaged. Far from accepting her words at face value he found his curiosity roused
to a degree she would have found alarming. For all that
she tried to pretend that there was nothing unusual in
journeying alone to so remote a place as Helmshaw, he
was quite undeceived. Ordinarily no respectable young
woman would do so. And yet there was nothing in her
that he found disreputable. Everything in her manners
and appearance spoke of a gentle upbringing. She was
no minx; naïve perhaps, but not of doubtful virtue. God
knew, he'd had enough experience to judge. And she had
spirit, enough anyway to stand up to Jed Stone. Recalling the incident and the perpetrators, Marcus felt only
contempt. It was fortunate that he'd been there to inter-
vene. She would have had no chance against such scum
as those and he could no more stand by and see a woman
assaulted than he could fly. Her self-control had been
impressive. Most young women would have been reduced
to hysterics by what had happened. Though much shaken,
she had not treated him to a fit of the vapours nor even
cried, though he could see she had wanted to. It was
unexpected and oddly touching, serving to underline her
vulnerability. At least he hadn't come too late that time.

Disturbed by his own train of thought, Marcus laid aside the paper and glanced once more at Claire who, apparently, was engrossed in her drawing. Then he rose and, having excused himself politely, left the room. Claire watched him go, feeling a strange mixture of relief and disappointment. With a conscious effort she forced her attention back to what she was doing.

Marcus stood by the garden wall, looking out at the view. The scenery was beautiful and it was pleasant to feel the sun on his face once more. The enjoyment of the moment was enhanced by the knowledge that but for good fortune and expert doctoring he might never have done so again. His health was improving daily and he would soon be able to dispense with the sling. The inaction of the past few days was beginning to chafe now. Besides, there were several matters requiring his attention. Foremost of these was the need to return to Netherclough and take up the reins of government there.

When he had left it all those years ago he had little thought to see the place again. Who could have foreseen the circumstances that would demand his return? His father would be turning in his grave if he knew that his scapegrace son was now Viscount Destermere. Not without reason either. Thinking of the wild days of his youth and the reckless pranks he had embarked upon, he knew his father had had much to bear. Perhaps if they had been closer... Marcus grimaced inwardly. After their mother's death, he and Greville were left to a succession of tutors before being packed off to school. They had seen little of their parent. It was Greville that he looked to for advice and guidance, not his father. Their last words together had been spoken in anger and yet, paradoxically, the old man might have been pleased with his son's performance since. India suited Marcus down to the ground; it provided a disciplined environment but also enough scope for an adventurous spirit. He had loved its diversity, its colour, its vibrant life. Once he had thought to see out his days there. Now fate had decreed otherwise. He had responsibilities and he must fulfil them. It was time to face down the ghosts of the past and go home.

Having come to that decision, he imparted it to his friend when they met a little later. Greystoke heard him in silence and then nodded.

'If that is what you wish to do then I will support you in any way I can.'

'Thank you. There is one more thing, George. Before I go, your sister and Miss Davenport must be told of my real identity.'

'If that is what you want.'

'I owe them that much.'

'Ellen will never breathe a word, and I believe that Miss Davenport is both sensible and discreet.'

Marcus nodded. 'It has sat ill with me to dissemble to those who have done so much towards my recovery. It's time they knew the truth.'

'Do you wish me to speak to Ellen?'

'Yes, as soon as may be. I will see Miss Davenport myself.'

He was waiting by the garden gate when Claire returned from her afternoon walk. At first she did not notice him, her attention on the steep track that led down off the hill, and her heart leapt to see the tall figure standing there. Suddenly she was conscious of her rumpled gown and windblown hair and of the fact that she was carrying her bonnet, not wearing it.

However, if he found anything amiss it was not apparent in his expression. He opened the gate to let her pass and then, offering her his arm, led her across the garden.

'Will you spare me five minutes of your time?' he asked. 'I should like to speak to you.'

'Of course.'

He found a convenient bench for them to sit on and, having seen her comfortably ensconced, favoured her with an explanation of recent events and of his identity. Claire heard him without interruption. More than anything else she was conscious of things falling into place: so many questions about this man had just been answered. Listening now, she wondered how she could have mistaken Marcus Edenbridge for anything other than the aristocrat he was. Everything about that tall commanding presence proclaimed it, from his physical appearance to his gentlemanly behaviour in championing her cause against Jed Stone and his cronies. It came as no surprise that he should seek out the men who killed his brother, even at the risk of his own life.

'I apologise for the deception,' he went on, 'and I ask for your discretion now. The true identity of Mark Eden must not become generally known.'

'You may be assured of my silence, sir.'

'Thank you.'

She paused, dreading to ask the next question, but needing to know the answer. 'May I ask when you intend to leave for London?'

'In three days' time.'

'I see.' Her spirits sank. It was hard to visualise this place without him somehow and she knew that his absence would leave a yawning gap.

'It is a necessary stage in my plans.'

'So you can announce the return of Viscount Destermere?'

'Exactly. London will be thin of company at present, but word will get round all the same.'

'Will you remain there, sir?'

'No. I shall travel into Essex and collect my ward before returning to Yorkshire.'

Her hand clenched around the ribbons of her bonnet. He was coming back! Then she registered the remainder of what he had just said.

'Your ward?'

'Yes, my brother's child, Lucy. She is six or thereabouts.'

'Have you never seen her before, then?'

'No, though, of course, I knew of her existence from Greville's letters.'

'Of course.'

'Her mother died when Lucy was born.'

'Poor little girl. She has lost a great deal in her short life. Six is too young to be orphaned.'

For a moment he regarded her shrewdly. 'Yes, you are right.'

'There is never a right time to lose one's parents, but children are so vulnerable.'

'Indeed they are.'

'I am sure she will welcome some stability after all the disruption she has endured.'

'In any event, I shall give her a home for as long as she needs it.' He smiled and for a moment the grey eyes warmed. 'When I return to Netherclough Hall I hope to have the honour of receiving you there, Miss Davenport, along with Dr and Miss Greystoke.'

At those words, Claire felt her heart miss a beat. She

would see him again after all. Almost immediately she told herself not to be so foolish as to refine upon it. He was merely being polite. He owed the Greystokes such an invitation. If she was included, it was because good manners demanded that he did not slight their friend. Once honour was satisfied they would have nothing more to do with each other. The man she had known as Mark Eden was gone, replaced by Viscount Destermere, one who was so far her social superior as to make even the thought of such a connection truly laughable. That was reality. He belonged to another world, a world of wealth, position and power. One day in the not-too-distant future he would marry—a young woman of his own class who would provide the heirs to continue his line. That too was reality and she acknowledged it. All that had happened here would one day be relegated to the back of his memory and she with it. It was an oddly dispiriting thought.

Chapter Four

Lying in bed later that night, Claire found herself unable to sleep for her mind was racing, turning over all she had learnt. It turned too on her situation. This interlude with the Greystokes had been a welcome respite from trouble but, having been here nearly a month, she did not deceive herself that it could continue. They had been more than kind, but she could not impose on them much longer. Besides which, the uneasy thought persisted that her aunt might have kept Ellen's letters and might remember them now. Her uncle had been made to look a fool, a situation that would not long endure if he so much as suspected there was a remedy. She must find a secure position and soon, a place her uncle would never think of looking.

And then the germ of an idea occurred to her. An idea that was both wild and wonderful together. Could it work? Would she dare suggest it? And if she did, what would be the response? Almost she could see the Viscount's expression, the cold reserve returning to those grey eyes. He could be an intimidating figure when he chose. Would he consider it the greatest piece of presumption? Would he even listen? Claire bit her lip. There was only one way to find out: she must seek an opportunity to speak with him alone and then ask him.

The first part of her plan proved quite easy; the following morning Dr Greystoke went out on his rounds at ten and Ellen left to call on someone in the town. Their noble guest was ensconced in the parlour, perusing the newspaper. Hearing the door open, he glanced up and, perceiving Claire, rose from his chair and made her an elegant bow.

'Miss Davenport.' His gaze swept her from head to toe. 'No need to ask if you are well.'

'Thank you, sir.'

Not knowing what else to say, she sat down on the edge of the couch and watched him resume his seat. She swallowed hard. It had all seemed so easy when she was lying in bed last night, but now that the moment had come it was a different matter. There was a knot in her stomach and her mouth felt dry. For all his polished manners he seemed so commanding a presence, so remote from her in every way. How could she have presumed to think he would agree to her request? And yet... She closed her eyes a moment and saw her uncle's face. Could she risk his finding her because she had lacked the resolution even to try to put her plan into action? Claire lifted her chin.

'May I speak to you, sir?'

He laid aside the paper. 'Of course.'

She had his attention. It was now or never. She took a deep breath.

'I would like a position in your household...as governess to your ward.' Before he could say a word she hurried on. 'My education is good. I can speak French and Italian and write a fine hand. I know about arithmetic and the use of the globes. I can play the pianoforte and sing and sew and draw. Miss Greystoke can attest to my family background and character. And I like children. I used to teach my younger cousins.'

It was out. She had said it. With thumping heart Claire waited. For a moment he did not move or speak though the grey gaze never left her face, and under their cool, appraising stare she felt her cheeks grow warm.

'I confess I am surprised, Miss Davenport,' he said then. 'Not by the quality of your education, but by your desire to become a governess.'

'As I told you, my parents are dead and I must earn my living, sir.'

'And what of your other relations? The ones with whom you live.'

'They cannot provide for me indefinitely. I always knew that I should have to find a suitable position one day.'

'And why do you think this suitable?'

'Your ward is of excellent family, she is motherless and she needs someone who will look after her.'

'Do you think that I will not look after her?'

'No, of course not. I never meant to imply any such thing.' She paused. 'But a young girl also needs a woman's presence.'

'True. How old are you, Miss Davenport?'

Her colour deepened but she met his eye. 'I am almost one and twenty.'

'Are you not a little young for the role?'

'By no means. I know how it feels to lose one's parents and how important it is for a child to feel secure, to know that there will always be a sympathetic female presence she can turn to for guidance, someone who will always have her best interests at heart, someone who will really care.'

It came out with quiet passion. In fact, it was not just the tone but the words that took him aback for he could not doubt the sincerity of either. He knew she was speaking from experience. Had her own life been unhappy after the death of her parents? Had that anything to do with the relatives she spoke of? His curiosity mounted and with it the feeling that there was something he wasn't being told.

'My estate at Netherclough is remote. Apart from the local village there is no society for miles around. How would you bear the solitariness of the place?'

'I should bear it very well, sir. I was born in the country and spent the first thirteen years of my life there. Thirteen happy years.'

He heard the wistful note and was unexpectedly touched by it. Even so he felt the need to probe a bit further.

'And when your parents died you went to live with your father's relations.'

'Yes.' Her heart began to beat a little faster.

'And your uncle resides in…?'

'Northamptonshire.'

'You *are* a long way from home, aren't you?'

Not far enough, she thought. Aloud she replied, 'Oh, not so far. Stage coach travel is improving all the time, is it not?'

'Is it?'

Claire could have kicked herself. Of course, a man like this would never use stage coaches. Why would he, with a stable of fine horses and numerous carriages at his beck and call?

'Surely your uncle would be most alarmed by your failure to return home,' he continued.

'Not at all, sir, since I should write and inform him of the altered circumstances.' It was a blatant lie but it couldn't be helped. She went on, 'Besides, he would be the last person to stand in my way. He told me so himself.' That part was true at any rate.

'I see. And what sort of salary would you require?'

This was something she had not considered and for a moment was thrown. What did governesses earn? Knowing a response was required of her she plucked a figure out of thin air.

'Thirty pounds per annum.'

'You set a high price on your skills, Miss Davenport.'

Her cheeks went scarlet. However, if he expected her to retract he was mistaken. Instead her chin lifted.

'My services are worth the money, sir.'

'That has yet to be determined.'

'Then you will employ me?'

If she had hoped not to betray too much eagerness she was wide of the mark. He could see it in her face. Moreover, it was underlain by something akin to desperation. She really wanted this job. Thinking carefully, he weighed up the possibility. His ward was certainly going to need a governess and that was a serious responsibility since whoever filled the role must fit the child to take her place in society one day. Such a person must be intellectually capable and of unimpeachable reputation. Miss Davenport, though young, was well educated and evidently of good family. George and his sister spoke well of her. Though he sensed a mystery somewhere, what did he actually know against her? Nothing, he decided. In spite of the somewhat unusual manner of her arrival in Yorkshire, he believed her reputation to be good. She was courageous; she had come to his aid when he needed it. It was clear that she needed the situation and he was in a position to help.

He remembered all too clearly how it felt when one could do nothing. For a second Lakshmi's face swam into his mind. Could he abandon another young woman to her fate? The world was a hard place when one did not have the protection of wealth. Claire Davenport was not asking for money; she was asking for the means to earn it and he respected that. Did she not deserve a chance? He threw her a cool, appraising look and made up his mind.

'Very well,' he said. 'Consider yourself hired—for a probationary period of three months. If we are both satisfied with the situation at the end of that time, the post will become permanent.'

For a second she wasn't sure that she had heard him correctly. Then it sank in and fierce joy swept through her.

'Thank you, sir. You won't regret it, I promise you.'

'See to it that I don't, Miss Davenport.' The grey eyes locked with hers. 'I give you fair warning that I expect the highest standards in every respect. If they are not met the arrangement will be terminated immediately. Is that clear?'

'Very clear, sir.'

'As long as we understand each other.'

Claire left him shortly afterwards and, unable to contain her elation, went into the garden. Once there she let out a whoop of joy. Three months! Three months to prove herself. And she would prove herself! She would try by every means in her power to make a success of this. Her uncle would never think of looking for her at Netherclough, and by the time her probation was complete she would have reached her majority. She would be free.

Alone in the parlour the Viscount stood awhile, gazing down into the fire. He was committed now. Time would tell whether the decision was the right one. Yet there was something about Claire Davenport that he found hard to dismiss: beneath that outward show of spirit was an underlying vulnerability. Moreover, he acknowledged that she was a very pretty girl. No doubt his ward would prefer someone young and attractive as a governess. What really mattered, of course, was competence. That would become evident soon enough. Three months would demonstrate whether his decision had been the right one or not.

Two days later he prepared to leave for London, having first taken his leave of his hosts and of Claire.

'We shall meet again very soon, Miss Davenport. In the meantime is there anything I can bring you from the capital?'

It had never occurred to her that he would even ask and the question threw her.

'I thank you, no, sir.'

'You must be the first woman ever to say so,' he replied, regarding her with the familiar cool appraisal that caused a fluttering sensation in her stomach. 'I half expected a lengthy shopping list.'

'Then you have been spared it.'

'So it would seem. I suppose I should be grateful.'

Thinking of the little money remaining to her, she knew there was no possibility of indulging herself, even if she had thought of it.

'I expect to be gone for two weeks or so,' he went on. 'I shall inform the housekeeper at Netherclough when to expect me. At that time I shall arrange for a carriage to collect you.'

It was an attention she had not expected.

'Thank you, sir.'

'It is my wish that you should be there when I return so that you can become acquainted with my ward from the outset. I think we should start as we mean to go on.'

'As you wish, sir.'

'Until then, Miss Davenport.'

He favoured her with a bow and then was gone. Watching his departing figure, she was conscious of a strange sense of loss.

The feeling stayed with her in the days that followed. He was such a charismatic figure that when he was absent the house felt different, not less friendly or less welcoming exactly and yet still lacking. Although she made every attempt to keep busy, Claire found herself counting the days until she should be able to take up her new position. It represented a first step into a larger world, one that only a few short weeks ago she could never have thought of entering.

Eventually the day came, a fortnight later, when a carriage arrived to transport her to Netherclough Hall. With very real regret she said farewell to Ellen and George Greystoke and thanked them for their kindness. Like his sister, George seemed genuinely affected to see her go.

'I wish you all good fortune in your new life, Miss Davenport,' he said as they stood together by the gate.

Ellen smiled. 'I hope you will be very happy, my dear.'

'I'm sure I shall be,' Claire replied. 'I'll write as soon as I can and tell you how I go on.'

'I shall look forward to that.' She took Claire's hand

for a moment and gazed very earnestly into her face. 'You know that you can always come to me if you need to, my dear.'

'Thank you.'

Claire gave her friend a last hug and climbed into the carriage. A liveried footman put up the steps and closed the door. As the vehicle pulled away she leaned from the window to wave. Only when her friends were out of sight did she settle back into her seat and look around her. The carriage was larger and more opulent than anything she had ever seen. Furthermore it was so well sprung that even the worst bumps in the road went almost unnoticed. The four bays that pulled it were spirited and swift, as different as could be from her uncle's carriage horses. He could never have afforded any as fine as these. Never would she have expected to ride in such style or comfort.

Glancing at the valise beside her, she was forcefully reminded that it contained all her worldly possessions. If the footman had been surprised by the lack of baggage, he was too well trained to betray it. Perhaps he had assumed her trunks would be following later. She smiled ruefully. A governess had no need of fine gowns. As long as her appearance was clean and neat it would suffice. A new chapter of her life was beginning and for the first time she had a measure of control over how it would unfold.

For a while she was so wrapped in thought that she paid no heed to the country through which they were passing, but eventually it impinged on her consciousness again and she found herself curious to see Netherclough Hall. By repute it was a very grand old house and set in a large attractive park. That at least would afford long walks in the fresh air and some pleasant scenes to sketch.

For all the Viscount's doubts she had no fear of solitude and had never minded her own company.

The thought brought her employer to mind again. It seemed strange to think of him in those terms but she knew she must accustom herself to it. Mark Eden was gone. She was entering the service of Viscount Destermere. There could be no hint of earlier familiarity. That had belonged to a set of extraordinary circumstances—circumstances that must never be alluded to in any way. It was not to be supposed that she would see very much of her employer anyway. Probably their paths would cross but rarely. The knowledge gave her a strange pang.

She was drawn from her thoughts when, at length, the carriage turned in through large wrought-iron gates that gave onto a long driveway between mature chestnut trees. Beyond it, rolling green parkland stretched away to wooded hillsides. With excitement and trepidation Claire craned eagerly for a view of the house. When it came into view round a bend in the drive she drew in a sharp breath. Netherclough Hall was an imposing residence built of grey stone, nestled in a fold of the hills. From its numerous chimneys and crenellated walls to the stone mullions and ancient porch it was in every way a nobleman's residence. Beneath its sloping grounds a river ran through trees among the water meadows.

The Viscount had not lied when he said his estate was remote, but far from feeling concerned Claire knew only a sense of satisfaction at the location. It was definitely the last place her uncle would ever think of looking for her.

Presently the carriage drew up outside the stone porch beyond which was a great iron-clamped door. Another footman admitted her to a flagged hallway hung with racks of antlers and ancient weapons. A great carved-oak staircase led to the upper floors. Claire looked round, trying to take it in, but just then footsteps announced the arrival of the housekeeper, a plump middle-aged woman in a neat grey gown and lace cap who introduced herself as Mrs Hughes. When the courtesies had been observed she offered to show Claire to her room.

This proved to be a light and pleasant chamber at the rear of the house, overlooking the gardens and the park. Comfortably furnished, it appeared to have been newly decorated. Elegant blue-and-gold hangings and thick rugs added a feeling of cosiness and luxury. A cheerful fire burned in the grate.

'I hope everything is satisfactory,' said Mrs Hughes.

'It's beautiful.'

The housekeeper smiled, clearly pleased by the reaction. 'I hope you will be happy here, Miss Davenport.'

'I'm sure I shall. Thank you.'

'Is the rest of your luggage to follow, miss?'

Claire knew a moment of acute embarrassment. 'No. Everything is here.'

The only indication of the older woman's surprise was a brief silence. Then she smiled again.

'Well, then, perhaps you would care to take some refreshment after your journey?'

'That would be most kind.'

Having removed her bonnet and spencer, Claire followed the housekeeper to a small parlour. A footman appeared a short time later with a tray. Mrs Hughes poured the tea and offered her guest a slice of seed cake. Thus fortified, Claire began to relax.

'This is a beautiful house,' she observed. 'Have you been here long, Mrs Hughes?'

'Thirty-five years. I took up my post in Lord Destermere's time. The older Viscount Destermere, I mean.'

'I see.'

'His sons were mere children then, of course. Who could have foreseen what tragedy would follow?' She shook her head. 'It will be good to have this house inhabited again.'

'I imagine it will.'

'The estate needs attention too, after all these months. Lord Destermere will find himself busy enough, I have no doubt.'

'Yes, I'm sure he will.'

'Not that anyone expected to see him again after he was packed off to India.'

'Packed off?'

'There was some scandal involving a young woman, I believe. Someone his father considered unsuitable. I never really knew the details.' She leaned forward confidentially. 'Master Marcus and his brother were rather wild in their youth. I put it down to them losing their mother when they were boys. Their father took her death hard and became very withdrawn. Just between ourselves, Miss Davenport, he didn't take the interest in his sons that he might have.'

Claire listened with close attention for the words stripped away some of the mystery surrounding her new employer. The story saddened her, too. Children were so vulnerable, as she had good cause to know. It could be no wonder that two bewildered little boys should look to their father for support and guidance. When their parent failed to provide it or show any interest they must have sought to get his attention in the only way they knew how.

'They got up to enough mischief as boys, but that was

nothing compared to what happened once they came down from Cambridge and went to London. They got in with a very fast set indeed. Gaming, drinking, horse racing, opera dancers. You name it.'

'That must have grieved their father.'

'There were some terrible rows, believe me,' replied Mrs Hughes. 'However, Master Greville calmed down a great deal when he married. In fact, it was the making of him.'

'Was his wife very beautiful?'

'Oh, yes, and so accomplished. The toast of London. He was very much in love with her.'

'How sad that she should have died so young.'

'Yes, indeed. He was almost distracted by her loss. For some time he couldn't even bear to look at his infant daughter.'

Hearing those words, Claire felt a sudden chill. Had history repeated itself? Her heart went out to Lucy, and for the first time the burden of her new responsibility was brought home to her.

'I really thought all would be well again after he inherited the title, but first there was the business of his wife's untimely demise and then the dreadful news of his own death.'

'But now Lord Destermere is returned. Perhaps all may yet be well,' replied Claire.

'I truly hope so.' Mrs Hughes set down her cup and saucer. 'And now perhaps you would like me to show you around the house?'

'Indeed I should, if it is no trouble.'

'No trouble at all, miss. Besides, it's such a rambling old place that it's easy to get lost.'

And so there followed a guided tour. The reception rooms were beautiful, and there was a library, which

Claire made a mental note to revisit as soon as possible, as well as the private apartments and a long gallery lined with family portraits. The last room they visited was the schoolroom. It was spacious and light and it too had been recently redecorated. Moreover, it was supplied with rugs, table and chairs, two small desks and a blackboard and easel. A shelf held a selection of old books and toys and an ancient rocking horse stood in one corner. There was also a fireplace with logs ready laid. Claire saw it with some relief, recalling the chilly room where she and her cousins had taken their lessons under Miss Hardcastle's exacting eye. This was cosy in comparison, though a glance at the books revealed they were too advanced, and thus unsuitable for a young child.

'We expect His Lordship tomorrow,' said Mrs Hughes.

Claire's heart gave a peculiar lurch. Tomorrow. She regarded the prospect with mingled excitement and trepidation. When she had told the Viscount that she liked children it had been the truth, but her experience of them was limited. Could she do the job? Could she give an orphaned child the care needed? Then she thought back to her own childhood and the benevolent influence of Ellen Greystoke. Surely those precepts would be good ones to follow, comprised as they were of firmness and kindness, always backed by sincere interest. Please God, she thought, let me get it right.

Chapter Five

It was therefore with mixed feelings that Claire awaited the Viscount's return the following day. In the event, it was late afternoon when a large and handsome carriage drew up before the house. From the resulting bustle among the servants it was clear who had arrived. Hastily smoothing her skirts she hurried to the hallway where Mrs Hughes was already waiting. Uncertain of what to expect and unwilling to push herself forward Claire remained in the background. And then he was there, a tall elegant figure in a travelling cape and high-crowned beaver hat. At the sight of him her heart began to beat a little faster. His presence seemed to fill the room somehow as though the house had been waiting only for his arrival to seem complete. In that moment she knew how much she had missed him. The realisation was disturbing, the sentiment inappropriate. Forcing her expression into what she hoped was a becoming calm she drew in a deep breath. Marcus, looking round the hallway, perceived her at once, the grey eyes missing no detail of her appearance from the dark curls to the simple sprigged muslin gown. She looked as neat as wax, he thought, favouring her with a bow.

'Well met, Miss Davenport. May I introduce your new charge?' He glanced down at the small figure at his side. 'This is my ward, the Honourable Lucy Edenbridge. Lucy, this is Miss Davenport who is to be your new governess.'

The child dropped a polite curtsy and stared at Claire with big blue eyes. She was clad in a blue cloak, and a straw bonnet partially concealed light brown curls. In one small hand she was clutching a toy. She looked lost somehow, and a little timid.

Claire smiled at her. 'Hello, Lucy. What a lovely doll.'

The child made no reply and lowered her eyes. Marcus glanced down and surveyed her keenly.

'You should answer, child, when you are spoken to.'

Lucy's cheeks reddened, but still she remained silent. Marcus raised an eyebrow. Fearing that the scene would escalate, Claire cut in.

'It's all right. This has been a big change and it will take her a while to find her feet and grow accustomed to all the new faces around her.'

'You may be right,' he replied.

Claire bent down so that she was on Lucy's level. 'What do you call your doll?'

There followed another silence. Then, very quietly, 'Susan.'

'That's a good name. It suits her very well. Shall we take Susan upstairs and show her where her room is? She must be feeling tired after such a long journey.'

After a moment the child nodded. Claire held out her hand.

'Come, then.'

Lucy looked up at her uncle and he nodded.

'That's right. You go along with Miss Davenport.'

A small hand stole tentatively into Claire's. The Viscount caught her eye.

'I will speak with you later, Miss Davenport. There are various points we need to discuss.' He paused. 'In the meantime, Mrs Hughes will send up a tray for Lucy. It has indeed been a long journey and she is tired. An early night is in order, I think.'

'Yes, sir.'

As Claire led the child away she was conscious of the penetrating gaze that followed them to the stairs.

In fact, he had been quite right. By the time Lucy was ensconced in her room and had eaten some supper she was pale with fatigue so Claire undressed her and put her to bed. As she tucked the sheet in she was aware that the child watched her with solemn, sleepy eyes.

Claire smiled. 'Would you like to have Susan with you?'

This elicited a nod. Retrieving the doll from a nearby chair, Claire handed it over and watched as it was tucked carefully under the covers. Then she gently brushed the child's face with her hand.

'Goodnight, dear. Sleep well.'

Within a very short time Lucy was asleep, clearly worn out by the journey and perhaps too by the anxiety of altered circumstances. As she looked at the forlorn little figure in the big bed her heart went out to Lucy. How lonely and frightened the child must be. She knew how it felt to be alone in the world and cast on the mercy of others, and that was at thirteen, not six years of age.

She remained in the room until she was quite certain that Lucy was fast asleep, and instructed the maid to leave a night light burning. If by some chance the child did wake up, at least she wouldn't be on her own in a strange place in the dark.

Having seen to her charge's immediate needs, Claire made her way to the drawing room, mindful that her employer had asked to speak to her. When she entered he was standing by the hearth. He had been leaning on the mantel, staring down into the flames, but hearing her come in he glanced up and then straightened.

'Ah, Miss Davenport. How is my ward?'

'Asleep, sir. As you suspected, she really was very tired.'

'Yes, I imagine she was. It was a long journey and there has been all the upheaval attendant on her removal. What she needs now is some stability.' He regarded her keenly. 'I take it that you have seen the nursery.'

'Yes, sir.'

He smiled faintly. 'It has been some years since I was there, and is no doubt lacking in some essentials. You may have whatever you need for the discharge of your duties. Money is no object. Just tell me what you want and I'll see that you get it.'

Somewhat taken aback, she thanked him. 'There are a few things missing,' she admitted, 'chiefly books suitable for a child of Lucy's age.'

'That will be rectified as soon as possible. In the interim she needs some time to grow accustomed to her new surroundings. It will all be very strange and frightening. Let her have plenty of fresh air and exercise, Miss Davenport. Then introduce her lessons gradually.'

'As you wish, sir.'

'This is her home now and I want her to feel at ease here.'

For the second time Claire was taken aback for there could be no mistaking the sincerity with which he spoke.

There was, besides, real compassion in the orders he had given and she was touched.

'I will do my best to see that she does, sir.'

'I am sure you will.' He paused, surveying her keenly. 'And what of you, Miss Davenport? Does your room meet with your approval?'

'Oh, yes. It is beautiful.'

Again she found herself caught unawares. She knew enough of life to realise that employers usually gave little thought to the comfort of their servants.

'Good. If you find you need anything else, tell Mrs Hughes and she will arrange it.'

'Thank you. That is most kind.'

For a moment there was silence and she felt acutely aware of that disconcerting grey gaze. Then he smiled.

'Then if there is nothing else I will not detain you.'

She dropped a graceful curtsy and retraced her steps to the door, pausing briefly to look over her shoulder. However, he had turned back towards the fire and seemed to have dismissed her from his mind. Claire opened the door quietly and slipped away. On returning to her room she sat down and began to write the promised letter to Ellen.

In the days that followed she heeded her instructions. The early autumn weather was pleasant, so it was no hardship to take her young charge out of doors. Besides which it gave Claire a chance to talk to her and find out more about her. Although she was shy and her education had been somewhat disrupted due to circumstances, Lucy was not unintelligent and had an enquiring mind. She was quick to learn the names of the flowers and trees and living creatures they encountered on these walks. When told a story she was an avid listener. Little by little Claire added to their activities, always taking care to vary them and to try to make them interesting.

She had not expected to see much of her employer at all, but he occasionally came to the nursery. One day, when teaching Lucy her letters, she looked up to see the tall figure in the doorway. Realising who it was, she felt her heartbeat quicken. Following her gaze, Lucy saw him too and paused in her task, regarding him uncertainly.

He smiled down at her. 'How are you today, Lucy?'

She reddened and lowered her eyes. 'Very well, thank you, Uncle Marcus.'

'What have you been doing?'

Lucy moved her hand so that he could see the copy-book in which she had been working. He surveyed it closely and the letters written in large childish script.

'Well done,' he said then. 'You're making good progress, I see.'

Lucy's blush deepened. Over her head he exchanged glances with Claire.

'Well done, Miss Davenport.'

She had half expected to hear irony in the tone, but there was none and her own face grew a little warmer.

'She is quick to learn,' she replied.

'I'm pleased to hear it. I should not like my niece to be an ignoramus.'

'I can assure you, sir, she is far from being anything of the sort.'

'Good.' Marcus looked down at his niece. 'Now, Lucy, copy out all those letters again. I wish to speak to Miss Davenport.'

Obediently the child returned to her task. Seeing her once again employed, he drew Claire aside.

'The books and materials you asked for have been

ordered,' he said. 'They should be here within the week. Is there anything else you require?'

'Not at present, thank you.'

'If you think of anything later, be sure to let me know.' He paused. 'Has the child's appetite returned? Is she sleeping properly?'

'Yes, sir, on both counts.'

'Does she seem to be settling down?'

'I think she is beginning to, yes, but it is likely to take a while before she really feels at home.'

'Yes, I suppose it will.' For a moment he surveyed her in silence. 'Well, then, I won't detain you further.' Throwing another glance towards his niece, he took his leave of them.

She watched the departing figure a moment and then went back to see what Lucy was doing. The child looked up, regarding her quizzically.

'What's a nigneraymus, Miss Davenport?'

Claire bit back a smile. 'A very stupid person. Not like you at all.'

'Oh.' Lucy digested the information thoughtfully. 'If I learn all my letters, will Uncle Marcus like me better?'

'He likes you now.'

'Does he?'

'Of course. Did he not bring you here to live with him?'

'Yes.'

'Well, then.'

'It's just that I don't see him very much.'

'Your uncle is very busy,' Claire replied. 'Netherclough is a big estate and it takes up a lot of his time.'

Lucy nodded slowly. 'Papa was always busy, too.'

'Gentlemen often are, but it doesn't mean they don't

care for you.' She put a reassuring hand on the child's shoulder and smiled, hoping that what she said was true.

As she and Lucy went for their afternoon walk Claire pondered the matter. She knew that after months without a master, Netherclough really did need Marcus's close attention. Very often she would see him ride out with Mr Fisk, the land agent, or else he would be closeted in the study with piles of paperwork. So far as the physical welfare of his niece was concerned he had shown a great deal of consideration and compliance. She lacked for nothing. The same was true of her education: the list of books and schoolroom materials Claire had submitted had not been questioned. It seemed he trusted her judgement and was prepared to back it financially. Of course, as he had intimated, money was no object. If Mrs Hughes was to be believed, the Edenbridge family was among the wealthiest in the country. However, when it came to the child's emotional needs the case was rather different. Marcus spent very little time with her, most of it comprising short visits to the nursery, as today. Although his manner showed interest, he seemed to hold himself aloof somehow as though, having seen to all the material aspects of his guardianship, he was absolved from deeper involvement. She hoped that, as time went on and matters fell into a routine, he might be able to spend more time with Lucy.

She had been so absorbed in thought that she hadn't paid much attention to the direction of their steps that afternoon, but realised now that once again Lucy had brought them to the paddock where several horses were grazing. It was clear at a glance that they were hunters, huge, powerful beasts all sixteen hands or more at the shoulder. Unperturbed by its size, Lucy was feeding one of them through the fence with handfuls of grass. It was clear that the child knew to hold her hand out flat and that she had no fear of the great teeth or the long tongue that whisked the grass away. As the horse munched she stroked its nose gently.

'You like the horses, don't you?' said Claire then.

Lucy nodded.

'Shall we find the head groom and ask if we can have a look around the stables?'

Lucy turned round, her expression animated. 'Oh, yes, please, Miss Davenport.'

And so they spent a delightful hour walking along the row of stalls and loose boxes and admiring the beautiful animals they encountered there. It was immediately clear to Claire that the Viscount and his late brother had a good eye for horseflesh. The head groom was Mr Trubshaw, a stocky, grey-haired individual with a weathered face and a thick Yorkshire accent, and he possessed a fund of knowledge about his charges. He told Lucy the name of each horse and a little of its history. She listened avidly, committing all the details to memory, and asked questions in her turn. Seeing her interest was genuine, he warmed to her very quickly and soon the two were chatting like old friends. Claire watched thoughtfully. Trubshaw had accomplished more in an hour with the child than Marcus had managed in weeks. Lucy was in seventh heaven here and that knowledge gave her an idea.

Later that evening, when Lucy was in bed, Claire inquired of Mather where His Lordship was to be found. The butler directed her to the small salon. It was the same room he had interviewed her in before, when they had spoken about books and teaching equipment.

Marcus was seated in a chair by the fire, but he rose as

she entered. Claire caught her breath. He was dressed in cream-coloured breeches and a coat of claret velvet over immaculate linen. A single fob hung from his waistcoat. His hands were innocent of adornment save for one gold signet ring. It was a simple costume, but she thought it would have been hard to find one more elegant or better suited to such a powerful physique.

'Good evening, Miss Davenport.'

She replied to the greeting and took the offered chair.

'How may I help you?'

'I wish to speak to you about Lucy.'

The dark brows twitched together. 'Is something wrong? Is she ill? Has she been misbehaving?'

'No, nothing like that. I wanted to ask if there is a pony in your stables that she might ride.'

'A pony?'

'Yes, the horses are all too big, you see.'

Undeceived by the innocent tone, he threw her an eloquent look. 'Is the child keen to ride?'

'Yes. I believe she has a real affinity with horses.'

She told him about the visit to the stables. He heard her in silence, thinking carefully as he did so. It was not an outlandish request. Horsemanship was one of the accomplishments expected of a young lady of Lucy's station, and it was healthy exercise besides.

'There is nothing in the stable that is suitable at present,' he replied, 'but I am sure that a pony could be found.'

'I know that Lucy would be delighted.'

'I'll speak to Trubshaw in the morning. He knows every horse within a twenty-mile radius of Netherclough.'

'He is most knowledgeable,' she replied.

'Yes, he is. It was he who taught me and Greville to ride. He'll be an ideal teacher for Lucy, too.'

'I have no doubt he will.' Claire took a deep breath. 'However, I was hoping that perhaps you might go out with her sometimes, sir.'

The grey gaze came to rest on her face while his own assumed an expression of hauteur. Feeling her cheeks grow warmer, Claire hurried on before her courage failed her.

'I know you have been very busy since your return, but this would provide a good opportunity for you to spend some time with the child.'

'What are you implying, Miss Davenport?'

'Nothing. It's just…'

'Just what?'

'It's just that I thought it might bring you together more.'

'Did you indeed?'

'I do not mean to criticise,' she said, 'but it is true that you have seen very little of the child so far and, well, she notices, sir.'

The grey eyes grew as cool as his tone. 'You think I neglect her?'

'No, of course not. Well, not deliberately anyway.'

'So you do think so.'

She swallowed hard. 'The only reason I said anything is because Lucy asked me if you liked her.'

'And what did you say, may I ask?'

'That I was sure you did.'

'How very reassuring to have your support,' he replied. 'However, it is not your place to discuss me with my niece.'

'She asked the question, sir, and I answered it. I intended no disrespect in doing so.'

For a moment he was silent. Almost she could feel the anger radiating off him and her heart sank. She had spoken too frankly and antagonised him. Perhaps now she had made the situation worse.

'If I have caused offence, I beg your pardon, sir.'

'As well you should. In future you will confine yourself to your duties, Miss Davenport, instead of interfering in matters that do not concern you.' He got to his feet. 'That will be all.'

Uncomfortably aware of having made a false step, she rose from her chair and dropped a curtsy before beating a retreat, aware as she did so of the fierce hawk-like gaze that followed her every step of the way. Only when she was safely in the hall did she let out the breath she had been holding. Her cheeks burned. How angry he had been. Yet in spite of that she could not regret having said it, even if he did ignore the words.

After she left him Marcus poured himself a glass of brandy and took a deep swig. Claire's assessment had been quite correct: he was angry. Angry with her for presuming to tell him his duty and angry with himself because he knew the words were merited. It was true he had been very busy since his return; Greville's death had left a vacuum and there were numerous matters requiring his attention. However, he realised now that in part they had been an excuse for avoiding his young niece. Having spent the last ten years soldiering, he was unused to children and unfamiliar with their needs. The journey from Essex had been more difficult than he had anticipated, for the child was withdrawn and shy of him. Though he spoke to her with the utmost gentleness he had hardly been able to get half a dozen words out of her. He had tried telling her stories about the animals in India that he thought she might enjoy but, though she heard him quietly, she had offered no response. Moreover, she ate very little and slept badly. Clearly the disruption of recent months was taking its toll on her. More than once he had been overwhelmed with a sense of inadequacy.

Claire had known what to say, he recalled. From the first she had instinctively known how to get past the barrier that Lucy had been protecting herself with. He sighed. He had spoken more harshly than he should have done, but her words had touched a nerve. At the same time, he acknowledged, she was offering him an opportunity. Could it work?

After the unfortunate interview in the salon, Claire had seen Marcus only twice in the following week, and that was when he had come to the schoolroom. As usual he had stayed only a short time, just long enough to see what his niece was doing and to ask about her progress. When he had spoken to the child it was always in a tone of quiet encouragement, but this had never elicited more than a few shy words from Lucy. Seeing it, Claire had been saddened. Were the two of them destined to remain polite strangers?

She had said nothing at all to Lucy about the matter of a pony. Marcus had promised to speak to Trubshaw, but would he remember? He *was* very busy. She wouldn't raise the child's hopes only to see them dashed. Nor would she raise the subject again with Marcus himself. It was too loaded a topic now. He had made no reference to their conversation and his manner to her was one of polite aloofness. It seemed that she and Lucy were both to be relegated to the periphery of his affairs.

It came as a surprise, therefore, when a footman came to the nursery to say that His Lordship desired Miss

Davenport and Miss Lucy to attend him in the stable yard after luncheon. Hearing the summons, Claire felt the first faint stirrings of hope. Had he kept his promise?

'Why does Uncle Marcus want us to go to the stables, Miss Davenport?'

'I don't know, dear. We must go and find out.'

When they arrived, the Viscount was already there, talking to Trubshaw. Seeing their approach, he greeted them both and then nodded to the groom. The man promptly disappeared into the stable and emerged a few minutes later leading a grey pony. Understanding the implication, Claire felt her heart soar even as her critical eye took in the details of the new arrival. A sturdy, shaggy little creature, the pony stood approximately twelve hands high. He had a bushy mane and tail and gentle brown eyes. A perfect choice, she thought, and her face lit with a smile for she could not but remember when she had been given her first pony. The memory was bittersweet.

Beside her Lucy's eyes widened.

'He's wonderful, isn't he, Miss Davenport?'

'Yes, he is.'

'May I ride him one day, do you think?'

'You had better ask your uncle,' she replied.

For a moment her gaze met his. Then Marcus looked down at the child and smiled. 'Of course you can ride him. He's yours.'

'Mine? To keep? Really?'

'Yes, really.'

Too overcome for speech just then, she flung her arms round him and hugged him. Taken totally by surprise, Marcus felt himself redden and then somehow, rather awkwardly, his arms were round the child and he was hugging her back. Then together they walked over to the pony.

'His name's Misty,' he said.

Lucy looked up at him. 'I like his name. It suits him.'

'Yes, I think it does.'

'How old is he?'

'Er…' Marcus looked at Trubshaw for help.

'Ten, my lord,' replied the other.

'He's older than me,' said Lucy.

'That's so he can teach you how to ride, miss,' replied the groom.

She nodded thoughtfully, then looked at her uncle. 'Can I ride him now?'

'Why not?' He lifted her up and sat her on the pony's back. 'Hold on to his mane. That's it.' He looked at the groom. 'Take her for a walk around the yard so she can get used to him.'

As they set off he watched for a moment or two and then glanced back at Claire only to see that she was already looking at him, her face lit with a dazzling smile. His heart missed a beat and for the second time that afternoon he was taken totally by surprise. She was more than a pretty girl, he realised then. Furthermore, the expression in those glorious eyes was joyful and tender and its warmth was directed at him. The effect was to take his breath away.

'Thank you,' she said.

Marcus collected himself quickly. 'He's hardly bloodstock,' he replied, 'but he's quiet and steady enough for the child to learn on.'

She nodded. 'Lucy adores him already.'

He followed her gaze back to the child and the pony, and then he smiled, too. 'I believe she does.'

'It will be hard to keep her away from him now, but

he will be so good for her, I know it. He'll build her confidence like nothing else could.'

'Yes, I think he will, and for that I owe you my thanks. If you had not mentioned the idea, it might not have occurred to me.'

'I'm very glad I did.'

'So am I.'

The sincerity in his voice was unmistakable, and the grey eyes looking into her face held an expression she had never seen there before. It disturbed and excited in equal measure, like the memory of his lips on her neck and throat. The recollection sent a shiver along her skin and she was more than ever glad he had known nothing of it. Besides, she reflected, in his fevered dream he had been kissing someone else.

Just then Lucy returned, bright-eyed and smiling, from her short excursion. Marcus lifted her down.

'Can I ride him again tomorrow?' she begged.

'Yes, I don't see why not,' he replied. 'If Miss Davenport doesn't mind.'

He looked over the child's head and met Claire's eye. Lucy looked up anxiously.

Claire laughed. 'No, I don't mind.'

'Will you teach me how to ride properly, Uncle Marcus?'

'If you wish.'

'Oh, yes, please.'

'Very well, but I warn you now. I shall expect you to try hard.'

'I will try hard, I promise.'

She tucked her small hand into his and gave the other to Claire. Then they walked back to the house together.

'Will Miss Davenport come riding with us too, Uncle Marcus?'

'If she wishes to,' he replied.

The grey eyes rested on Claire. Her heart leapt. It would be wonderful to ride again. She had always loved it, but the opportunities had been few and far between in recent years for it was a pursuit that found little favour with her aunt. Equally quickly she knew it would not be possible to take up the invitation. She had no riding clothes and no means of getting any either with the few meagre shillings remaining to her.

'I'm afraid I cannot,' she replied.

'Why not?'

'I regret that I have no suitable costume.'

'I see.'

Much to her relief he didn't pursue it. In any case, she realised, he must have understood how the case was. He had seen every gown she possessed many times. Her salary would be paid quarterly and wasn't due for weeks yet. Besides, if he went out alone with Lucy it would strengthen the relationship between the two of them and that could only be to the good.

Chapter Six

Having tucked Lucy into bed that night Claire took herself off to the library to find a new novel. It was her favourite room, a warm, comfortable place with wonderful old chairs in which it was possible to curl up and lose oneself in a good book. She was perusing the shelves when a footman entered with the intelligence that His Lordship desired her presence in the study.

Wondering what it could possibly be about, Claire made her way there. The Viscount was seated behind a large desk. He had apparently been reading some papers, but looked up as she entered and smiled faintly. After inviting her to sit, he opened a drawer in the desk and took out a small box.

'It occurs to me that if Lucy is to learn to ride she will require a riding habit and some boots. I would like you to attend to it.' Opening the box, he took out a pouch of coins and laid it on the desk. 'That should cover the expense.'

'Yes, sir.'

'It also occurs to me that you might require an

advance on your salary.' He laid another pouch beside the first. 'Shall we say ten pounds, to cover immediate expenses?'

Claire felt warmth rise to her face. Ten pounds! It was more money than she could ever recall seeing at one time in her whole life.

'I should have thought of it earlier,' he continued, 'but there have been many matters requiring my attention. I apologise for the oversight.'

'I...not at all.' She sought for the right words, feeling oddly tongue-tied. 'Thank you.'

'I have some business in Harrogate tomorrow. I thought perhaps you and Lucy might like to come along. I understand from Mrs Hughes that there are some good drapers in the town and an excellent seamstress. You can get Lucy's riding habit made up there. Order one for yourself at the same time. There is enough there to cover the cost.'

Claire felt her face grow very warm and the hazel eyes that met his were bright with indignation. Somehow she controlled her voice.

'I thank you, sir, but I cannot accept such a gift. It would be most improper to do so.'

He raised one eyebrow. 'Miss Davenport, when my ward has learned to ride it will be necessary for you to accompany her when I cannot. That being so, you will require the appropriate costume to do it in. It is a vital part of the equipment you require to do your job—like the horse and the saddle.' He paused. 'I take it there will be no difficulty attached to my providing *those?*'

Hearing the ironic tone, she lifted her chin. 'It is not at all the same thing.'

'I beg to differ. I can see very little difference.'

'Perhaps not, but I assure you, sir, that I can.'

'Your opinion in this matter is of no moment, Miss Davenport, since it is my wish as your employer that you should ride with my ward. And as your employer I expect my wishes to be obeyed.'

The tone, though perfectly level, was implacable. She knew it would be fruitless to argue, but only suppressed the desire with great difficulty. Had it been Mark Eden she would have yielded to the impulse—with Marcus Edenbridge she could not. It was infuriating, like the suave expression on that handsome face. How arrogant he could be at times and how determined to get his own way.

Though he guessed quite accurately at the thoughts behind the hazel eyes, he remained undeterred. Following up his advantage, he continued, 'Should you see anything else that Lucy might need, you should feel free to make the purchase.'

'As you wish, sir.'

'Quite so, Miss Davenport.'

Her hands clenched in her lap as she wrestled with a strong desire to hit him. She mastered it and tried to focus on what he was saying.

'The carriage will leave at nine o'clock.'

'We will be ready, sir.'

'Until tomorrow, then.'

It was clearly dismissal. Claire retrieved the purses from the desk and rose from her chair. She was halfway to the door when he recalled something else.

'Incidentally, I have asked Dr and Miss Greystoke to honour me with their company for dinner next Thursday. I would be pleased if you would join us.'

Taken unawares, she heard him with surprise and then with pleasure. It would be wonderful to see her friends again. Gathering her wits, she nodded.

'I should be delighted.'

'Good.' He favoured her with a charming smile. 'That's settled, then.'

After she had left him Claire returned to her room. Laying the two purses on the table, she regarded them thoughtfully. With that one casual gesture he had rescued her from financial embarrassment. Moreover, he didn't have to do it. She could not have asked him for money, particularly since she was essentially here on a trial basis. It was within his rights to withhold any payment until that period was over. Yet he had given it anyway. It was an act of kindness and one she had not looked for. But then there was the matter of the riding habit. He must have guessed what her response would be and had met it most adroitly, leaving no possibility of refusal. The knowledge of her defeat still rankled. For a moment his face returned to her mind.

'Impossible man!' she said aloud.

Attempting to dismiss that provoking image, she turned her thoughts to the morrow. With a trip to town in the offing, she would be able to rectify some of the deficiencies in her wardrobe. It occurred to her that, having seen every gown she possessed, he must have realised how the matter stood. The thought that he had assessed her wardrobe and found it wanting was mortifying. Worse, he was right. It was inadequate and unsuited to her present role. It had been foolish of her to think otherwise. By suggesting this trip he had saved her from some potentially embarrassing situations, damn him!

As she had anticipated Lucy was eager for the forthcoming treat and both of them were ready at the appointed time. The carriage stood waiting, a liveried footman by the open door. The Viscount was already in the hall-way. Looking at that tall elegant figure, Claire knew a moment's misgiving. However, nothing of their earlier encounter was apparent in his manner. On the contrary he glanced at the clock and smiled.

'You are punctual, Miss Davenport.'

Unable to think of a reply, she merely inclined her head.

He gestured toward the door. 'Shall we?'

Having lifted Lucy into the vehicle, he held out a hand to Claire. For a few brief seconds she could feel the firm clasp of his fingers. His touch seemed to burn through her glove. Then, having spoken to the coachman, he climbed in after her and seated himself opposite as the carriage moved forwards. Aware of his presence to the last fibre of her being, she arranged her skirts and hoped that nothing of her feeling showed in her face.

Fortunately Lucy diverted his attention with a question. He answered her with his customary patience and showed no sign of irritation when it was followed by two more. Now that the barriers were starting to come down, he clearly wanted to encourage the child to talk to him. As she watched the scene it occurred to Claire that he would be a good father as well as an indulgent uncle for there could be no doubt he would have children of his own one day. The thought was pleasing and unwelcome together. Before she could ask herself why, Lucy broke in.

'Uncle Marcus used to live in India, Miss Davenport.'

'So I believe,' replied Claire.

'When we were travelling from Essex he told me stories about it.'

'Oh?'

'Yes, all about hunting tigers and riding on elephants.'

'How exciting!' Then, recalling her defeat the previous evening, she smiled. 'Perhaps he'll tell you another story now. I'm sure you'd like that, wouldn't you?'

'Yes, I would, if you please, Uncle Marcus.'

Torn between disbelief and amusement the Viscount threw Claire a most eloquent look. It was met with an innocent expression that did not deceive him for a moment and he was strongly tempted to deliver a severe set down. Then he saw Lucy's eager face and knew he could not. After making a mental note to deal with Miss Davenport later, he favoured them with a tale about crossing a river on an elephant which had chosen to take a cooling shower while its passengers, of whom he was one, were still aboard. Lucy laughed in delight.

'Was anyone watching, Uncle Marcus?'

'Roughly half the population of the local village, as I recall.'

'What did you do?'

'The only thing I could do. I adopted a stiff upper lip and pretended to be quite unconcerned.'

Lucy giggled and, unable to help herself, Claire laughed, too. He regarded his audience with a pained expression.

'This really is most unkind of you both.'

That had the effect of sending Lucy into fresh peals of laughter, as he had known it would. Claire was both impressed and touched by the way he engaged with the child, and by his ability to take a joke; his expression now was far removed from the haughty individual she had spoken to the previous evening.

Sensing her regard, he looked up and for a moment met her gaze. Then the light of humour faded a little and was replaced by a different kind of warmth altogether.

Conscious of that look, Claire felt her heart miss a beat and she quickly looked away.

Seeing her unease, Marcus was annoyed with himself. He had been caught off guard when he should have been prepared, for he had already felt the effect that her laughter could have. Once again it lit her face and made her look beautiful. She laughed sincerely, from the heart, without any trace of affectation. He realised too that it pleased him to see her laugh like that. Hitherto her demeanour, though pleasant and courteous, had always seemed a little reserved, but in unguarded moments she had revealed another side to her personality, one that was fun-loving and light-hearted. It suited her. More, he found it intriguing. Almost at once he brought himself up short. As Lucy's governess and a member of his staff she was strictly off limits. He had appointed her to the post because it suited him; it was convenient and she was eligible and he wanted to help. Now he realised, somewhat belatedly, that he had not been completely impervious to her charms either.

Claire, sensitive to the atmosphere, felt the change in his manner and upbraided herself for being too forward. It must not happen again. She had not failed to recognise the expression in his eyes when he looked at her and was appalled. Her security depended on keeping this post and she would only do that if her behaviour was above reproach. There could be no familiarity between them. Besides, their social positions made it quite impossible that he would consider her as anything more than a diversion. That kind of liaison could have only one end. It was a lowering thought. Worse was the knowledge that she would forfeit all respect if she was ever to be so foolish as to encourage such attentions. Besides, as she knew full well, there was already a woman in his heart.

* * *

In many ways it was a relief when the carriage reached its destination and drew up in the main thoroughfare. The Viscount turned to Claire.

'I shall leave you here for the time being,' he said. 'Wakely will accompany you and carry your packages. I shall return in two hours' time.'

'Very well, sir.'

'In the meantime I trust that you will have a productive shopping expedition.'

'I am sure we shall, sir.'

The footman opened the door and, having let down the steps, handed Claire and Lucy out onto the street. The Viscount nodded farewell and the vehicle moved on. For a moment or two Claire watched it depart and then took Lucy by the hand.

'Come. Let us see what this place has to offer.'

In fact, their investigation of the town's shops was enjoyable and rewarding. Moreover, she and Lucy were the objects of almost fawning attention by the traders they met for the mode of their arrival had been noted. Such a handsome equipage could only belong to a wealthy man and the crest on the door left people in no doubt as to his identity. Two elegantly dressed females attended by a footman were certain of the warmest welcome everywhere they went. Claire was torn between amusement and alarm. It had not occurred to her that they would attract such notice. On the other hand, it was a novelty to be afforded the undivided attention of every shopkeeper they encountered. The latter almost fell over themselves to offer help and advice.

The first stop was the draper's shop recommended by Mrs Hughes, where bolt after bolt of fine cloth was displayed for her inspection. Eventually she settled on two lengths of figured muslin, in blue and jonquil respectively. They were totally unexceptionable, perfect for her newfound role. Along with them she chose a soft lilac mull. It was simple and plain, but it would make an elegant dress for the forthcoming dinner party with the Greystokes. The fabrics were relatively inexpensive, too, which meant that she could save the remainder of her money in case of need.

When it came to the matter of riding habits Lucy had decided ideas of her own. Rejecting the draper's suggestion of a dependable brown serge, she chose a deep blue velvet instead. Claire didn't argue. It was a pretty colour and it enhanced the child's blue eyes. She chose the brown fabric for herself.

Having purchased the cloth, they went next to the seamstress where they were ushered into an immaculate parlour and served tea while dress patterns were discussed at length. Delighted to have the custom of such exalted clients, the seamstress went into raptures over their chosen materials and assured them both of her ability to contrive the most stylish and elegant gowns imaginable. The conversation about styles and trimmings and measurements went on at such length that eventually Lucy grew bored and plumped herself down in a chair to play with her doll.

At last all the arrangements were complete and they escaped from that establishment to move on to the milliner and thence to the bootmaker. After two hours they had spent what seemed to Claire to be a truly prodigal sum of money. At the same time she had to acknowledge that it was very pleasant to have the means to do it and to be free to choose what she liked rather than what her aunt considered suitable for a young lady. That thought produced others less welcome and, as they walked along the street, she prayed that her uncle would never think to look for her in Yorkshire. In a momentary fit of panic she wished she were safely at Netherclough again, concealed from the public gaze. Then she took a deep breath and told herself not to be so foolish. It couldn't possibly hurt to enjoy one simple shopping trip.

While Claire and Lucy were thus engaged, Marcus had gone to call upon Sir Alan Weatherby, the local magistrate. He had sent a letter some days earlier, announcing his intention. The missive aroused both curiosity and surprise in the recipient, but he received the visitor with considerable pleasure. The news of Marcus Edenbridge's return from India had aroused considerable interest in the town, and, with his assumption of the Destermere title, made him a personage of some importance in the neighbourhood. However, in this case the matter was more personal: Weatherby had been a friend of the late Lord Richard Destermere, and had stood as godfather to his sons.

'Welcome back, Marcus,' he said, taking the other's hand in a hearty grip.

'Thank you, sir. It's good to be back.'

For a moment the two men were silent, regarding each other in mutual appraisal. Then Weatherby smiled.

'I see that India agreed with you, my boy.' He clapped him on the shoulder. 'Come, let us go into the study and celebrate your return with a glass of wine.'

Once the niceties had been observed, the older man set down his glass and regarded the other with a shrewd gaze.

'I sense there is more to this than just a social call.'

'Yes, good though it is to see you.' Marcus paused. 'It is about my brother I would speak.'

'A sad business, Marcus. A bad business in every way.'

'You saw Greville before he died.'

'Yes, he paid me an unofficial visit in the guise of David Gifford. He told me about his mission here—as a magistrate it was my job to lend him whatever assistance I could. I was glad to do it, too. The Luddite crew have stopped at nothing in the pursuit of their evil ends.' Weatherby paused. 'Your brother paid a heavy price for trying to stop them.'

'Yes, he did, but I intend to bring his killers to justice.'

'You can count on my full support.'

'Thank you, sir.'

'Someone found out what he was doing and silenced him. The killing had all the hallmarks of an execution.'

'You saw his body?'

'Yes.' Weatherby's hand clenched on the arm of his chair. 'As soon as I heard the name David Gifford I knew who it was. Later I visited the scene of the crime—a deserted barn on the edge of the moor. My guess is he was somehow lured to the spot and then killed.'

'Have you any idea whom he might have met that evening?'

'No, but he must have thought it important to be there.'

'Was he following a lead, perhaps?'

'Who knows? At any rate he must have been getting close if someone felt the need to silence him.'

'Who else knew about his mission here?'

'Only Sir James Wraxall. He's also a magistrate and he owns several mills.'

'So he would also have an interest in helping to catch the wreckers.'

'Absolutely. He was most keen to help. It was he who provided Greville's cover by hiring him as a wagon driver at the Gartside mill.'

'Did he know David Gifford's real identity?'

'No, only that his task was to find and destroy the Luddite group.'

'I see.' Marcus drank the rest of his wine and set down the glass. 'Well, this has been a most helpful conversation, sir.'

'What are you going to do?'

'I don't know yet. First I need to find out who my brother's associates were, and who he was due to meet the night he died.'

'I'll make some discreet inquiries. If I find out anything at all, I'll send word.'

'I'd appreciate it.'

'In the meantime I trust you're settling back to life in England.'

'Yes, though I little thought I'd ever return.' Marcus smiled. 'It has been good to see Netherclough again. And it's not just my home now—my niece lives there, too.'

'Ah, yes, Greville's child. I have not seen her since she was a baby.'

'Lucy is six now.'

'Good Lord! Is she really? At all events, it's too young to be cast adrift in the world. Lucky for her she has you, my boy.'

'I'll try to live up to expectation.'

'I'm sure you will.' The older man eyed him keenly. 'Meanwhile, you need to think about the future. As Viscount Destermere it is incumbent on you to marry and get heirs to carry on the family name. Find a good woman, my boy. I did and I've never regretted it.'

Marcus grinned. 'I'll keep it in mind.'

* * *

Having taken his leave, he returned to town to collect Claire and Lucy. Both looked to be in good spirits so he assumed the shopping expedition had been a success. On enquiry he was proved right.

'It was most satisfactory, sir,' replied Claire. 'I hope your business was concluded equally well.'

'Indeed it was, Miss Davenport.'

His expression was enigmatic and not for the first time she found herself wondering at the thoughts behind those cool grey eyes. However, he seemed disinclined to talk after that and, as Lucy was busy with her doll, Claire occupied herself agreeably by admiring the view from the window. Thus the rest of the return journey passed in companionable silence.

In the days following, Claire's time was spent in the schoolroom or in the grounds where she and Lucy walked when the weather was fine. The estate was beautiful, for some of the trees were changing colour and the rolling green acres of park and woodland were tinted with gold and russet hues. Sometimes they walked along the banks of the river and looked for a kingfisher or watched the brown trout finning against the current. At others they walked in the woods and collected handfuls of burnished conkers from the horse chestnut trees, and listened to the songs of the wild birds.

When it rained and they were compelled to remain indoors, Claire used the long gallery for exercise, thinking up games to play. It was during one of these that Lucy's gaze came to rest on one of the portraits.

'Papa,' she said then.

Claire came to stand beside her. 'Your papa?'

'Yes. Aunt Margaret said he's with the angels now, like Mama.'

'I'm sure she's right.'

'She said he wasn't coming back.'

'Do you miss him, Lucy?'

'I suppose so. Only I never saw him much. He was always very busy, you see.'

Claire did see, all too well. She put her arm round the child's shoulders and drew her closer.

'You have your Uncle Marcus, though, and you have me.'

Lucy nodded. 'I like Uncle Marcus. He makes me laugh.' She paused. 'I like you too, much better than Great-Aunt Margaret. She was old and cross.'

'Was she?'

'Yes. I was glad when Uncle Marcus came for me.'

Although the words were said matter-of-factly, Claire felt her heart go out to the little girl who had never known what it meant to be part of a loving family.

'Are you happy here, Lucy?'

The child looked up at her with solemn eyes that were somehow much older than their six years. Then she nodded. Claire breathed a sigh of relief. It was often hard to know whether children were happy, but at last Lucy seemed to be adjusting to her new environment and to the people in it. She pointed toward the next picture. It was of two young men in sporting costume. Both carried guns under their arms and were accompanied by several dogs. A brace of pheasant lay at their feet.

'See, there's your papa with Uncle Marcus.'

'How old were they?'

'About seventeen, I'd say.'

'That's quite old, isn't it?'

Claire supposed it was when you were six. She smiled. 'Yes, quite old.'

Pleased to have the thought confirmed, Lucy turned back to the portraits.

'Who is that lady there?'

'I'm not sure.'

'That is your mother,' said a voice behind them.

They turned in surprise to see Marcus there. Neither of them had heard him approach. Claire wondered how long he had been there and how much of the conversation he might have overheard. He came to join them in front of the painting.

'She's very pretty,' said Lucy.

'Yes, she is,' he replied. 'You look like her.'

'Do I?'

'I think so.'

Lucy surveyed the portrait with wistful eyes. 'I wish she was here.'

'If she were, I think she would be very proud of you.'

That drew a faint smile. Claire, looking over the child's head, met his eye and smiled, too. Then she turned back to the pictures and by tacit consent they strolled on a little way, eventually coming to a halt before another canvas. This time a haughty nobleman stared down at them out of the frame.

'My father,' said Marcus, by way of explanation.

Looking at the cold, aloof expression on that face, Claire remembered what the housekeeper had told her earlier.

'I can see the family likeness,' she observed.

'There is a physical likeness,' he acknowledged. 'Otherwise we were chalk and cheese, and it wasn't a case of opposites attracting.'

'I'm sorry to hear it.'

'He did have a lot to put up with admittedly. Greville and I were no saints. We sowed some wild oats between us. The old man was glad to see the back of me in the end.'

'Was that why you went to India?'

'I was sent to India in consequence of a scandal,' he replied. 'At the time I fancied myself in love with a most ineligible young lady. We planned an elopement to Gretna Green, but my father found out and scotched the scheme just in time.'

'Just in time?'

'Yes. He was right in that instance. The marriage would have been an unmitigated disaster. Of course, I only realised that with the wisdom of hindsight.'

'And so you found solace with the East India Company.'

'Very much so. The place suited me very well and the Company offered the possibility of an exciting and varied career.'

'And you never looked back?'

'At first, but less and less as time went on. Eventually I came to see that what I'd believed to be love was merely boyish infatuation.'

'I see.'

'Do you think me fickle?'

She shook her head. 'No, just young—and perhaps a little foolish.'

'I was certainly young, and very foolish. However, India changed that. You might say I grew up there.'

'It must have been exciting.'

'It was, some of the time.'

'I should like to hear about it.'

'Some time perhaps,' he replied.

The tone was courteous enough and the words accompanied with a smile, yet she knew that there had been an indefinable shift, as if an invisible barrier had come down between them. Clearly there were things about those years in India that he did not wish to discuss, and she had no right to trespass there. Was the mysterious Lakshmi among them? What had happened? Clearly he had been very deeply in love with her. In that case, why had he returned to England without her? Surely a man like Marcus Edenbridge wouldn't give a snap of his fingers for social convention. In his position he didn't need to. Perhaps the boot was on the other foot and the lady had not cared enough for him. Perhaps she had loved someone else and jilted him.

Before further contemplation was possible a maid-servant arrived to inform them that some parcels had arrived. Marcus excused himself and she and Lucy took themselves off to investigate. The parcels in question proved to be from the seamstress. The next hour was spent trying on the finished garments. Claire could not but admire the workmanship. It was very fine indeed and far better than she could have done herself. The new muslin dresses were neat and functional, but the lilac evening gown was a more elegant creation, fitting close at the bust and then falling in graceful folds to her feet. The bodice, though modest, revealed her figure to advantage. In comparison to London fashion she supposed it to be unremarkable, but it was, nevertheless, a more fashionable gown than any she had owned before and she knew full well she would enjoy wearing it. The riding habit was neat and elegant, the severe lines of the military-style jacket relieved by gold frog fastenings. It fitted like a glove to the waist before falling away into the · full skirt. A jaunty little hat trimmed with ostrich feathers completed the ensemble. The shade and style were well suited to her figure and colouring, and at a stroke transformed her from girl to woman of fashion. The thought was both welcome and disturbing. It occurred to her to wonder what her employer would think of the transformation. Then she told herself not to be foolish. He probably wouldn't even notice. Uncle Hector never seemed to notice such things. At the very most a new gown had called forth a grunt from that quarter. Fortunately no one else was likely to see it, so it would not attract undue attention.

Meanwhile, Lucy had been parading up and down in front of the mirror, admiring her new riding habit from every possible angle. The colour was a perfect foil for her brown curls and blue eyes. Lifting the hem of her skirt, she stuck out a toe to see the effect of the fabric against the polished leather of a new boot. Then she smiled as her gaze met Claire's in the glass.

'Now Uncle Marcus can teach me to ride,' she announced.

Chapter Seven

The first lesson was duly arranged for the following afternoon. Claire accompanied her young charge to the stable yard where Marcus was already waiting. He smiled to see Lucy's new costume and bade her turn around so he could view it from every angle.

'Very pretty,' he said then.

'I chose the material,' she confided.

'You chose well.' He tweaked one of her curls and then turned to Claire. 'I'll take her out for an hour or so and let her get used to the saddle.' He glanced at her muslin frock. 'I take it you're not accompanying us today.'

'No, sir. I thought it best if I did not.' Seeing him raise an eyebrow, she hurried on. 'This being the first time Lucy has ridden. The fewer distractions she has the better.'

The grey gaze met and held hers in a long and level stare. Recalling an earlier conversation, she felt her heart begin to beat a little faster. Was he annoyed? However, to her relief he merely nodded.

'Well, you may be right on this occasion. However, in future I shall expect you to come along, Miss Davenport.'

'As you wish, sir.'

'I do wish it.'

Conscious of that penetrating gaze, Claire tried to appear unconcerned. However, it wasn't easy when he was standing so close. With no little relief she watched him turn his attention to his niece, lifting her easily onto the pony's back. She listened as he showed the child how to sit and how to hold her reins. Lucy hung on his every word.

Once she was ready he swung onto his own horse. He looked as if he belonged there, she thought, a born horseman. There was an elegance about the tall, lithe figure, and a suggestion of contained strength. She watched him take the pony's leading rein and touch his horse with his heels. Then they set off, followed at a respectful distance by Trubshaw. Claire watched until they were out of sight and then retraced her steps to the house.

Lucy took to the experience of riding like a duck to water and the following day saw her and Claire in the stable yard again. This time, both were dressed to ride. The Viscount made no comment on Claire's appearance and merely greeted her with his customary courtesy.

In fact, he had noted the habit with approval, his critical gaze taking in every detail. It was elegant and quietly stylish and, he thought, it became her very well indeed, showing off her figure to perfection. And what a figure! A man could span that waist with his hands. Even the sober colour looked good on her too, he thought, complementing her dark curls and enhancing those wonderful hazel eyes. He smiled wryly. It remained to be seen whether she could ride. He had selected a pretty bay mare for her, a willing creature but well mannered withal.

Whatever doubts he might have had on that score were

soon allayed. She had an excellent seat and a light hand on the reins. Moreover, she looked very much at home in the saddle. He found himself wishing they were alone so that she might really put the mare through her paces. For some time they rode at Lucy's pace, but then, feeling the need for something more challenging, he reined in and told Trubshaw to go on ahead.

'We'll catch up in a minute.' He looked across at Claire. 'These horses need to stretch their legs.'

At the thought of a gallop her eyes brightened. Part of her suspected he was also testing her, but she didn't care. Once again she was aware of his regard and felt rising warmth along her neck and face. To hide her confusion she kept her eyes on the departing figures. When she judged they were far enough away she threw him a quizzical glance. He met and held it.

'Well, Miss Davenport?'

For answer she touched the mare with her heel. The horse sprang forwards into a canter. Out of the corner of her eye Claire saw the Viscount's chestnut drawing level. She grinned. So he wanted to test her, did he? She leaned forwards a little and gave the horse its head. The mare accelerated into a gallop, her neat hooves flying across the turf. Exhilarated by the pace and the rushing air Claire laughed out loud. Behind her she could hear the thudding hoofbeats of the other horse and then a moment later saw it draw level. A sideways glance revealed a grin on its rider's face. In that second she knew he was deliberately keeping pace and had no intention of being outrun. The two horses swept on up the slope to where Lucy and Trubshaw were waiting. Claire reined in and then leaned down to pat the mare's neck. Lucy was agog.

'It was a draw, Miss Davenport. I was watching.'

Claire laughed. 'I think you're right.'

'I'm going to ride like that one day,' the child continued.

'Yes, but not just yet,' said Claire.

'Certainly not,' agreed the Viscount. Then, seeing Lucy's crestfallen expression, he softened the blow. 'You'll learn soon enough.'

As they set off again he reined his mount alongside Claire.

'How do you like the mare?'

'I like her very well.'

'I thought you might. She was a lady's horse before, and is of a sweet temperament.'

'Her owner must have been sad to part with her.'

'I imagine so. However, I could hardly have mounted you on one of my hunters.'

Claire threw him a swift sideways glance in which dismay was clearly registered. Surely he hadn't bought the horse on her account? That was ridiculous. He must have had the animal for some time. Yet she couldn't recall having seen her when she and Lucy visited the stables before. Furthermore, the mare was no more than fifteen hands and finely made, certainly not up to a man's weight. As the implications dawned she felt a strange sensation in her breast. It was a feeling compounded of gratitude and alarm. He had already shown her a great deal of consideration. More than she had any right to expect.

Although he could not follow her train of thought he could not mistake the expression of dismay on her face and he mentally rebuked himself for his clumsiness. He had meant to let her think the horse had been part of his stable.

'I purchased her along with Lucy's pony,' he said. 'As

I told you, I shall require you to accompany my niece when I cannot.'

The tone was cool and firm and precluded argument. Claire avoided his eye and kept her gaze straight ahead between the horse's ears.

'Yes, sir.'

It was the only reply she felt able to give. He was her employer and his wishes prevailed. More than that, she had enjoyed herself too much today to want to forfeit the chance of riding in future. Now that she was on a horse again she realised how much she had missed it.

Somewhat to her disappointment, business occupied him for the next few days so she and Lucy had to go out without him. Trubshaw was in attendance as usual but the Viscount was conspicuous by his absence. Claire tried hard not to miss him but, though it was undoubtedly a pleasure to ride, it wasn't the same somehow. She was annoyed with herself for feeling the lack. For goodness' sake, she was too old for what amounted to a schoolgirl crush! He certainly wouldn't be giving her a moment's thought. Why should he? He had hired her to do a job. If he showed her any additional courtesy it was on account of what had gone before and, perhaps, because of her connection with the Greystokes.

That last proved a calming thought. The Viscount valued Dr Greystoke's friendship very highly and was also beholden to Ellen for her previous care of him. He would not risk offending either by his treatment of Claire. Having got a new perspective on the situation, she cringed inwardly when she remembered her response to his kindness. What a vain little fool she must appear. As if a man like Marcus Edenbridge would look twice at a governess! Why should he? He could have his pick of all the eligible young women in the land. Mortified now, Claire resolved to demonstrate a different kind of behaviour when next they met.

That proved to be on Thursday when the Greystokes came to dine at Netherclough. Claire was relieved to learn that they were to be the only company that evening. It meant there was no one else to note her presence and perhaps mention it to others later. Her whereabouts would remain secret. She dressed with care, selecting her new lilac gown. It was simple and elegant without being ostentatious, and the colour suited her. As she had no other jewellery her only adornment was her locket. Nevertheless she was not displeased by her appearance when she looked in the glass. It should at least pass muster. Affording her reflection a last wry smile, she left her chamber and made her way to the drawing room.

She arrived to find the guests talking to their host, but at her entrance they greeted her with expressions of pleasure, which she returned with equal sincerity.

George gave her a beaming smile.

'Good to see you, Miss Davenport, and how very well you look.'

Ellen echoed the sentiment. 'Indeed you do, my dear. And what a delightful gown.'

The Viscount, listening, knew the words for truth. As he hadn't seen the frock before he gathered it must be a new purchase. Clearly the trip to Harrogate had been productive. The colour of the fabric became her well, suiting her dark curls and fresh complexion, and his critical eye could find no fault with the cut or the style. It epitomised simple, understated elegance. She seemed to have an instinct for it. He noted that she was wearing the silver locket again. It was a pretty trinket, but amethysts would go better with that gown. Even so it showed off her figure well and, he reflected, a figure like hers should be shown off. It was beautiful. His imagination stripped away the dress and contemplated what lay beneath. He caught his breath. With an effort of will he forced the image away and his attention back to his guests.

A short time later dinner was announced. He offered his arm to Miss Greystoke while her brother led Claire in. Throughout the meal, though he kept up his part in the general conversation, Marcus found his attention repeatedly returning to Claire. Yet his critical eye could discern not the least hint of awkwardness in her demeanour, and her manners were impeccable. Far from seeming out of place, she looked as though she belonged.

Once the meal was over the two ladies withdrew to the drawing room, leaving the men to talk over their brandy and cigars. Claire had been looking forward to having the opportunity for private speech with Ellen, and when at last the two of them were alone she seated herself on the sofa beside her friend.

'Now tell me all,' Ellen said. 'And especially about your young charge.'

She listened avidly as Claire supplied the details.

'I am so glad that all is well. I gathered as much from your letter, but it's always reassuring to hear it from your own lips.'

'I have nothing to complain of,' said Claire. 'The Viscount takes a great interest in Lucy's education and provides whatever I ask for in that regard.'

'Excellent.'

'He is most solicitous about the child and seems anxious to ensure her happiness.'

'So it would seem.' Ellen paused. 'Has he said any

more about finding the men responsible for his brother's death?'

'No, but that does not mean he has abandoned the scheme.'

'At least he can use his position to enlist the help of the authorities. That must be far safer than adopting a false identity.'

'I cannot think he will do so again, not now he has Lucy to consider.'

Had they known it, the conversation in the dining room was turning on a similar theme.

'Have you taken further action?' asked George.

'I called upon Sir Alan Weatherby in Harrogate last week. He is my godfather—was Greville's too—and is a local magistrate besides. He is most anxious to have information about the wreckers. Rest assured, if he learns anything I shall know of it soon after.'

'Then he knows the truth?'

'Yes. Sir James Wraxall also knew of Greville's mission here, though not his true identity. He knew my brother by the pseudonym of David Gifford.'

'Wraxall knew?'

'Yes, and lent his full support to the scheme.'

'I suppose he would, being a local magistrate. All the same he is not a popular man in the district.'

'Magistrates rarely are popular,' said Marcus.

'Wraxall is a mill owner, too. He was the first to cut wages.'

'Ah, I see.'

'I am glad you have chosen this way to find your brother's killers.'

'I hope the disappearance of Mark Eden didn't cause you any difficulties?'

'None at all. As you asked, I gave it out that he had gone to stay with relatives further north. I left the destination suitably vague.'

'I am much obliged to you, George.'

'No offence, but I rather hope Eden does not return.'

The Viscount smiled wryly. 'Really? I rather liked him.'

'Seriously, Marcus.'

'Seriously, George, so do I.'

A short time later they rejoined the ladies in the drawing room and the conversation was directed into other channels for a while. Then George suggested some music. The Viscount's grey eyes gleamed. Recalling the story-telling episode on the way to Harrogate, he looked straight at Claire and seized his opportunity for revenge.

'Perhaps Miss Davenport will oblige us with a song.'

As he had foreseen, Claire could hardly refuse. He watched as she got up and moved to the pianoforte. When her back was to the others she threw him a most eloquent look. His grin widened. Enjoying himself enormously, he followed her to the instrument and riffled through the sheet music until he found the piece he was looking for. Then he handed it to her.

Torn between annoyance and amusement Claire took it from him, scanning it quickly. In fact it was neither difficult nor unfamiliar as she had suspected it might be. He wasn't that unkind, she decided. All the same she would have preferred not to be the centre of attention. Thank goodness it wasn't a large company.

'I'll turn the pages for you,' he said.

Undeceived by that courteous offer she nevertheless returned him a sweet smile.

'How very kind.'

The grey eyes held a decidedly mischievous glint, but he vouchsafed no reply and merely stationed himself beside her. Supremely conscious of his proximity but unable to do anything about it, she turned her attention to the music. Then, taking a deep breath, she settled down to play.

After hearing the opening bars Marcus's amusement faded and was replaced by pleasure and surprise; she played and sang beautifully, more so than he could ever have supposed. He had expected competence, but not the pure liquid notes that filled the room. Her voice was clear and true and had besides a haunting quality that sent a shiver down his spine and seemed to thrill to the core of his being. He had heard the song countless times, but never so movingly rendered. When at last it came to an end he was quite still for some moments before he recollected himself enough to join in the applause. He wasn't alone in thinking the performance good. Greystoke too had been much struck by it.

'Wonderful!' he said at last. 'First class, Miss Davenport.'

'I had a first-class teacher,' she replied, looking at Ellen.

'There can be no doubt about that,' Marcus replied. 'You are both to be congratulated.' This time there was no trace of mischief in his face when he looked at Claire. 'Please, won't you play something else?'

Her heart beat a little faster for he had never used quite that tone before. It was unwontedly humble. Controlling her surprise, she could only acquiesce.

'Yes, of course.'

Turning to the pile of music, she drew out a piece at random. It was much more difficult and she was glad of it for it meant she wouldn't be tempted to look at him

instead. However, she soon became conscious that he felt
no such constraint. Her skin seemed to burn beneath that
penetrating gaze and only with a real effort of will could
she keep her expression impassive and her concentration on the music. Soon enough the melody claimed her
and filled her soul. Marcus saw her surrender to it and
felt all the passion of that skilled performance as he too
was transported. He knew then that he was listening to
something quite out of the ordinary, something that both
awed and delighted, and he didn't want it to end.

When it did he was first to lead the applause. However,
the others were not far behind him. George Greystoke
got to his feet.

'Bravo, Miss Davenport!'

She received their praise with a gracious smile and
then rose from the piano stool, insisting that Ellen be
allowed her turn. When her friend bowed to the pressure
Claire retired to a seat across the room. Marcus's gaze
followed her, but he remained by the pianoforte and
presently turned his attention to his guest, consulting
with her about the choice of music and then waiting to
turn the pages as she played. He was, thought Claire, a
most courteous host, and, seeing him now, his attentions
to herself did not seem so marked at all, but rather the
good manners of one accustomed to moving in the first
circles. It was foolish to refine on a look or a gesture.
He would treat any female guest with the same polished
courtesy.

The remainder of the time passed agreeably enough
until, soon after the tea tray had been brought in, the
Greystokes took their leave.

'It has been a most delightful evening,' said Ellen as
they stood together in the hallway.

'I hope to have the pleasure of seeing it soon repeated,' Marcus replied.

He shook hands with George and then came to stand by Claire to wave the guests off.

'Miss Greystoke is right,' he observed as the carriage pulled away. 'It has been a most delightful evening.'

Claire glanced up at him and smiled. 'Yes, it has.'

They remained there together until the vehicle was lost to view round a bend in the drive, and then turned and walked back into the hallway. For a moment they paused, neither one speaking. Aware of him to her very fingertips, wanting to linger and knowing she must not, she forced herself to a polite curtsy.

'I'll bid you a goodnight, sir.'

Marcus wanted to detain her, but could think of no valid reason for doing so. Instead he took her hand and carried it to his lips.

'Goodnight then, Miss Davenport.'

Reluctantly he watched her walk away and then returned to the drawing room and poured himself a large brandy from the decanter on the table. He tossed it back in one go and poured another. As he did so he glanced across the room to the pianoforte and, in his imagination, heard Claire singing and knew again the *frisson* along his spine. He also knew that what he felt was a damn sight more than admiration for fine musical skill. When they had been alone together after the guests had gone he had wanted to take her in his arms. No, he corrected himself, what he had really wanted to do was carry her up the stairs to his bedchamber and make love to her all night.

Almost immediately he felt self-contempt. Claire Davenport was not some trollop to be used for an idle hour's amusement. She was a respectable young woman. She was Lucy's governess, for heaven's sake. A role he had appointed her to. Any liaison between them would make that position untenable and he would be responsible for ruining her reputation and then for causing her to leave. Only a real cur would do that. Only a cur put his own desire before the welfare of the woman he claimed to care for. For both their sakes there could be no familiarity between them. It was not only his feelings and hers that were involved here, but Lucy's, too. She was beginning to settle into her new home, to trust him. It was obvious that she was also growing attached to her new governess. Could he be responsible for the loss of yet another person she cared for? Could he put her through that? It needed but a moment's thought to know the answer. There must be no advances to Claire, no matter what it cost him. Had she been living with the Greystokes it might have been different, but the minute he hired her he had put her out of reach. The irony did not escape him.

Claire returned to her room and retired to bed, but sleep would not come. Her thoughts were troubled and her mind raced. Every time her eyelids closed Marcus's face was there. His words echoed in her memory. She could still feel the warmth of his hand on hers. The memory set her pulse racing, like that other memory of his lips on her skin. When he was near it was hard to think of anything else. His presence drew her as a moth to a flame and, just as surely, she knew that yielding to temptation would mean getting badly burnt. Men of rank might dally with their servants, but they did not marry them.

The knowledge brought with it a feeling of over-whelming sadness. If things had been different…if they had met under other circumstances…but she could not imagine any circumstances under which they would have met. Her uncle, though a gentleman, did not move in such exalted circles. He was flattered by the notice of a man like Sir Charles Mortimer. What would he have said to the notice of a viscount? What would have been his reaction if such a man had offered for her hand? She knew the answer too well: the offer would have been accepted immediately and she would have been expected to comply. Her heart beat a little quicker at the thought. If she had been promised to a man like Marcus Edenbridge would she have sought to escape the match? The answer brought another wave of warmth to her neck and face. Just as quickly she realised how ridiculous it was even to consider the possibility. Ridiculous and dangerous. She was not safe yet. This post was her refuge, her protection. She would do nothing to jeopardise it, no matter what her personal inclination.

In the morning she would resume her duties as though nothing had happened. When she and Marcus Edenbridge happened to meet, she would behave with the utmost propriety. Never by word or sign would she let him suspect what she felt for him. This evening, delightful as it had been, was a one-off occasion, a favour perhaps for past aid. It would not happen again. He had discharged his obligation and in future his socialising would be done among his social equals. The knowledge gave her a pang; she had enjoyed herself this evening. It had given her a glimpse of another world, one to which she would never belong. It served to reinforce how very different were their social positions.

In the days that followed the Viscount behaved with the utmost propriety when their paths crossed. He visited the nursery each day and took a keen interest in what Lucy did, but he never lingered or tried to interfere in any way.

To Claire he was unfailingly civil, but never more than that. Just occasionally the grey eyes betrayed a stronger emotion, but it was never given further expression.

He also rode with them less frequently, having many other matters requiring his attention. Although she missed him, Claire was grateful for the distance between them. Sometimes she would look from her window and see him ride out across the estate, sometimes alone, but more usually with the land agent. Then she would know that she and Lucy would be riding with Trubshaw that day. Her young charge made good progress and gained in confidence. Soon she was clamouring to be let off the leading rein. The next time that Marcus appeared in the nursery she petitioned him on that score.

'I've been riding for three weeks now, Uncle Marcus. Can't I please ride Misty without being led?'

He dropped to one knee so that they were face to face and then he smiled. 'I don't see why not.'

Lucy flung her arms round his neck. 'Thank you, Uncle Marcus.'

He returned the hug and looked over the child's shoulder to Claire.

'The pony is quiet enough. I think she'll come to little harm,' he said. 'In any case, one learns by doing. Is that not so, Miss Davenport?'

'Indeed it is, sir.'

Lucy looked at him solemnly. 'Will you come with us, Uncle Marcus?'

He grinned and ruffled her hair. 'I have a lot of things to do today.'

She threw a conspiratorial glance at Claire. 'But I might fall off.'

'Well, you might,' he agreed. 'But then you'll just have to get back on, won't you?'

'Yes.'

The tone and facial expression were so forlorn that Claire was unable to restrain a grin. Her young charge was clearly not above using feminine wiles to get her own way. Even so she didn't expect him to succumb. His expression said very plainly that he knew what she was about, but to her surprise she saw him smile.

'Oh, all right, then, you ghastly brat. I'll come.'

Undismayed by this mode of address, Lucy smiled up at him.

'But only if you have completed all of your lessons first,' he added, with belated severity.

Desperately wanting to laugh, Claire turned away and fixed her attention on the view from the window. The Viscount stood up, regarding her with a speculative expression.

'You will inform me later, Miss Davenport, if Lucy has not done everything she ought.'

'Yes, sir.'

He looked at his ward and jerked his head towards the desk. With the sweetest of smiles Lucy returned to work. Seeing her once more bent over her copybook, he turned back to Claire. Though she had assumed an expression of becoming gravity she was unable to hide the laughter in her eyes. It was fascinating, all the more so because she was quite unconscious of the effect it had on the beholder. If they had been alone, he would have taught her about the dangers of exerting fascination. As it was he could not permit himself that very attractive luxury so, reluctantly, he made her a polite bow instead and then took his leave.

Claire didn't set eyes on him again until they met in the stable yard that afternoon. However, apart from a brief, polite acknowledgement of her presence he focused his attention on his ward. Claire was glad of it. It also afforded an opportunity of watching them together. He was, she thought, a good teacher, for he was quiet and firm in delivering instruction, but always ready to praise. As always, Lucy hung on his every word, clearly eager to please him. She learned quickly. He had only to tell her something once and she remembered it.

As she was off the leading rein a groom and not Trubshaw attended them. And as it was Lucy's first solo outing the pace was necessarily gentle, but Claire didn't mind. It was just pleasant to be out of doors on so fine a day and in so beautiful a place. All the trees were turning now, the foliage a glorious display of red and russet and gold, and the autumnal air was rich with the scent of leaf mould and damp earth. It was good to be alive on such a day. She glanced at her companions. It was good to be in such agreeable company. Even if it could not last for ever she would enjoy it now.

Lulled by the easy pace and the beauty of her surroundings, Claire was totally unprepared for the sudden violent eruption of a pheasant from the long grass at her horse's feet. For one heartbeat she had an impression of beating wings and a squawking cry and then her startled mount shied violently, throwing her hard. Earth and sky and trees spun crazily for some moments afterwards, so she lay quite still until the scenery had stopped moving and she could get her bearings again. Then she was aware of someone beside her and of anxious grey eyes looking down into hers.

'Claire, are you hurt?'

For a second she did not reply, being aware only that he had used her Christian name, a mode of address that he had never employed before. Then she shook her head.

'I...I don't think so. Just a little dazed, that's all.'

'Can you sit up?'

A strong arm brought her to a sitting position and supported her there. She managed a wan smile. 'Nothing broken, I think,' she said. 'Only my pride is a little bruised.'

'That will mend. Can you stand?'

'Yes, I think so.'

She made to rise, but was saved the trouble for his arm was round her waist, lifting her onto her feet. It stayed there while the groom was despatched to retrieve her horse. Feeling somewhat foolish and not a little self-conscious, she disengaged herself from his hold and took a tentative step away. Without warning the ground shifted under her feet and she swayed. If he had not caught her she would have fallen.

'I think that's the end of your ride for today,' he said. 'We must get you back to the house.'

'There's really no need. I'll be all right in a minute or two.'

'Nonsense! Your cheeks are the colour of paper. You need to go and lie down for a while.'

'Really, I...'

'Don't be a little fool. If you get back on that horse now you'll be off again within a minute.'

He guided her to his own horse and without further consultation she was lifted in a pair of powerful arms and transferred with consummate ease onto the front of his saddle. As the implications dawned Claire paled further. Surely he could not be intending to... It seemed that he was for, having given orders to the groom to lead the mare back, Marcus swung up behind her. Then, taking the reins in one hand, he locked the other arm around her waist. Claire tensed, her heart racing.

'I can ride home,' she protested. 'There's really no need...'

In mild panic she tried to resist the arm. For answer it tightened a little, pulling her closer.

'I think otherwise,' he replied, 'and for once you're going to do as you're told, my girl.'

With that he turned the horse for home. Seeing there was no help for it, Claire capitulated, lapsing into warm-cheeked silence. As he glanced down at her his lips twitched.

'What, no furious counter-argument?'

'Would it do any good?'

'Devil a bit,' he replied.

It drew a wry smile in return. She might have known how it would be. Being used to a life of command, this man had an expectation of getting his own way, and an infuriating habit of succeeding, too. In any case she didn't feel much like arguing. Her head was beginning to throb now and, in spite of her assertion to the contrary, she was no longer convinced that she could have ridden back by herself. Moreover, there was something comforting about having the responsibility removed and she felt grateful for that solid and reassuring presence.

Lucy regarded her somewhat anxiously. 'Are you all right, Miss Davenport?'

'Not quite right,' she replied, 'but I shall be better soon.'

'It was a naughty pheasant, wasn't it?'

'Very naughty.'

Marcus grinned. 'If I see it again I'll shoot it.'

Satisfied with this, Lucy nodded and trotted along beside the groom.

Claire sighed. 'I should have been better prepared. Then I would not have fallen off.'

'You could scarcely have avoided it,' Marcus replied. 'The bird was well concealed and there is nothing like a pheasant for putting a rider on the ground.'

The tone was both humorous and kind and not what she had been expecting. There was also an unusually gentle expression in the grey eyes. Seeing it, Claire felt her pulse quicken. Not knowing quite what to say, she lapsed into silence.

'It's all right,' he said. 'You don't have to talk if you don't want to. Lean your head on my shoulder and rest.'

Claire reclined against him and closed her eyes. The gentle motion of the horse and the warmth of the man were soothing and gradually she began to relax. There would probably be some bruises tomorrow, but all things considered she'd got off lightly.

They returned to the stables some twenty minutes later. Marcus instructed the groom to see to Lucy and then dismounted, lifting Claire down after. Just for a moment she had a sensation of weightlessness before he sat her down gently on the cobbled yard, surveying her with a critical eye. She still looked a little pale though not quite as much as before.

'Can you walk?'

She replied hurriedly in the affirmative, dreading that if she did not he would carry her. The idea of presenting such a spectacle to the watching servants filled her with horror. Much to her relief he did not gainsay her this time, but merely offered her his arm, and his free hand to Lucy.

'Come then, let us go in.'

He escorted them in and sent Lucy to change before escorting Claire to the door of her room.

'I will have Mrs Hughes send up some water,' he said.

'You must have a hot tub at once. If not you'll be as stiff as a board tomorrow.'

Claire's cheeks turned a deep shade of pink. Gentlemen did not commonly refer to such things in front of ladies, yet he seemed quite unembarrassed. He was also right. A hot bath would help enormously. Lowering her gaze from his, she nodded.

'Thank you.'

'After that you must lie down for a while until you feel better.'

'But Lucy…'

'I will see to Lucy. You just concern yourself with getting well again.'

With that he left her. Claire slipped thankfully into her room and closed the door, leaning upon it in relief.

In fact, Marcus was right. A hot tub and a lie down did much to restore her. She was right though about incurring some bruises, but Mrs Hughes had come to the rescue with tincture of arnica so the discomfort was considerably lessened. It was from the housekeeper that she learned about the Viscount's plans to host a soirée.

'It is to be a fairly small gathering,' said Mrs Hughes, 'but it will be so pleasant to see company at Netherclough again.'

Claire felt the first stirrings of apprehension. Company posed a possible threat to her anonymity here. However, she forced a smile. 'Yes, I'm sure.'

'His Lordship wishes to establish his return in the neighbourhood,' the housekeeper continued, 'and that can only be to the good, can't it?'

'Oh, yes. When is the event to be?'

'On Tuesday next. There's a deal of work to do before

we can pass muster, of course, but I doubt not we'll pull it off.'

'I'm sure you will.'

'Perhaps he'll ask you and Miss Lucy to come down for a while.'

Claire's stomach lurched. The possibility had not occurred to her and now occasioned real alarm. She had no desire for anyone to see her here. It wasn't that she thought they'd find a governess of any interest at all, but gossip spread and a careless word in the wrong place might mean her uncle somehow got to hear of it. Then she would be lost. When she had asked for this job it was in part because Netherclough was remote. It had not occurred to her that her employer would entertain. Too late she realised it had been a foolish oversight on her part.

In the days that followed this conversation she waited in trepidation lest the Viscount should approach her to solicit Lucy's presence in the drawing room. If he did she would be obliged to accompany her charge. She could not risk arousing suspicion by refusing or making difficulties. As he hadn't mentioned the occasion to her at all, perhaps it was because he had no intention of having either of them there.

But on his next visit to the nursery, he explained, 'I would have asked you to bring Lucy down tomorrow evening,' he said, 'but the affair is not due to start until eight, which is really too late for her.'

Claire seized her chance. 'Yes, sir, you are quite right.'

'It's a pity but, on this occasion, it can't be helped.'

'She is also shy and might feel daunted at the prospect of so many strange faces.'

He looked thoughtful. 'I had not thought of that.'

Claire felt flooding relief. He seemed to have accepted what she said. She was off the hook and, perhaps, when she and Lucy did eventually appear in company, all need for circumspection would have passed.

On the evening of the soirée he came to say goodnight to his ward. He had got into the habit now and Lucy clearly derived pleasure from seeing him.

'You look very nice, Uncle Marcus,' she said, surveying the tall figure clad in impeccable evening dress.

Claire silently agreed with the assessment. He wore a dark coat with cream-coloured breeches and waistcoat and immaculate linen. It was simple, almost severe, but it enhanced every line of that lean, athletic form. She thought it would be hard to find a more elegant figure, or a more striking one. He was, she acknowledged, a very handsome man.

He smiled down at the child. 'I hope the rest of the ladies will be so easily pleased.'

Hearing the words, Claire experienced an unexpected pang. Of course there would be ladies present. Moreover, they would be ladies of his social class. Some, no doubt, would be single and on the lookout for a husband. He was, she knew, a most eligible bachelor. Annoyed with herself for thinking such thoughts, she tried to dismiss them. A man like Marcus Edenbridge could set his sights as high as he liked. Not only would he never look her way, but, once married, the secluded rural idyll she had enjoyed would be shattered for good.

They bade goodnight to Lucy and then withdrew to the passage outside the door. Marcus paused a moment, surveying Claire keenly.

'Are you all right, Miss Davenport? You look a little pale.'

'I am quite well, thank you, sir. Just a little tired, that's all.'

'Perhaps an early night, then?' he suggested.

'Yes,' she replied. 'That was my intention.'

He bade her a goodnight, favoured her with a polite bow, and then was gone. Claire waited until he reached the end of the passage and headed down the stairs. Then very quietly she followed, stopping in the shadows on the landing, watching him descend to the hallway. The sound of horses' hooves and wheels on gravel announced the arrival of the first guests. She saw them enter, heard him greet them, speaking and smiling with the polished assurance that so characterised him.

Looking at the beautiful clothes of the arriving guests, Claire became painfully conscious of her plain muslin frock. It soon became clear too that several of the ladies were young and very attractive. From their smiles it seemed that their host was making quite an impression. But then he was the kind of man that women did notice. She sighed. When she had come to Netherclough she had wanted to preserve her anonymity. Now she had got her wish. Marcus wouldn't give her another thought. Why should he? He had plenty of other distractions now. She was merely the governess and could be nothing more. For just one moment she wished she could be down there too, wished she could be one of that elegant gathering. Then he might glance across the room and, seeing her there, might smile and come across and solicit her hand for a dance. How would it be to dance with him? She would never know. Sadly she turned away and went to seek solace in the library.

* * *

It was gone eleven before the last of the guests departed and Marcus had waved them off. The evening had been a success in that it had fulfilled its aim of reacquainting him with the wealthy and aristocratic neighbours he had not seen for over ten years. On the other hand, having re-established the connection, he was reminded why he hadn't missed them. With a wry smile he acknowledged that he had been scrutinised and weighed and measured, mostly by the matrons with unmarried daughters. Their fawning attentions left him in no doubt they considered him a good catch. Yet for all their undoubted accomplishments the young women present were lacking somehow. They were either too diffident or too conscious of their own social consequence. At some point he knew he would have to marry and get heirs to continue the family name, but he had seen nothing tonight that remotely tempted him. The thought of a London Season held little appeal either.

Unlike Greville, he suspected he would not find his soul mate among the society beauties. The woman he loved was lost to him for ever and he had never found her like again. He wondered now if he ever would. The past ten years had not been without female companionship, of course, but now he found it hard to remember their faces. They had given their bodies willingly and he had satisfied a need with them, but his heart had remained untouched. Having experienced the grand passion, he found it hard to settle for less.

Recalling the simpering smiles and downcast eyes that had been his lot for much of the evening, he found himself wishing Claire had been there. She would not have looked out of place in such a gathering. On the contrary, her appearance there would have put a few noses out of joint. Moreover, there was nothing diffident or arrogant about her and she was invariably agreeable company. He realised then that he had missed her. A glance at the clock revealed the advancing hour. It was probable that she had retired long since. Conscious of disappointment, he made his way upstairs.

As he passed along the corridor he saw that the library door was slightly ajar. The gleam of light beyond suggested that the room wasn't empty. Curious, he pushed the door further open and glanced in. The pool of candlelight revealed another presence and he smiled in recognition. Claire was curled up on the sofa by the fire, clearly engrossed in the book she was reading. For a moment or two he watched her, his gaze taking in every detail from the dark curls to the small foot peeping out from the hem of her dress, then he pushed the door to behind him and crossed the room to join her.

Hearing a footstep, she looked up and perceived him there. Her heart skipped a beat as she saw who it was. Then, belatedly aware of her informal pose, she straightened quickly.

'No, don't get up,' he said. 'I didn't mean to disturb you. In truth, I didn't think anyone was in here till I saw the light.'

She glanced at the clock and with a start of surprise noticed the late hour. Surely it had been only eight-thirty the last time she looked? Before she could say anything Marcus disposed himself casually on the sofa beside her. Then he glanced at her book.

'What are you reading?'

Very much aware of that charismatic presence and trying not to show it, she replied, *'Sense and Sensibility.'*

'I see you find it absorbing.'

'Very much so. The author is both perceptive and witty.'

'Indeed she is.' He smiled faintly. 'You enjoy reading novels, then?'

'Of course.'

'You do not subscribe to the view that they are unsuitable reading matter for young females?'

'Certainly not. That is the kind of nonsense my uncle used to spout.' Then she stopped, suddenly aware that she had no idea of where he might stand on the issue.

Seeing her expression, Marcus interpreted it correctly. 'No, I do not share that view. Losing oneself in a good story must rank as one of life's great pleasures.'

'Why, so I think.'

'Your uncle is of a conservative disposition, I take it.'

'Yes, sir.' She might also have added, *and humourless, joyless and cold,* but bit the words back, having no wish to allude further to her background. It might prompt more awkward questions. Instead she changed the subject. 'Did you have an enjoyable evening, sir?'

'Tolerably so,' he replied.

Her unwillingness to talk about her relatives had not escaped him, but he knew better than to try to force her confidence.

'I have thought on what you said earlier about Lucy's shyness,' he continued, 'and I am determined that she must be helped to conquer it. As opportunity permits I would like you to bring her down to the drawing room. With you to support her she will soon grow accustomed to company.'

Claire heard him with sinking heart, but knew she couldn't refuse. 'As you wish, sir.'

'She must learn to take her place in society, and if anyone can help her it will be you, I think.'

'You underplay your own role, sir.'

He smiled faintly. 'I am not skilled with young children as some are, but I'm learning.' He took her hand and carried it to his lips. 'But then I have a good example to follow, do I not?'

Claire felt her face grow hot, not only on account of the words but the warmth of the fingers pressing hers and the unmistakable expression in his eyes.

'You are kind, sir.' She made to rise. The hold on her hand tightened a fraction.

'You are not leaving?'

'I think I must.'

'What are you afraid of?'

'I…nothing.'

'Then why are you trembling?'

'I'm not trembling,' she lied.

'Are you afraid of me?'

'No, sir.' That much was true, she thought. It was not him she feared now.

'Good. I would not have you so.' He smiled. 'Therefore will you not stay awhile?'

Claire fought down the temptation to say yes. 'It is late, sir.'

For a moment she thought he would insist, but to her relief he sighed and let go of her hand. 'Yes, I suppose you are right.' He rose with her. For a moment or two they faced each other in silence. 'Goodnight, then, Miss Davenport.'

'Goodnight, sir.'

Dropping a polite curtsy, Claire walked away, conscious of the grey eyes watching her retreat. Her heart was thumping, her hand burning from his touch. More than anything she would have liked to remain and more than anything she knew she must not. Marcus Eden-bridge was forbidden fruit and she dared not forget it.

Chapter Eight

The day after the soirée Claire was returning from a walk with Lucy when they met the Viscount in the hall. With him was Dr Greystoke, who was clearly on the point of departure. He looked round and, seeing Claire, smiled.

'Miss Davenport, how very good to see you again.'

'I am happy to see you too, sir.'

'I hoped I might see you for my sister entrusted me with a message. She begs you will do her the favour of visiting next time you are free.'

'I should be delighted. I am free on Friday afternoon.'

'Excellent. I'll send the carriage over for you.'

Before she could answer, Marcus interrupted. 'There is not the least occasion to do so. Miss Davenport is welcome to have the use of one of my carriages.'

She looked up quickly, but his expression revealed nothing. 'Thank you, sir, if you are sure it will not be inconvenient.'

'Not the least bit,' he replied.

'That's settled, then,' replied Greystoke, beaming. 'I'll tell my sister to expect you on Friday.'

With that he bowed and then he and his host moved away to the door. As she and Lucy continued on towards the nursery Claire reflected on the pleasure of the forthcoming visit to Ellen. It would be good to see her friend again, though she had not expected to be able to do so in such ease and style. It had been kind of Marcus to offer the carriage, though by doing so he spared the Greystokes' coachman an additional journey. That must have been the reason, she decided.

When she returned to her room later it was to find a long, narrow box on the table beside her bed. For a moment she frowned, wondering what it was, knowing it certainly didn't belong to her. Then she saw the note underneath. Rather apprehensively she opened it and read:

Please accept this as a small token of my appreciation for your help in settling Lucy into her new home.

Claire opened the box with trembling hands and then gasped to see the necklace that lay on the satin lining within. Made of silver and set with amethyst flowers, it was quite the prettiest thing she had ever seen. The stones would complement her lilac gown to a nicety. That realisation, and the implication that followed hard on its heels, brought a rush of colour to her face. Then her hand stole to her cheek in dismay. There was no possibility of her accepting this. It would be utterly wrong to do so. No single lady could accept such a gift from a man unless he was a close relative or perhaps her fiancé. To take it would be a gross breach of etiquette and, worse, would be morally compromising. She must return it at once.

For fully five minutes she paced the floor, turning over in her mind various schemes for doing so. She could wait until she knew he was out of the house and then leave it on the desk in his study. But that would mean writing a note to go with it. How to phrase such a note, though, so that it would be firm and courteous together? Perhaps she could leave the box without a note. She sighed. That would look rude and cowardly, too. There was only one way and that was to talk to him face to face. It wasn't a solution she greeted with enthusiasm.

Summoning her courage, she went in search of him and was informed by Mather that His Lordship was in the study. Seeing her come in, the Viscount rose from his chair and greeted her with a smile.

'Miss Davenport. What a pleasant surprise.' He gestured to a chair. 'Won't you sit down?'

'I'll stand if you don't mind, sir.'

One arched brow lifted a little. 'As you wish. How may I be of service?'

Claire laid the box containing the necklace on the desk in front of him.

'By taking this back.' Drawing a deep breath, she hurried on before her courage failed her. 'It was a most generous thought and I am grateful for it, but you must see it is absolutely impossible for me to accept this gift.'

'Why?' he asked.

She had half expected wrath or indignation, but this left her staring in disbelief. 'Why?' she echoed. 'You know why.'

'I don't think I am obtuse, but in this instance I fail to see why at all.' He favoured her with a quizzical look. 'Do explain it to me.'

'Well, because I…because it's inappropriate.'

'Ah, you don't like it.'

'Yes, I do like it. It's beautiful, but…'

'But?'

'You must know that a lady may not receive such

gifts from a gentleman.' Claire paused, feeling the room growing hotter. 'Particularly not from a gentleman who is also her employer.'

'Who says so?'

'I say so.'

'But I wish you to have it, and as your employer I have the final word on the matter, I think.'

'Not this time,' she replied.

'I beg your pardon?'

Her gaze met and held his. 'I think you heard me perfectly well, sir.'

'You know, arguing with your employer is a bad habit, Miss Davenport.'

'I have no wish to argue with you.'

'You are arguing now.'

'No, sir, I'm *telling* you that I cannot accept this gift.'

For a moment there was a tense silence as she waited for his anger. What came instead was a penetrating stare.

'You suspect an ulterior motive perhaps?'

'I suspect nothing, but I cannot take it.'

'You have earned it.'

'You pay me well enough already, sir. I do not require any additional remuneration.'

'But I wish to give it.'

She shook her head. 'The matter is closed.' Seeing him about to interrupt, she pre-empted him. 'Please.'

There was an appeal in her eyes that would not be resisted. He made a vague gesture with his hand.

'Very well, since you feel so strongly about it let us say no more on the subject.'

Feeling immeasurably relieved, Claire dropped a polite curtsy and left quickly before he could change his mind. Marcus made no attempt to stop her, merely looked thoughtfully at the box on his desk. Then he sighed.

* * *

For the next two days Claire avoided him but when they did meet he made no reference to their earlier discussion. Nor did he seem in any way displeased. It was almost as though the incident had never happened.

On Friday, the day appointed for her visit to Helmshaw, the Viscount's barouche duly appeared at the door. She had wondered if he would forget, but it seemed his memory was good. Once again Claire was conscious of being beholden to him. At the same time she was grateful, too. As always where Marcus Edenbridge was concerned she seemed to experience contradictory feelings.

On her arrival at the Greystokes' house she was greeted at the door by Eliza. Seeing who it was, the maid smiled and then stared wide-eyed at the carriage standing at the gate. Recovering herself quickly, she bobbed into a respectful curtsy.

'Miss Greystoke is expecting you, ma'am.'

She showed the guest into the parlour. Ellen looked up and smiled.

'Claire, I am so glad you are come.' She looked at the maid. 'Eliza, bring us some tea, please.'

As the maid departed the two women sat down on the sofa.

'It is so good to have you back here,' said Ellen then, 'if only for a short time. I have missed you very much.'

'And I you.'

'I suppose I should be thankful that you are only ten miles off and not a hundred. You are treated well?'

'I have no cause for complaint.'

'I am glad.' She paused. 'I confess I did feel anxious when first you took the post. It is good to know that the anxiety was unfounded.'

Claire's heartbeat quickened a little. 'But why should you be concerned?'

'It was because I wondered about Lord Destermere's motives in hiring you and on such a handsome salary.' Ellen coloured faintly. 'I am quite ashamed—I see now that my suspicions were unworthy.'

Listening to this and recalling the recent past, Claire felt her own face grow pink. 'Lord Destermere is many things, but he is not dishonourable.'

'No, I truly believe he is not.' Ellen paused. 'It's just that when one has seen a little of the world such thoughts inevitably occur. You are a very attractive young woman after all.'

'You have no reason to be concerned, though I thank you for it all the same.'

Her companion smiled and then changed the subject and they chatted agreeably until Eliza came in with the tea.

'I am sorry that George is not here,' said Ellen. 'He had hoped to be, but at the last minute he had to attend a birth in Gartside.'

'Your brother is an excellent physician. The people here are fortunate.'

'Goodness knows there is need.' She paused. 'I wonder, when we have had our tea, if would you walk with me into Helmshaw? There is something I should like you to see.'

'I'd be glad to come with you, but let us take the carriage. It is at our disposal after all and it will be better than keeping the horses standing too long.'

'As you wish.'

Thus it was that half an hour later they embarked on the short journey to Helmshaw.

'We must tell the coachman to wait in the square. The carriage will not be able to negotiate the narrow lanes.'

Claire was puzzled now, but made no demur, trusting to her friend's judgement. They alighted in the square and turned off it along a narrower thoroughfare. Having followed this for perhaps a hundred yards, Ellen turned off again, this time along a narrow muddy lane with mean houses on either side. Ragged children played nearby. Presently she stopped outside a door halfway down the row, and knocked. A girl of about eight opened it.

'Who is it, Meg?' said a voice from within.

'Miss Greystoke, Ma.'

On hearing the name a woman looked up from the stool by the hearth. She was probably in her early thirties, but looked ten years older. In her arms she held a baby. With them were five other children, ranging in age from two to about twelve years. They eyed the newcomers with solemn-eyed curiosity.

'Come in, Miss Greystoke,' she said.

As they stepped over the threshold Claire saw with a sense of shock that the house had just one room. Apart from the table and two rough benches, the only other furniture was a bed in the far corner and a wooden dresser. A small fire burned in the hearth and a meagre pile of wood lay in a box nearby. The room was clean but cold, for the heat reached only a few feet beyond the hearth. The younger children were huddled together on the bed for warmth. The air smelled of damp. By the look of things the small heap of potatoes on the table was dinner for all of them.

'Mrs Dobson, I have brought a friend today. This is Miss Davenport.'

'Pleased to meet you, ma'am. Any friend of Miss Greystoke's is welcome here.'

'I came to see how little Sarah is doing,' Ellen continued. 'Is her cough improving?'

Mrs Dobson glanced down at the baby. 'Aye, ma'am, a little, thank you.'

Her voice shook as she spoke and now that her eyes had become accustomed to the dim light Claire could see she had been crying.

'Has something happened, Mrs Dobson?' she asked.

To her horror the woman burst into tears. Then, clearly overcome with embarrassment, she began to apologise.

'I'm so sorry, ma'am. It's just that I don't know which way to turn.' She took a deep, shuddering breath. 'Since my Jack died things have gone from bad to worse. The landlord came for his rent yesterday. 'Tis already weeks in arrears. If we don't pay up by the end of the month, he'll evict us.'

Claire stared at her, appalled. 'But where will you go? What will you do?'

'I have no more idea of that than you do, ma'am. My oldest boys have tried to get work, but there's none to be had.' She glanced across the room to the two in question. 'In the meantime there's seven mouths to feed and the baby ill. If it hadn't been for Miss Greystoke's kindness, we'd have starved by now.'

'What happened to your husband?'

'He died the night Harlston's loom was destroyed by the wreckers.' She dashed away fresh tears with the sleeve of her shabby gown. 'He'd volunteered for the work to try to earn a bit more money. They shot him through the heart.'

Listening to her story, Claire turned cold. That had been the night Marcus had been wounded. She recalled with dreadful clarity the morning she'd found him on the moors, and the wagon bringing the dead back for burial. Unbeknown to her one of those men had been Jack Dobson. The tragedy of it struck her with force.

'I am so very sorry to hear of your loss.' Even as she spoke, the words sounded woefully inadequate. Worse, she hadn't even brought any money with her that day. There was no practical help she could offer.

'Thank you, ma'am.'

Ellen took a small bottle from her reticule. 'I have brought some more medicine for the baby.' She put it on the table and, unobtrusively, a small knotted handkerchief alongside. Claire guessed that it contained coin.

'God bless you, ma'am, for your kindness, and Dr Greystoke, too. Pray thank him for us.'

'No thanks are necessary,' Ellen replied.

They left shortly afterwards, retracing their steps along the lane. For a while they did not speak, each of them lost in thought. Claire was more than ever conscious that, but for fortune, she too might have been reduced to destitution and worse. She knew very well how it felt to be alone and penniless and frightened.

They reached the corner of the lane and turned into the wider thoroughfare beyond. Two men were standing by a doorway opposite, engaged in quiet conversation. One then went inside. The other turned to leave. As he did so he looked round and stopped in his tracks. Claire found herself looking straight at Jed Stone. She paled. His expression changed too and a wolfish smile played about his lips as the predatory gaze hardened. In an instant all the details of their encounter in Gartside returned with force. Sickened, she turned away, but not before Ellen had seen the look on her face. She shot a swift glance at the man opposite and then back at Claire.

'Is anything wrong, my dear?'

'No, nothing.'

Claire took her friend's arm and hurried on, terrified that Stone might try to bar their way. However, he made no move in their direction at all. Rather he remained where he was, staring after them with the same lupine smile on his lips.

'Who was that man?' asked Ellen. 'He seemed to know you.'

'I don't know. Perhaps he has seen me before in town.'

'Yes, that must be it.'

To Claire's relief Ellen did not pursue the matter and five minutes later they reached the waiting carriage without further incident. However, as the vehicle pulled away Claire saw Stone again, this time watching them from the corner of the road that led off the square. She knew that he must have followed them and the thought made her distinctly uneasy. Then she became aware that Ellen was speaking to her.

'I hope you will forgive me, my dear, but I must confess to an ulterior motive in taking you to meet the Dobsons today.'

Claire regarded her quizzically. 'Motive?'

'Yes. I was wondering...' She hesitated. 'I was wondering, do you think that some sort of employment might be found for them on the Netherclough estate?'

Claire stared at her in surprise for a moment but, now the words were out, it seemed an obvious solution. She wondered that she had not thought of it herself.

'I don't know,' she replied, 'but I could certainly ask.'

'Would you?'

'I'd be glad to.'

'The family has a good reputation in the town. Mr Dobson was known for being a hard-working man and his wife is a good woman. I have done what I can, but it is precious little. If they do not get real help soon, I fear the worst, especially for the baby.'

Claire nodded. 'When I return to Netherclough I shall speak to Mar…Lord Destermere at the earliest opportunity.'

'Bless you. It would mean so much if—' She broke off. 'But I must not get ahead of myself here. There may be no position for them after all.'

'They shall not be allowed to starve. Netherclough is a large estate. There must be something they could do.'

'I hope it may be so. These times have brought so much hardship to the people hereabouts. Old Mrs Grundy told me yesterday that Sir James Wraxall has cut his workers' wages to seven shillings a week.'

'Seven shillings! Are you sure?'

'Quite sure. Mrs Grundy's son works in one of Wraxall's mills.'

'But people could scarcely manage on eight shillings,' Claire replied.

'I know, but that is of no concern to men like Wraxall. He alone seems to prosper in these hard times. Only six months ago he was able to buy Beardsall's mill when its owner went bankrupt.'

Claire was sickened. How could such a wealthy man behave with such callous unconcern for those who depended on him? Indignation rose like a tide and along with it the knowledge of her own impotence.

Ellen's words stayed with her, even after she had taken her leave. As the carriage began the return journey, Claire was doubly determined to try and do something for the Dobsons. She was realist enough to know that she couldn't save everybody caught up in the economic depression, but it might be possible to help one family at least.

* * *

Mindful of her promise to Ellen she sought an interview with her employer the very same evening. On learning from Mather that His Lordship was in the study, she presented herself at the door. The Viscount was reading through some paperwork but, on seeing her there, looked up in surprise. Then he rose and smiled.

'Miss Davenport, what an unexpected pleasure. Won't you sit down?'

Claire sank into the offered chair and folded her hands in her lap to stop them trembling. Now that they were face to face it was suddenly less easy to broach the subject. The affairs of people like the Dobsons were hardly his concern. Would he consider her request the grossest piece of presumption?

'I hope you enjoyed your visit to Miss Greystoke,' he said.

'Yes, thank you.'

'Good. I'm glad to hear it.'

Claire bit her lip, knowing she must speak and not quite knowing how to begin. The silence stretched.

'Was there something you wished to discuss?' he prompted.

'Yes.' She took a deep breath. This was her chance. 'I was wondering…well, hoping that you could offer employment to the Dobson boys.'

He raised one arched brow. 'And who, pray, are the Dobson boys?'

'Their father was killed when Harlston's machines were attacked. He was one of the escort. Do you remember? The night you were shot?'

'I could hardly forget it,' he observed.

'No, I suppose not. Well, the thing is that Mr Dobson's death has meant that his family is destitute. He left a wife and six children. The oldest boys have tried to find work, but there is none to be had. If they don't get help soon, the whole family will be evicted and left to starve.'

'May I ask how you know all this?'

'Ellen took me to visit the family this afternoon. Mrs Dobson is a good woman and does the best she can, but their plight is pitiful indeed. Ellen tries to help, and Dr Greystoke too with medicine for the baby, but there is only so much they can do, sir.'

'Ah, yes. Miss Greystoke is known for her charitable works, is she not?' He paused, regarding her keenly. 'Is she behind this request, by any chance?'

Claire felt her cheeks grow warm. 'She asked if I would speak to you.'

'I see.'

'She understands perfectly that there may be nothing for them here. Only…'

'Only?'

'Netherclough is such a large estate and it requires so many staff. She…we wondered if places might be found for two more. In the gardens, or the stables perhaps?'

'I do not run a charitable institution, Miss Davenport. While I can sympathise with the plight of people like the Dobsons, I cannot change the times we live in.'

'No, but you can help to make things a little better.'

The grey eyes met and held hers. 'I do not need you to tell me what I can and cannot do.'

'I'm sorry. I did not mean to be presumptuous. It's just that I'd hoped…'

'Hoped what?'

'That you might at least consider it.'

'If such aid is offered to one family, it sets a precedent for others.'

'It could be done discreetly.'

'Perhaps. If there was work available. As it is, Netherclough is fully staffed. I'm sorry.'

The tone expressed finality and Claire knew it was useless to pursue the matter and stupid of her to have assumed he would help. Rich men stayed rich because they didn't give money away unless they had to. For a split second Ellen's words about Wraxall leapt to mind and with them a surge of indignation and impotent anger. She had thought Marcus was of a different stamp. Trying to force the lid down on her temper, she rose from her chair and faced him.

'I quite understand, sir. I'm sorry to have bothered you with this. After all, the Dobsons can always go to the workhouse.'

With that she swept out of the room, leaving Marcus staring after her in slack-jawed astonishment. A moment later he was on his feet.

'Claire! Claire, come back here!'

The only reply was swiftly retreating footsteps. He swore softly. For a second he was sorely tempted to go after her but resisted it, knowing that if he did he might do something he'd regret. Like giving her a good shaking perhaps. Had he not treated her with consideration? And was he to be treated to such a display of scorn just because he had refused this one request? A totally unreasonable request at that?

'Damn!'

He flung out of the chair and went to stand by the hearth, glowering down into the flames. No one had ever spoken to him like that. Certainly not a governess. Miss Davenport needed to learn her place—or lose it. That thought gave him pause. He drew in a deep breath. By rights the vixen should be given her marching orders, but he knew perfectly well he wasn't going to dismiss her. Lucy would be upset by it. He couldn't do that to the child, even though such a step would have the advantage of ridding him of an argumentative, troublesome little jade.

After she left him Claire marched straight to her room there to pace the floor, fists clenched. Her face still burned and the memory of the recent interview did nothing to cool it. He could have intervened! He was the richest man in the county! With a shaking hand she dashed away the tears that started in her eyes. She had expected so much more than a flat refusal to help.

For some minutes she paced, until her anger cooled a little. Moving to the window, she stared out at the beautiful gardens and rolling parkland beyond. How was it that some people had so much and others so little? And should not the rich help the poor when they could? She did not grudge the wealthy their good fortune. There had always been social inequality and always would be, but what about fair treatment? The labourer was worthy of his hire. How could men like Wraxall justify paying seven shillings a week and causing families to starve? How could honest employment be withheld by those who had the power to give it?

Claire sighed and sat down disconsolately on the edge of her bed. Gradually as her anger cooled it gave way to more rational thought. She should have realised that the Viscount would be more likely to refuse than to accede to her request. A house like Netherclough was always properly staffed. It ran like a well-oiled machine. It occurred to her then that most of its employees were drawn from the local area. Indeed, its owner was a key employer in his way. And he paid fair wages. The admission brought her back to earth with a jolt.

Claire knew then that she had absolutely no right to criticise or to tell him what he ought to do. Had he not shown her kindness up to now? Recalling the attentions she had received, she began to feel guilty. Mingled with it was shame for losing her temper. She had spoken to him as she might have done to an intimate. Yet this man was among the foremost in the land. Not only that, he was her employer, the being who held her fate in his hands. The realisation of the true extent of her folly acted like a bucket of cold water. How could she have been so stupid? He had made it clear at the outset that continued employment was dependent on satisfactory completion of the probationary period. The latter still had well over a month left to run. Instead of getting on with her job she had allowed her feelings to run away with her and behaved like an idiot. If he gave her notice to quit, it would be no more than she deserved. Truly appalled now, she knew that she owed him an apology—and soon.

For a while she deliberated. Should she go now or wait, hoping his anger might have cooled by the morrow? But then she had her duties to perform and likely would not see the Viscount at all. She certainly couldn't imagine him visiting the nursery and even if he did it was not the right place to say what needed to be said. No, it must be now. Pausing only to bathe her face and tidy her appearance, she retraced her steps to the study and knocked on the door.

'Come!'

Claire swallowed hard and, summoning all her courage, went in.

At first he didn't look up from the desk, seemingly absorbed in the papers before him. She had leisure to observe the sharp crease between his brows. Heart thumping, she took a tentative pace forward and stopped again. Then he did look up. For just a split second the grey eyes registered surprise. Then it was gone. She could detect no sign of outward anger, but the steely expression was infinitely worse.

'Well?'

It was hardly a promising beginning, but she knew there was no possibility of leaving before she had atoned for her behaviour. As he waited, Marcus knew a moment of intense and gloating satisfaction. So she had thought better of it, had she? As well she might. He leaned back in his chair, relishing the moment.

'I wish to apologise, sir, for what I said earlier. It was quite uncalled for and unpardonably rude.' She took a deep breath. 'I beg your pardon.'

For the second time he knew surprise, though now his expression gave no hint of it. He could not mistake the note of sincerity in her words either. Indeed, she looked abject. The hazel eyes met his in mute appeal. As they did so every vestige of his former satisfaction vanished and was replaced with quite a different feeling.

Mistaking his silence, Claire felt sick inside. She had failed. He had not forgiven her. His anger was still very much alive. And why would it not be? She made a vague, despairing gesture with her hand.

'That's all I came to say, sir.'

With that she turned away and walked towards the door. She never reached it for Marcus was out of his chair and across the room in three strides. Seizing her by the wrist, he pulled her round to face him. For just one second, grey eyes burned into hazel before he drew her close and brought his mouth down hard across hers in a searing kiss. He felt her tense and try to resist him. It availed her nothing. His mouth demanded her response, to acknowledge what was in her heart. Crushed in that powerful embrace, Claire felt her blood race, every part of her alive to the touch and taste and scent of him. Unable to escape, or to ignore the sudden igniting of that inner fire, she abandoned herself to his kiss.

When at last he drew back a little and looked into her eyes, it was to see an answering recognition and his heart leapt.

'I suppose it's my turn to apologise now,' he said, 'but for the life of me I cannot. I've wanted to do that for weeks.'

She shut her eyes as the enormity of the situation dawned. He shook her gently.

'Look at me, Claire.'

Unable to resist the appeal in his voice, she obeyed.

'Now tell me you feel nothing for me.'

'I cannot tell you that for it would be false. But this cannot be.'

'Why not?'

'Because it's wrong. Surely you see that?'

'No, I don't. How can this feeling be wrong?'

'Because of who we are. Because of our different situations. I will not be a rich man's plaything, Marcus.'

'Is that what you think this is about?' he demanded, stung.

'Isn't it?'

'I have never thought of you in those terms.'

'Then why did you kiss me like that?'

'Because I couldn't help myself.'

'Was this why you gave me the governess post here?' she asked.

'No, of course not.' His hold slackened. 'Do you really think me capable of such a calculating act?'

She shook her head. 'I'm sorry.'

'Besides, it was you who sought the post, remember?'

'Yes, I remember.'

For a moment there was a tense silence. Then the grey eyes narrowed.

'Why? Why did you want this place so much?'

She swallowed hard. 'I told you—I had to earn my living.'

'No, there's more to it than that, isn't there?' She tried to turn away but his hands on her shoulders prevented it. 'Tell me why, Claire.'

'I…it's something I should have told you long since. Only I did not know how.'

Marcus waited. Unable to withstand that scorching gaze, Claire averted her eyes and for several seconds was silent. Suddenly she wanted to tell him everything and yet part of her feared his response. Would he be angry with her for withholding the truth? There was only one way to find out.

'It concerns my uncle.'

That certainly wasn't what he had been expecting. 'Your uncle? How so?'

'He became my legal guardian after my parents died. He was…*is* a man of stern principles and not given to demonstrating affection, even to those nearest to him. In consequence we were never close.'

'That is hardly to be wondered at.'

'Although he provided for my material needs in childhood, I always knew that one day I should have to earn my living. That much had been made clear. In any case the thought of leaving did not distress me greatly. I expected that he would find me a situation.'

'And did he?'

'Yes, as the intended wife of one of his friends. A man old enough to be my father.'

'Good God! But of course you refused the offer.'

'Yes, I refused.' She took a deep breath. 'My uncle was furious. He said he would not be forsworn and that the marriage would take place no matter what.'

'But he could not compel you to wed against your will.'

'You have never met my uncle, sir. He would not hesitate to use force and told me as much. I knew him well enough to understand it was no idle threat.'

Marcus's jaw tightened. 'Did he hurt you, Claire?'

'No. I pretended compliance. He is so used to being obeyed he could not conceive of disobedience in any member of the family. Having lulled him into believing he had won, I packed a bag and escaped out of the bedroom window one night.'

Torn between indignation and amusement he shook his head. 'And then?'

'After that I knew I had to get as far away as possible and to the one person in the world I knew would help me.'

'You refer to Miss Greystoke, I collect. You had kept in touch then?'

'I received a letter from her not long after I arrived at my uncle's house, and I was permitted to reply—under my aunt's direction. That was all. None of Ellen's subsequent letters ever reached me, though she told me she wrote several times.'

The grey eyes hardened. 'They were kept from you?'

'I believe so. But in spite of that I never forgot her. She had always been so kind to me, you see. I just prayed that when I reached Helmshaw she would still be there.'

As he listened to the tale it seemed to Marcus that many pieces of a puzzle had just dropped into place.

'It was fortunate for you that she was,' he replied, grim-faced.

'Yes, and fortunate for me that you came along when you did.'

Remembering the incident in Gartside, he felt a surge of unwonted anger. The idea of any man laying hands on her was intolerable. He had let Jed Stone off far too lightly. And yet was he much better? Had he too not forced his attentions on her, a vulnerable young woman who was under his protection? He should keep her from harm, not be the cause of it. *'I will not be a rich man's plaything.'* The words smote his conscience hard.

'I did what any self-respecting man would have done.'

'No, not just any man.' The hazel eyes met and held his and, seeing the expression there, he felt his heart miss a beat. 'And then you gave me this situation and with it the means to support myself,' she went on. 'It was like the answer to a prayer.'

For a moment he was silent, regarding her with a level gaze. 'You need have no fear that I shall divulge your whereabouts to your uncle.'

'Thank you.'

'I think it unlikely he would trace you this far in any case but, even if he did, he will not remove you from this house.'

'I'm sorry. This might still put you in a difficult position with the law.'

'But you cannot now be far off your majority.'

'In a few more weeks I shall be one and twenty. Then his authority over me will be at an end.'

Marcus knew a moment of inner relief. He had not the least fear of meeting her uncle—indeed, would rather have relished doing so—but the legal aspect of the matter was trickier. Technically the brute did have the right to remove her from the house and compel her return. In the same instant he knew he would never permit that to happen. The idea of any young woman being forced into such a marriage was repugnant, but when that woman was Claire it became unthinkable.

He looked down into her face. 'Why didn't you tell me, Claire? Did you not trust me enough?'

She met his gaze and, interpreting it correctly, her heart thumped harder. 'I'm so sorry. I know it was wrong of me, but I was afraid you might turn me away.'

'I would never turn you away. Nor would I ever let harm come to you.'

He drew her closer and kissed her mouth, gently this time, and just for a moment. Then he drew her against him, holding her close, breathing in the fragrance of her hair. It felt right to hold her in his arms; she belonged there. He had known that feeling only once before, and had never thought to feel it again. He wanted her now with every fibre of his being, wanted to carry her to the couch and continue this to its delightful conclusion. But he knew he could not. He could not take advantage of her innocence or her vulnerability.

Claire heard him sigh and felt his hold slacken.

'Forgive me,' he said then.

It took every ounce of her willpower not to reach out for him, not to surrender to the heat in her blood. The memory of his kiss burned still. She could feel yet the warmth of his hands, the lean hardness of the body pressed against hers. It was like being on the brink of a lake of fire and wanting nothing more than to plunge in and be consumed. The expression in his eyes left her in no doubt he felt it, too, that he wanted her just as much. Was this what her parents had felt for each other?

The memory jolted her back to reality. What they had felt was love, not passion merely; the kind of love that finds expression in a lifetime's commitment, not in a dishonourable and furtive liaison. Marcus might want her, but his heart was given elsewhere. She knew beyond all doubt that she cared for him, that she had always cared for him, but she could never be his mistress. While she was not fool enough to think he would ever marry her, she could at least retain his respect and his regard. It was all she had.

'I should go,' she said.

Unable to follow all the thoughts behind the hazel eyes, he recognized the resolution in her expression. He knew also that she was right.

'Go then, Claire, if you must. I'll not prevent you.'

With unconcealed relief she saw him stand aside. Before he could change his mind she slipped past him and out of the door, fleeing for her room and not daring to look back.

Grim-faced he stood on the threshold, watching her retreating figure. Part of him was tempted to go after her and to bring her back, but he knew he must not. His fists clenched at his sides and slowly he turned away, shutting the door behind him. Then he let out the breath he had unconsciously been holding. As he calmed a little and more rational thought intervened he could only regard his behaviour with abhorrence. There could be no repetition of what had happened today. Somehow he must find the self-discipline to live in the same house with her, to see her every day, and behave as though they were merely polite acquaintances brought together by circumstance. In the meantime he could only hope that she would forgive him.

True to his intention he avoided her for several days, deciding that they both needed space and time to try to put the incident behind them. In any case there were many matters requiring his attention and he spent hours closeted with Fisk, discussing estate business. Sometimes, when he looked out of the study window, he caught a glimpse of her walking in the gardens with Lucy. Once he heard them laughing together and wondered what had caused their amusement. It was good to hear a child's laugher around the place. He wondered suddenly if Lucy was ever lonely. While she had her governess there were no children of her own age to play with. Recalling his own childhood adventures with Greville, he knew that his brother had been an important part of his life. It came to Marcus then that he would very much like to have children of his own.

A sound at the door brought him back to the present. Mather was there to say that John Harlston had called.

'Ah, yes. Show him in, Mather.'

'Yes, my lord.'

A few moments later Harlston appeared. The Viscount smiled and held out his hand.

'Thank you for coming, Mr Harlston.'

'My pleasure, sir.'

Having invited his guest to sit and plied him with a glass of sherry, Marcus got straight to the point.

'I have asked you here in order to enlist your help in catching the Luddite wreckers.'

The other regarded him with some surprise. 'I will certainly do all in my power.' He paused. 'You have a plan?'

'Yes. I intend to set a trap.'

'A trap? How?'

'If you are in agreement, word will get out about the delivery of a replacement power loom to your mill. There will be a wagon and a suitable escort, but no loom—only a contingent of militia concealed beneath the tarpaulin, and another riding behind the convoy just out of sight.'

Harlston considered it and then nodded slowly. 'By heaven, it might just work.'

'I believe it might.' The Viscount paused. 'However, secrecy is essential if the wreckers are to take the bait. The fewer people who know about it, the better. The escort need not know until the last minute. As for the militia, only Major Barstow needs to be told initially. I believe we may rely on his discretion.'

'What about the other mill owners?'

Marcus met and held his gaze. 'I would prefer to say nothing for the time being.'

'Very well, sir. I'm sure you have your reasons.'

'I do, and they are good ones.'

'Will you apprise Major Barstow or shall I?'

'I will speak to him. I intend to be one of those in the convoy.'

'You, sir?' Harlston's astonishment was plain. 'Forgive me, but have you considered? It is most dangerous work.'

'I am fully aware of that, Mr Harlston, but I have special reasons for undertaking it. I am also well able to defend myself should the need arise.'

'Of course you are, but…'

'It is pointless to try to dissuade me on this point. My mind is made up.'

'As you will. May I ask when you are proposing to put the plan into action?'

'At the end of the month. That will afford us plenty of time to see that everything is in place.'

'If it works, and there is no reason to suppose it will not, the area will be rid of that murderous crew once and for all.'

'That is my intention.'

Harlston regarded him steadily for a moment. 'May I ask why you take such a keen interest in the matter, sir?'

'I cannot answer that at present. Suffice it to say that the business of catching these men is important to me for several reasons.' Marcus paused. 'I must ask you to trust me.'

'Very well, sir.'

'Thank you.'

The two men shook hands and Harlston left a short time later. For some minutes after his visitor had gone Marcus remained alone in the study, turning over the details of the plan in his mind. It was simple but, in his experience, the simplest ideas were often the best. When Harlston said it was dangerous he had spoken the truth, but Marcus would not ask other men to do what he wasn't prepared to do himself. Besides, this was also personal. One way or another he intended to bring Greville's killers to justice.

He tossed back the remainder of his sherry and rang the bell for Mather. When the butler appeared shortly afterwards he was directed to send for Mr Fisk. The land agent duly arrived a few minutes later.

'You wished to speak with me, my lord?'

'Yes. Am I right in thinking that one of the estate cottages is currently standing empty?'

'That is correct, my lord. It has been vacant since old Ramsbottom died. He had no surviving family.'

'Quite so. As it has been uninhabited for several months, the place may possibly need some renovation to make it habitable. You will put matters in train immediately.'

'Certainly, my lord.' Fisk paused. 'Am I to understand that the cottage is about to be tenanted again?'

'Yes.'

'Very good, my lord.'

'That will be all, Mr Fisk.'

Having dismissed his agent, the Viscount sat down at his desk and began to pen a letter to Ellen Greystoke.

Chapter Nine

Claire strolled along the river bank while Lucy ran on ahead collecting brightly coloured leaves. From time to time she would run back and show Claire a particularly prized specimen, which was duly admired. The afternoon was cool but fine and, feeling the need to escape the confines of the house, Claire had not hesitated to take her young charge out for a walk. Besides, the place was peaceful and pleasant, affording plenty of opportunity for private reflection.

After that last momentous encounter with Marcus she had not set eyes on him, and correctly surmised it was deliberate policy. In many ways she was glad of it. He had the good sense to avoid temptation. She smiled sadly. The temptation was not all one-sided as she knew full well. She had come to care for him more deeply than she could ever have dreamed possible. It was a passion that could never be realised for to do so would render her position here untenable. She must not jeopardise that. It wasn't going to be easy to keep a cool head. In spite of good intentions they would be thrown together, and each time would make it harder for both of them. Somehow she must find the strength of mind to resist the attraction he represented, even though every part of her longed to succumb. He could never be for her. Eventually, he would marry a lady from among the *ton* and bring her here to be mistress of Netherclough. His wife would be a fortunate woman, she thought.

Claire's twenty-first birthday was drawing near. In a little over four weeks she would be a free agent. Uncle Hector would have no authority over her and it wouldn't matter if he did find out where she was. No doubt there would still be an unpleasant scene in which he would castigate her for ingratitude, but she could bear it. Besides, she was under the Viscount's protection. Even her uncle would think twice before crossing such a powerful man. She just hoped that Ellen would not be subjected to any disagreeable scenes for her part in all of this.

By a strange coincidence it seemed that her friend had also been thinking of her, for the following morning brought an unexpected communication:

My Dearest Claire,

Forgive the brevity of this letter but I have so little time to write at present. Even so, it would be most remiss of me if I did not apprise you of the most recent developments regarding the Dobson family. Yesterday I received a letter from Lord Destermere to say that he had lately been informed of their attempts to find employment following Mr Dobson's untimely demise. His Lordship informs me that a vacancy exists in his household for a kitchen maid, and wonders if the situation would suit Mrs Dobson. The position is offered along with a vacant cottage on the Netherclough estate. Furthermore, he undertakes to find suitable situations for the eldest Dobson boys.

I lost no time in imparting all this to Mrs Dobson, and you can well imagine the family's joyful response on receiving the news. My own gratitude towards Lord Destermere can scarcely be expressed, but I have written to thank him for his great kindness. However, I also know that sincere thanks are due to you too, dearest Claire, for helping to bring this about. God bless you.

Your affectionate friend,
Ellen

For some moments Claire was too stunned to take it in, but on rereading the letter discovered she had not been mistaken. Heart full, she felt tears start in her eyes. He had listened after all, but even in her wildest dreams she had never expected he would exert himself so far. For the first time in days her spirits soared. What had made him change his mind? Was it perhaps that he too had come close to death the night Mr Dobson was killed? Or perhaps it was just that, on reflection, he had decided it would not be too difficult to accommodate one more family at Netherclough? Did he understand what happiness he had given to others by his actions? She folded the letter carefully and put it in her pocket. No matter what it cost her she must thank him, too. It was the least she could do.

As it happened she did not need to seek him out because he came to the nursery not long afterwards. Lucy saw him first and the child's face was lit with a smile.

'Uncle Marcus!'

'Hello, Brat.' He lifted her into his arms so that their faces were level. 'I hope you've been behaving yourself.'

'I know all my letters now.'

'I don't believe you.'

'I do, don't I, Miss Davenport?'

Claire smiled. 'Perhaps you should say them.'

Marcus assumed an expression of mock severity. 'I quite agree. Otherwise I will only have your word for it.'

Rather self-consciously Lucy proceeded to recite the alphabet faultlessly. Marcus grinned.

'I am amazed! I never thought to have such a clever niece.'

'Miss Davenport is teaching me to read now.'

'Is she so?' He glanced past the child to Claire. 'Then no doubt you will be able to read to me very soon.'

'Yes, I shall,' Lucy replied, the tone suggesting total confidence. 'Shan't I, Miss Davenport?'

'I am quite sure of it,' said Claire.

'Very well, then. Far be it from me to hinder your progress.'

Lucy eyed him speculatively. 'Are you going away again, Uncle Marcus?'

'Going away? No, why?'

'I haven't seen you for days and days.'

'I know. That is why I wondered if you would like to go riding with me this afternoon?'

'Oh, yes, please!'

'All right, then.' He set the child down. Then he looked at Claire. 'I will see you in the stable yard at two o'clock.'

It was evident that she was to be included in the expedition. Outwardly then everything would appear the same. Only the two of them knew it was not. However, if he could keep up his part of the pretence, she could do no less. It would also give her an opportunity to thank him for his intervention in the Dobson affair. But there was more to it than that, as she quickly acknowledged: she was looking forward to seeing him, to being in his company again. In spite of herself she had missed him in these last few days.

They rode out as usual that afternoon. Claire took care to let Lucy monopolise his attention, and watched the interaction between the two of them. He kept his horse to a slow walk to allow for the pony's shorter paces and, whenever the child spoke to him, he gave her his full attention. Now that she was gaining competence he allowed her a gentle canter, a development that brought a glow of excitement to her eyes.

'Will you let me ride to hounds one day, Uncle Marcus?'

'One day,' he replied, 'when you are more competent. Then I will take you out myself.'

Lucy's smile widened. 'You can come too, Miss Davenport.'

Claire smiled in return. 'Well, thank you very much.'

'Then we can all go together.'

'We'll see.'

As Lucy turned to impart the news to the groom, Marcus reined his horse alongside Claire's.

'She is making excellent progress,' he observed.

'Yes, she is a natural rider.'

'I did not mean in horsemanship alone. She is making progress in every way. More indeed than I could have hoped.' He threw her a sideways glance. 'And that is due to you.'

Claire felt her cheeks grow warm. 'She is a delightful pupil, bright and eager to learn.'

'She has grown much attached to you in the last two months.'

'And I to her.'

For a moment or two they rode on in silence. Then she turned towards him.

'I wanted to thank you for what you have done to help the Dobson family. Ellen wrote and told me.'

'Did she?'

'Yes. You cannot know how much it means to them. To all concerned.'

'Do not cast me in the role of hero. It was done with extraordinarily little effort on my part.'

'You underplay it, sir. If it were not for your intervention, their situation would be dire indeed.'

'Well, at least now they won't end in the workhouse.'

'I should not have said that.'

'Yes, you should.' He paused, surveying her keenly. 'And you were quite right, of course. But do not be under any illusions—my actions were not the result of altruism.'

'What, then?'

'I believe I acted in the hope of pleasing you.'

She met his gaze, but could detect no sign of teasing. On the contrary there was an expression there that made her heart beat a little faster.

'Then you succeeded.'

'I'm glad to hear it. I could not long withstand your disapproval.'

Her colour deepened. 'I am far too outspoken.'

'Yes,' he replied, 'but like the voice of my conscience, hard to ignore.'

She smiled ruefully. 'It was most presumptuous of me and I am sorry for it.'

'Since you are in such a penitent mood I shall take full

advantage of the fact. I intend to hold a ball at Netherclough three weeks from now. I would like you to attend.'

Claire's stomach turned over. 'A ball?'

'Yes, it is a genteel entertainment involving a lot of dancing.' Seeing the speaking look that greeted his sally, he grinned.

'I must refuse, sir, though I am grateful for the invitation. It would not be appropriate.'

His smile vanished. 'Damn it, Claire, I don't want your gratitude, and I'll decide what's appropriate and what is not.'

'I cannot, sir.'

'Cannot or will not?' he demanded.

'Cannot, sir. You must see that. The more people who see me, the more likely that my uncle will get to hear of my whereabouts.'

Seeing the anxiety in her face, he felt some of his annoyance ebb. 'Your uncle has no acquaintance here who might tell him. There can be no danger, I think.'

Claire shook her head, unconvinced. 'All the same…'

'Even if he did discover your whereabouts, I would not let him take you from Netherclough.'

'He would have the law on his side.'

'True, but litigation takes time, and by then you would have achieved your majority.'

'How I wish I had.'

The words were delivered with quiet passion and struck him forcibly. What kind of brute was this uncle that he should inspire such feelings of dread?

'You have not long to wait now,' he replied. 'In the meantime it will do you good to enjoy yourself. Come to the ball, Claire.'

'I have no gown.'

'I'll buy you one.'

'No, sir.'

He threw up a hand in despair. 'I am thwarted at every turn.'

'I am truly sorry, sir.'

She really was, but knew that she could not yield the point.

'Think about it,' he said. 'I'll not press you for a final answer now.'

In the event all thoughts of the ball were driven out of her head for a while, because two days later Lucy contracted a feverish cold and was confined to bed. Initially it was thought to be merely a childish ailment that would probably cure itself in a day or two. However, the little girl grew more listless and lethargic and her appetite disappeared altogether. Claire grew concerned enough to go and see Marcus.

'I think we should have a medical opinion, sir.'

He reached for the bell pull. 'I shall have Dr Greystoke summoned immediately.'

The physician was not long in coming but though he examined the child thoroughly he could find nothing more seriously wrong than a bad cold.

'Will she be all right?' asked Marcus as they walked together down the stairs.

'Yes, though she may feel poorly for a few days yet.'

'What brought it on?'

'It is hard to say. A slight chill perhaps,' Greystoke replied. 'Keep her warm and quiet and see that she drinks plenty of fluids. For the time being she must have no excitement or exertion.'

'Very well.'

'I will call again tomorrow to see if there has been any improvement in her condition.'

After the physician had left, Marcus returned to the sickroom to find Claire there already. He came over to stand by the bedside.

'How is she?'

'Sleeping now. I'll sit with her for a while.'

'Are you sure? One of the maids could do it.'

'I would rather stay—for the time being.'

'As you wish.' He regarded her keenly for a moment. 'Is there anything you need?'

'Thank you, no.'

'If you think of something, just let one of the servants know.'

'I will.'

'Very well. I will come back later and see how she does.'

After he had left Claire watched the child sleeping for a while and then moved to the window. For some minutes she stood there, looking out onto the garden. It had been raining earlier and the fallen leaves lay dark and sodden on the pathways and flower beds where a few late blooms drooped over the dark earth. A lowering sky promised more rain. She shivered. The place seemed strangely bleak and forlorn after the previous weeks of autumn sunshine.

Turning away from the scene, she took a glance at Lucy and, seeing that the child still slept, returned briefly to her own chamber to fetch her book. It would help to pass the time. Having accomplished her goal, she settled herself in a chair and began to read.

Lucy woke about an hour later and complained of thirst so Claire gave her some water. Then she read to her for a while until the child dozed again. Marcus returned not long after, moving quietly across the room to join her.

'How is she?'

Claire gave him a summary of the situation.

'I think the sleep will do her good.' He paused. 'As for you, I think some luncheon is in order. You must be hungry by now. I've told Mrs Hughes to prepare something. Meanwhile, one of the maids will sit with Lucy.'

His thoughtfulness touched her and she was glad to obey. Much to her surprise he led her to a small dining room where a table had been set for two. He intended to join her then. She looked around, taking in the cheerful fire and cosy furnishings. It was far more intimate than the main dining room, and at this season much warmer, too. It occurred to her that she should not be here alone with him like this, that it could only lead to further complications, but somehow she didn't care.

If he thought anything amiss it wasn't apparent in his manner or expression. On the contrary, he seemed to enjoy her company and her conversation. For a while the latter turned on general topics but then, gradually, to matters closer to home.

'I spoke to Trubshaw yesterday about the oldest Dobson boy. It seems he has an affinity with horses and has the makings of a fine stable lad.'

Claire smiled. 'I am so glad.'

'The younger brother has yet to find his métier, but no doubt that will become clearer with time.'

'Thank you for all you are doing for them.'

'I am doing nothing at all. I mention the matter only because I thought it would interest you.'

'It does, very much, and you are too modest about your role in bringing it all about.'

'Now the conversation grows dull. Let us speak of other topics, I beg you.'

'Then may I ask whether you have got any further with your plan to apprehend the men responsible for the attack on Harlston's loom?'

'Yes, matters are in train. With the aid of the militia I intend to arrange a trap.'

'You, sir?'

'Who else? This matter is dear to my heart.'

'You must have been very close to your brother.'

'When we were growing up I thought he was one step removed from God. Wherever he led, I followed. Usually into another scrape.'

'I can imagine. You must have missed him when you went abroad.'

'I did, but India provided enough excitement and challenge to keep me busy.'

'And romance, too.'

'Yes, that, too.'

His fingers tightened on the stem of his glass and for a moment there was silence. For a moment she was tempted to ask, but quickly stifled the impulse. Presently the conversation moved in other directions for the remainder of the meal. At length Claire laid down her napkin.

'I should go back and see how Lucy is faring.'

'Let us go along together,' he replied.

She had not expected it, but merely inclined her head in acquiescence. They walked together back to Lucy's chamber. He did not speak again and she would not break into his private thoughts, though the very air between them seemed charged somehow.

Lucy was awake but clearly feverish. Marcus frowned and laid a hand on her forehead. It was hot to the touch and there was hectic colour in her cheeks. The tray of food nearby was untouched. He turned to the maid.

'Fetch a cup of warm milk.'

As the woman hastened to obey, Marcus peeled off his coat and hung it on the chair she had vacated. Having done so, he wrung out a cloth in the basin on the washstand and laid it on the child's forehead.

'It's nice and cool,' he told her. 'It will help your headache.'

Lucy regarded him with solemn eyes. 'Shall I be better soon, Uncle Marcus?'

'Of course you will.'

'I want to go out riding.'

'And you shall, but not today.'

The words brought welling tears and seeing them Claire came to sit on the other side of the bed.

'It is raining today, dear,' she explained. 'If you took Misty out he might catch a cold, too. You wouldn't want that, would you?'

Lucy looked thoughtful and then slowly shook her head. 'No. He must stay in his stable.'

'That's right,' Claire went on. 'All the horses are staying in today.'

'Even yours, Uncle Marcus?'

'Even mine,' he replied. 'Miss Davenport is right. I should not like them to catch cold. It's even worse for horses than for humans.'

'Is it?'

'Very much so. You have to take great care of them.'

The threatened tears subsided and he gave Claire a grateful look. She had a light touch, he thought. Where had she learned it? All at once he felt curious about her earlier life. Although he knew the broad outline now, she had remained reticent about much of it. Yet was he not reticent also? On some matters anyway. Recalling their earlier conversation he felt a twinge of guilt. He could hardly demand frankness when he was not prepared to give the same.

A few moments later the maid returned with the milk. At first Lucy refused to touch it, but by a mixture of joking and cajolery they persuaded her to drink half of it. After that she began to doze again.

'I think she'll sleep for a while now,' he said.

Claire nodded. 'It's the best thing for her.'

'I'll stay awhile. Just until she drops off. Then the maid can take over for a while.'

'As you wish, sir.'

She took her leave of him and, not wanting to return to her own chamber, made her way to the library. It was her favourite room and one she visited often for, among other things, it contained a handsome collection of novels. Having selected a new book she ensconced herself on the sofa by the fire. Outside the wind flung a squall of rain at the window. Claire smiled. In here it was warm and cosy. She curled up and settled down to read.

However, after a few minutes she found her attention wandering and instead of the printed pages it was Marcus's face she saw. She could not forget the gentleness and concern he showed for his young ward. It was an aspect of his character that she had not expected—such matters were usually considered a woman's domain, beneath the notice of men. Yet he had made it his business to know how matters stood and was not above getting involved either. He must have felt a great affection for his late brother. Did he see something of Greville when he looked at Lucy?

The thought of Greville led to others, less welcome.

Marcus had told her that he had a plan for the apprehension and arrest of those responsible for his brother's murder. It disturbed her to discover he meant to be directly involved but, knowing him as she did, she could not imagine that he would stand on the sidelines while others took the risks. What if something were to happen to him? He had been lucky once, but he might not be a second time. She shivered at the implications, unable to conceive of a world where he was not. She could endure to live without him if she had to, provided she knew he was safe and well. It was all that mattered.

Chapter Ten

As the doctor had predicted, Lucy soon rallied from her cold and, within another couple of days, was sitting up in bed playing with her doll. She was impatient to get up, but Marcus would not allow it and refused to be swayed by pleas or tears.

'When your fever is down at night as well as the mornings then you may get up,' he said. 'Not until.'

To sugar the pill he devoted considerable time to her amusement, telling her stories and playing simple card games. When he could not be with her Claire took over. Between them they kept the child calm and entertained.

Once or twice when Lucy was resting Claire took the opportunity to go for a walk round the gardens. Having spent several days cooped up indoors, she felt the need for some fresh air and exercise. It was while she was returning from one of these excursions that she was waylaid by one of the servants who slipped out of a side door as she was passing. With some surprise she recognised the face.

'Mrs Dobson! What a pleasant surprise. How are you?'

'I am very well, ma'am, I thank you.'

'And your children?'

'Well too, ma'am.'

'I am glad to hear it.'

'I've been watching out for a chance to speak to you, Miss Davenport. I want to thank you for all that you've done for me and mine. Miss Greystoke told me as how you'd spoken to His Lordship on our behalf.'

'I was glad to do so.' Claire smiled. 'I hope that you and your family are comfortably settled now.'

'It's like a dream come true, ma'am. Sometimes I have to pinch myself to make sure I'm really awake. If it wasn't for you we'd have had to go on t'parish.'

'Thank goodness it didn't come to that.'

'I thank God for it every day. It must have been divine providence brought you to us.'

More like Ellen Greystoke, thought Claire. Her friend was subtle in achieving her ends.

'I beg you will not mention it, Mrs Dobson. My part in the matter was very small. Lord Destermere must take all the credit.'

'We're beholden to His Lordship and no mistake, but I want you to know that I and my family won't forget what you did. Not ever.'

After they parted Claire returned to her room to divest herself of bonnet and gloves. However, she had not taken two paces into the room when she stopped short with a gasp of surprise. Lying on the bed was the most beautiful ball gown she had ever seen. Made of spangled white sarsnet, it was trimmed with silver ribbons. On the floor lay a pair of white satin slippers. For a moment she could only stare. Then she realised how it had come there and her hand stole to her cheek. If a necklace was an inappropriate gift from a gentleman, how much more was this gown? And yet it was so lovely.

Reverentially she lifted it off the bed and held it up against her. The fabric shimmered with every movement. It needed only a glance to see it became her well. For a few more seconds she wrestled with temptation. Then she was struggling out of her muslin gown. The ball dress was a perfect fit, almost as if it had been made for her. It fitted close to the waist, but was cut low to reveal her shoulders and the soft swell of her breasts. The dress floated away in graceful folds to her feet. It was altogether a more daring gown than any she had ever worn in her life, shocking and wonderful together. The slippers fitted perfectly, too. For a moment or two she pirouetted in front of the glass, turning this way and that to gauge the effect. It was glorious, a gown fit for a queen. *Yes,* said an inner voice, *but not for a governess.* Claire went hot and cold by turns as the implications of the scene dawned on her. She could not accept this gown any more than she could have accepted the amethyst necklace, and Marcus knew it. They must have this out, and soon.

Dressed again in her plain muslin frock she felt more equal to the task of confronting him. Enquiries as to his whereabouts led her to the library. He was sitting at a small table, apparently studying some ledgers, but he rose as she entered. Ignoring the offer of a chair, she stood instead.

'You should not have done it, sir.'

'Done what?' he asked.

'I refer to the new gown.'

'Ah. It seemed necessary.'

'How so?'

'You said you had not got a ball gown.'

'I may have said so, but that did not mean I wished you to buy me one.'

'No, I wished to do that.'

'It's all wrong, sir.'

'Oh? I rather thought the style would suit you very well. Perhaps the gown does not fit?'

Claire controlled herself with an effort. 'There is nothing wrong with the style or the fit.'

The grey eyes gleamed. 'Ah, you tried it on, then? Good.'

'I said I wasn't going to the ball.'

'Yes, I heard you,' he replied, unperturbed. 'However, it is my wish that you should attend.'

For a moment she was speechless, but only for a moment. 'You have no right to insist.'

'No,' he admitted. 'It's a total abuse of power.'

'And knowing that you will still do it?'

'Absolutely. It's one of the great advantages of position.'

'Sometimes, you are quite odious!'

His lips twitched. 'I wonder that you can bear with me at all.'

'Now you are roasting me.'

'You look even more attractive when you are annoyed, you see.'

'Will you be serious for a moment?'

'If you insist.'

She made a vague gesture with her hand. 'How can I make you understand?'

'All I understand is that I want you to be present. It is a ball, not a punishment.'

'I do not think of it as a punishment. You know my reasons for refusing.'

'Yes, just as I know they are groundless. I want you to come and enjoy yourself. Please say you will.'

He paused, his gaze searching her face. She sighed, knowing he wasn't going to yield on this.

'All right, I'll come, but it is for this once only.'

'Thank you.' He rose then and took her shoulders in a gentle clasp. 'It makes me happy to hear you say that.'

'Sir, I…'

'You know my feelings for you, Claire.'

It was so tempting to take the words at face value. How much she would have liked to believe them. The warmth of his hands through her gown, his nearness, filled her with a deep longing, but it was a feeling she didn't dare give in to. Apart from the impossibility of it leading to anything but pain and disaster, she would never accept second place in any man's affections. With an effort of will she detached herself from his hold.

The dark brows drew together. 'What is it, Claire? What's wrong?'

'Why are you doing this? Why pretend you care for me when we both know you love another?'

He stared at her, thunderstruck. 'What are you talking about?'

'Lakshmi,' she replied.

There followed a moment of complete silence in which the hawk-like gaze searched her face. Then, very steadily, he said, 'How do you come to know that name?'

'You spoke it in delirium. Not once, but several times.'

'I see.'

She watched him turn away as though wrestling with some powerful emotion, and she felt her throat tighten. It was as she had suspected. Lakshmi ruled his heart still. The knowledge hurt, but it was better than pretence. At least now the matter was out in the open.

'It is something I have never discussed with anyone,' he said then. 'Not even George Greystoke, but you deserve the truth if anyone does.' He turned again to face her. 'Do you want my story, Claire? I warn you now it is not pleasant.'

Her heart beat a little faster for there was an expression on his face that she had not seen there before. It sent a shiver down her spine. Feeling suddenly in need of support, she sank into a chair. Nevertheless, she knew she must listen.

'I will hear it, if you are willing to tell me.'

'Very well.' He paused, eyeing her keenly. 'The events I am about to relate took place some eight years ago. Lakshmi was an Indian princess, a young woman of extraordinary beauty and goodness. We met by chance when I was able to do her a trifling service. From the first there was a powerful alchemy between us. Our time together was brief, a matter of days only, but I knew then that she was the woman I wanted to marry and spend the rest of my life with. My feelings were returned. However, because of our respective positions there were obstacles to our being together. I should have followed my instinct and taken her away while I had the chance. There would have been all manner of trouble, but we could have surmounted it. Instead I hesitated, fearing to embroil her in a major scandal.

'While I hesitated, her father married her off to the rajah of a neighbouring state, a man old enough to be her grandfather. My despair at losing her was equalled only by the rage I felt for my earlier procrastination. So I threw myself into my work in an attempt to forget her. However, about a year later I had news of her again. Her elderly husband had sickened and died. In accordance with the traditions of that country the old prince's body was to be cremated. His widow was to commit suttee. In other words, she must go to the fire with her husband.'

Claire regarded him in horror. She had heard of the custom. Until now it had seemed unreal, part of the exotic fabric of a foreign culture. Seeing her expression, Marcus nodded.

'You may imagine my feelings on learning that. At any rate I was determined to save her and, taking a detachment of men, left immediately for Kathor. It was three days' ride away, but we travelled fast, pausing only to rest the horses when we had to. We cut half a day off the time but, even so, we came too late. When we reached the burning ground the ceremony had already begun.' He paused, taking a deep breath, seeing again the pyre and the flames. 'I tried to fight my way through the crowd, but it was too dense and prevented me. It also got ugly, for the people of that place believe the custom to be holy and resent interference. I was dragged from my horse and would have died too had my men not intervened and got me away.' One hand went to the scar on his cheek. 'I carry this as a permanent reminder of that day.'

Claire paled, appalled, for this calm relation of events was worse than any deliberate dramatisation could ever have been.

'Oh, Marcus. I'm so sorry. What a terrible thing.'

He was struck less by her evident sympathy than by the use of his name. It was the first time she had ever done so and was all the more telling for being entirely unconscious. In that moment he felt as though a barrier had come down.

'As I said, it was a long time ago.'

'I think it would not matter how many years passed by. Such a thing could never be forgotten.'

'No, we just learn to live with the memories.'

Claire was very still. Suddenly a lot of things had become clear. She was both honoured and moved by his confidence, for she could never have supposed he would open up to her in that way. At the same time it raised other questions. Almost as if he heard the thought, Marcus regarded her steadily.

'I shall never forget her, but one cannot cling to the past, Claire. Life goes on and time lessens the intensity of pain. Lakshmi is not your rival.'

'I see that now.'

'I hope you do.'

She returned his gaze. 'Besides, there are newer hurts to salve, are there not?'

'If by that you mean my brother, then, yes.'

'Can hurts be salved in blood?'

'This one will be, I promise you.'

Looking at the expression in the grey eyes, Claire shivered. This was a side to his character that she had only glimpsed before, but there could be no mistaking its deadly intensity. He would do what he set out to do, no matter how long it took, and his enemies could expect no quarter.

Much later, as she lay in bed, she reflected on that conversation and the story he had told her, unable to sleep for the images it evoked. She could only imagine the horror of it, the horror and the terror. Such things left an indelible impression upon the memory. No wonder Marcus had been so reluctant to speak of it. And yet perversely it was a part of him, a part of who he was. Having been afforded a glimpse of his past and the events that had shaped him, she found herself eager to know more. For all that air of quiet strength and invincibility there was also a hidden vulnerability about him, the person who all his life had wanted to be loved—and to love in return. Yet through some malign fate he had always lost those he cared for. How much she would have liked to be the woman who made him whole, the woman who had his heart. What he had offered her was passion, but she knew it was not enough and never could be. Without love there could be nothing.

As Marcus had intimated, Lucy was able to leave her room the next day and she and Claire re-established their usual routine soon after. In the meantime preparations were in train for the forthcoming ball and an endless stream of carts and wagons arrived at Netherclough Hall delivering everything from candles to chalk. Mrs Hughes spent several hours closeted with the Viscount while the arrangements were discussed in detail. Everyone who had been invited had returned an acceptance. Clearly it was to be the social event of the year in Yorkshire.

As the day came closer Claire found herself looking forward to the occasion and became caught up in the excitement around her. Though she had attended various social functions when she lived at her uncle's house, none had been as splendid as this promised to be. In all probability this was the only chance she would ever have to experience such a glittering event. The thought of the spangled sarsnet gown filled her with guilty pleasure. It would be perfect for the occasion, as Marcus had known when he ordered it. Would he still approve his choice when he saw her wearing it? The thought of his approbation brought a glow of warmth.

Lucy begged to be allowed to attend the ball, but to no avail. Marcus was adamant. However, he did promise that he and Claire would come and say goodnight before the guests arrived that evening. With that she had to be content. Meanwhile she was making excellent progress in the schoolroom, for she was a keen and conscientious pupil, soaking up information like a sponge. In teaching Lucy, Claire had followed similar principles to the ones that had been used in her own early education, before the stifling regime she had endured in her teens. She wanted the child to learn to think for herself and to be able to apply her knowledge. Along with the basic school work were the practical lessons in music and art, dancing and deportment. Where possible Claire tried to make the lessons fun, and devised all manner of different strategies until she found the ones that suited her pupil. She was devoutly thankful that the task was rendered much easier by having an able and willing mind to deal with.

Marcus, watching it all in his quietly observant manner, was impressed. He had taken a gamble when he had hired Claire, but it had paid off. The three-month probationary period had been a safety clause, but he knew now he wouldn't need to apply it. He couldn't visualise anyone else in the role. Though he had met her only three months earlier, it seemed in many ways a lot longer. She had become such a part of everyday life that he felt as though she had always been there. Somehow he couldn't imagine life without her, a future without her.

However, before he could contemplate the long-term there were matters closer to hand that must be attended to. The ball would be a pleasant interlude, but more importantly it would announce to the world that a new master was in residence at Netherclough. It would emphasise his presence and the role he intended to play in local affairs. All the main players would be present. It behoved him to know them better for they would also have an influence on what would follow.

After his travels abroad he had come to see the impor-

tance of every section of society, not merely the aristoc-
racy. Men like John Harlston, with his association in
trade, might be viewed with disdain by the upper classes,
but they created the wealth that made the country strong.
When trade resumed its normal levels again Marcus
knew that the mills would come into their own, like the
mines and the iron foundries. They were fundamental
to the life of the county and of the country. As he told
Claire, he could not isolate himself from them in an ivory
tower of privilege.

They had gone out riding and, while Lucy trotted
on ahead a little way, he had reined his horse alongside
Claire's. It seemed entirely natural to him now that he
should talk to her about his ideas for the future. Unlike
many of the women he had met in the past, she had a
sharp mind that was concerned with more than fashion
and lap dogs. She was quick to assimilate ideas and was
a good listener too, but she could also hold her own in
conversation and he often used her now as a sounding
board for ideas he wanted to explore.

'Netherclough is at the heart of things,' he said. 'I want
this gathering to reflect that, for the county families to
rub shoulders with professional men. Society is changing,
Claire. We must change with it or be left behind like so
many fossils in the social bedrock.'

She returned him a wry smile. 'If the French had
understood that they might never have had a revolution.'

'We have our revolution too, though it might be termed
industrial.'

'It is proving bloody, too, in its way.'

'Blood will have blood, Claire.' He turned his head
to meet her gaze. 'I am coming to understand how the
lure of profit may turn ordinary men into killers.'

She frowned. 'I don't follow.'

'It is my belief that Greville was killed because of something he learned, not only because he was a government agent.'

'You think he knew the identities of the wrecker gang?'

'Possibly, though they are just the tools employed to do a job. I think he may have discovered who they worked for.'

'Then you think someone is orchestrating the attacks?'

'I'm certain of it. Just as I'm certain that the wrecking of machines in this locality is about more than workers' wages.'

'But what else is there?'

'I told you—profit.' He paused. 'When one cannot make progress in an investigation a good rule is to follow the money.'

'That's a rather cynical philosophy, is it not?'

'Cynical but accurate. Someone stands to make a great deal out of the misery of others and he has manipulated events to suit his purpose.'

'But who would do such a thing?'

'A ruthless and dangerous man.'

'Have you proof?'

'Not yet, but I *will* get it.' He regarded her steadily for a moment. 'Not just for Greville, but for all those other poor fellows who have been murdered in the name of greed and ambition.'

'And so you will spring your trap.'

'Yes. When the sprats are caught I'll find out what I want to know. Then I'll go after the big fish.'

As the ramifications dawned, she paled a little. Seeing it, he surveyed her shrewdly. 'I cannot watch from the sidelines while others take the risks on my behalf, Claire.

I knew the danger when I undertook this mission, and I must see it through. Besides, soldiering is my business.'

'Even so…' she began.

'There is only one way to lead, Claire, and that is from the front.'

Chapter Eleven

'You look beautiful, Miss Davenport!' Lucy's gaze took in every detail of the white sarsnet gown with unqualified approval.

Claire smiled. 'Thank you. I'm glad you like it.'

In truth she had taken a lot of time and trouble over her appearance this evening. One of the maids had helped to dress her hair so that the dark curls were piled high before falling in graceful ringlets over her shoulders. The white gown was a perfect foil for her warm colouring. Around her neck she wore the silver locket. Long gloves and satin slippers completed the outfit.

'You look like a princess in a fairy tale.'

'It's kind of you to say so.'

'It's true.' Lucy looked over Claire's shoulder. 'Isn't it, Uncle Marcus?'

She had not heard him come in and turned to see the tall figure in the doorway.

'You have excellent taste, child,' he replied. For a moment his gaze swept across Claire and the grey eyes warmed. 'A princess indeed.'

Her cheeks went pink. 'Thank you, sir.'

Under that close scrutiny she was more than ever aware of that charismatic figure and the raw, sensual power he exuded. Dressed in immaculate evening dress he looked every inch the aristocrat that he was. The dark coat might have been moulded to fit those broad shoulders. Pale breeches, snowy linen and cream-coloured waistcoat were plain almost to the point of austerity, and yet the overall effect was breathtaking. Once again it would have been impossible to find a more elegant or eye-catching figure.

He bent to give his ward a goodnight hug and tucked her in. Then he turned to Claire and offered his arm.

'Shall we?'

As they walked toward the staircase she glanced up at him once or twice, but could gain no clue from his expression as to the thoughts that lay behind the facade. Yet she somehow sensed his approval and her heart sang. No matter what came after, there would always be this night to remember, the night when for a few hours anyway she had been transported into another world where there was no ugliness or sorrow, only beauty and light and music. A world where he was.

In fact, Marcus was supremely conscious of the young woman beside him. He had not been exaggerating when he had likened her to a princess. She looked all of that and more. As he had imagined, the gown was stunning, serving as a glorious foil for the beauty of the wearer. It showed off every curve and line to perfection while tantalising him with the thought of what lay beneath. Did she know how lovely she was, or how powerful an impression she was making? He glanced down at her, but there was not the least trace of flirtation or coquetry in her manner, and she appeared quite unconscious of the effect she was having. It was probably just as well, he reflected. If she knew what was going through his mind that expression of calm serenity would vanish in an instant.

His attention was eventually diverted by the arrival of the first guests, and Claire slipped away into the salon, hoping that Ellen and her brother would arrive very soon. In fact, she had not many minutes to wait before she heard their names announced. With them was Sir Alan Weatherby. George Greystoke performed the introductions.

Weatherby beamed at her. 'A pleasure to make your acquaintance, Miss Davenport, and how pretty you look! By Jove, I wish I were thirty years younger.'

Claire smiled and blushed at the compliment. Greystoke smiled.

'You look wonderful,' he said. 'That really is a beautiful gown.'

'Thank you, sir.'

Ellen smiled at her friend. 'It suits you very well, my dear.'

'It's enough to make every woman here green with envy,' said Weatherby.

'If Miss Davenport will favour me with the first dance, I'll make a few men envious too,' replied Greystoke.

When eventually the orchestra struck up, he led her out onto the floor. After that, introductions were sought by several other gentlemen, including Major Barstow, who solicited the next two dances. A handsome moustachioed figure in a dashing uniform, he had caught the eye of many ladies present. Claire put him in his midthirties. He had easy, unaffected manners and she found herself taking an instant liking to him.

From across the room Marcus watched their progress. Both of them danced well, he saw, and they made a striking couple. From the Major's expression it seemed that Claire had made quite an impression. Forcing his gaze away from the pair, the Viscount gave his attention to his own partner. The girl was not unattractive, but every time he spoke to her she seemed able to reply only in monosyllables and soon he gave up the attempt at conversation. By the end of the dance he was glad to relinquish her hand to her next partner. A glance at the other participants revealed that Barstow had retained Claire for the cotillion. It appeared she had no objection to offer. Indeed, from her smile it seemed to be most agreeable to her. The Viscount's grey eyes narrowed and his smouldering gaze followed them across the floor.

Claire was enjoying herself enormously. Major Barstow was an excellent partner and a witty conversationalist, which made him excellent company. However, knowing it would expose her to gossip if she permitted him any more dances, she pleaded thirst.

'Of course, how thoughtless of me,' he replied. 'I'll find you some refreshment at once.'

He hurried off to execute the commission. While she waited she heard her own name being spoken nearby. It was a woman's voice, one of the party accompanying Lord and Lady Frobisher.

'She's the governess apparently. One wonders what Lord Destermere can be thinking of.'

'I beg your pardon,' replied her male companion, 'but I should say it's very easy to understand what he is thinking of. She's a very attractive young woman.'

The words were followed by others in a murmured undertone. The latter elicited a gasp and a rap on the arm with a fan.

'Shocking, Henry! I am sure it is no such thing. Destermere would never lower himself so far.'

'Of course not, I spoke in jest. I had it from Weatherby that she's connected in some way to the Greystokes,' replied her companion. 'It seems the good doctor is a particular friend of Destermere's. From India, don't you know?'

'Oh, I see.' The woman's tone was suggestive of disappointment. 'All the same, it is rather singular, is it not? I mean, she's little more than a servant after all.'

Claire's jaw tightened and she had to fight the desire to turn round. She would not give them the satisfaction of revealing she had overheard them. Fortunately Major Barstow returned a few moments later with two glasses of punch. They had hardly taken a sip when another voice cut in.

'Major Barstow, won't you introduce me to this delightful creature?'

She looked up to see a stranger. Seemingly in his early fifties, he was a rather stooped figure with sandy-coloured hair. His freckled face was thin and angular, the thin-lipped mouth like a slash. It gave him a slightly reptilian appearance. At his side was a stout young man who bore him a striking facial resemblance.

Barstow stiffened slightly, but then acknowledged them with a polite bow.

'Miss Davenport, may I present Sir James Wraxall and Mr Hugh Wraxall?'

The reptilian mouth widened in a smile that never reached the pale blue eyes. 'Charmed, Miss Davenport.'

Beside him his son echoed the sentiment and smiled too, revealing stained teeth. His gaze travelled from Claire's face to the front of her gown where it lingered. She felt her skin crawl.

'May I have the honour of the next dance?' he asked.

Unable to get out of it, she was forced to accept with a good grace and allow herself to be led away to the ballroom. They took their places in the next set. It soon became clear that Hugh Wraxall was not an accomplished performer and, worse, he kept squeezing her hand in a manner that was both embarrassing and distasteful. Each time the figures brought them together he leered at her cleavage. The music seemed to go on for ever. When it finally stopped she breathed a sigh of relief, wanting nothing more than to escape, but it seemed the ordeal wasn't over yet.

'Don't think I shall release you so soon, Miss Davenport. I claim the next.'

Before she could reply a tall, familiar figure cut in. 'I'm sorry to disappoint you, Wraxall, but this one's mine.'

Hearing that familiar voice Claire felt her heartbeat accelerate and a moment later she was looking up into Marcus's face. For a brief moment an expression of annoyance flitted across Wraxall's features; then it was masked with an unctuous smile. He bowed and retreated, leaving the field to his rival. Claire smiled at her rescuer.

'Thank you.'

'My pleasure,' he replied. Then *sotto voce,* 'How on earth did you get waylaid by that charmless oaf?'

'I wasn't quick enough with an excuse.'

'That's most unlike you.'

She threw him a speaking look, which seemed not to disconcert him in the least. Rather the grey eyes gleamed.

'True sir, but in this instance I am grateful.'

'Good.' He paused. 'How grateful exactly?'

He watched her cheeks turn a delightful shade of pink. 'Odious man!'

He laughed. Then the orchestra struck up the next dance and they took their places in the set. For a little while they were separated by the moves of the dance, but when she rejoined him at last he pursued it.

'You do not answer my question.'

'Nor shall I.'

'Then you must demonstrate the feeling instead.'

Her eyes widened a little. 'How so?'

'By dancing the next with me as well.'

They parted again for a while. Claire, moving through the intricate sequence of steps, was aware of his gaze following her. The knowledge set her pulse racing.

'Well?' he inquired when she returned to him. 'Have you considered my request?'

'I have, sir.'

'And?'

'I accede to it.'

'Excellent. Of course, it would have made no difference at all had you refused.'

The tone was both teasing and provocative, but the expression on that handsome face was less easy to read.

'No, I suppose not,' she agreed. 'You have a habit of getting your own way.'

The grey eyes gleamed appreciatively. 'Indeed I do, ma'am.'

He was as good as his word, for when the dance ended he made no move to lead her aside, but waited while the next set formed around them. Once again Claire was uncomfortably conscious of eyes turning their way. Seeing that fleeting expression, he squeezed her elbow gently.

'Don't let them trouble you, Claire. It will do them good to witness my standards.'

At his words of praise her heart leapt, and she looked

up quickly to see him smile. Suddenly all her former
anxiety melted away like frost in the sun. As the measure
began, Claire forgot everything else and then there were
only the two of them and the music and the moment. It
felt so right to be here with him, to feel his hand on hers
as he led her through the figures of the dance, to see the
warmth in his eyes when he looked at her. When she was
with him she felt truly alive. This one night was all they
would ever have, but she knew it would remain with her
as long as she lived.

Marcus had also taken note of the eyes turned their
way and was both amused and gratified. Curiosity had
been aroused, it seemed. He knew full well every man
there would like to be in his shoes, but for this little
space at least he had Claire all to himself. The notion
was pleasing. It felt right to have her beside him like this.
She danced well too, her movements light and graceful,
as though it were the most natural thing in the world.
Somehow it went against the grain to acknowledge that
he would have to yield her up to other partners, but good
manners dictated that he must later solicit other young
ladies for a dance. After Claire, their company would be
at best insipid.

When at length the dance was over he led her aside
and paused a moment, looking down into her face. Then
he carried her hand to his lips.

'I regret that I am engaged elsewhere, but I leave you
in good company this time.' He glanced to where Ellen
Greystoke was talking with Sir Alan Weatherby.

Following his look she smiled. 'Very good company,
sir.'

Then, having spoken to the others briefly, he reluctantly relinquished her hand and bowed before taking
his leave. For a moment or two she watched his retreat-

ing back, then forced herself to look away and give her attention to her present companions.

Her hand was solicited again several times by other gentlemen before she eventually sat down to eat supper with the Greystokes, along with Sir Alan Weatherby and Major Barstow. She found her companions most agreeable and entertaining, and the conversation and laughter flowed easily. Once she looked around the room for Marcus and located him at a table across the room. Among the aristocratic guests gathered there were the Frobishers. Quickly she looked away again, for seeing him there was a pertinent reminder of who he was. That was his milieu, the society to which he naturally belonged and which she could only be part of for this one brief night.

Later she watched him mingle among the other guests, laughing and talking with his habitual polished ease. She could discern absolutely no difference in his manner whether he spoke to a mill owner or a lord. If some sections of the company regarded his behaviour askance, they kept their opinions to themselves. A viscount could afford eccentricity, and if he saw fit to invite the professions into his home then he was entitled to do it. However, she knew that every aspect of this occasion would be discussed in minute detail on the morrow. She smiled to herself, well able to visualise those scenes.

Marcus had shown her some attention this evening, more perhaps than he needed to. Had it aroused jealousy in other female breasts? Was this going to make her the butt of local gossip for weeks to come? She ought to feel concerned, but for the life of her she could not regret it.

Just then his voice broke into her reverie. 'Shall we have some music? Miss Greystoke, can I persuade you?'

Ellen murmured something in reply and then rose, following their host to the pianoforte in the corner of the room. Claire watched them select the music and then Ellen seated herself and began to play. The music was gentle and soothing and she listened with close attention until the piece finished, joining the applause enthusiastically. Her friend played two more pieces before relinquishing her place at the instrument to Lady Frobisher's daughter, Mildred. Though Claire had no objection to hearing someone else play, the heat of the room was increasing and she began to feel the need for a little fresh air, so with a smile and a brief word she excused herself. Having slipped away from the crowded reception rooms, she turned into the corridor and headed for the conservatory. It wasn't far and it would be an ideal sanctuary for a while.

Her instinct had been correct, for here among the scented greenery it was blessedly cool and the air sweet and fragrant. She breathed deeply, enjoying it. From somewhere behind her she could hear the music still, though more faintly now, but all the bustle and conversation was absent. The only other sound was of tinkling water from a small fountain. It was restful here, a place to pause awhile and dream. Marcus's face drifted into her consciousness unbidden. He should be pleased tonight: the ball had been an unqualified success. The new Viscount Destermere was well and truly established. She smiled. He looked the part too, every self-assured and arrogant inch of him.

The sound of the door opening drew her back to reality and she turned quickly. Her eyes, accustomed to the dimmer light now, made out a man's figure. For a second her heart leapt. Surely it couldn't be he? The figure made its way towards her.

'Ah, there you are, Miss Davenport.'

She froze, recognising the voice of Hugh Wraxall, and in an instant her former hope was dashed.

'Saw you slip away,' he went on. 'Followed you here.'

Claire regarded him with alarm and distaste. The slurred tones suggested he had been drinking, not enough to render him incapable, but certainly enough to be a nuisance.

'I came in here for some fresh air,' she replied. 'I'm going back now.'

He stood across the path, barring her way. 'What's the hurry?'

'Pray excuse me.'

'Not yet. I think you and I should get to know each other better.'

'I have no desire to know you better, sir.'

Hearing the icy tone his expression changed. 'I'll wager you wouldn't be so damned haughty if the handsome Viscount were here.'

Claire's fists clenched at her sides as she strove to keep control of her temper. 'Please let me pass.'

'Touched a nerve, have I? Thought as much.' He leered at her, wafting a reek of foul breath in her face. 'Had you written down as a fancy little piece from the start.'

His answer was a sharp slap across the face. For a second he reeled, holding his smarting cheek. Then his expression grew ugly.

'You'll pay for that, you haughty little madam.'

He grabbed hold of her arm, dragging her close. Seeing his face looming over hers, she turned her head aside and the intended kiss grazed her cheek instead.

'Let go of me!'

'Oh, no, my dear, I'm not done with you yet.'

His arm tightened around her waist. Pressed against

him, Claire could feel his arousal through the thin material of her gown. With each passing moment the danger of her predicament became increasingly obvious and she struggled to free herself from that noxious embrace, but he was strong. She heard him laugh. The sound roused her to renewed effort.

'Get your filthy hands off me! Let me go!'

'You heard the lady,' said a voice from the doorway.

With unmitigated relief Claire recognised Major Barstow. Taken quite by surprise, Wraxall stared at the newcomer and then his face darkened.

'Mind your own business,' he snarled.

Barstow strode forwards and a second later had him by the throat. With a strangled croak of surprise Wraxall released his hold on Claire. The Major shook him hard, regarding him with contempt the while.

'You nasty little cur! I'll teach you to lay hands on a lady.'

'Mind your own business, soldier boy.'

'This is my business.'

As he spoke Barstow let go of his grip and Wraxall launched a haymaker in reply. It missed by a wide margin, but Barstow's clenched fist hit its intended target and sent the other reeling backwards. As he staggered, Wraxall's heel caught the stone edging round the plant border and he lost his balance to fall sprawling among the greenery in the flower bed. There he groaned once and lay still. Claire stared at him in horror and then looked up at her rescuer.

'Thank you, sir.'

'A pleasure, ma'am, believe me.'

Claire drew in a deep breath to steady herself, trying not to think of what might have happened but for the

Major's timely intervention. Seeing her trembling, Barstow put a gentle arm about her.

'It's all right, Miss Davenport. He cannot harm you now.'

This time the bodily contact was comforting, not threatening, and she managed a wan smile. 'I am much in your debt, sir.'

'Nothing of the sort,' he replied. 'Come, let us leave the loathsome brute and find more congenial company. I'll escort you back to the salon.'

She nodded gratefully and allowed herself to be led from the conservatory.

'I am so grateful for your help back there, Major Barstow. If you hadn't come along when you did...'

He stopped and drew her gently round to face him, letting his hand rest lightly on her shoulders. 'Say no more about it, Miss Davenport.'

'How did you know I was there?'

'I didn't. To tell the truth, I thought the conservatory was empty. I wanted a cigar and it seemed like the ideal place.'

'I see.'

He smiled down at her. 'It's a bit of a vice, but perhaps it does have its uses after all.'

'Indeed it does, sir.'

'Will you be all right now?'

'Yes, perfectly.'

He took her hand and carried it to his lips. 'Then I shall adjourn to the terrace for my cigar.'

'I think you have earned it, sir.'

He laughed. Then she became aware that he was looking beyond her and glanced round. As she did so her heart missed a beat to see the tall and familiar figure on the threshold of the lighted doorway. Marcus! For a moment he stood there motionless, his expression thunderous, the grey eyes like chips of agate. His gaze raked her from head to toe.

'I came in search of you,' he said then, 'but evidently too late.' He threw them an icy smile. 'Forgive me. I see I am *de trop.*'

With that he turned on his heel and strode away. Claire paled. Surely he could not have thought that she and Barstow… Almost immediately she knew that was exactly what he did think. Appalled by the implications, she was rooted to the spot. Barstow glanced from her to the Viscount's retreating back. For a moment he seemed nonplussed. Then one eyebrow lifted slightly and he glanced down at his companion. Claire, pale before, had turned pink with mortification. However, he was too much the gentleman to remark upon it.

'I think perhaps I should return you to your friends, Miss Davenport.'

'Thank you, sir, I would be most grateful.'

Together they walked back into the salon. Determined not to reveal her inner turmoil, Claire lifted her chin and fixed a smile on her face. As they entered, the heat hit her at once. The room seemed stifling now, and heavy with the scent of beeswax and perfume and the press of human bodies. All around her conversation and laughter rose in a wave and a feeling of desolation swept over her. Suddenly, her magical evening was ruined.

Marcus returned to the ballroom and found a glass of wine. He tossed it back in one go and then set down the glass with a snap. No one looking at that expressionless face could have guessed at the thoughts behind. However, the grey eyes were more eloquent. He took a deep breath to steady himself. So she preferred the handsome Major, did she? His fists clenched at his sides. If he hadn't had a house full of guests, he'd have run the man through. Part of him still wanted to go back and call the bastard out. And yet why was he surprised? Claire was a lovely young woman. He'd seen the way men looked at her. What red-blooded male wouldn't want her? The handsome Major had lost no time in securing her affections. All too successfully it appeared.

As the evening drew to a close and the guests began to depart Claire was reminded of her social obligations. When her companions announced their intention to go, she accompanied them to the hall. She must smile and bid everyone farewell. Nothing of her inner feelings must be allowed to show in her face either. So far as anyone else was concerned the evening had been a huge success.

Marcus was already there, speaking to some of the departing company and, although his glance acknowledged her presence, she was glad that they didn't have to talk. Her initial mortification had crystallised into anger now; he had been so quick to judge her, so ready apparently to believe the worst. He hadn't even waited to speak to her, or to hear her side of the story.

As she watched him with his guests her chin lifted. If he could play a part, so could she. Accordingly she stepped into role, smiling and laughing, as the people departed. She tried not to think about what would happen when everyone had gone and they were alone together.

The clock was striking three before the last of the carriages rolled away from the door. Claire saw it go with a sense of relief. She was tired now and wanted nothing more than to collapse into bed and fall into a deep and dreamless slumber. However, it appeared that Marcus had other ideas.

'A word with you, Miss Davenport,' he said, glancing past her towards the study.

The imperious tone rekindled her resentment and she made no move to obey. 'I'm very tired, sir. Can it not wait until tomorrow?'

'I will not keep you long.'

Seeing there was nothing for it but to face the coming storm, she nodded. 'Very well.'

He stood aside to let her precede him into the room. Then he closed the door behind them. For a moment they faced each other in silence. Almost she could feel the anger radiating off him. With more calm than she felt, Claire regarded him with a level gaze.

'There was something you wished to say, sir?'

'You know damned well there is. I refer to your unseemly conduct with Major Barstow.'

'Unseemly!' The fragile hold on her temper began to slip. 'How *dare* you?'

He stared at her in disbelief. 'How dare *I*? Can you deny that he held you in his arms?'

'I have no wish to deny it.'

'I see.'

'No, you don't.'

He gave a short, harsh laugh. 'I suppose I imagined that tender scene.'

'Your imagination is greatly overworked.'

'I know what I saw.'

'Major Barstow had just saved me from an unpleasant encounter with Hugh Wraxall. I was still shaken and the Major was merely being kind.'

'That's one way of describing it!' He paused and the

dark brows drew together. 'What encounter with Hugh Wraxall?'

'A little earlier I had gone into the conservatory for some fresh air. Unfortunately, Wraxall followed and trapped me there. He was drunk and he...he laid hands on me. Major Barstow came along in time to stop it.'

The hawk-like gaze rested on her face. 'Did Wraxall hurt you?'

'No, it was merely disagreeable.'

The thought of any other man touching her at all was unbearable. That one should have taken liberties filled him with fury. Part of him felt relief that it hadn't gone further, but another part was unwilling to let it go.

'You should not have wandered off alone,' he replied. 'It leads to such misunderstandings.'

'I told you, I needed some air.'

His breast was filled with conflicting emotions: he wanted to take her in his arms; he wanted to shake her. His inner demon refused to lie down and be quiet.

'Some air? How very convenient.'

'What do you mean?'

'Do you really expect me to believe such a tale?'

'But it's the truth.'

He turned, glowering down at her. 'Is it? Or is it rather that Wraxall inconveniently interrupted the tryst you had planned with Major Barstow?'

'What!' Claire glared back. 'You cannot believe that.'

'All the evidence points that way, does it not? Having dealt with the interloper and seen his plans in ruins, the good Major brought you back to the main company, but not before he afforded himself the solace of a comforting embrace.' He paused. 'An embrace which you evidently found most agreeable.'

'It wasn't like that.'

'It looked very much like that from where I was standing.'

'You saw what you wished to see.'

'I had the evidence of my own eyes.'

Claire's chin lifted to a militant angle. 'If Major Barstow and I had wished for intimacy, do you really think that we would have chosen to meet in a public corridor when there are a hundred secluded places in this house?'

His lip curled in a sneer. 'Oh, like the conservatory, for instance?'

'Why are you so determined to think the worst of me? Why will you not hear me, or take my part?'

For a moment there was silence as her gaze searched his face, and for a second there was a flicker of something like pain in his eyes.

'Why do you persist in lying to me?'

'I'm not lying to you.'

'Can I trust you, Claire?'

Her heart thumped painfully hard and a lump formed in her throat. 'If you do not know the answer to that, Marcus, then we have nothing more to say to each other.'

With that she turned on her heel and walked away, leaving him staring in impotent wrath at the empty doorway.

Chapter Twelve

For the next few days Claire barely set eyes on Marcus and when their paths did cross he treated her with a cold civility that was worse than his initial anger. All the ease of their earlier relationship vanished as though it had never been, and overnight they became like distant strangers. His indifference and his apparent belief in her unseemly behaviour confirmed her in the opinion that his feelings had never been as deeply engaged as her own. He had been amusing himself with her company, but nothing more.

When she learned from Mrs Hughes that, in the days following the ball, he had accepted several invitations to call upon his wealthy neighbours, her suspicions were confirmed. It was clear he meant to cast a much wider net. There were many eligible young ladies among the local gentry and several of them were very pretty girls. Perhaps he meant to choose a wife from among their number. At any rate he would never consider a governess for such a position, and she had been a fool to attach any significance to the attention he had shown her.

Her birthday was only a week off, and with it the end of the three-month probationary period. It marked the end of a chapter. After what had happened she knew there was no alternative now but to leave Netherclough for a new position elsewhere and try to forget Marcus Edenbridge. It was a thought that filled her with dread. In spite of everything she could not imagine a life without him, a house where he was not. However, it was impossible to stay here. She felt certain that Ellen would let her stay in the interim if need be, but hoped the gap between this situation and the next would not be too lengthy. She would not want to impose on her friend for long. With a heavy heart she began to scan the advertisement columns in the newspaper.

Her search produced two possibilities, both in London. Before she could apply for them she knew that Marcus would have to be informed. He would need to make alternative arrangements, too. Besides, she would need a character reference. She had to hope that enough goodwill remained for him to provide it. In many ways it would be to his advantage to do so—he would be rid of her and Lucy could start afresh with someone else.

The thought of breaking the news to Lucy caused a sharp pang. In the past weeks she had come to care for the child very deeply and knew it would be desperately hard to leave her behind. It was an additional disruption that the little girl could do without. What signal did it send out when everyone she relied on seemed to abandon her? Claire was saddened to think that she too would be letting Lucy down, and yet there was no other choice now. And if it had to be done, then perhaps the sooner the better. Waiting for Marcus's next visit to the nursery, she steeled herself to speak to him and ask for the necessary interview.

He heard her request in stony silence and she wondered if he would refuse, but at length he favoured her with a nod.

'Very well, Miss Davenport. Come along to the study this evening.'

For the rest of the day she tried not to think about it but somehow it kept intruding on her thoughts, like his face as he looked at her. The grey eyes were bleak with no spark of their former warmth. His voice too was cold. Clearly he still thought the worst. Heartsick, she knew that the matter was beyond remedy now, that her only recourse was to get away as soon as possible and put the whole sorry business behind her.

She presented herself at the study at the appointed hour. He was seated behind the desk, but rose at her entrance and offered her a chair. She declined it, fearing that if she sat down her legs might refuse to let her stand again after.

'I have come to tell you that I am seeking a new situation and to give you notice, sir.'

His brows twitched together and he shot her a piercing look. 'Indeed?'

'I do not wish you to think me ungrateful for all your past kindness,' she went on, 'but in the light of recent events I feel it is better for all concerned if I go.'

'Go where exactly?' he demanded.

'To London, sir.'

'I see.' He paused. 'Is this what you really want?'

She swallowed hard. 'I feel it is the right thing, sir.'

'Will you not reconsider?' There was another pause.

He made a vague gesture with his hand. 'After all, Lucy is growing attached to you, I believe.'

'I am very fond of her, but she is young and will soon form a new attachment.'

For a long moment he said nothing, only regarded her steadily. The grey eyes seemed even bleaker. 'Are you quite resolved to go, then?'

'I believe I must, sir.' She hesitated. 'There is one more thing…the matter of a reference.'

'Oh, yes, of course. Do not concern yourself over that.'

'Thank you, sir.'

Marcus cleared his throat. 'There is also the question of remuneration…'

'You have already advanced me part of my salary. You owe me nothing more.'

For another long moment they regarded each other in silence. Then she made him a polite curtsy and bade him a good evening. With that she hurried back to her room and closed the door, leaning upon it as the tears welled in her eyes.

Marcus rose from the desk grim-faced, and paced the room several times. Eventually he came to a halt by the hearth and stood for a while gazing moodily into the flames. When Claire had asked to speak to him he had not expected that it would be to announce her departure. In anyone else he might have suspected a fit of pique, but her quiet resolution was very different. It left him feeling strangely shaken.

Over the past few days he had had time for calmer reflection and knew that his earlier behaviour had been a complete overreaction. Unusually, he had let his temper get the better of him, but somehow he hadn't been able to help himself. Even now the thought of her in Barstow's arms was enough to goad him to wrath. At the time he hadn't cared to ask himself why. He had thought himself immune to the green-eyed god, but now he realised he was not. Once he had believed he could never care for another woman as he had for Lakshmi. He had believed his heart was dead. Over the past weeks he had been drawn insensibly closer to Claire Davenport: her beauty, her intelligence, her wit, her laughter had all acted on him like sunlight after a lengthy period of darkness. Her strengthening relationship with Lucy was another factor. More than just a gifted teacher, she was genuinely kind and compassionate to boot. Small wonder then if other men should notice her many talents and be charmed in their turn.

For a moment Major Barstow's face impinged upon his consciousness and his fist tightened. The man was personable and good-looking. Why should Claire not find him attractive? It was evident that the feeling was mutual or he wouldn't have gone to the trouble of arranging a tryst. How mortified he must have been to have it all spoiled by a little cockroach like Hugh Wraxall. For a moment Marcus knew a sense of gloating delight. However, it faded almost as quickly as it had come. What replaced it was sweeping desolation.

His mood was not improved when, the following afternoon, Claire did not turn up to ride. He had informed her that morning that he would be accompanying his ward, but only Lucy arrived in the stable yard.

'Miss Davenport has a headache, Uncle Marcus, and begs you will excuse her.'

His hand tightened round the handle of his riding whip. 'Has she?'

'Yes.' Lucy regarded him with solemn eyes. 'Are you all right, Uncle Marcus?'

He forced a smile. 'Of course, never better. Are you ready?'

'Oh, yes.'

'Then let us go.'

He lifted her onto the pony and slid her foot into the stirrup. Then he mounted his own horse, reining in alongside the little grey. Sensing his preoccupation, Lucy remained silent, her solemn gaze going to his face from time to time, but not daring to interrupt his unwontedly sombre mood.

Unaware of her scrutiny, Marcus could think only about Claire. He strongly suspected that the headache was an excuse—she was avoiding him. At first he had been sorely tempted to go back to the house and fetch her himself, but a moment's reflection told him he could not. Besides, as he now acknowledged, she was probably right. The less they saw of each other, the better. The realisation didn't make him feel better though; up until that point he hadn't realised how badly he had wanted her company. It was quite clear that she, on the other hand, didn't wish to see him. Thinking about his behaviour towards her, he could hardly blame her now.

He stayed out with Lucy for an hour and then walked with her back to the house. The child went off with a maidservant to change her clothes and Marcus headed for his own chamber. He was halfway down the corridor when he met Claire. Both of them stopped short and there followed an awkward silence. He was about to make a sarcastic comment about her absence, but one look at her face stopped the words on his tongue. She was pale and the hazel eyes spoke of inner pain. The sight of it filled him with remorse.

'Is your headache better?' he asked.

The tone suggested concern and it took her aback. 'A little better, thank you.' She paused. 'I hope you and Lucy enjoyed your ride.'

'Indeed. We missed you.'

Claire felt her throat tighten. 'I'm sorry.'

'Don't make yourself uneasy about it.'

'Is Lucy gone to her room?'

'I believe so.'

'Then I must go and find her. Please excuse me.'

With that she hurried away. Marcus remained quite still, staring after her, wanting to call her back and yet not knowing how.

Having seen Lucy safe in bed that evening, Claire returned to her room and began drafting out her letters of application for the new governess posts. Now that the decision was made she must expedite it with all speed. However, the words would not flow and it took half a dozen attempts before she had produced something satisfactory. Then she made two fair copies. When they were done she folded and sealed them and wrote out the directions. Finally she took them down to the hallway and placed them on the table, for collection by the footman next day. They would be despatched first thing in the morning.

In many ways it was a relief to have taken some action. If a reference was required, then there was a good chance of her getting one of those posts. She trusted Marcus to write what was fair. In any case it was to his advantage to do so. She glanced once at the study door, but it was firmly closed. With a sigh she made her way back to her room, thinking that an early night would not come amiss.

Needing something to take his mind off present domestic concerns, Marcus took himself off to the library in order to finalise his plans for the capture and arrest of the Luddites. He remained ensconced there for much of the evening, going over the details of the scheme until he was sure that every aspect had been covered. A week from now the trap would be set and, with any luck, well and truly sprung. Then the wrecker crew would be brought to justice for their crimes.

It was late when eventually he left. Retracing his steps, he came at length to the gallery and paused there awhile, looking up at the portrait of his brother. It was a good likeness, he thought, capturing the lithe elegance and the handsome features very well. What it didn't show was the quick mind behind those watchful grey eyes. For a moment he met and held his brother's gaze and in his imagination he heard Greville's voice.

'Don't let me down, Bro.'

Marcus's jaw tightened and he drew in a deep breath, mentally repeating the vow he had made months before. Come what might, he wouldn't fail. With a last glance at the portrait he walked away. A few minutes later he reached the hallway and was heading for the study to collect some papers when he noticed the letters on the table. For a moment their significance didn't register, but a closer inspection revealed that they were addressed to some unknown people in London. His brows twitched together as he recognised the elegant handwriting. For a moment he was quite still. Then, as their significance sank in, he felt a sudden cold chill. Turning away abruptly, he strode to the study, closing the door behind him.

* * *

When Claire came down next day the letters were gone. The matter was out of her hands. Breathing a sigh of relief, she made her way to the nursery. She and Lucy spent a productive morning on reading and basic arithmetic and then, the day being fine, they went out for a walk in the afternoon. When they returned it was to see two carriages waiting at the front door. Lucy eyed them with curiosity.

'Visitors, Miss Davenport.'

'For your uncle, I imagine,' Claire replied.

'Who are they?'

'I don't know. Something to do with business perhaps.'

A few moments later she saw John Harlston emerge from the house. She recognised him from the ball. A few paces behind was Sir Alan Weatherby. They didn't notice her or Lucy because they were still some distance off, but instead climbed straight into the waiting coaches and drove away. Watching them depart, Claire found herself wondering at the nature of the visit. She knew his friendship with Weatherby went back years, but Harlston was a different matter. The connection there went back to the time when Marcus had been living under another name, when he had ridden escort on the wagon bringing the new power loom. It brought back unpleasant and frightening memories. She knew instinctively that this visit was related to those events.

Marcus had told her himself that he was devising a trap for the wreckers. He would enlist the help of men like Weatherby and Harlston, and no doubt the local militia. Major Barstow's face flitted into her mind. He too would have a role to play if the plan went ahead. And if it did, what then? Would more men die before it was

over? Would Marcus be among them? She glanced down
at the child beside her and shivered inwardly.

She and Lucy had taken their afternoon tea by the fire
when the footman entered.

'A letter for you, ma'am.'

It was from Ellen and, from the appearance of the
scrawled hand, had evidently been written in haste.
Claire broke the wafer and opened it.

My Dearest Claire,
    Be on your guard. Your uncle has arrived in
Helmshaw. He came to the house this morning.
You need have no fear that George or I have told
him anything. Neither will the servants betray
your whereabouts. However, I have since learned
from some acquaintances that your uncle has been
asking questions in the town. Have a care, I beg
you.
Your affectionate friend,
Ellen

Claire's stomach lurched and for several heartbeats
she experienced a sensation akin to panic as her uncle's
unforgiving countenance imposed itself on her consciousness. She had always known him to be firm of
purpose. When no trace of her had been found at the
coaching inns on the London road he must have begun
to consider other possibilities. Her aunt must have kept
Ellen's letters, or at least remembered the address. They
must have put two and two together.

Forcing herself to think calmly, Claire studied the note
again. Her friend would not betray her. Her uncle had no
acquaintance in Yorkshire so far as she was aware and

it was highly unlikely he would meet any of Viscount Destermere's circle. Netherclough Hall was the last place he would think of looking.

She was so preoccupied with these thoughts that she failed to hear the door open. Only Lucy's exclamation of delight alerted her to Marcus's presence. Claire returned to the present with a start and hastily refolded the note, shoving it into her pocket. Then she rose to face him. For a moment the hawk-like gaze surveyed her keenly, but with an effort of will she met it, hoping that her demeanour revealed nothing of her inner anxiety.

In fact, very little escaped him where she was concerned and certainly not the ashen colour of her face when he had first entered. She had started, too, as though she had seen a ghost. When he looked into her face he could see the anguish there. It hit him hard for he knew that, in part, he had been the cause of it. The days since the ball had taken a heavy toll on both of them, for he was not immune, either, to the effects of their sudden estrangement. He had tried so hard to hold aloof, to busy himself with work or social calls, but even then he found himself thinking of her, listening for the sound of her step or her voice. In spite of his best efforts he had missed her. He missed their conversations, missed her acute observations, her laughter. He had driven her away because a better man had won her affections. All at once he was sickened by self-contempt.

To cover his feelings he bent down and engaged Lucy in conversation for a while. He listened to her childish prattle as she showed him the work she had been doing and read to him from her primer. Once again he was conscious of how far she had come in a relatively short time, and knew it was due to Claire. His conscience prodded him again. How was he ever going to explain her departure? Lucy would be heartbroken. And it was all so unnecessary. If it hadn't been for his accursed temper it wouldn't have happened. Calling himself all kinds of fool, he knew he must try to put things right as far as possible. That meant making his peace with Major Barstow and with Claire and wishing them well.

His plans for dealing with the wreckers had thus far involved close liaison with Weatherby and Harlston. However, as commander of the militia, Barstow was an important figure in the scheme, an irony that didn't escape Marcus. Knowing he couldn't put the moment off any longer without detriment to his plans and wanting to try to smooth things over anyway, at least as far as possible, the Viscount had requested the Major to dine with him and the others that evening.

To the Major's credit he showed no signs of resentment or ill will over what had happened at the ball. He kept up his part in the conversation at dinner and, when the meal was concluded and they settled down to discuss business, readily agreed to do all he could to assist in the apprehension of the Luddite group.

'My men are at your disposal, sir. The sooner these murdering brutes are caught the better.'

Marcus, already ashamed of his previous behaviour, began to feel distinctly guilty. He knew he owed Barstow an apology and was determined to offer it. His opportunity did not arise until his guests were on the point of departure. Having bidden Weatherby and Harlston a goodnight, he detained Barstow in the hall.

'Would you be so kind as to give me five more minutes of your time, Major?'

There was a fractional hesitation, but then Barstow inclined his head in acquiescence, following his host into a nearby salon. For a moment or two they faced each other in silence. Then Marcus took the initiative.

'I would like to thank you for your help in this current undertaking, Major.' He paused. 'And to apologise to you for my former rudeness.'

'I assure you that I have no recollection of it, sir,' replied the other.

'You are generous. More so than I deserve.'

Barstow regarded him with a speculative eye. 'Is it possible that Your Lordship has formed a mistaken impression?'

'How so?'

'It is a delicate matter because it concerns a lady. One for whom I have the highest regard.' He paused. 'May I speak frankly?'

The Viscount held down his resentment. 'Very well.'

The Major favoured him with a short and unvarnished account of what had happened on the evening of the Netherclough ball. Marcus, listening, might have been turned to stone. Inwardly his heart was thumping. The account tallied in every respect with Claire's. There was no indication at all that the speaker held her in anything other than esteem. He had merely done what any gentleman would have done under the circumstances. Furthermore, there was a soldierly directness about Barstow that Marcus recognised and respected, and he knew the words for truth. As the implications hit him he felt his heart leap.

'Then you're not courting Miss Davenport? She doesn't…'

'My lord, I would be the happiest of men if Miss Davenport ever deigned to look my way. Unfortunately, she has not done so and, I fear, never will.' He looked Marcus straight in the eye. 'I believe her affections are engaged elsewhere.'

With that he bowed and took his leave, though in truth his host was hardly aware of his going. All Marcus's consciousness was drawn inwards to the dawning understanding and magnitude of his own folly. When he thought of the accusations he had flung at Claire, not to mention his subsequent behaviour, he was appalled. She had told him the truth and he, in a fit of jealous pride, had refused to listen. Her words returned to haunt him: *Why are you so determined to believe the worst of me?* He could not forget the look of hurt in her eyes. She had asked for his trust and he had refused to give it. His fists clenched. No wonder she wanted to leave.

Come what may, he knew he couldn't let her go, that she had become as necessary to him as the air he breathed. He had known it since the day she had given her notice. Remembering the letters on the hall table, he knew she meant it. The thought filled him with despair. London be damned, he thought. She belonged here, with him. The question was how to make her see that. Would she hear him? Could she ever forgive him? After what had passed between them he was going to need all his powers of persuasion.

Claire was surprised the next day when a footman delivered a politely worded request to attend her employer in the library that afternoon. Surprise was followed swiftly by misgiving. What now? There was no way of refusing the summons either, as she was at first inclined to do. Then she reflected that it must be important if he felt the need to call her away from her duties. Leaving Lucy with a maidservant, she set off for the library.

He was already there when she arrived and for a moment or two was unaware of her presence. He was leaning upon the mantel above the hearth, one booted foot resting casually upon the fender as he stared down into the fire. Her heart began to beat a little faster. Very deliberately she closed the door.

Hearing the sound, he came out of his reverie and looked up. When he saw her there, his gaze brightened.

'Come in…please.'

He watched her cross the room to join him and asked her to sit down.

Claire took the offered chair and waited. He seemed different today, somehow. The former aloofness in his manner was entirely absent. It had been replaced by a very different expression that was much harder to interpret. If she hadn't known better, she would have said it contained a hint of awkwardness.

'I asked you to come here in the hope of ending the estrangement that has lately existed between us,' he said.

She looked up in surprise, but said nothing.

'You may be aware that several guests came to dine here yesterday,' he continued. 'One of them was Major Barstow.' He saw her cool, quizzical look and hurried on. 'Before he left he favoured me with an account of what happened on the night of the ball. I realise now that I placed entirely the wrong construction on what I saw.'

'*I* told you that.'

'Yes, I know and I'm sorry for doubting you.' He took a deep breath. 'I apologise, Claire.'

Her fists clenched in her lap and for a long moment she was silent. Then she rose stiffly to face him. 'Thank you, sir. And now if you'll excuse me I must return to my duties.'

He regarded her in disbelief. 'Is this all I am to expect?'

'What else would you like me to say, Marcus?' The hazel eyes burned with contained fire. 'You have insulted me, you have doubted my word, and you have told me in the plainest terms that I am not to be trusted. Only when you heard the truth from another man were you prepared to believe it. Only then did it occur to you that you might have been wrong. Why would you not believe *me?*'

His cheeks, warm before, paled a little as the force of the accusation struck him. 'Claire, I'm sorry. I should have believed you, I know that now.' He took a deep breath. 'But I was so jealous that I could scarcely think at all. When I saw you in Barstow's arms, I thought that you and he…well, you know what I thought.'

She stared at him, incredulous. 'Jealous? Of Major Barstow?'

'Yes. I thought that he had succeeded in winning your affections.'

'I had never even met him before!'

He sighed. 'How long does it take to know your own heart? It was not until I saw his arms about you that I woke up to the true nature of my own feelings.' His eyes met hers in anguished appeal. 'I love you, Claire. It has been growing so gradually that I was hardly aware of it.'

'Love? Is that what you call it?' She rounded on him, fury apparent in every line of her body. 'When you believed in my guilt, as you were so ready to do, you could not wait to be rid of me. You positively encouraged my departure. Your only concern was to wonder what you were going to say to Lucy.'

'It wasn't like that, I swear it. I never wanted you to go.'

'You gave a good impression of it, though.'

'A mistaken impression. I need you here.'

'Why?' she retorted. 'Has it just occurred to you that my departure might be inconvenient?'

'Inconvenient! Is that what you think?'

'Yes. After all, there is Lucy to consider.'

'Lucy needs you, it is true, but I need you, too.'

'Why, Marcus?'

'Because you have become so much a part of things that I cannot imagine what life would be like without you.' He paused, watching her closely. 'Did it not occur to you that I might want you to stay for yourself?'

'I could hardly be expected to believe that, could I?'

He sighed. 'I can understand why you might not.'

She turned away from him, trying to conquer the emotion that swept through her.

'Stay here,' he continued. 'Let me protect you. It isn't safe for you to leave.'

The knowledge of her vulnerability was borne upon him even more strongly. Having a good deal more experience of the world than she, he was appalled to think of what might happen if she left Netherclough. She would be easy prey for the unscrupulous, never mind the ever-present threat of her uncle.

'I'm not sure it's a good idea for me to remain, Marcus.'

His heart gave an unpleasant lurch. 'There's no other serious possibility. Surely you see that?'

'London is a big place. One could be anonymous there, I think.'

'I could force you to stay, Claire. I would too if I thought for one minute it would do any good.'

That brought her round in an instant. 'You cannot keep me here.'

He regarded her steadily. 'There are a dozen ways I could do it. Netherclough is remote and I am the law here.'

Her colour fluctuated delightfully. 'You wouldn't dare!'

Even as she spoke she wasn't sure that was true.

'Oh, I'd dare, believe me, but what would be the use?'

'No use at all,' she replied.

'Exactly. I know you too well. Besides, I want you to stay out of choice, not compulsion.'

For the length of a dozen heartbeats they faced each other in silence. Her anger had ebbed now to be replaced with uncertainty and sadness. He saw it in her face. Knowing himself to be the cause, he felt only remorse. He could not blame her, only hope she might forgive him—in time. Meanwhile he had to make her see sense.

'I beg you to reconsider, Claire. Please don't go.'

The tone was humble, almost pleading, unlike any she had heard him use before.

'I don't know, Marcus. I can't think properly.'

'Take all the time you need. Just promise me you'll think it over. That you won't do anything rash.'

She hesitated a moment, then nodded. 'All right.'

He let out the breath he had been holding. 'Thank you.'

She left him then, too rapt in thought to be aware of the gaze that followed her until she was out of sight.

Chapter Thirteen

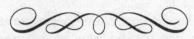

A sleepless night brought Claire no further help, and she arose next day feeling unrefreshed and heavy-eyed. Being in need of some fresh air, she took Lucy out for a walk later that morning. It also gave her leisure to reflect.

More than anything else she wanted to stay at Nether-clough, to be where Marcus was. How much she wanted to believe him when he spoke to her of love, but did the word mean the same thing to both of them? Was his interpretation about passion only? Was it merely a passing fancy that would vanish as soon as it was gratified? Marriage had never been mentioned. She believed now that it never would be. Men of his rank married women of their own class. Anything else was dalliance, mere amusement. That was not the kind of love she sought, although she knew it existed. Instinctively her hand went to the locket round her neck, feeling its reassuring presence.

'Are you all right, Miss Davenport?'

Claire looked down with a start and saw the child's face with its quizzical expression.

'Oh, yes, quite.'

'You looked as if you were far away.'

She smiled. 'Yes, I was for a moment. I'm sorry.'

'Shall we walk down to the river?'

'What a good idea.'

Lucy smiled and tucked her hand into Claire's and together they followed the path through the water meadow. Forcing everything else to the back of her mind, Claire gave the child her full attention. Whatever else, Lucy was not to blame for what had happened.

After an hour in the fresh air they retraced their steps to the house, both of them feeling invigorated and ready for some tea by the nursery fire.

'Will you tell me a story when we get back, Miss Davenport?'

'All right.'

'The one about Cinderella?'

'If you like.'

And so when they returned Claire told her the story again, acting it out and putting on different voices for the different parts, holding her young charge enthralled to the end.

'That's my favourite story.'

'Why that one?'

'I like the bit at the end with the shoe, where the prince realises it's her.' Lucy replied. 'Although I still think he should have known it was her in the first place.'

'Yes, he should,' Claire agreed. 'But perhaps she looked very different. After all, she was wearing a ball gown before.'

'But I can still tell it's you when you're not wearing a ball gown. I think the prince must have been quite stupid.'

'Yes, or else his eyesight wasn't very good.'

Lucy giggled. Then, a movement in the doorway caught her attention.

'Uncle Marcus.'

He came to join them and, smiling at Lucy, received a shy smile in return. Over the child's head Claire met his gaze, but his expression gave nothing away.

'Might I have a word, Miss Davenport?'

They walked aside a few paces.

'There are matters I should like to discuss with you,' he said. 'I would be grateful if you'd meet me in the study this afternoon. Shall we say at three?'

Once again she was conscious of feeling torn, of wanting to be alone with him and at the same time dreading it. Every time she saw him it became harder to try and pretend that her emotions were under control. How easy it would be to surrender, to throw caution to the winds and let her heart rule her head. She had wondered before how women could allow love to overrule common sense. Now she knew.

'As you wish, sir.'

'Until three then,' he said.

As the morning wore on her anxiety increased. Would he press her for an answer? He had told her she might take time to reflect. Perhaps his definition of time meant something different. Knowing the nettle must be grasped, she duly presented herself at the appointed hour. However, on entering the study she checked in surprise. Marcus was dressed to ride. A pair of pistols lay in an open case on the desk. Beside them the light gleamed softly on the hilt of a sheathed cavalry sabre. As the implications dawned she looked from them to him in sudden alarm, all other thoughts driven from her mind.

'You are going after the wreckers tonight.'

'Sooner. I mean to take advantage of the last hour of daylight to ride for the rendezvous with Barstow.'

'I see.'

'If the plan works this district will be rid of the wreckers for good.'

'Yes.'

He heard the determined neutrality in her tone and threw her a shrewd glance. 'It has to be done, Claire.'

'I know, but cannot the authorities deal with the matter?'

'The authorities are dealing with it,' he replied. 'Sir Alan Weatherby is fully apprised of the situation, as are John Harlston and Major Barstow.'

'That is not what I meant and you know it. Surely there can be no necessity for you to go.'

'It is most necessary.'

'I understand why you think so, but there are other considerations now.' She paused. 'What about Lucy? If you are shot and killed, what happens to her? Have you considered that?'

He gave her a wry smile. 'I don't intend to get shot.'

'You didn't intend to last time.'

'On this occasion it is we who are setting the ambush. If the wreckers take the bait and attack the wagon, they won't find a loom beneath the tarpaulin, but a dozen riflemen instead.'

'Will they take the bait?'

'I've arranged for news to leak out that Harlston is bringing in a replacement loom. I'm gambling that the wreckers won't want to let that happen.'

She knew with sick certainty that they would not. The simplicity of the plan could not be faulted, or its potential deadliness doubted.

'More men will die, Marcus. Perhaps you among them.'

He surveyed her with studied nonchalance. 'Would it matter if I were?'

'You know it would.'

For a moment neither of them moved and the only sound in the room was from the crackling logs in the hearth. Then, somehow, his arms were round her and he was clasping her to his heart.

'You don't know what it means to me to hear you say that.'

He bent his head and kissed her gently on the mouth. Claire closed her eyes, letting her body relax against him. The kiss grew deeper and more passionate, a long, lingering embrace that set her pulse racing and turning her blood to fire. Then he drew back a little.

'I love you, Claire.'

'Then don't go tonight.'

'I must, you know that.'

'Think, Marcus, I beg you. Let the militia deal with this.'

'It is an affair of honour, Claire.'

'What use will honour be if you are killed?'

Forcing his eyes away from hers, he gestured to the mantelpiece and for the first time she saw the letter there.

'I have no intention of getting killed,' he said, 'but I've been in enough battles to know that there is always a chance. You asked me if I had considered the consequences. The answer is yes. For that reason I have left instructions. Should the worst happen, I would be grateful if you would see that they are carried out.'

Claire paled and her throat felt suddenly dry. 'Marcus, I...'

'Will you do it? There is no one I'd trust more.'

At first she wasn't quite sure she had heard him correctly, but there could be no mistaking the look in his eyes. 'I…yes, if you wish.'

'Thank you.' He drew closer and she felt his hands on her shoulders. 'Now kiss me, Claire.' Again the wry smile appeared. 'After all, it may be the last time.'

She shook her head. 'A keepsake for you to take into battle, Marcus? I won't do it.'

For answer he pulled her hard against him. 'Kiss me, you contrary little witch!'

A second later he matched the deed to the words, his arms tightening about her as the kiss grew deeper and more passionate. It seemed to go on for a long time. Then he drew back, looking down into her face.

'If I'm to die, I'll do it as a happy man.'

Anger replaced fear and she pulled free of him. 'Damn you, Marcus Edenbridge! Damn you to hell! This business with the wreckers means more to you than anything else, doesn't it? More than me or Lucy or Netherclough?'

'That's not true.'

'It is true. You're so caught up in the past you're willing to sacrifice all our futures to it.' She threw him a fulminating look. 'I only hope that if someone tries to shoot you tonight, they aim for your head. It's the only place a shot wouldn't do any damage!'

With that she turned on heel and marched to the door. Marcus bit back an exclamation. He wanted to run after her, to talk to her and try to make her understand, but a glance at the clock revealed that it was half past the hour. It was time to go if he was to make the rendezvous by dark. He didn't want to leave things like this with Claire, but there was no choice now. Reaching for the sword belt, he buckled it on and then shoved the loaded pistols into his belt.

A discreet cough at the door caused him to look up quickly and for a moment his heart leapt, hoping it might be her. Instead a servant entered to say that his horse was saddled and ready at the door.

'Very well, I'll be there directly.'

The man withdrew and Marcus sighed. Taking a last look around to make sure he hadn't forgotten anything, he threw a cloak around his shoulders, donned a hat and strode out into the hall. Minutes later he was mounted and heading the horse up the drive.

When she left him Claire had no clear idea of where she was going, following the corridor blindly, but presently found herself by the exit that led to the rear garden terrace. Opening the door, she slipped out, needing to escape the confines of the house for a while. Marcus's words were still ringing in her ears. Why would he not listen? Why were her powers of persuasion so ineffective? She crossed the terrace and descended the steps, heading off down the gravel path beyond. For a while she walked on, regardless of the chill or the direction until her anger began to abate.

Gradually, it was borne upon her that she and Marcus might never meet again. The men he sought were dangerous. They had almost killed him once before. What if, in the darkness and confusion, a stray shot should find him? *I only hope that if someone tries to shoot you tonight, they aim for your head.* Claire bit her lip. Dear God, what had she said? It was in that second, as the possible ramifications became clear, that pride and anger evaporated and were replaced with anguish. If anything happened to him, it would be like losing a part of herself. Beside that, their argument paled into insignificance. She could not let him go without telling him the truth.

For the first time she looked around, taking stock of her surroundings. Her steps had taken her some distance from the house and brought her to the edge of the herb garden. She could see two figures there at work, an older man and a boy. They straightened on seeing her and touched their caps respectfully. She acknowledged their presence with an inclination of the head, her gaze lingering on the lad. He looked familiar. For a moment she couldn't place him, then memory returned and she smiled.

'You are one of Mrs Dobson's boys, are you not? Is it Peter?'

'Luke, miss. Peter's my older brother. He works in t'stables.'

'I see. And you are learning to become a gardener.'

'Aye.' He gestured to the area he had been working on. 'Clearing t'herb beds today, miss.'

'And do you like the work?'

'I like it well enough, miss.'

'Well, then, I'd better leave you to it.'

He nodded and touched his cap again, before returning to his task. Claire walked away down the path, aware now of the low sun and the chill air. It had been foolish to come out without a pelisse or gloves. Foolish, too, to let Marcus go without a word of support from her. He would do what he thought he must. What mattered now was to wish him well in the endeavour. She could only pray it was not too late.

Her thoughts were rudely interrupted when a man stepped out from behind a hedge and blocked her path. She drew in a sharp breath and looked up quickly. Her heart lurched as she found herself face to face with Jed Stone. Suddenly the sense of cold intensified and she shivered inwardly.

'What are you doing here?'

He gave her an insolent smile. 'I came to look for you, Miss Davenport. In fact, I've been hanging around for a couple of days in t'hope of meeting you.'

'Why?'

'Someone else is looking for you, too.'

'I don't understand.'

'Your uncle?'

Her heart began to beat faster. 'What have you to do with my uncle?'

'Word went out in Helmshaw that he were looking for you.'

'What of it?'

'Seems he's very concerned about you.'

'Is he?'

'Oh, aye. You know you really shouldn't have run away from home. Bein' a minor an' all.'

'My actions are no business of yours.'

'The world's a dangerous place for a young lady alone. It's my duty as a good citizen to see that you're returned to your guardian.'

Claire felt the first prickling of fear, but forced herself to face him down. 'You wouldn't know duty if it leapt up and slapped you in the face.'

His smile never wavered, though it didn't reach his eyes. 'What would the authorities say, if they knew t'Viscount were harbouring a minor without her guardian's knowledge or consent?'

'I neither know nor care. Nor is it any business of yours.'

'It is when there's a handsome reward for t'information.'

His words gave her a real jolt. The possibility that her uncle might offer money for information should have occurred to her. It was a measure of his determination to find her. It was also the greatest misfortune that the matter had been brought to Stone's attention. A chance of easy gain would be irresistible to this man. With far more calm than she felt, Claire met his eye.

'So go and claim it, then.'

She made to pass him, but he sidestepped, blocking the way. For the first time she realised they were out of sight of the house and the light was fading.

'I intend to do better than that,' he said.

'What do you mean?'

'There's a reward for information, but an even bigger one for returning you to your guardian.'

Her heart began to thump. He took a step closer. Seeing his intent, she turned and ran, but he had hold of her in three strides. Claire shrieked. Then a hand closed over her mouth. There followed a brief, unequal struggle before she was gagged and bound, after which her captor swung her up into his arms and carried her away.

She was taken down the path leading to the perimeter hedge and thence out into the lane beyond before being dumped unceremoniously into a waiting cart. Stone climbed in beside her and, favouring her with a nasty smile, threw an old blanket over her, concealing her from public view. His companion whipped up the horse and the vehicle rumbled away. Sick with fury and fright, she struggled to free her hands but the knots held good. Above the rumbling wheels she heard Stone laugh.

From the shadow of the hedge Luke Dobson watched the departing vehicle, wide-eyed. Claire's scream had reached the two workers in the herb garden and his older mentor had sent him to investigate. Knowing he must do something, but not being quite sure what, the boy hesitated. Should he go back and tell his companion what had happened or should he follow the cart? Instinct told him to keep sight of the cart. It held Miss Davenport. His ma would take it much amiss if anything were to happen to the lady she considered to be the family benefactress. Remembering her words on the subject, Luke set off in pursuit of the vehicle.

Marcus rode at a steady pace to the rendezvous on the moor, taking care not to push his horse too hard. The animal was fresh and champing at the bit, but he would not indulge it yet; he might need its strength and speed later. In his mind's eye he went over every detail of the plan and was satisfied that nothing had been overlooked. The only unknown factor was whether the rebels would take the bait. On the other hand, would they let Harlston bring in a replacement for the loom they had smashed before? As he had told Claire, he was gambling that they wouldn't.

This day would see the end of the Luddite threat in this part of Yorkshire. He sighed, wishing he could say as much for his own problems. Claire's face swam into his mind. Almost he could feel the crackling tension of that last encounter. At the same time he could still feel the warmth of her in his arms, the taste of her mouth on his. Just the thought of her excited passions he once thought he would never know again. He wanted her with every particle of his being, needed her, loved her. Somehow he must make her understand that, make her believe him.

These thoughts were uppermost in his mind until he reached the meeting place half an hour later. It was dark now, but by the flaring light of half a dozen torches he could see Major Barstow and a dozen mounted men. Seeing the new arrival, Barstow smiled.

'Good evening, my lord.'

Marcus returned the greeting. 'Are you ready to go hunting, Major?'

'Indeed we are.'

The Viscount glanced toward the wagon some yards in front. Drawn by four heavy draught horses, its deadly load was concealed by a tarpaulin stretched across a wooden frame. Four armed outriders waited alongside. Two linkmen stood in front with torches. Looking at them, Marcus experienced a moment of *déjà vu*. It sent a chill along his spine. This time he was determined the boot would be on the other foot. He turned back to Barstow.

'Are your men ready, Major?'

'They are, my lord.'

'Very well. Let's get them on their way.'

The Major gave the order and the lumbering vehicle moved off. Marcus waited until he calculated that it and its escort were a quarter of a mile ahead, then nodded to Barstow. At the signal his men doused the remaining torches and a few moments later the column of mounted men moved forwards.

Claire had long since given up any hope of freeing her hands and lay still now. Half smothered by the dirty blanket and jolted by the movement of the vehicle, she fought the rising tide of panic that threatened to overwhelm her. Where was Stone taking her? In the conversation about her uncle he had mentioned Helmshaw. Would he risk being seen there under these circumstances? Surely if he took her into town she would be able to attract attention somehow. There must be someone who would come to her aid. Miserably she thought of Marcus. By now he would be at the rendezvous with Major Barstow's men. When, eventually, he returned to Netherclough she would be long gone. He would have no clue as to her where-abouts. By the time he found out it would be too late. She would never see him again.

Suddenly she became aware that the cart was slow-ing. Then it stopped altogether. Surely they had not travelled above two miles, not nearly enough to have reached Helmshaw. Before further thought was possible the blanket was thrown aside and for a moment she found herself looking at Stone. She shivered inwardly as he bent towards her. To her considerable surprise he untied the gag round her mouth. She eyed him uneasily.

'Why have we stopped?'

'This is where we part company,' he replied.

'I don't understand.'

'You will soon enough.'

He climbed out of the cart and hauled her out after him, setting her down on the track. Then he untied her wrists. Taking a firm grip on her arm, he led her round the side of the vehicle. Her heart lurched. For the first time she saw the dark mass of the waiting coach partly concealed against the trees at the side of the lane. Stone felt her hesitate and his grip tightened.

'Come, miss. Don't be shy.'

'Where are you taking me?' Even as she spoke she guessed the truth.

'I'm sure your uncle will be glad to see you again,' he said in a conversational tone. 'He's been most anxious to find you.'

Claire hung back, trying unsuccessfully to break his hold. The grip tightened and dragged her on.

'Of course,' he continued, 'I'd like to have spent a bit longer with you myself, for old times' sake, but I don't suppose your uncle would approve of that. In any case I've other matters to attend to this evening and other places to be. Still, it's good to know you'll be in capable hands.'

She stumbled on down the track beside him, knowing it would be useless to try to appeal to his better feelings. Where she was concerned he had none. Moreover, it was clear he was enjoying his revenge.

A few moments later they reached the coach and a familiar dark-clad figure stepped out. Her stomach lurched. Uncle Hector!

Then they were face to face and the cold eyes fixed her with a gimlet stare for a moment before passing on to Stone. The latter smiled.

'The young lady, sir. As promised.'

'You have done well,' her uncle replied.

He produced a leather pouch from the folds of his cloak and tossed it over. Claire heard the clink of coins. Then he jerked his head to the waiting vehicle. Stone dragged her to the door and, when she tried to resist, lifted her off her feet and bundled her unceremoniously inside. Having seen her safely stowed, her uncle climbed in after. She had a glimpse of Stone's grinning face in the gathering dusk before the door slammed and the coach moved away.

Breathing hard from his exertions, Luke Dobson flung himself down behind a bush, staring at the departing vehicle. Presently Stone and his companion returned to the cart. He watched them climb aboard and then they drove off too, taking the fork in the road that led to the moors. The boy frowned, wondering what could possibly take them up there with night almost upon them. When they were out of sight he emerged from his hiding place, knowing now that he had to get back to Netherclough at all costs. Then he would go to the kitchens and find his mother. She would know what to do.

Feeling the coach gather speed, Claire's panic increased. Knowing she must fight it, she drew in a deep breath and tried to think. Somehow she had to get away. Eyeing the far door, she weighed up her chances. If she jumped from the moving coach, she risked a broken ankle or worse, but it was a chance she was prepared to take. There was no other. In desperation she made a lunge towards the door, but a hand like a vice closed on her arm and pulled her roughly back. Then Davenport slapped her hard across the face. She gasped, her hand clutching her burning cheek.

'Don't attempt that again,' he said. 'There's no escape for you now.'

Her stomach knotted. 'What do you mean to do?'

'What I intended to do from the outset. That is to see you married to Sir Charles Mortimer.'

'I will never agree to that.'

He regarded her coldly. 'I rather think you will.'

The knot in her stomach tightened. 'Please, Uncle, I beg you, don't do this.'

'You have made me a public laughing stock and you have caused me to look a fool in the eyes of my friend. I intend to rectify that. Tomorrow you *will* become Lady Mortimer.'

Anger vied with surprise. 'That's impossible. It is at least three days' travel to Northamptonshire.'

'You are not going back to Northamptonshire,' he replied, 'only as far as Sir Charles's country house near Barnsley—where you and he will be married.'

Claire paled. 'Never! I'd rather die than be wed to that disgusting, lascivious old man.'

He slapped her again, harder, across both cheeks this time, rocking her head back and forth and bringing water to her eyes.

'You will marry him,' he replied dispassionately, 'be assured of that. Then I have no doubt your husband will tutor you in the subject of wifely submission. He and I see eye to eye on such things. He will very soon bring you to heel.'

Claire turned cold as the implications dawned. Barnsley was hardly any distance at all. They would arrive the following day. Her stomach churned.

'We cannot be married,' she protested, her voice shaking. 'The banns have not been published.'

'It is of no consequence. Sir Charles has obtained a special licence. His brother is a bishop and will officiate at the ceremony in the private chapel at Mortimer House.'

Claire paled, her hands clenching in her lap. Her uncle surveyed her with a cold and knowing eye.

'In the interim you will have my company and, when we reach our destination this evening, I intend to teach you about the follies of disobedience and ingratitude. When I'm done with you, my girl, you will be only too glad to marry Sir Charles.'

Marcus scanned the gloom ahead, listening intently, but could detect no sign of human life. They had ridden for several miles now without challenge. In keeping with the plan, the wagon and its escort had been sent along a different road this time, one more open and less susceptible to ambush. He hoped that detail would lend authenticity to the scheme and help convince the wreckers to take the bait. They had to believe Harlston was being extra cautious this time. The information had been deliberately leaked in the appropriate quarter some days since. Marcus smiled grimly. He wished he could have been there, but felt certain that Sir Alan Weatherby had done a good job.

A staccato crack rang out in the darkness up ahead. Barstow held up his hand and the column stopped, every man there straining to hear. The still air carried the sound of two more shots and then shouting voices.

The Major grinned. 'I think they've taken the bait.'

As he spoke the sound of shouting increased and then there was a crash as of something falling and a volley of shots. He drew his sword. The sound was repeated as a dozen more blades were drawn free of their sheaths. Raising the weapon aloft, he ordered the charge.

The horses leapt forwards and the noise of shots was drowned by the sound of galloping hooves. Barely a minute later, the wagon came into view. By the light of the torches Marcus could see several bodies stretched out around the wagon and swaying figures locked in hand-to-hand combat. The mounted force swept down on the attackers. Seeing the arrival of armed reinforce-ments, the wrecker crew saw too late the full extent of the trap that had been sprung. Seriously outnumbered and on foot, the survivors of the first deadly fusillade were no match for mounted men and swinging sabres. Some abandoned the fight and tried to run, but were pursued in their turn.

Marcus reined in, looking swiftly about him as the militia mopped up the remnants of the rebel force. As he did so he saw a movement out of the corner of his eye and turned his head in time to see a dark figure emerging from the shadow beyond the wagon. And then the man called out.

'Eden!'

Just in time Marcus saw the pistol aimed at him and

flung himself sideways as the weapon discharged in a spurt of flame. He felt the breath of the passing ball on his cheek. A moment later he hit the ground and rolled, coming to his feet in time to see the dark form retreating into the darkness. Marcus raced after the fugitive figure, rage lending wings to his feet. He heard the sound of a heavy thud and a muffled curse that told him his enemy had stumbled and fallen. A second later he was on the man and they rolled, locked in a deadly struggle. In the process the other's hat fell off and moments later Marcus's clawing fingers ripped off the handkerchief round the face but even before he saw, he knew who it was.

'I hoped I'd catch up with you, Stone.'

'I've looked forward to it too, Eden.'

A second later Marcus felt a fist connect with his jaw and returned the blow with interest. He heard the other man grunt in pain. But Stone was tough and fighting for his life. He came to his feet, facing his enemy, breathing hard.

'I thought I'd killed you before.'

Marcus smiled grimly. 'You're not a good enough shot.'

He ducked the punch aimed for his head, but took one in the midriff. For a moment he staggered, caught off balance. Stone laughed.

'I promised you'd get yours, you bastard, and I mean to deliver.'

Without warning he bent and drew the knife from his boot, lunging forwards in one fluid movement. Marcus leapt back to avoid the blade, dodging and weaving to evade the savage edge. However, Stone was fast and dangerous and several times it passed close, slashing fabric. Marcus set his jaw, waiting for a chance. In desperation he feinted, pretending to stumble. Stone saw it and lunged for his breast. A moment later, Marcus's hand closed on his opponent's wrist and twisted hard. He heard sinew crack and then a muffled expletive. The knife fell. Before Stone could recover a boot came up into his groin with brutal force, doubling him over in agony. As he slumped forwards Marcus's knee caught him in the face, snapping his head up and pitching him backwards. Stone fell and lay still, groaning. Breathing hard, Marcus lifted his arm and wiped blood and sweat from his face with the sleeve of his coat.

Then he became aware of other figures approaching and looked up to see Major Barstow and four of his men. As the latter moved in to secure the prisoner, Barstow eyed Marcus.

'Are you all right?'

The Viscount nodded. 'I'll live.'

'The rest of the Luddite gang are dead or taken,' said Barstow. He glanced toward Stone and then at his men. 'Sergeant Carter, put this one with the others.'

'Yes, sir. At once.'

As the sergeant moved to obey, Marcus held up a hand.

'One moment. There's something I want to know first.'

'You'll not learn anything from me, Eden,' said Stone.

Marcus stepped in closer. 'Who killed David Gifford?'

A flicker of surprise registered for a moment in the other's face. 'What's it to you?'

'Who killed him?'

Understanding dawned in the other's face. 'You're another bloody government agent.'

'I am many things.' Marcus paused. 'You haven't answered my question.'

'Nor shall I, since I'll hang either way.'

No sooner were the words out than Stone gasped as a

powerful hand closed round his tender privates. A second later the point of a blade pierced his breeches and punctured the skin beneath. Sergeant Carter, face thrust close, favoured him with a winning smile.

'The gentleman asked you a question, you murdering bastard. Either you answer him or I cut off your balls.' The blade moved a little deeper.

Stone yelped. 'All right! All right!'

'So talk, scum.'

'It were Sir James Wraxall—he shot him in t'back.'

For a moment there was silence. Marcus fixed Stone with a cold eye.

'Why?'

'He knew Gifford were working for t'government to find out who were behind t'machine breakin'.'

'Wraxall is a magistrate. Why should he work against the man who was trying to stop it?'

'Because it were Wraxall as were behind t'attacks. When t'looms were smashed, some of t'mill owners couldn't sustain t'financial loss and went under.'

'And then Wraxall bought up their mills for a song,' said Marcus.

Stone nodded. 'He's made himself rich.'

'Yes, with your help.'

'What were we supposed to do? Wraxall paid well. You can't feed a family on eight shillings a week.'

'So you turned to murder.'

'Those men took their chances.'

'Yes, and so will you, you bastard. At the end of a rope.'

'Aye, he'll dance to a different tune, my lord,' said Sergeant Carter.

Stone frowned and glared at Marcus. 'My lord? Who? What's he talking about?'

'A matter of identity. Mine, to be precise.'

'Lord Marcus Edenbridge, Viscount Destermere,' Carter explained.

For a second Stone didn't move, his expression registering first incredulity and then anger. Then both were hidden behind a slow smile.

'Viscount Destermere?' he said. 'Well, well, who'd have thought it, eh?'

'Life's full of surprises, isn't it?' Marcus replied.

The insolent smile widened. 'Oh, yes, my lord, it certainly is. More than you know.'

With that he began to laugh. Marcus regarded him with disgust for a moment and then turned to Carter.

'Take him away.'

The soldiers led Stone off to join the other prisoners. Barstow looked at the Viscount.

'There's something else I think you ought to see, my lord.'

He turned his horse and led the way back toward the wagon onto which his men were lifting the injured. The bodies of the slain lay where they had fallen. It was beside one of these that Barstow eventually stopped. Then he turned to Marcus.

'See for yourself.'

The Viscount turned his attention to the corpse and found himself looking down into the face of Hugh Wraxall. A round, dark hole in the forehead told how he had died, the eyes still wide with sightless astonishment. Suddenly sickened, Marcus turned away and met Barstow's gaze.

'He's paid a heavy price for his part in all this.' He glanced across at the prisoners. 'When all is said and done these men were just pawns in a larger game. I think it's time we went to find the main player.'

Chapter Fourteen

When Marcus and the militia arrived at Wraxall's mansion they were met at the gate by Sir Alan Weatherby. Then they went in to confront Wraxall. As Marcus had expected, he first denied all knowledge. Then he blustered for a while and finally, on learning of his son's death and the destruction of all his plans, fell into a tight-lipped silence. Weatherby stepped forward.

'Sir James Wraxall, you are under arrest.'

'For what crimes?'

'For murder, among others.'

'Murder? Don't be ridiculous.'

'I accuse you of murdering the late Viscount Destermere and of being instrumental in the deaths of at least half a dozen other men.'

'Viscount Destermere died in an accident. It's common knowledge,' Wraxall replied. 'Besides, I never laid eyes on the man in my life.'

'Perhaps you knew him better as David Gifford,' said Marcus.

For a moment the cold eyes widened a little.

'I see you know the name.'

'I…it is familiar to me.'

'I know it is. When you discovered he was working for the government, you promised him your support to help break the Luddite group.' Marcus paused. 'Later, when he got too close to the truth, you lured him to a remote spot and killed him.'

Wraxall licked dry lips. 'You can't prove any of it.'

'We have proof and to spare. Not all your underlings were killed tonight. And when they're offered the chance to save their necks they'll testify against you, enough to hang you several times over.'

'I had no part in it. It was all my son's doing.'

Marcus surveyed the cold reptilian face with disgust. 'I have long thought of the moment when I would be face to face with my brother's killer and could run him through. Now it has come and I know I will not dirty my sword with you. Let the law take its course.'

As Wraxall was led away Marcus let out a long breath. His godfather regarded him in silence for a moment, understanding something of the thoughts behind that impassive face.

'So it ends,' he said.

'Yes.' Marcus met his gaze. 'Wraxall will hang, but what of the others?'

'Some of them were guilty of murder, too.'

'But not all. What they did was wrong, but they were also driven to desperation by circumstances over which they had no control.'

Weatherby regarded him in frank astonishment. 'Are you suggesting they deserve mercy?'

'Who am I to say what they deserve? What I do know for certain is that they can't feed their families on eight shillings a week.'

'Many others are in a similar plight and yet did not resort to crime.'

'True, but then everyone has a different breaking point.' Marcus made a vague gesture with his hand. 'Can anything be done to prevent more deaths?'

'I don't know,' Weatherby replied. 'If some of these men are prepared to give evidence against Wraxall, then the death sentence *might* be commuted to transportation instead. But it's a long shot, I warn you.'

'Will you try?'

'I'll try, but I promise nothing.'

'Thank you.'

'Since when did you become so tender-hearted?

Marcus returned him a wry smile. 'Let's just say I must be mellowing with age.'

'I think there is more to this than meets the eye and I'm curious. Will you come back with me and dine?'

'I thank you, no. I must return to Netherclough. There is someone there I must see.'

His godfather grinned. 'Would that someone happen to have dark curls and beautiful hazel eyes?'

'She would.'

'Well, don't let me delay you, my boy.'

They walked together back to Weatherby's carriage and his godson waved him off. Then Marcus remounted his horse and headed for home.

He rode steadily, wanting time to reflect. Besides, weariness was setting in now and the bruises he had acquired earlier were making their presence felt. Yet in spite of that he felt a sense of release as though months of pent-up tension had lifted and gone. His promise to Greville was fulfilled. It was time to move on.

He knew now where his future lay and what he wanted

from it. He had seen enough of fighting and bloodshed and death to last a lifetime. What he craved now was peace, the chance to build something worthwhile. He must look to the estate entrusted to him and the people in his care. One day he would pass Netherclough to his own son. That thought led to others and Claire's face drifted into his mind. After all that had passed between them, did he still have a chance? He sighed. Just then, out of nowhere, Greville's voice came to mind again, this time speaking in tones of mild reproof.

'Faint heart never won fair maid. Get to it, Bro.'

Marcus shook his head and smiled. Then, touching his horse's sides with his spurs, he urged it to a canter.

He arrived home half an hour later to find the butler in the hallway waiting for him. From the man's expression it was clear that something was amiss. The Viscount frowned.

'What is it, Mather?'

'It's Miss Davenport, my lord.'

'What about her? Speak, man!'

'She's gone, my lord.'

'Gone where?'

'We don't know, my lord. She's been kidnapped.'

'Kidnapped?' Marcus stared at him. 'Who kidnapped her?'

'I think you should speak to young Dobson, my lord. He saw it.'

'Where is he?'

'I took the liberty of asking him to wait in the small salon. His mother is with him, my lord.'

The Viscount strode into the salon. At his entrance the pair sprang from their seats, regarding him in trepidation.

'I'm sorry, my lord,' Luke burst out. 'I would have stopped 'em if I could, but there were two on 'em.'

Marcus regarded the small tearstained face and then said, 'I'm sure you would have.'

'Are we going to lose us places now?'

'No, of course not.' He took the child gently by the shoulders. 'Just tell me what happened, lad.'

Luke took a deep breath and then began to explain. Marcus heard him first with incredulity and then with mounting anger. With an effort he controlled it. What had happened wasn't the boy's fault and he was already frightened.

'Did you recognise the men who took her?'

'One of 'em were Jed Stone, my lord.'

Recalling the man's laughter earlier that evening, the Viscount was suddenly filled with a sense of foreboding.

'Are you sure?'

'Begging your pardon, my lord,' said Mrs Dobson, 'but Stone once worked in t'same mill as my late husband. We know 'im all right.'

'He's a bad 'un,' said Luke. 'Pa said so.'

'Your father was right,' replied Marcus. 'Did you recognise the man with him?'

'Aye, my lord. It were Jake Harcourt. He lived in t'same street as us before we came here.'

'What about the third man, the one in the carriage?'

'I were too far away to see 'im properly, my lord. An' it were goin' dark.'

'No matter, you've done well, Luke. Now I need you to do one more thing for me.'

'Anything, my lord.'

Marcus looked down at the earnest little face. 'Go to the stables and tell Trubshaw to harness Lightning and

Wildfire to my racing curricle. Tell him I want it at the door in ten minutes.'

'At once, my lord.'

When Luke had gone the Viscount strode into the hall, calling for Mather, and then rattled off a series of instructions before heading to the study where he reloaded the pistols. As he worked his mind turned over all he had been told. He knew that the real perpetrator of the kidnap had to be Claire's uncle. Just how he had come to meet Stone was less clear. However, it was a devilish partnership.

He finished what he was doing just as his valet appeared bearing a clean coat and another cloak. Marcus divested himself of his torn and soiled garments and donned the others swiftly. Then he thrust the pistols back into his belt. Pausing only to retrieve a purse from the top drawer of the desk, he strode back into the hallway. The sound of wheels on gravel announced the arrival of the curricle.

Five minutes after that he was heading the horses out of the main gate and onto the highway. He knew full well it would have been faster to ride, but there were Claire's needs to be considered, for he had no intention of returning without her. Davenport would be heading south, but would no doubt put up for the night at an inn along the way. There were not so many places of good repute that it would be hard to find him.

The thought of Claire's terror fuelled his rage. Now he understood why she had been so afraid of her uncle discovering her whereabouts. The man was a ruthless blackguard. While he could understand Davenport wanting to find his niece and secure her return, why would he go to such extreme lengths? Her majority was not far off now. Surely he might more easily have washed his hands of her. What was the point of compelling her to return? Unless, of course, he had another end in view. An unwelcome possibility occurred. Surely the old reprobate wasn't still planning to try and force Claire into the marriage she had shunned before?

The more he thought about it the more likely it seemed. She had said her uncle was of a vengeful nature and not one to tolerate disobedience. Marcus heard her words in his mind: *He is nothing if not tenacious.* The realisation turned him cold. The idea of Claire married to anyone but himself was unthinkable. It came to him then that he loved her beyond all reason, too well to try to compel her to remain at Netherclough if she did not want to. Only let him rescue her from her uncle's clutches, and then he would do whatever she asked.

They had a good hour's start, but the curricle was light and swift and drawn by two of the best horses in his stable. Besides, Davenport would not be expecting pursuit. Marcus smiled grimly. He was confident of his ability to catch them. Focusing all his attention on the team, he settled down to drive.

Claire had no idea how long they travelled for time had lost all meaning. All she had been able to glimpse in the darkness was the verge speeding away beyond the window and each minute carrying her further from Netherclough and from Marcus. What would he think when he returned to find her gone? What if he did not return at all? What if he had been injured or killed? She shut her eyes, trying not to succumb to the terror that lurked on the edges of thought.

Having delivered that dire account of his intentions, her uncle had not spoken since. Nor did she wish for conversation, preferring to be alone with her thoughts.

Her cheeks still smarted from the blows he had struck. They were merely an earnest of what was to come. At the thought her stomach churned, for she knew him well enough to know he meant every word. Could she withstand such a beating? Recalling how he had dealt with even the slightest transgressions before, her throat tightened. This would be far worse. Dear God, let her have the courage to endure it. The knowledge of what submission meant made her feel physically sick. Better to die than be bound for life to a man like Sir Charles Mortimer, to be compelled to yield her body to him whenever he chose. For a moment Marcus's face flashed into her mind. In despair she closed her eyes and leaned back against the padded upholstery.

At some point she must have dozed off, for she came to later to find that the coach was slowing. As the vehicle stopped she could see a building set back off the road. It didn't look much like an inn, but more like a private house. Her heart thumped. Was this where they would be staying? It seemed so, for the door of the carriage opened and her uncle got out, commanding her to follow. There was nothing for it but to obey. Trembling she stepped down, shivering as the chill air insinuated itself through her clothes, looking fearfully around. The house was in darkness save for a light burning in an upper window. She could see no other vehicles or any sign of life. Further reflection was denied for her arm was seized in a firm grip and she was led toward the house.

'Where is this place?' she asked.

'It belongs to an acquaintance,' he replied. 'However, he has had to go away on business so we shall be quite alone.'

Claire swallowed hard, her steps lagging. The hold on

her arm tightened and she was drawn inexorably toward the door. It was opened by a hard-faced woman in a mob cap and shawl. It was clear that she recognised Hector Davenport and the thin lips formed a smile.

'Good evening, sir.'

He returned the greeting brusquely and strode inside, drawing his niece with him. The woman glanced at Claire, taking in her slightly dishevelled appearance and the lack of bonnet and cloak, but if she was surprised she made no comment.

'Is my niece's room prepared?' Davenport demanded.

'Quite ready, sir.'

'And the meal too?'

'Everything is ready, sir, just as you ordered.'

'Good. Then you may go. I shall not require you again tonight.' He paused. 'Nor do I wish to be disturbed under any circumstances. Do you understand?'

'Very well, sir.'

The woman bobbed a curtsy and withdrew. Hector Davenport strode to the stairs, dragging Claire with him. With thumping heart she stumbled up the flight to the next floor and along a passageway with several rooms leading off. Her uncle stopped by one of these, opened the door and thrust her inside. Claire stumbled again, only just retaining her balance. He followed her over the threshold. Trembling, she looked around. The room was quite large, but cold and spartan in appearance. The walls and floor were bare of covering or ornament, the only furnishings a narrow bed, a single chair and a washstand with basin and ewer. Her eyes flicked to the window. Her uncle noted the direction of her gaze.

'Do not imagine that you will escape this time, Niece. The window is barred and the door will be securely locked. I shall go and sup now and leave you at leisure to repent of your folly.' He paused. 'When I return, we shall discuss that subject further.'

With that he left her, locking the door behind him. Claire listened to his retreating footsteps and heard him descend the stairs. With pounding heart she flew to the door and tried the handle. It yielded not a whit. She turned next to the window but, as he had told her, it was barred with stout iron rods. She had no hope of moving them. Disconsolately she turned back to the room, wrapping her arms about her to ward off the chill, and then sank down onto the bed in despair. She was lost. Even if Marcus were to follow he would never find her. Unbidden, the tears welled in her eyes. It was hopeless. Her uncle had outwitted every chance of rescue by using a private dwelling. Furthermore, the place was remote and set back off the road. Even if she screamed for help, no one would come.

As time passed the room seemed to grow colder and Claire began to walk up and down in an attempt to keep warm. The hearth was empty save for a few blackened embers and a heap of ash. From the look of it, it hadn't been used for some time. She knew the lack of fire and food was no oversight. Her uncle had never intended to provide any. He intended to make her pay for every bit of the inconvenience and embarrassment she had caused him. This waiting was no mere chance either. It was designed to give her time to speculate on the punishment to come, a deliberate and sadistic ploy to increase her fear and soften her will. It was a calculated piece of cruelty, and that knowledge reignited her anger and resentment. Instead of weakening her resolve, it strengthened it. She would not let him win, could not let him win when the whole of her future hung in the balance.

She stopped pacing and looked round the room again, this time with a sharp, analytical eye. Clearly the window and door afforded no chance of escape. Which left just one possibility. She crossed to the hearth and, bending under the mantel, looked up the chimney. At the bottom anyway the flue was wide enough to take a person. Stepping into the hearth, she straightened and then began to explore the brickwork. After perhaps half a minute her questing hands found what she was looking for, the jutting bricks inside the flue that provided footholds for the sweeps and their boys. She had no idea how long ago this particular chimney might have been swept, but a bit of dirt was a cheap price to pay for freedom. Taking a deep breath, she began to climb.

Chapter Fifteen

The flue was dark and cold and smelled strongly of damp and soot. The footholds were small and she tried them gingerly, feeling her way for the next one. Her fingers sank into soft powder and little falls of it rustled past her shoulders. She prayed it wouldn't be enough to be noticeable among the ashes below. As she moved upwards the chimney soon began to narrow. There was no chance of being able to climb to the top, but she didn't need to. All that was required was to get clear of the hearth so as to be invisible from the room below. When she was sure that she had gone high enough she braced herself against the sides of the flue and waited.

The clock on the landing struck nine. As the last note died away, a door opened downstairs. A moment later footsteps sounded on the stairs. Claire's heart pounded. Straining to catch every sound, she waited dry-mouthed. The footsteps stopped outside the door and she heard the key turn in the lock. Someone took two paces into the room and checked. Then she heard an exclamation. Her uncle! She heard him move further into the room, probably to look under the bed. It was the only place someone could be concealed. Apart, of course, from her present hiding place. She bit her lip, her muscles trembling with reaction and the effort of maintaining her precarious position. A few seconds later she heard a soft oath and then he strode out of the room and back along the passage. His footsteps clattered on the stairs and she heard his angry tones calling for the housekeeper.

Heart pounding now Claire climbed down from her hiding place, regaining the hearth. A glance across the room revealed the open doorway. Her heart leapt in silent exultation. In moments she had crossed the intervening space and was peering cautiously into the passageway. It was empty. She made her way to the far end, praying that her guess was right and there would be a back staircase, one the servants would use. Her luck held. Furthermore, it was in darkness. She made her way down, guiding herself with the banister rail. A few moments later she was on the ground floor. A high window afforded enough light to make out a nearby doorway. From the far end of the house she heard voices, her uncle's and that of a woman: the housekeeper. Claire's heart thumped painfully. Turning the handle of the door, she slipped through it into the room beyond.

Stale cooking smells announced a kitchen. A swift glance around revealed the dark bulk of the outer door opposite. She moved towards it and lifted the latch, but the door didn't move. Locked! For a moment she fought panic. Her fumbling fingers felt for the key and discovered it, still in the lock. She turned it and tried the latch again. Still the door refused to open. There must be a bolt somewhere. Reaching upwards, she felt for it. Sure enough it was there. Stealthily she slid it back. This time when she tried the latch the door opened. A swift look around revealed there was no one in sight, so she slipped out and pulled the door to behind her. She was free.

With slow care she made her way to the corner of the building and peered round. A second later she caught her breath and flattened herself back against the wall, for her uncle was standing on the driveway, lantern in hand, speaking to his coachman. The housekeeper stood just a few feet behind him. Claire swallowed hard, scarcely daring to breathe. A few moments later the crunch of gravel announced movement and someone heading her way. Heart in mouth she waited, motionless. The footsteps came closer. She could make out the man's dark shape only feet away. Praying he wouldn't look round, she watched with bated breath as he strode on past, heading for the buildings opposite. Claire let out the breath she had been holding and then peered round the corner again. The coast was clear. She began to move cautiously away from the house.

Moments later a woman's voice called out a ringing challenge. Claire threw a horrified glance over her shoulder and saw the housekeeper standing in the doorway. Knowing the shout would bring her uncle in seconds, she picked up her skirts and ran, tearing along the drive and out onto the road. Behind her she could hear running feet. The sound spurred her to renewed effort; if her uncle caught up with her now it was all over.

Knowing the centre of the road was muddy and slippery, she tried to keep to the sides, ignoring the twigs and brambles that slashed at her and snagged on her clothes. Several times she stumbled and nearly went down, but fear kept her going. She could no longer hear the sounds of pursuit, but knew better than to stop, for any minute now the coach would be following in her wake and much more quickly, too.

She was perhaps half a mile up the road when her parched lungs and pounding heart forced her to pause. The night was very still, the cold, damp air carrying every sound. For a second or two she could hear nothing. Then her ears caught the muffled thud of hoofbeats that could only be a carriage driven at speed. It was coming her way. In desperation she looked wildly around and then plunged off the road into the bushes at the side. Half a dozen paces later she hit a stone wall. Stifling a cry, she stumbled along it, turning her ankles on the uneven ground. Then her foot met something big and solid, and she half fell across the fallen tree. Behind her the sound of hoofbeats grew louder. A few more seconds and the carriage would be on her. Claire threw herself flat along the length of the tree trunk so that she was between it and the wall.

The carriage thundered past. Claire remained quite still, listening to the sound diminishing in the distance. Then, cautiously she raised herself on one elbow and peered over the top of the tree trunk. The night was still again, but she knew she couldn't leave her hiding place yet. When her uncle found no trace of her in the next mile or so he would return and cover the ground again, more slowly this time. She took a deep breath, forcing herself to think. Her uncle couldn't search properly in the darkness and this stretch of road was lined with trees and undergrowth. If she held her nerve, she might evade him yet. And so she waited. For the first time she began to feel cold, for the damp had soaked through her clothes and shoes and the chill was biting. She had never felt so alone in her life.

For the first time since her escape she had time to think about Marcus and her throat tightened. She knew now that he was the reason she could never submit to

an arranged marriage with another man. There could
never *be* another man. The thought of their last meeting weighed doubly heavy on her heart. How much she
regretted the angry words she had flung at him and how
much she would have given to have felt his arms around
her again.

The sound of hooves and wheels invaded her consciousness and she stiffened, listening. There could be no
mistake; the carriage was returning as she had guessed it
would. Her uncle knew full well the sort of distance she
would be able to cover on foot in the time available and,
having found no trace of her further along the road, was
now going over the ground again. For one brief moment
she felt a surge of pleasure at the thought of having foiled
his plans yet again. His rage and frustration must be at
boiling point and she was glad of it. What she felt for
him now was hatred and that was stronger than fear.

The vehicle drew nearer, but now it was moving at a
walking pace. Peering over the fallen tree, she glimpsed
the light of the carriage lamps through the trees. The
window was down and her uncle was leaning out, his
gaze scanning the darkness, his face a mask of cold
fury. Claire dropped low again, listening intently. The
carriage drew level with her position and stopped. She
held her breath. Her heart beat so loudly she was certain
her uncle must hear it. For fully half a minute nothing
moved and the night was silent. Then the vehicle began to
move forwards again at the same pace. Claire remained
still. Fifty yards further on, the carriage stopped again.
She could visualise her uncle's angry gaze peering into
the undergrowth, looking for any trace of movement,
listening for any sound that might reveal the presence
of his quarry. How long before he realised there was
little chance of finding her in the darkness? Trying to

anticipate his next move, she suspected it would be to wait until first light. How far would she be able to get? She was alone, penniless and on foot. He must rate his chances of recapturing her very highly.

At last the carriage moved on and was lost to view. When she was sure it was out of earshot she stood up and with infinite care made her way through the bushes to the road. Then she was off and running again, determined to put as much distance as possible between herself and that awful house.

After two more miles the trees and bushes died away and only stone walls bounded the highway. No wonder her uncle had turned back so quickly. There was no place to hide here and the walls were too high to be climbed easily. On either side was only yawning darkness. There was a pain in her side now and her wet dress clung round her legs, impeding her progress. Yet she couldn't stay here. She had to find somewhere to take shelter if need be.

The stitch got worse and forced her to a walk, but she kept moving nevertheless. However, the road was climbing and beyond isolated trees there was still no sign of any kind of cover. Then her ears caught a sound. She paused, listening intently, and her heart missed a beat. There could be no mistaking the sound of hoof falls. In a moment of terror she froze, unable to go forwards or back. Her uncle had not given up after all!

It was several seconds before she realised that the vehicle was coming towards her, not from behind. The relief was almost overwhelming, so much so that she remained where she was in the middle of the road. The driver was almost on her before he saw the pale figure looming out of the darkness. He reined in hard. She heard a muffled expletive and then there was a confusion of flying hooves as he brought the startled and plunging horses under control.

'What the hell do you think you're doing, walking in the middle of the road like that?' demanded a furious voice. 'I might have killed you, you bloody idiot!'

Claire's heart leapt for she recognised the voice instantly.

'Marcus!'

The driver of the vehicle stared at the filthy and dishevelled figure now pooled in the lamplight at the side of the vehicle.

'Christ! Claire?'

The relief of hearing his voice was so great that she began to shake. Then he was beside her and she was being swathed in the warm folds of a huge cloak and held very close to a broad chest.

'Oh, my love, my sweet Claire, I thought I'd lost you.'

'He came for me, Marcus. He made me go with him.'

'My poor darling. My dearest love.'

At the sound of those endearments her throat tightened, making speech impossible, and she began to shiver violently with cold and reaction. Wasting no time on further speech, he swept her into his arms and lifted her onto the seat of the curricle before climbing up himself. Then, with the practised ease of a skilled whip, he turned the vehicle round and began to retrace his route.

Afterwards Claire had only a hazy memory of that part of the affair. Some time later she was carried into what appeared to be an inn, and there followed a confused impression of voices and hurrying footsteps. Then she was put down gently in a chair by a cheerful fire and two large warm hands were chafing her cold ones.

'Drink this.'

A mug of hot and fragrant liquid was held to her lips. She took a sip and felt it carve a path to her stomach. As the spiced wine warmed her she became aware of a familiar figure seated on the stool at her side.

'I was afraid you'd been killed,' she said. 'But you're all right. You're all right.'

His jaw tightened. 'Never mind me. It's you I'm concerned about just now.'

In truth he was appalled by the sight of her physical condition, revealed in ghastly detail by the lit room. Appalled and deeply angered. To judge by appearances she had been confined in a coal cellar. What the hell had happened in the time before he found her? What kind of a brute was that uncle of hers? He fought down the vengeful feelings rising in his breast, knowing he'd have to wait to learn the truth. What mattered now was to get her warm and clean again and safely tucked up in bed.

A few minutes later the landlord appeared to say that the room was ready. Hearing that, Claire got shakily to her feet, feeling both the effects of fatigue and spiced wine and wondering if there was sufficient strength in her legs to get her up the stairs. The answer was never known because Marcus had no intention of putting the matter to the test. Lifting her with casual ease, he carried her to an upper room and set her down before a cheerful fire. Glancing round, she was aware of a large bed and, blessedly, a tub of hot water.

She was vaguely aware of the door closing, but when she looked over her shoulder it was to see that Marcus was still this side of it. Surely that couldn't be? Before she could say a word he moved closer.

'Come here. We need to get you out of those wet things.'

Her eyes widened a little. 'We?'

'That's right.'

Under her astonished gaze he shrugged off his coat and rolled up his shirtsleeves. The implications sent a rush of warmth from her neck to the roots of her hair.

'But, Marcus, you can't…'

It seemed however that he could, for a moment later the cloak was plucked from her shoulders and tossed aside. Then his hands were on her shoulders again, this time turning her gently round. Their warmth through the damp fabric sent a shiver along her skin. The voice of her conscience said this was wrong. That he should not be here doing this. And yet perversely it felt right. His touch should have frightened or disgusted her, but it did not. The feeling it aroused was quite different. He drew the torn and filthy gown off her shoulders and down over her breasts, freeing her arms from the sleeves, and let it fall. Then he undid her petticoat and stays with the practised ease of a man completely at home with female clothing. Moments later she was standing in her shift. The grey gaze warmed. Following its downward glance she was suddenly aware that the sodden fabric was clinging to her flesh and revealing a great deal more than it concealed. She saw him smile and then reach for a chair, pushing her gently down into it. Then he knelt and lifting her feet in turn, removed her shoes. She felt his hand brush her leg as he unfastened the garters that held her stockings and rolled them down, drawing them off her feet.

'Come,' he said.

He led her to the tub, and paused a moment to remove the pins from her hair. It tumbled in disordered curls about her shoulders. Finally he reached for the fastening of her chemise. When she was completely naked he lifted her into the tub. In an instant she was enveloped in delicious warmth.

Kneeling beside her, he took a cloth and soaped it thoroughly. Then he wiped her face, cleansing away the dirt. Claire winced. For the first time he noticed the dark bruise along her cheekbone. His brows drew together. Immediately his gaze looked for further evidence of abuse, but mercifully found none. He rinsed the skin clean and then washed her hair, vigorously at first to remove the dirt, then gently the second time, massaging her scalp with his fingers, loosening the tension in her neck. Then he rinsed her hair with clean water from the jug. Soaping the cloth again, he moved on to her arms and hands, cleansing away the mud and grime, and thence to the smooth, soft skin of her neck and shoulders and back. Her body was beautiful, he thought, more so than he had envisaged, and he had thought about it often.

Under the soothing strokes of the cloth and the pervading warmth of the water Claire, at first as tense as a bow, began insensibly to relax. The spiced wine, taken on an empty stomach, made her feel pleasantly light-headed. In one part of her mind the voice told her this was shocking and deeply immoral, but another, stronger voice, replied that she didn't care. All that mattered now was to be here with him, to feel his hands on her skin and to revel in the new and wonderful sensations they aroused. Every particle of her body felt deliciously alive, as though she had been asleep before and was only now awakening to a dimension hitherto un-guessed at.

A firm hand closed round her ankle and, lifting her leg, drew it straight. The cloth soaped its length, beginning at her foot and moving slowly along her calf to her knee and thence to her thigh, repeating the exercise with the other leg. Laying the cloth aside, he soaped his hands and began to massage the skin of her neck and shoulders. Gradually, as the skilful fingers continued their work, the knotted muscle relaxed and became pliant. Claire sighed in contentment. It felt blissfully good.

His hands moved down, gently stroking her breasts, brushing the nipples to tautness. Claire drew in a sharp breath for the touch sent a shiver of pleasure rippling through her entire being. Deep within, a familiar spark rekindled and glowed into life and became flame. The shiver along her flesh intensified. And then his mouth was on hers in a soft kiss, gentle and tender, offering only itself, demanding nothing. Her lips parted beneath that soft pressure, her mouth yielding itself to his.

Then he drew away and took the cloth again and rinsed the soap off her. When it was done he drew her to her feet and lifted her from the tub, wrapping her in a warm towel. Without any evidence of haste he dried her hair and then moved on to the rest, moving his hands over her body with slow and deliberate thoroughness. Her flesh, warm from the bath, burned beneath his touch. He turned her to face him, drawing her against him in a warm and gentle embrace, and kissed her again. Her arms stole around his neck and then she was kissing him back, pressing closer, drawing his face down to hers.

Marcus felt the flaring warmth in his groin, instantly aroused, wanting her. A week ago, a day even, and he would have lain her down on the rug by the fire and followed his desire to its conclusion. It was still very tempting, but he knew now it wasn't enough. With a supreme effort of will he drew back a little and looked into her face.

'Are you sure, Claire? I cannot pretend I don't want you, but nothing is going to happen without your consent.'

'I love you, Marcus.'

His heart leapt, for he had never thought to hear those words from her.

'And I you,' he replied. 'I think I did not know how much until I had almost lost you. Yet when I remember some of the things I said before, I feel only shame.' He paused, looking into her eyes. 'Can you ever forgive me for doubting you?'

She put a finger to his lips to silence him. 'I told you, there is nothing to forgive. Besides, my own angry pride was much at fault.'

'You had every right to be angry after the way I have behaved. I cannot think of it now without abhorrence.'

'We both said things in haste that we did not mean.'

'Do you really want to leave Netherclough, Claire? If you do, I'll not prevent you or blame you, even though losing you would be like losing a part of myself.'

She shook her head. 'I don't want to leave. I never did.'

'Then stay, I beg you, and for good this time.' He looked down into her face. 'Marry me, Claire.'

Her heart performed an erratic manoeuvre in her breast that was followed a moment later by flooding happiness.

'Yes,' she replied. 'Oh, yes.'

For a while after that no speech was possible. Afterwards it was unnecessary. He carried her to the bed and, stripping off the remainder of his clothing, joined her there. Then he made love to her, continuing what he had begun before, fanning the embers of the banked fire, restraining his own desire to increase hers, wanting it to be perfect for both of them. He wanted her, but he wanted all of her, not out of fear or compulsion but of her own free will, and so he was gentle and infinitely patient, exploring her anew, making his ultimate possession an act of homage.

No longer afraid of the feelings she had hidden for so long, Claire returned his passion, knowing that this was what she had both desired and refused to acknowledge. Now she yielded herself up to his lovemaking with every part of herself, holding nothing back, wanting to be part of him. Her lips sought his now, teasing, provocative, and passionate by turns, her arms twined about him, her entire being revelling in the nearness of the body pressed against hers. She quivered, feeling his lips travel from her mouth to cheek and temple, ear and throat and breast, kindling her flesh until it seemed that every part of her glowed like a brand. Awareness became a fusion of different sensations: the coarse linen sheet beneath her back, the smell of woollen blankets and tallow candles mingled with wood smoke and the warmth of flesh on flesh, the hardness of the muscles in his arms and shoulders, the erotic, musky scent of sweat on his skin.

She felt his hand slide from her waist along her hip to her thigh and thence to the hidden cleft between, gently stroking. The movement sent a delicious shudder through her body. As he continued stroking, sensation intensified and she gasped, feeling a sudden shockwave of pleasure. Then his weight was pressing her down into the bed, his knee parting her thighs and he entered her, gently at first until the initial resistance was past and then more strongly, the rhythmic strokes thrusting deeper, sending pleasure coursing through every fibre of her being, her body arching against him in ecstasy. She felt him shudder and heard him cry out and then the sudden exhalation of breath as the tension left him afterwards.

And then she lay in his arms, feeling his body curled around hers, both of them drowsing and deliciously sated, protected by a cocoon of warmth. Here with him there was no fear or disgust, only delight, for this was where she belonged. With him she had found the love she had dreamed of for so long.

Claire woke the following morning with a delicious sense of well being. She yawned and stretched lazily, opening her eyes to the new day. As memory returned her heart leapt. He had come for her. Against all the odds he had found her. Just knowing he was near made her feel absurdly happy and all the adventures of the previous evening seemed like an evil dream now from which she had awoken. Recalling too the wonderful sensations of his lovemaking, she reached out for him.

Her hand found only empty space. Coming to full wakefulness, she sat up and looked around. He had gone. Her heart began to beat a little more quickly. Climbing out of bed, she realised suddenly that she had no clothes. The ones she had been wearing yesterday were good for nothing but rags now and the rest of her things were at Netherclough. She reached for a blanket and wrapped it around herself.

A knock on the door diverted her attention. A few seconds later Marcus entered the room. For a moment he surveyed her keenly, his gaze taking in every detail of her appearance, from the dark curls tumbled about her shoulders to the small bare feet just visible below the hem of the blanket. Then he grinned.

'Good morning. You're looking much better.'

'I feel much better,' she replied, very much aware of the sudden acceleration of her heartbeat.

'I've brought you these.' He held up the garments on his arm. 'They're not exactly in the first style, but they're all I could get hold of. They're more or less your size, I think.'

The grey eyes rested on her critically and she was conscious of warm colour rising from her neck.

'Thank you,' she replied.

He laid the clothes over the back of a chair and crossed the intervening space, taking her in his arms and following the gesture with a lingering kiss. Then he looked down into her face.

'Are you hungry?'

'Yes.'

'Good. I've ordered some breakfast downstairs. Then, when we've eaten, we'll go home.'

'Oh, Marcus, I thought yesterday that I would never see you or Netherclough again.'

He smiled. 'I'm not so easy to get rid of. Nor would I let another man steal you away from me.'

'I was so afraid.'

He drew her close to his breast, letting his lips brush her hair. 'There is no need to be afraid, my darling. I won't let him hurt you again.'

Thinking of the narrowness of her escape and of the consequences if she had failed, Claire shuddered. Marcus felt that tremor and frowned, vowing silently that nothing should hurt her again if he could prevent it.

When eventually he left her she dressed hurriedly in the borrowed garments. As he had said, they were hardly stylish but they were at least clean and serviceable. Then she arranged her hair as best she could. Having made herself as presentable as possible under the circumstances, she made her way downstairs. A servant directed her to a small private breakfast parlour.

Marcus had been looking out of the window, but turned when he heard the door open, and then smiled.

Feeling oddly self-conscious, she allowed him to lead her to the table and ply her with ham and eggs and hot coffee. Only when they had finished eating did he bring the conversation round to the events of the previous evening.

Claire gave him a summary of all that had taken place. He listened without interruption, only his expression revealing the anger he felt. Only the part about her eventual escape brought a smile to his lips.

'You're as courageous as you are beautiful,' he said.

She could detect not the least trace of mockery in his tone and the look in the grey eyes reflected only sincerity.

'It wasn't bravery,' she replied. 'Only self-preservation.'

'Your uncle should be horsewhipped. He may yet be if we ever meet.'

Claire paled. 'He will come after me, I know it.'

'Let him. It will avail him nothing. He will not lay hands on you ever again, I swear it.'

Unaccountably a lump formed in her throat.

'Don't be afraid, Claire.'

'I'm not—now.'

'If I had been there, this whole sorry business would never have happened.'

'It wasn't your fault,' she replied. 'Just bad timing, that's all.' She paused. 'But you have not told me your story yet. What happened last night? Did your plan work?'

'Yes. The Luddite group is finished. In that neck of the woods anyway.'

She listened intently and in mounting horror as he outlined what had taken place. It was almost inconceivable that a man in Wraxall's position should stoop to such baseness, and she could feel no pity for his impending fate.

'So your brother is avenged,' she said. 'And you have fulfilled your promise.'

He nodded. 'Yes. It's a strange feeling in many ways, and a relief too that it is over.' He paused. 'Now I can think about the future, our future. I want to build something worthwhile, Claire, and that will only be possible with you beside me.'

Her heart leapt, both for the tone of the words and the intensity of his expression. 'We will build a future together, Marcus. A wonderful future. I know it.'

He raised her hand to his lips. 'You do me a greater honour than I deserve.'

'Let's look forward, not back.' She smiled up at him. 'After all, there is so much to look forward to.'

Chapter Sixteen

Marcus was just about to hand her into the curricle when another carriage pulled up outside the inn. She recognised it in a moment, and the familiar figure that got out. Her cheeks paled.

'My uncle,' she murmured.

Marcus, following the direction of her gaze, frowned and laid a hand over hers, but before he had time to say anything, Davenport's gaze came to rest on the handsome racing curricle and the tall, elegantly clad man beside it. For a second or two he didn't recognise his niece in the young woman with him. Then he saw her and his expression lit with triumph. Claire swallowed hard. Moments later her uncle was crossing the intervening space. She glanced from him to Marcus, who seemed not to be in the least perturbed, but merely watched as Davenport strode towards them. Having reached the curricle, he threw a cold glance at his niece and then another at her companion.

'Forgive me, sir,' he said, 'but I must ask you to hand that young woman into my custody.'

Marcus raised an eyebrow and raked Davenport from head to toe with a haughty look. 'And who might you be, sir?'

'I am Hector Davenport and the girl is my niece.'

He was favoured with the briefest of bows. 'Lord Destermere, at your service.'

For a second Davenport didn't move. His cold eyes registered surprise, but he recovered at once and bestowed on the other a thin smile.

'Your servant, my lord. May I say how much I regret the trouble that you have been put to by this wayward wretch?'

'Your niece has been no trouble. On the contrary.'

'You are generous, my lord.'

'Not in the least. My only concern is that you should have caused the lady to be removed from my house in such an underhand manner.'

'It was necessary, my lord.'

'Indeed?'

'You have been grievously imposed upon. I do not know what tale the girl has told you in order to trick her way into your house, but she is as devious as she is headstrong.'

The Viscount's grey eyes grew colder. 'Devious? How so?'

'She left home some months ago, without my knowledge or permission.'

'Ah, she ran away? Why would she do that, I wonder?'

Davenport's cheeks reddened a little. 'She is a disobedient and ungrateful girl. A most advantageous match had been arranged for her but she, in a fit of contrariness, saw fit to go against the judgement of her elders and betters.'

Marcus shook his head. 'Dear me, I can hardly credit it.'

Claire threw him a speaking look, which he affected

not to notice. Evidently, though, her uncle took the words at face value.

'It is indeed difficult to grasp the extent of such wilful folly,' he continued. 'The girl has put me to a good deal of trouble, but now that I have found her again, I shall take her off your hands.'

'As you did yesterday,' replied Marcus.

'She gave me the slip yesterday, but she will not do so again, I assure you. I shall have the knot tied by tomorrow night.'

'And what has the lady to say to this?' asked Marcus, glancing at Claire. 'It seems from her behaviour that she still does not desire this marriage.'

'I will never agree to it,' she replied.

Marcus looked at Davenport. 'There you have it. It looks to me to be a hopeless case. The lady does not wish to marry your choice of husband.'

Davenport stared, as though he could not believe his ears. 'I beg your pardon?'

'In fact,' Marcus went on, 'I don't wish her to either. You see, I intend to marry her myself.'

'You intend…'

'That's right, and she has done me the honour of accepting my proposal.'

Davenport's face suffused with colour when he saw the smile that passed between the other two and he controlled himself with a visible effort. 'Your ruse will not work, my lord. I am the girl's legal guardian and until she comes of age she is mine to dispose of as I see fit.'

Claire, who had been listening to the exchange in mounting concern, felt her stomach give a strange lurch as another realisation struck her. Then a smile lifted the corners of her lips and she turned to Marcus.

'What is the date today?'

'The thirtieth, why?'

'It's my birthday!'

Marcus grinned and turned to her uncle. 'It looks as though your guardianship has just lapsed, sir.'

For a moment there was an awful silence in which Davenport surveyed them in impotent wrath.

'Very well, then, you have made your choice, Claire. I'm done with you. I wash my hands of you.'

'Is that a promise, Uncle?'

'Wicked, ungrateful wretch!'

Seeing him raise his hand, Claire shut her eyes instinctively, anticipating the blow. However, it never reached her for the fist was arrested in mid-air by a grip of iron and held there. In utter astonishment Davenport found himself looking into a pair of cold grey eyes.

'I have always disliked men who abuse women,' said Marcus, 'and you, sir, are one of the most contemptible examples of the species. The only reason I don't thrash you as you deserve is out of consideration for the lady, who I know would dislike a public scene.' He paused, lowering his voice. 'But understand this—if you ever lay a hand on her again, I'll kill you.'

Looking at that flinty expression, Davenport was left in no doubt that he meant it. His face, red before, went pale, but he vouchsafed no answer. Marcus's lip curled, but he released his hold.

'Get out.'

Pausing only to cast upon them a look of loathing, Davenport turned on his heel and strode back to his carriage. He flung in and slammed the door. Moments later the vehicle was drawing away. As Claire watched him go, she was conscious of a huge weight being lifted off her shoulders. She glanced up at Marcus, who was still staring wrathfully after the departing carriage.

'God help me,' he said, 'I have never wanted to knock a man down half so much in my life.'

'He's not worth the effort,' she replied.

'No, you're right. All the same it would have given me immense satisfaction.' He turned and folded her in his arms. 'His tyranny over you is at an end.' Then he grinned. 'Mine, however, is only just beginning.'

'I believe I shall be better able to withstand yours.'

'Can you really bear the thought of a lifetime of me, to say nothing of my wretched temper?'

'There is no one else I would rather share my life with.'

'The sentiment is returned.' Then another thought occurred to him. 'I haven't even wished you a happy birthday yet.' His mouth descended on hers in a long and lingering kiss that set her heart thumping. Then he looked into her face. 'What would you like as a present?'

'I already have what I want.'

'It seems a poor reward to me,' he replied.

Dashed poor, agreed Greville. *Have to do better than that, Bro.*

Marcus grinned. 'How about a diamond ring?'

Claire returned the smile. 'All right, I'm persuaded.'

'I hope it's going to be this easy to get my own way after we're married.'

'Don't count on it.'

'I was afraid you'd say that.'

Clasping her fingers in his, he helped her into the curricle and then climbed up beside her, taking hold of the reins and the whip. Then he glanced down at his companion.

'Home, my lady?' he asked.

'Home, my lord,' she replied.

* * * * *

His Counterfeit Condesa

For Catherine Pons, whose friendship
has made life so much richer

Chapter One

Spain 1812

Sabrina surveyed the laden wagon and the damaged wheel and mentally cursed both. Her gaze travelled down the dusty road that snaked through rock and scrub towards the distant sierra. The sun was already past the zenith and they still had many miles to cover before they reached their destination. Now it looked as though they were going to be much later than planned. The wagon driver, a short, wiry individual of indeterminate age, kicked the wheel rim and flung his hat to the ground, muttering an imprecation under his breath. Then he turned towards her, his swarthy face registering an expression that was both doleful and apologetic.

'*Lo siento mucho, Doña* Sabrina.'

'It's not your fault, Luis. This wagon wasn't up to much in the first place,' she replied in Castilian Spanish as fluent as his own.

'It is no better than firewood on wheels,' he replied.

'Or rather, not on wheels any more. Next time I see that donkey, Vasquez, I shall kill him.'

She shook her head. 'He is an ally, even if he does supply poor transport.'

'*Dios mio!* With allies such as this, who needs to worry about the French?'

'Even so.'

Luis sighed. 'Very well. I shall let him off with just a beating.'

'No, Luis, tempting as it is.' She turned back to the wagon. 'All that matters now is to get this thing fixed so that we can make the rendezvous with Colonel Albermarle.'

Another voice interjected calmly, 'There's a wheel-wright in the next town. It's no more than five miles from here.'

She turned towards the speaker, a man of middle years whose black hair showed strands of grey. His tanned face was deeply lined but the eyes were shrewd and alert. Though he was not tall, his stocky frame suggested compact strength.

Sabrina nodded. 'All right, Ramon. You and I will ride into town and fetch help. Luis and the others can stay here and guard the wagon.'

With that she swung back astride the bay gelding and waited while Ramon remounted his own horse. She nodded to Luis and the three men with him and then turned the horse's head towards Casa Verde.

Town was an overstatement she decided when they reached it about an hour later. It was no more than a large sleepy village. Many of the buildings were ram-shackle affairs with cracked walls and sagging pantile roofs. Chickens scratched in the dirt and a hog sunned itself beside an adobe wall. Ragged children played knucklebones before the open door of a house. The narrow street led into a small dusty plaza and Sabrina glanced at her companion.

'Where can we find the wheelwright?' she asked.

'Garcia's premises are located behind the church.' Ramon nodded in the direction of the imposing white-washed building on the far side of the square. 'Not far now.'

They found the place with no difficulty but discovered the proprietor and two others engaged in removing a wheel from a large supply wagon. Another similar vehicle stood nearby, laden with barrels and sacks. A group of red-coated soldiers stood beside it, laughing and talking among themselves. Sabrina and her companion exchanged glances.

'I'll go and speak with Garcia,' he said.

She took his horse's reins and watched him cross the intervening space. The wright glanced up from his work. There followed an interchange lasting perhaps two minutes. Then Ramon returned, his expression sombre.

'The man has just begun a new job,' he said. 'He will not be able to help us until tomorrow.'

'What!'

Ramon gestured to the two supply wagons. 'He says he must fix those first.'

'But we're supposed to rendezvous with Albermarle in Ciudad Rodrigo this evening.'

'I think that won't be possible. He says the English soldiers are before us and their commanding officer needs these wagons in a hurry.'

'Yes, and we need ours in a hurry,' she replied. 'I'll speak to the officer. Perhaps he may relent.'

Ramon grimaced. 'I doubt it.'

'We'll see.'

Sabrina swung down off her horse and thrust both sets of reins into his hands. Then, taking a deep breath, she walked across to the group of soldiers by the waiting wagon. As she drew nearer the two facing her looked up, becoming aware of her presence. Their expressions registered surprise and curiosity. Seeing it their companions glanced round and then the conversation stopped. Sabrina fixed her attention on the man immediately in front of her.

'I need to speak to your commanding officer.'

'That would be Major Falconbridge, ma'am.'

'Can you tell me where he is?'

'Over there, ma'am,' the soldier replied, nodding towards a dark-haired figure crouching beside one of the draught horses tethered nearby.

Sabrina thanked him and went across. Though the Major must have heard her approach he didn't look up, his attention focused on the horse's near foreleg. Strong lean fingers ran gently down the cannon bone and paused on the fetlock joint.

'Major Falconbridge?'

'That's right.' The voice was pleasant, the accent unmistakably that of a gentleman.

'I am Sabrina Huntley. May I have a word with you, sir?'

He did look up then and she found herself staring into a tanned and clean-shaven face. Its rugged lines had nothing of classical beauty about them but it made her catch her breath all the same. Moreover, it was dominated by a pair of cool, grey eyes, whose piercing gaze now swept her critically, moving from the tumbled gold curls confined at her neck by a ribbon, and travelling on by way of jacket and shirt to breeches and boots, pausing only to linger a moment on the sword at her side and the pistol thrust into her belt. As it did so a gleam of amusement appeared in the grey depths. Then he straightened slowly.

'I am all attention, Miss Huntley.'

Sabrina's startled gaze met the top buttons of his uniform jacket and then moved on, giving her a swift impression of a lithe and powerful frame. Her heart skipped a beat and just for a moment her mind went blank to everything, save the man in front of her. With an effort she recollected herself and, adopting a more businesslike manner, explained briefly what had befallen the wagon.

'I must get to Ciudad Rodrigo tonight. I need the services of the wheelwright at once.'

'I regret that I cannot help you,' he replied, 'for as you see his services are already engaged.'

'My business is most urgent, Major.'

'So is mine, ma'am. Were it not so I would have been delighted to oblige you.'

'Can you not delay your repairs a little?'

'Indeed I cannot. I must deliver these supplies today or my men won't eat.'

The tone was even and courteous enough but it held an inflection of steel. She tried another tack.

'If I do not get help my men and I will be forced to spend the night in the open.'

'That's regrettable, of course, but fortunately the weather is clement at this season,' he replied.

Her jaw tightened. 'There is also the chance of encountering a French patrol.'

'There are no French patrols within twenty miles.' He paused, eyeing the sword and pistol. 'Even if there were I think they would be foolhardy to risk an attack on you.'

Her green eyes flashed fire. 'You are ungallant, sir.'

'So I'm often told.'

'Would you leave a lady unaided in such circumstances?'

'Certainly not, but on your own admission you have several men to help you.' He paused. 'May I ask what your wagon is carrying?'

There was an infinitesimal pause. Then, 'Fruit.'

One dark brow lifted a little. 'I think your fruit will be safe enough, ma'am.'

Sabrina's hands clenched at her sides. 'I do not think you understand the seriousness of the case, Major Falconbridge.'

'I believe I do.'

'I must have that wheelwright.'

'And so you shall—tomorrow.'

'I have never met with so discourteous and disobliging a man in my life!'

'You need to get out more.'

Hot colour flooded into her face and dyed her cheeks a most becoming shade of pink. He smiled appreciatively, revealing very white, even teeth. Sabrina fought the urge to hit him.

'For the last time, Major, will you help me?'

'For the last time, ma'am, I cannot.'

'*Bruto!*'

The only reply was an unrepentant grin. Incensed, Sabrina turned on her heel and marched back to where Ramon waited with the horses. The Spaniard regarded her quizzically.

'Do I take it that the answer was no?'

'You do.'

Grabbing the reins, she remounted and turned her horse towards the gate, pausing only to throw Falconbridge one last fulminating glance as she rode on by. As the Major's grey gaze followed her he laughed softly.

Some time later the army supply wagons set out. Falconbridge rode alongside, keeping the horse to an easy pace. From time to time he let his gaze range across the hills but saw nothing to cause him any concern. For the rest, his mind was more agreeably occupied with the strange encounter in the wheelwright's yard. He smiled to himself, albeit rather ruefully. His response to the lady's plight was ungallant as she had rightly said. No doubt his name was mud now. All the same he wouldn't have missed it for worlds. It had been worth it just to see the fire in those glorious green eyes. For a while there he had wondered if she would hit him; the desire had been writ large in her face. The image returned with force. He knew he wouldn't forget it in a hurry.

Her unusual mode of dress had, initially, led him to wonder if she was one of the camp followers, but the cut-glass accent of her spoken English precluded that at once. Her whole manner was indicative of one used to giving orders. He chuckled to himself. Miss Huntley didn't take kindly to being refused. Under other circumstances he would have behaved better, but he had told the truth when he said he needed to deliver the supplies promptly. She had told him her destination was Ciudad Rodrigo. His smile widened. Without a doubt he'd be meeting her again and soon.

These reflections kept him occupied until the town came into view. He saw the supplies safely delivered and then headed straight to the barracks. He arrived at the quarters he shared with Major Brudenell to find the former already there, seated at the table. Though he was of Falconbridge's age the likeness stopped there. Hair the colour of ripe wheat offset a lightly tanned face whose chiselled lines bespoke his noble heritage. He looked up from the paper on which he had been writing, vivid blue eyes warmed by a smile.

'Ah, Robert. Everything go as planned?'

'Yes, pretty much.'

'The men will be pleased. That last barrel of salt pork was so rancid it could have been used as a weapon of terror. If we'd fired it at the French they'd have been in full retreat by now.'

Falconbridge smiled. 'Maybe we should try it next time.' He nodded towards the paper on the table. 'Letter home, Tony?'

'Yes. I've been meaning to do it for the past fortnight and never got the chance. I must get it finished before I go.'

'Before you go where?'

'The Sierra de Gredos. Ward has me lined up for a further meeting with El Cuchillo.'

The name of the guerrilla leader was well known. For some time he had been passing information to the English in exchange for guns. Since the intelligence provided had been reliable, General Ward was keen to maintain the relationship.

'You'll be gone for a couple of weeks then.'

'I expect so.'

Falconbridge glanced towards the partially written letter. 'I sometimes think war is hardest on those left behind.'

'As a single man you haven't got that worry.'

'Nor would I seek it, notwithstanding your most excellent example.'

Brudenell shook his head. 'I am hardly an excellent example. Indeed it has been so long since I saw my wife that she has likely forgotten what I look like.'

'That must be hard.'

'Not in the least. Ours was an arranged marriage with no choice offered to either party. I am quite sure that Claudia enjoys an agreeable lifestyle in London without being overly troubled by my absence.'

The tone was cheerful enough but Falconbridge glimpsed something very like bleakness in those startling blue eyes. Then it was gone. Privately he owned to surprise, for while he knew that his friend was married, he had only ever referred to the matter in the most general terms, until now. The subject was not one that Falconbridge would have chosen to discuss anyway. Even after all this time it was an aspect of the past that he preferred to forget.

It seemed he wasn't going to be allowed that luxury as Brudenell continued,

'Have you never been tempted to take the plunge?'

'I almost did once but the lady cried off.'

'I'm sorry to hear it.'

Falconbridge achieved a faint shrug. 'Don't be. It was undoubtedly a lucky escape. Ever since then I've preferred to take my pleasure where I find it.'

'Very wise.'

'You condemn matrimony then?'

'Not so,' said Brudenell, 'though I would certainly caution against arranged matches.'

'Advice I shall heed, I promise you.'

'Of course, you might meet the right woman. Have you considered that?'

'I've yet to meet any woman with whom I would wish to spend the rest of my life,' replied Falconbridge. 'The fair sex is charming but they are capricious and, in my experience, not to be trusted. Brief liaisons with women of a certain class are far more satisfactory.'

'You are a cynic, my friend.'

'No, I am a realist.'

What Brudenell might have said in response was never known because an adjutant appeared at the door. He looked at Falconbridge.

'Beg pardon, Major, but General Ward requires your presence at once.'

'Very well. I'll attend him directly.'

As the adjutant departed, the two men exchanged glances. Falconbridge raised an eyebrow.

'This should be interesting.'

'A euphemism if ever I heard one,' replied his companion.

'Well, I'll find out soon enough I expect.'

With that, Falconbridge ducked out of the room and was gone.

It was late afternoon of the following day before Sabrina and her companions crossed the Roman bridge over the Agueda River, and reached the rendezvous in the Castillo at Ciudad Rodrigo. After the siege in January that year, the French had been driven out by British troops. Capture of the town and the big artillery batteries on the Great Teson had opened up the eastern corridor for Wellington's advance into Spain. The Castillo was a hive of activity. The guards at the gate of the fortress recognised the party in the wagon and sent word of their approach, so that by the time they drew to a halt in the courtyard Albermarle was waiting. The Colonel was in his mid-fifties and of just above the average height, but for all his grey hairs he was of an upright bearing and the blue eyes were sharp and astute. When he saw Sabrina his craggy face lit with a smile.

'You're late, my dear. I was getting worried.'

'We had a damaged wheel, sir, and it took longer than expected to repair.'

'Unfortunate, but these things happen. Any other trouble on the way?'

For a moment Major Falconbridge's face swam into her memory. She pushed it aside.

'No.'

'Good.' He eyed the oranges on the wagon. 'And the guns?'

Sabrina nodded to Ramon. He pushed aside part of the top layer of fruit and lifted the sacking on which it rested to reveal the stocks of the Baker rifles beneath. Albermarle smiled.

'You've done well, my dear, as always.' He eyed her dusty garments and then went on, 'Lodgings have been arranged for you nearby. You'll find Jacinta there with your things. When you've had a chance to bathe and change we'll have dinner together.'

'That sounds delightful, sir.'

'Good. We'll talk then.'

Sabrina rejoined him some time later, elegantly gowned in a sprigged muslin frock and with her hair neatly dressed. The meal was good and so far removed from the rations of the last few days that she ate with real enjoyment. Her companion kept the conversation to general topics but, knowing him of old, she sensed there was something on his mind. In this she was correct, though the matter was not broached until they had finished eating and were lingering over the remains of the wine. The colonel leaned back in his chair, surveying her keenly.

'Have you thought any more about our last conversation, my dear?'

'Yes, and my answer is the same.'

'I thought it might be.' He smiled gently. 'Does England hold no charms for you then?'

'I barely remember the place, much less my aunt's family. It is kind of her to offer me a home but I would feel like a fish out of water. My life has revolved around the army. Father could have left me behind in England when he went abroad, but he chose not to and I'm glad of it.'

'I have known your father a long time. John Huntley was always an unusual man, some might even say eccentric, but he is brave and honourable and I am proud to count him among my friends. He is also a very fine cartographer.'

'Yes, he is, and it's thanks to him that I have received such an unusual education. How many young women have been where I've been or done what I've done?'

He chuckled. 'Precious few I imagine.'

'I have sometimes thought that it might be pleasant to have a permanent home and to attend parties and balls and the like, but the bohemian life is not without its charms, too. I suppose the habit has become ingrained, even though Father is gone.'

'You miss him, don't you?'

'It has been four months now, but not a day passes when I don't think of him.'

'His capture was a severe blow to the army.'

'I can't bear to think of him languishing somewhere

in a French prison. I cling to the hope that one day he will be freed and I shall see him again.'

'When the war is over who knows what may happen?'

She sighed. 'I think that day is far off.'

'I know how lonely you must be without him.' He hesitated. 'Did you never think about settling down?'

'Marriage?' She shook her head. 'I have never been in one place long enough to form that kind of attachment.'

'Just so, my dear, and it worries me.'

'There is no need, sir, truly. Father took pains to ensure I was well provided for.'

'It is a godfather's privilege to be concerned,' he replied.

She returned his smile. 'When I find another man like you I may consider settling down. In the meantime it is my duty to do my part for king and country.'

'Are you sure, my dear?'

'Quite sure.' She paused, her gaze searching his face. 'There's something in the wind, isn't there?'

'Am I so transparent?'

'I've known you a long time, sir.'

'True. And you're right. There is a mission in the offing.'

'May I know what it is?'

'Even I don't have all the details yet. All I can tell you is that it is top level. I have a meeting in the morning with General Ward and Major Forbes.'

'Major Forbes is one of Wellington's leading intelligence officers.'

'Yes, he is.' He paused. 'What is more, he has asked that you should be present at the briefing tomorrow.'

Her astonishment was unfeigned. While she had

undertaken several missions in the last year they were all low-key affairs involving relatively small risk. This appeared to be rather different. Curiosity vied with a strange feeling of unease. What kind of mission was it that required her involvement? What part would she be asked to play?

For a long time after she retired that night she lay awake pondering what her godfather had said. It wasn't just the business of the mysterious mission. It was the matter of her future. At some point the war would end and, God willing, her father might be released. However, conditions in French prisons were notoriously bad and she had to face the possibility that he might not survive. What then? Likely she would have no choice but to return to England. However, she had been independent too long ever to live by someone else's rules. Her aunt meant well but the prospect of life in a small town held no charms. Besides, the only career open to a woman was marriage, an indescribably dull fate after a lifetime of adventure. Happily, that was one problem that wouldn't affect her. She had learned early that, when it came to matters of the heart, what men said and what they meant were very different things.

For an instant Captain Jack Denton's image returned, along with its false smile and equally false assurances. Of course, she had been much younger then, barely fifteen. Having no mother or older sisters to advise her, she had been easy prey for a handsome face and polished manner. They had met at her first dance. Ten years older than she, Denton's attentions had been flattering, and had awakened something inside her whose existence had remained unknown till then. He had recognised it at once. And he had been clever, careful not to move too fast yet leaving her in no doubt of his admiration. Smiles and soft looks and compliments developed into brief stolen meetings, always when her father or his friends were not by, and eventually a tender kiss. It had kindled the spark to a flame that lit her whole being. Utterly infatuated, she never questioned his sincerity or the depth of his feelings.

She swallowed hard. No woman in her right mind would risk making that mistake again. Nor would any woman risk her reputation so foolishly. Her relationships with men were almost entirely professional now. On those occasions when she met them socially she was unfailingly courteous but also careful to keep them at arm's length. It was better to be free and independent. The only person she could rely on was herself.

In the meantime she must find out what Ward and Forbes were planning, and the only way to do that was to accompany her godfather tomorrow.

Falconbridge lay on his cot, staring into the darkness, his mind too crowded with thoughts for sleep to take him. The meeting with General Ward was still vivid. Though his skills as an intelligence agent had been used many times on different missions, Falconbridge knew this one was different. If it succeeded it could change the whole course of the war, but the hazards were great for all sorts of reasons. It had been madness to agree to do it. The fact that Ward had given him a choice showed that he knew just how much he was asking. However, the offered inducement was also considerable—for an ambitious officer. Ward was fully aware of it, of course, and calculated accordingly. He knew his man. There was no knowing if this would work, but doing nothing was not an option. Had it involved only himself,

Falconbridge would have taken on the challenge without demur, even knowing the risks were great. As it was... He had expressed his reservations in the strongest possible terms, and been ignored, of course. He thumped the pillow hard. The General had made up his mind and would not be deterred. It argued a degree of calculated ruthlessness that was almost enviable.

The meeting was arranged for ten o'clock. Sabrina had dressed with care for the occasion, donning a smart primrose-yellow gown. Her hair was neatly arranged beneath a pretty straw bonnet. Having surveyed her reflection in the glass with a critical eye she decided the outfit would pass muster. She and Colonel Albermarle presented themselves at the appointed time. Knowing the army as she did, Sabrina had expected a lengthy wait, but to her surprise they were shown straight in.

General Ward was seated behind the desk at the far end of a large room, and Major Forbes was standing beside him. Both men were poring over a map. As they entered Ward looked up.

'Ah, Colonel Albermarle.' As the Colonel came to attention, Ward rose from his seat and bowed to Sabrina. 'Miss Huntley.'

Sabrina returned the greeting and accepted the offer of a chair. For a moment there was silence and she saw the General exchange glances with Forbes. Then he drew a deep breath.

'We have requested your presence today in order to put forward a proposition, Miss Huntley.'

'A proposition, sir?'

'Yes. One of the carrier pigeons recently returned bearing a coded message. In essence, the Spanish agent who sent it has obtained vital military documents concerning French troop movements. However, his responsibilities in Madrid make it impossible for him to deliver the information to us. Like everyone else in senior government positions he is watched, and cannot afford to do anything that might appear unusual. That means someone must go and collect the information from him.'

Sabrina's brow wrinkled for a moment. 'But surely it would be equally suspicious, sir, if he were suddenly visited by a total stranger.'

'Ordinarily it would. However, the gentleman's wife is celebrating her birthday next week and he is holding a ball at his mansion near Aranjuez to mark the occasion. It is to be a lavish affair. Everyone who is anyone will be there. It will also provide a perfect opportunity to get hold of the information he has obtained.'

She nodded slowly. 'I can see that, but I confess to being at a loss as to my role in all this.'

'Our agent is to impersonate this gentleman's cousin, the Conde de Ordoñez y Casal. The real one lives on his estate in Extremadura. Apparently he prefers the pleasures of country life to those of the city and almost never goes there.'

'But isn't there a chance someone will know him and spot the deception?'

'It's an outside chance but one we have to take,' the General replied.

'I still don't understand how all this involves me.'

'The Conde de Ordoñez is a married man. As such, his wife would certainly attend the ball with him. Our agent must therefore be so accompanied.' Ward glanced at Forbes who nodded. 'My informants tell me that Ordoñez's wife is French and blonde. As I am sure you will appreciate, ma'am, there are not many blonde-haired women hereabouts, and even fewer who speak fluent French as well as their native tongue. Your skill in both languages is well known to us.' He paused. 'And you have helped us before.'

'You want me to pose as the Conde's wife?'

'Just so.'

Beside her Colonel Albermarle gave an exclamation of astonishment and disgust.

'The whole thing is highly improper, sir, and I would in no way sanction it,' he said. 'Besides, which, it would be unthinkable to put my goddaughter in such a danger-ous situation.'

The General regarded him with a cool and level stare. 'I have not said all.'

'You mean there's more to this confounded business, sir?'

'Yes. We are not expecting Miss Huntley to take such a risk without offering something in return.'

Ward paused and glanced at his companion. Forbes smiled.

'Your father is unfortunately confined in prison in France,' he said. 'Negotiations are underway for the release of certain English military personnel in exchange for high-ranking French officers currently in our hands. If you agree to help us we'll make your father's release part of those negotiations.'

Sabrina swallowed hard as she tried to marshal her thoughts. 'If I were to agree, what guarantee would there be that my father would be released?'

'We would ensure the man we offered in exchange was of sufficient importance that the French would be most unlikely to refuse.'

'How soon would my father be free?'

'In a matter of weeks.'

A matter of weeks! Her heart thumped in her breast. Her father need not die in a foreign prison after all. They would be reunited at last. Surely that was worth any risk, wasn't it? She bit her lip, unable to ignore the ramifications of her decision. If she agreed she might be putting her life on the line; would be reliant on the help and cooperation of a complete stranger. She did not think that Ward and Forbes would have chosen anyone but the best for this task; they couldn't afford to. All the same, this man's first care was to see that those plans got back to Wellington. If it came to a choice between that and her safety it didn't take a savant to work out which would come first. She would be expendable. The intelligence service needed those plans and its agents were prepared to go to considerable lengths to get them. That also included the ruthless exploitation of her emotions. Her father was of no real monument to them. Had it been otherwise they would have negotiated his release already. The knowledge caused the first faint stirrings of anger. It was an emotion she couldn't afford. Forcing it down she met the General's gaze with apparent composure.

'May I have some time to reflect?'

'Time is of the essence. The ball is eleven days hence. The journey will take nine. I need an answer today.'

Her godfather laid a gentle hand on her arm. 'You don't have to do this, my dear. Your father would never ask it of you. I know how much he means to you and I care for him, too, but as your guardian I urge you to think most carefully.'

'I cannot leave him to die in prison, sir.'

'Consider, Sabrina. You know nothing about this man they would have you accompany.'

'I assure you, sir, that the gentleman is of good

family,' Ward replied. 'He is the younger son of the Earl of Ellingham and is currently carving out a distinguished career for himself as a member of Wellington's intelligence staff.' He paused. 'His background might be considered among the best in England. Good enough, one would think, to be a fit companion for your goddaughter.'

Seeing Ward's haughty expression, Albermarle reddened. 'My goddaughter is also of good family, General. John Huntley has no reason to be ashamed of his connections.'

'I never meant to imply any such thing, Colonel.'

Recognising the signs of impending wrath on her godfather's face Sabrina interjected quickly. 'I am sure you did not, sir.'

Albermarle threw her a swift glance and held his temper. 'Connections are all very well,' he went on, 'but what is the man's character?'

'I have never heard anything to his detriment. On the contrary, he has shown himself to be capable and resourceful in the undertaking of his duties.'

'I am quite sure of that or you would never have chosen him. What concerns me is his moral character. After all, my goddaughter will be alone in his company for weeks. Her reputation…'

'Will be untarnished,' said Ward. 'The proprieties will be observed, sir. Miss Huntley will take her maid, as befits a lady of rank, and our agent will be accompanied by some of his men, in the guise of servants.' He paused. 'It goes without saying that arrangements for accommodation will be quite separate.'

'My goddaughter will have more than just her maid for protection. If she goes at all I insist upon Ramon and Luis attending her as well.'

Forbes raised a quizzical eyebrow. 'Ramon and Luis?'

'Partisans, I believe,' said Ward.

'Two of my father's most trusted companions, sir,' Sabrina explained. 'They have guided him on numerous expeditions and have accompanied me on every mission I've been on. They are most able men.'

Forbes and Ward exchanged another glance. Then the latter nodded.

'Agreed.'

However, Albermarle wasn't finished. 'Apart from the dubious nature of this proposal, Aranjuez is deep in the heart of enemy territory,' he said. 'If anything were to go wrong there would be no possibility of outside help. The consequences mean death or imprisonment.'

'That's true,' said the General. 'It is a risk, albeit a calculated one.'

'In my view the whole thing is utter madness, but the final decision is not mine.'

Ward turned to Sabrina. 'Then may we know your mind, madam, or do you wish a little more time to consider?'

Sabrina knew that time would make no difference in this case. The choice was made as soon as he had talked of her father's freedom.

'I'll do it.'

There came a muffled exclamation from Albermarle, but he said nothing.

Ward smiled. 'Good. It's a brave decision, Miss Huntley. Believe me, we are most grateful.'

'Does your agent know about all this?' she asked.

'Yes, he was briefed earlier.'

'What did you offer him?'

For a second he seemed taken aback, as much by

the dryness of her tone as by the directness of the question, but he recovered quickly. 'Promotion to Lieutenant Colonel.'

'I see.' An ambitious man, she thought. That knowledge wasn't particularly reassuring. 'When do I meet him?'

'At once,' replied Ward. He glanced at Forbes. 'Tell him to come in.'

Sabrina closed her eyes for a moment, willing herself to calm. She must do this thing. There was no other choice. Her father's liberty was all that mattered. She heard the Major's footsteps cross the floor and then the sound of the door opening. He spoke briefly to someone outside. Two sets of footsteps returned. She clasped her hands in her lap to keep them still and forced herself to look up. Then her heart leapt towards her throat and she found herself staring into the grey eyes of Major Falconbridge.

Chapter Two

Suddenly it was harder to breathe and her cheeks, so pink before, went pale. Impossible! It couldn't be he! Of all the men in His Majesty's army… Sabrina came out of her chair and darted a glance at Ward and then at Forbes but saw nothing in their expressions to contradict it. Dear God, what had she agreed to? The idea of walking the length of the street with this man was unappealing, never mind spending weeks in his company. The temptation to renege on her promise and walk away was almost overpowering. Then she thought of her father and took a deep breath.

If Major Falconbridge had noticed aught amiss it wasn't evident. Having observed the necessary social courtesies he got straight to the point.

'I believe that you are to accompany me on this mission, Miss Huntley.'

Somehow she found her voice. 'Yes, sir.'

'I take it that you understand exactly what that entails.'

'I understand.'

'All the same, I should be grateful if you would afford me an opportunity for private speech later.'

With an effort she kept her tone neutral. 'As you will, Major.'

In fact, Falconbridge had seen the fleeting expression of dismay when she realised who he was. Under any other circumstances such a meeting would have been most entertaining, but just now he felt no inclination to laugh. For a moment he had expected her to refuse point-blank to enter into the bargain, but then she had seemed to regain her composure. Forbes had apprised him of her situation and he understood now just how much her father meant to her. After their first meeting Falconbridge knew he must be the last man in the world she would ever have chosen to go anywhere with, let alone Aranjuez. He also knew that his memory hadn't done her justice. From the beginning he had considered her attractive. Seeing her now he realised she was much more than that—spirited, too. However, looks and spirit were only part of it; she had other attributes. Ward had assured him of her linguistic ability in French and Spanish and of her usefulness to them in the past. It still hadn't stifled his doubts. Yet somehow those documents had to be obtained and brought back for Wellington. Promotion and the release of John Huntley, though highly desirable, were secondary considerations.

His thoughts were interrupted by General Ward. 'You will complete your briefing today and leave for Aranjuez in the morning.'

Sabrina's heart lurched. So little time! Then she reflected that it might be better so; if she had more space to consider she might well refuse to go through with it. This man unsettled her too much. Such a mission required clear-headedness and a certain amount of detachment. The knowledge that she was failing in both areas only added to her mortification.

Ward drew the meeting to a close shortly afterwards. Since Falconbridge was to be detained for a while he asked for directions to Sabrina's present accommodation.

'I will call upon you there very soon,' he said.

With that they said their temporary farewells and she and Albermarle left the room. For a while they walked in silence, but when they were away from the headquarters building he paused and drew her round to face him.

'Are you quite sure you know what you're doing, my dear? This mission truly is most dangerous.'

She nodded. 'I know but my mind is made up.'

'Very well. It's your decision, of course, but I cannot pretend that I like it.'

The words stayed with her long after he had gone. Though her reply had sounded confident, she was far from feeling it. However, the die was cast. Unwilling to spend too long thinking about the possibly dire consequences of her actions, she turned her mind to the practicalities. She would need to speak to Jacinta and then the two of them would pack all the necessary items for the trip. Later she would talk to Ramon and Luis. It was all very well for others to commandeer their services for this mission, but it was not the usual low-key affair, nor were they soldiers being paid to risk their lives. They needed to know of the dangers and be given the chance to opt out if they wanted to.

Jacinta listened impassively while Sabrina explained where she would be going. She did not go into details about why, since it was classified information, but only said that it concerned her father's safety, an explanation that she knew the maid would accept without question.

'Aranjuez?' she said then. 'I know of it, of course, but I have never been there. It will be interesting to see.'

'It will also be dangerous, Jacinta. Are you sure you want to come?'

The girl lifted one dark eyebrow. 'Do you think you can prevent it?'

Sabrina smiled ruefully. 'I doubt it, but I wanted you to know what you're agreeing to first.'

'If it were not for your father I would be dead now. He saved me after French dragoons burned and looted my village, and gave me a place in his household. Never shall I forget what I owe to him.' Jacinta's dark eyes burned now with inner fire. Her face, too angular for beauty, was nevertheless arresting and it concealed a sharp brain. In her mid-twenties, she had been with the Huntleys for the last five years. Ordinarily she never spoke of the past and Sabrina did not pry, though she knew the broad outlines of the story. If Jacinta wanted her to know the details she would tell her.

'I miss Father so much.'

'I, also,' Jacinta replied, 'but he is a brave and resourceful man. God will surely help him to win through.'

'I pray he may.'

'Meanwhile, not everything can be left to God. We play our part too, no?'

'As well as we can.'

Jacinta turned towards the clothes press. 'Then perhaps we should begin by relieving the Almighty of the task of packing.'

They were thus engaged when a servant appeared to

say that Major Falconbridge had just arrived. Sabrina drew in a deep breath. This had to be faced and it would be as well to get it over with.

He was waiting in the small salon. Hearing her step he turned, watching her approach. For a moment or two they surveyed each other in silence. Then he made her a neat bow.

'Miss Huntley. Thank you for receiving me. I am sure you must be busy.'

She kept her expression studiedly neutral. 'It is of no consequence, sir.'

'I shall not keep you long, but there are things that must be said.' He gestured to the open French windows that gave out onto the garden. 'Will you oblige me?'

As he stood aside to let her pass, she was keenly aware of the gaze burning into her back. It was one thing to be with this man in the company of others and quite another to meet him alone. It ought not to have bothered her; after all, the army had been a large part of her life. She was quite used to the company of men but none of them discomposed her like this one. But then none of them had his rugged good looks either, or that confoundedly assured manner. He had presence, no doubt about that. It was only enhanced by the scarlet regimentals; the jacket with its gold lacings might have been moulded to those broad shoulders. She had thought she was tall, until now. It gave him an annoying advantage since she was forced to look up all the time.

It was warm in the garden, the sunlight brilliant after the relative gloom indoors. They walked a little way down the path between the flower beds until they came to a wooden bench. There he paused.

'Shall we sit awhile, Miss Huntley?'

She made no demur and watched as he joined her. His gaze met and held hers.

'I'll come straight to the point,' he said. 'I was not… am not…in favour of your coming on this mission. It is difficult and dangerous and certainly no place for a woman.'

'And I am the last woman you would have chosen into the bargain.'

One dark brow lifted a little. 'I did not say so.'

'You didn't have to,' she replied. 'But then you are the last man I would have chosen, so in that way there is balance.'

'I am well aware that our first encounter was not calculated to make us friends, Miss Huntley, but personal feelings do not enter into this. My objections are based solely on the risks involved.'

Sabrina's chin lifted. 'It was my choice to come, Major. The risks were explained to me.'

'Were they?'

'Colonel Ward made it clear that capture would probably mean death.'

'Death is the best you can hope for if you are captured,' he replied. 'Before that there is always interrogation, and the French are not noted for their gentleness in such matters.'

'Are you afraid I would talk?'

'Everyone talks by the third day, Miss Huntley.'

Suddenly the sunshine wasn't quite as warm as it had been. 'Are you trying to frighten me, sir?'

'No, only to make you fully aware of what you are agreeing to.' He paused. 'The fact that you are a woman brings very particular perils.'

It was impossible to mistake his meaning and, under that cool scrutiny, she felt a hot blush rising from her neck to the roots of her hair. Immediately she was furious with herself. He saw the deepening colour and thought it became her. It was a most agreeable foil for her eyes.

'I consider the end to be worth the possible perils,' she replied.

'General Ward told me about your father. I'm truly sorry.'

The tone sounded sincere and it took her by surprise. 'If there is any chance that he might be released I have to take it. Surely you see that?'

'I understand your motives and applaud your courage, but…'

'You cannot dissuade me. I am set on going.'

'Very well, but know this: I shall expect you to obey my orders to the letter. Both our lives may depend upon it.'

'I understand.'

'I hope you do because I shall not brook disobedience.'

The threat was plain and she had not the least doubt that he meant it. Did he think her so unreliable?

'I assure you, Major, that I will do nothing to jeopardise the success of this mission.'

'Good.' He paused. 'Then we may be able to deal tolerably well together after all.'

It was, she knew, an oblique reference to their first encounter. Unwilling to go there she sought safer ground.

'There must be many things I need to know, about the Condesa de Ordoñez, I mean.'

'I shall brief you on those while we travel. There will be time enough for you to assimilate the details.'

'As you wish.'

He stood. 'Until tomorrow morning then, Miss Huntley.'

Sabrina rose, too, and held out her hand. It was in part a conciliatory gesture. Whatever had happened before, it must not be allowed to get in the way now.

'Until tomorrow, sir.'

She had wondered if he would shake hands with her or consider a curt bow sufficient. Strong fingers closed around hers and, unexpectedly, lifted her hand to his lips. The touch sent a tremor through her entire being. For a moment the grey eyes held hers, but she could not read the expression there. Then she was free and he turned to go. She watched until he was lost to view.

Early next morning, as the trunks were loaded onto the carriage and the horses put to, Sabrina came down to find her godfather and her large travelling companion already waiting. With a small start of surprise she saw that Major Falconbridge had changed his uniform for civilian dress. He was clad now in fawn breeches, Hessian boots and a coat of dark blue superfine that might have been moulded to his shoulders. Snowy linen showed at wrist and throat and a single fob hung from a cream-coloured waistcoat, completing an outfit that was at once simple and elegant. It also enhanced every line of that powerful frame and rendered it more imposing.

Unwilling to let her mind travel too far down that road, she turned her attention to their escort. Ramon and Luis were reassuring presences. As Jacinta had told her, when asked they had made it quite clear that they took their presence on this journey as read. Nor would they be dissuaded.

'Your concern does you credit, *Doña* Sabrina,' replied Ramon when she had told them her plans, 'but I believe

I will make up my own mind.' The words were quietly spoken but carried an undertone that she recognised all too well.

She made a last-ditch attempt. 'Aranjuez is far behind French lines.'

'*Madre de Dios!* Can it be true?' Luis threw up his hands in mock horror. 'In that case, Ramon and I shall remain safely here and tell your father later that we let you go alone into the lion's den. I am sure he will understand.'

'My father would not ask this of you.'

'Your father is not here,' said Ramon, 'which means that we two are *in loco parentis* until his return.'

'Loco is right,' replied Luis, 'but even crazy parents are better than none, eh?'

Unable to think of an immediate answer to this, Sabrina had given in. With Ramon and Luis now were two of Falconbridge's men, Corporal Blakelock and Private Willis. She recognised them from the encounter in Casa Verde. Both men seemed to be in their mid-twenties but there the resemblance ended: Blakelock's thin, rangy frame and shock of fair hair were a complete contrast to Willis's shorter, more compact build and straggling brown locks. They touched their caps and greeted her respectfully, neither one giving any indication that they recalled what had taken place that day in the wheelwright's yard. She wondered whether it was natural tact on their part or whether Falconbridge had spoken to them. They were to travel in the chaise with Jacinta. Ramon and Luis would take it in turns to drive the coach. The entourage certainly looked like that of a wealthy man and, in this instance, appearances were everything.

Sabrina had not expected that the farewell to

Albermarle would be easy, and in this she was right. The craggy face surveyed her for a moment in silence and the blue eyes softened.

'God bless you, my dear. I wish you all good fortune.' He hugged her closely. Then he shook hands with Falconbridge. 'Take care of her, Major.'

'You have my word on it, sir.'

Albermarle handed Sabrina into the carriage before turning back to the man beside him and bestowing on him a vulpine smile. Then he leaned closer and lowered his voice so that only the two of them could hear.

'If you let any harm come to her I'll personally cut out your liver.'

The Major met his eye. 'I'll try by every means to keep her safe, sir.'

'You'd better.' Albermarle smiled at Sabrina and watched her companion climb into the coach. Then he stepped back and rapped out a command to Luis on the box. The horses leapt forwards.

Sabrina drew in a deep breath as the coach pulled away; this was it, the beginning of the adventure. Yet she knew nothing about this man with whom she was to spend the next few weeks. This was only the second time they had been alone together. She would have preferred it to have been somewhere other than the close confines of the carriage, for she was only too keenly aware of the virile form opposite. Just then she would have given a great deal to know what he was thinking, but his expression gave nothing away.

What was running through his mind just then was a strange mixture of emotions. Chiefly he wished with all his heart that she had not come. He was also hoping with all his heart that their mission would go without a hitch. The thought of what might happen if she ever fell into enemy hands turned him cold. Any woman would have been in danger, but a woman who looked like Sabrina... It was why he had tried to talk her out of coming along. She really was lovely. The green travelling dress and matching bonnet became her well, enhancing the colour of her eyes. The shade was unusual, reminding him just now of sun-shot sea water. Those same eyes darkened to emerald when she was angry, he remembered. At that moment their expression was unfathomable. He sighed inwardly. Like it or not she was with him now and he knew it would be better if they could at least get along. The fact that they didn't was, he admitted, in great measure due to him.

'It doesn't seem quite real, does it?' he said then.

The words were so exactly what had been going through her own mind that she wondered if he had somehow read her thoughts.

'No, indeed it doesn't.'

She wondered if he would attempt to make polite conversation now. In truth she had no wish for it. However, it seemed that was not his intention.

'Since we are to spend some time together perhaps I should begin by telling you something of the lady you are to impersonate.'

She acknowledged privately that it was an adroit touch. He had her full attention now. 'I would be glad if you did. I know so little, apart from the fact that the Condesa is French—and blonde.'

'Her family's name was De Courcy. They came from Toulouse but left France during the revolution, just before the Terror, and settled in Asturias where, I understand, the family had lands.' He paused. 'Marianne de Courcy married Antonio Ordoñez three years ago.'

'Was it an arranged marriage?'

'Yes, though with the consent of both parties apparently.'

'Children?'

'A son called Miguel.'

'And they live retired.'

'Happily for our purposes, yes. The Conde prefers country life.'

'All the same, there might be someone at this party who knows him or his wife.'

The grey gaze met hers. 'Let us hope not, for both our sakes.' He reached into the inner pocket of his coat and drew out the object that reposed there. 'Incidentally, you will need this.'

'What is it?'

'A small detail, but an important one if our subterfuge is to be believed.' He held up a gold ring.

She stared at it for a moment and then at him. 'I had not thought of that.'

'How should you? It is a husband's concern, is it not?'

He reached across and took her hand, sliding the ring on her finger. It fitted well, almost as though it belonged there. However, she was not so much aware of the gold band as of the hand holding hers, a strong lean hand whose touch set her pulse racing. It lingered a few seconds longer and then relinquished its hold. He smiled faintly.

'The adventure begins, my dear, for better or for worse.'

They settled into silence for a while after this, each occupied in private thought. Sabrina's gaze went to the window but in truth she saw little of the passing country-side. The presence of the wedding band on her finger was a tangible reminder of the role she was expected to play now. It might have been easier if the man opposite had been a less charismatic, less attractive figure. A plainer, duller man might have made it easier to concentrate. She forced her attention back to what she had been told, committing the detail to memory. She couldn't afford to make a slip. Thus far she had not allowed herself to think too far ahead but now the implications of their mission crowded in, and the dangers it posed to them both.

At noon they stopped to rest the horses and to partake of a light luncheon. The inn was humble but clean and boasted a vine-covered terrace to the rear overlooking the hills. It was a far more appealing prospect than sitting indoors, and Sabrina readily agreed when he suggested they repair thither to eat. It was good to be out of the swaying vehicle for a while, and to have the opportunity to stretch her cramped limbs. While the Major bespoke luncheon, she walked to the end of the terrace and stood for a while looking out towards hills now hazy in the heat that shimmered over rock and scrub. Nothing moved in the stillness save a buzzard circling high on the warm air currents.

'It is a fine view, is it not?'

She had not heard him approach but a swift glance revealed the tall figure at her shoulder. His closeness was disconcerting so she returned her gaze to the hills.

'Very fine.'

'Spain is a beautiful country, at least those parts of it I have seen.'

She nodded. 'Yes, it is. My father always thought so, too.'

The mention of her father brought unwelcome emotions to the fore and she resolutely changed the subject.

'The journey has made me hungry. Shall we eat?'

He could hardly miss the hint and smiled faintly. They moved back under the shade of the vines. The meal was simple and unpretentious: tender, home-cured ham, slices of Manchego cheese, green olives, pieces of spicy chorizo, freshly baked bread and a jug of red wine, but Sabrina had no fault to find with it. On the contrary, she ate with enjoyment. The ham was particularly good, almost melting in the mouth.

Falconbridge owned to some surprise, initially wondering if she would turn up her nose at such plain fare. Perhaps the lengthy travels with her father had accustomed her to such things. It pleased him to find it so. This mission would be difficult enough without being saddled with a captious female.

For the most part they ate in silence. When at last they had finished he leaned back in his chair, surveying her keenly.

'Would you care to walk a little? It may be some time before we get another chance.'

She nodded acquiescence and rose with him. By tacit consent they strolled together towards the arroyo some hundred yards off.

'I find that I know nothing about you, or almost nothing,' he said then.

She glanced up at him. 'What do you want to know?'

'Now that's a leading question.'

'I have nothing to hide.' That wasn't completely true but she had no intention of mentioning Jack Denton. Anyway it had no bearing on their mission.

'Then tell me a little about your background, the things that General Ward did not say.'

'There is not a great deal to tell. My mother was a Frenchwoman whose family fled Paris when the revolution came. She died when I was twelve. Father refused to leave me with relatives and brought me with him to Iberia.'

'An unusual upbringing for a young woman.'

'I suppose it must seem that way to other people, though I have never considered it so.'

'You clearly have a gift for languages.'

'We spoke both French and English at home so the facility came early. I learned Portuguese and Spanish after my father's posting to the Peninsula.'

'I see. Did you never have any formal schooling?'

'I had a governess when I was little. My father also taught me many things; more perhaps than most young ladies learn.'

'Such as?'

'Such as learning how to defend myself.'

Recalling their first meeting, Falconbridge smiled. 'So the sword and pistol weren't just for show, then?'

'Hardly.'

'Have you ever been called upon to use them?'

'Yes. Father's work took us to some remote places and once we were attacked by robbers. Fortunately Ramon and Luis were with us and we were able to drive our attackers off, but it's not an experience I would choose to have again.'

'I can well believe it,' he replied. His curiosity mounted. 'Did you never settle in one place?'

'No, though there were some fairly lengthy spells in different locations.'

'Did it not bother you to be always on the move?'

'Home was wherever we happened to be. So long as Father and I were together I didn't mind.'

'His capture must have come as a severe blow.'

'Yes, it did.'

'I take it you were not there on that occasion.'

She shook her head. 'My horse was lame and Father was only going to be away for two or three days. That was four months ago. I have not seen him since.'

'I'm so sorry.'

Sabrina was struck again by the apparent sincerity in his tone. It was much at variance with the man she had met before.

'I should have been with him,' she said. 'Perhaps then I could have done something to help.'

'If you had been with him, my dear, you would have been killed or captured yourself.'

'Perhaps.'

'Soldiers are not known for their chivalrous behaviour.'

She smiled innocently. 'So I've noticed, sir.'

'Touché!'

Her riposte had been justified, he admitted. All the same he hadn't missed the mischievous glance that had accompanied it. There had been no malice in the look. On the contrary, it had been quite unwittingly seductive. The fact that it had been unintended made it all the more effective. He smiled in self-mockery. Any overture to Miss Huntley would likely result in him getting shot, or run through with a sword. She was more than capable of holding her own. It didn't displease him. Whatever else, it meant that the journey wasn't going to be dull.

Their stroll had brought them to the arroyo, but the stream in its stony bed was reduced to a mere trickle now. A few stunted trees clung to the margins. Heat struck upwards from the baked earth and carried with it the scent of wild thyme and dry grass.

'Despite the shortcomings of some members of the

military,' he continued, 'you are fortunate to have a friend in Colonel Albermarle.'

'He has been kindness itself. He and my father go back many years.'

'When this mission is over you will see your father again.'

'I pray that I may. I cannot bear to think of him in a foreign prison.'

Her expression grew wistful and he was unexpectedly touched. Her affection for her parent was clearly genuine, as was her desire for his freedom. Her youth made her seem more vulnerable. Once again he felt the weight of his responsibility.

'How old are you, Sabrina?'

'I'm nineteen.' Her eyes met and held his. 'How old are you?'

His lips twitched. 'Eight and twenty.'

'Now you know about me will you not tell me something of yourself?'

'You will find it dull. Unlike you I had a most conventional upbringing: Eton, Cambridge and the army. As the younger son I was expected to carve out a career for myself. My father bought me a commission and then let me get on with it.'

'Do you have any sisters?'

'One. Her name is Harriet. She is four years younger than I and married now with children of her own.'

'And your brother?'

There was an infinitesimal pause. 'Hugh, who is two years older.'

'Are you close?'

'Not especially.' It was, he thought, a massive understatement. The antipathy he had come to feel for his brother had, at one point, come perilously close to hatred.

'Is he married?'

The grey eyes glinted. 'Yes. His wife is called Clarissa and they have two children.'

It had been easier to say than he had imagined. It was said that time salved all wounds; it must have made more of a difference than he had ever envisaged.

Sabrina smiled. 'I find it hard to see you as an uncle.'

He regarded her steadily. 'Do you?'

'Yes, the soldier in you seems to preclude it.'

'In truth I have seen little of my nieces and nephews,' he admitted, 'but that is due to the demands of the army and not to any shortcomings of theirs. I happen to like children.'

The statement was surprising and oddly pleasing. It was a side to him that she would never have suspected. They turned and began to walk back towards the inn.

'How came you to be involved in army work?' he continued. 'It is an unusual occupation for a young woman.'

'It was at my own request,' she replied. 'I wanted to do something towards the war effort.'

'A noble aspiration, but not entirely without risk.'

'The risk has been minimal, until now.'

He regarded her steadily. 'You've taken a dangerous gamble, my dear.'

'So have you.'

'True, though I think the odds are stacked more in my favour.'

Sabrina was unable to decipher what lay behind that for the tone was compounded of several things.

'The odds are always stacked in a man's favour,' she replied.

'Doesn't that worry you?'

'Of course, but then much depends on the man, does it not?'

'And I have done little to impress you thus far.' He paused. 'I admit that on the occasion of our first meeting my behaviour was abysmal. I suppose there's no chance of my being forgiven?'

'Not the least chance, sir.'

He sighed. 'No, I imagine not.' There followed another brief pause. Then, 'Did you deliver your fruit safely, by the way?'

For a moment she stared at him, unable to believe her ears. Then she saw the gleam in his eyes and, unable to help herself, gave a gurgle of laughter.

'Yes, I did deliver it, no thanks to you, you odious man.'

His enjoyment grew. 'I knew you wouldn't disappoint me.'

It was hard to know what to make of that either, but she had a strong suspicion he was quizzing her.

'Anyway,' she continued, 'it wasn't just fruit.'

'What then?'

'Guns for the army.'

'Good lord! Did your godfather know?'

'He sent me.' Seeing his expression she lifted one finely arched brow. 'Why should he not? The risk was small. Besides, I can take care of myself.'

'No doubt,' he replied, 'but now that responsibility falls to me.'

'A worrying thought, sir.'

'Do you doubt my ability to protect you?'

The green eyes gleamed in their turn. 'Well, yes. Did

you not abandon me to spend a night in the open with five men and a broken wagon?'

'Wretch! You're not going to let me forget it, are you?'

'Certainly not,' she replied.

At this point all his preconceived ideas had vanished; she was unlike anyone he had ever met. In his experience young women did not usually meet his eye in just that way, and certainly didn't engage in verbal sparring. Beauty and wit were an attractive combination. She wasn't afraid of him either. He wasn't even sure if she liked him. On balance, he suspected not.

They returned to the inn and paid their shot before resuming the journey in a more companionable silence. Sabrina's gaze went to the window but in truth she saw little of the passing countryside. Her mind was focused on the man sitting opposite. Thus far she had not allowed herself to think too far ahead, but now the implications of their relationship crowded in. For the first time in her life she was thrown together with a man whom she knew hardly at all and in circumstances that required a certain amount of intimacy. Falconbridge was unlikely to do anything that might jeopardise the success of their mission, and he didn't seem the type to force unwanted attentions on any woman. However, she had learned early not to put her trust in appearances. Faith was a loaded pistol and she had a brace of them, should the need arise.

As for the rest, the villages they passed were few and mean, little more than clusters of hovels whose inhabitants eked a subsistence living from a grudging soil. It didn't shock her for she had seen it many times on her travels, but it did occur to her to wonder where they would spend the night. In the past she had slept in many places and knew that she would infinitely prefer a well-kept barn to a dirty inn. Even sleeping in the open was better than that. She decided to ask. The answer was immediately forthcoming.

'We shall stay at La Posada del Rey.'

'The King's Inn. It sounds quite grand.'

'I doubt if the king would be seen dead there,' he replied, 'but at least it's clean and well run. I've used it before on occasions.'

'I'm sure it will be satisfactory.'

'Don't expect luxury or I fear you'll be disappointed.'

Sabrina laughed. 'I became accustomed to rough living very early on. A clean inn is a luxury compared to a bed on open ground.'

He regarded her in surprise, not so much on account of her reply as the way in which laughter lit her face. It occurred to him again that she was rather more than just a pretty girl.

'I hope never to subject you to such rude accommodation,' he replied. 'Rather I promise you a comfortable chamber all to yourself.'

Though the words were blandly spoken they were also meant as reassurance and she knew it. The matter of their sleeping arrangements had been on her mind since they had set out. She suspected he had guessed as much, and also that she would rather have died before mentioning the subject.

'I shall hold you to that, sir.' Her tone was equally bland.

The grey eyes gleamed. 'I was certain you would, my dear.'

Unsure what to make of that she searched his expression for clues, but the rugged features gave nothing away.

Chapter Three

The journey resumed uneventfully next morning and, over the next few days, they made good progress, whiling away the time in conversation and sometimes with cards. Sabrina also took the opportunity to learn as much as possible about the woman she was impersonating. Her companion supplied as much detail as he could. All the same, she could already see potential pitfalls, such as the fact that she had never been to the Languedoc. Falconbridge did not seem unduly unconcerned.

'The Condesa must have been very young when the family left Toulouse,' he said. 'It's entirely possible she wouldn't recall very much anyway.'

'That's fortunate. There may be French officers present at this party.'

'I imagine there will. Try to steer the conversation away from potentially dangerous topics.'

She smiled faintly. 'If things look dangerous I'll ask the officer to talk about himself. Then I won't have to do more than nod and smile for the next hour or so.'

'You think any man could speak for so long about himself?'

'In my experience it's usually a favourite topic of conversation; present company excepted, of course.'

The dulcet tone elicited a faint smile. 'I'm relieved to hear it. I should hate to think that I was such a bore.'

'Hardly that.' Sabrina thought that *bore* was the last word she would use to describe him.

'Another load off my mind,' he replied. 'Is your knowledge of men so extensive?'

With those words Jack Denton's image resurfaced and with it a recollection of hurt and humiliation. She pushed it aside, forcing herself to remain collected. 'How am I to take that?'

'Given your unusual upbringing, you must have met many of my sex. Were they all such confoundedly dull dogs as your remark suggests?'

'No, not all. Some were good company.' She was minded to add a rider to that but refrained.

'Indeed? And did your father allow you to keep such company?'

An indignant retort leapt to mind immediately. Just in time she caught the sardonic glint in his eye and realised he had been quizzing her again.

'That was an outrageous suggestion.'

'Yes, I suppose it was.' He didn't look or sound repentant. 'I find myself curious, you see.'

'About what?'

'Given your bohemian lifestyle it cannot have been easy to meet eligible young men.'

'I never thought of them in such a way,' she replied. 'Some were my father's friends, others were officers whom I met in the course of events.'

'But none for whom you felt a particular partiality?'

'No,' she lied.

'You're never going to tell me that they looked upon you with similar indifference.'

'I really have no idea. You'd have to ask them.' Another lie, she thought. Somehow it went against the grain to tell a falsehood to this man, but the truth was a nest of hornets and best left alone.

He continued to regard her steadily. 'And yet you have been of marriageable age for some time.'

'You make it sound as though I were quite on the shelf.' The words were spoken without rancour.

'I beg your pardon. It's just that most young ladies I've ever met are on the lookout for a husband from the time of their coming out.'

'I never had a coming out,' she replied, 'so perhaps that has coloured my view of the matter. In any case I was enjoying my life too much to want to relinquish it for marriage.'

'You think that all enjoyment ends with marriage then?'

'I don't know. I didn't mean to imply that all marriages are dull, especially not where the couple marries for love. That must be agreeable, surely.'

'I'm sure it is.'

She eyed him curiously. 'Did you never wish to wed?'

There followed a brief hesitation. 'I once fancied myself in love but, as it turned out, I was mistaken.'

'Oh. I'm sorry.'

'No need,' he replied. 'Besides, I am now happily married to my career. Romantic entanglements are for other men.'

They lapsed into silence after this, each seeking refuge in private thought. Unable to tell what lay behind that impassive expression, Sabrina could only ponder his words. He had spoken lightly enough but she sensed that more lay beneath. Clearly he considered marriage an unnecessary encumbrance and perhaps in his line of work it really was. The thought caused an unexpected pang. Even in the short time she had known him he had made an impression, more so than any man of her acquaintance—apart from one. While she didn't equate the two, the first had taught her a valuable lesson. Since then she had kept her male acquaintances at a courteous and professional distance. She intended to do the same now. Her father was the reason she had become embroiled in this affair. His freedom was what really mattered. She must not forget it.

As usual they stopped that evening at an inn and Falconbridge requested rooms and a private parlour in which to dine. The *patrón* was delighted to welcome such exalted guests and assured them that he could offer a most excellent parlour. However, he regretted that he only had one bedchamber available. Falconbridge cursed inwardly. He had always realised this was a possibility but had hoped that it wouldn't arise. He glanced at Sabrina who was just then engaged in conversation with Jacinta. Mistaking that look entirely, the *patrón* hastened to reassure him that it was a large room.

'A truly commodious chamber, *señor.* The lady will be most pleased.'

Falconbridge seriously doubted that. Unfortunately, with dusk coming on, further travel was out of the question. The road was dangerous after dark. He had no desire to run into any of the brigands who frequented the hills, or a French patrol if it came to that.

'We'll take it.'

'*Si, señor.* You won't be disappointed, I guarantee it.'

Just then disappointment was the last thing on Falconbridge's mind, which was turning instead on Sabrina's probable reaction. In spite of the extraordinary circumstances in which they found themselves, a shared bedchamber was a step too far and, hitherto, separate accommodation had been obtained as a matter of course. Thus the proprieties had been observed. He could well understand the importance of that to any woman. Now though, matters were about to become deucedly awkward. Taking Sabrina aside he explained the situation briefly, watching her face, bracing himself for the explosion of wrath, which must surely follow.

'I'm truly sorry about this,' he said, 'but it cannot be avoided. There isn't another decent inn for twenty miles.'

Contrary to his expectation she didn't fly into a passion or refuse to stay a moment longer, though she could not quite conceal the expression of alarm fast enough to escape his notice. He could not know how hard her heart was thumping.

'We'll have to manage as best we may,' she replied.

Once again he owned to surprise and, privately, to relief. She was proving to be a much easier travelling companion than he had ever envisaged.

When inspected, the room was indeed quite spacious and, she noted with relief, it was clean. It was dominated by a large bed. A dresser and washstand occupied much of one wall. A low divan stood opposite. It was the first time she had been in a bedchamber with any man, other than her father. Major Falconbridge's presence was different in every way from the gentle reassuring figure of her parent. Somehow he seemed to fill the space.

'You take the bed,' he said. Then, glancing at the divan, 'I'll sleep over there.'

She nodded, forcing herself to a calm she was far from feeling, reminding herself that she had elected to come on this mission. What had happened was a temporary but unavoidable inconvenience. When their luggage had been carried up, Falconbridge took himself off for a mug of beer, leaving the room free for Sabrina. She was grateful for the courtesy. With Jacinta's help she washed and dressed for dinner, donning a green muslin gown. A matching ribbon was threaded through her curls. Sabrina surveyed her reflection critically. It was hardly sensational but at least she looked neat and presentable.

'It will serve,' she said.

Jacinta smiled. 'It looks very well.'

'Good enough for present circumstances.'

Sabrina did not add, 'and for present company'. In all likelihood Falconbridge would not notice what frock she had on. Not that there was any reason why he should. Theirs was a purely business arrangement. He had never given the least sign that he was attracted to her at all, and that, of course, was a great relief.

A short time later she heard a tap on the door. On being bidden to enter Falconbridge stepped into the room. For a moment they faced each other in silence; his practised eye took in every detail of her costume. He had no fault to find. The cut of the gown was fashionable and elegant. That shade of green really suited her, too, enhancing the colour of her eyes. For the rest she looked as neat as wax.

'I need to change,' he said. 'I beg you will forgive the intrusion.'

'Of course.'

He spoke to Willis, who had been waiting outside the door. The acting valet touched his forelock to Sabrina and then busied himself with a chest of clothes. Jacinta eyed both men with cold disapproval and then, with determined slowness, began collecting up her mistress's discarded garments.

Sabrina bit back a smile and, taking a book from her own travelling case, retired with it to the divan on the far side of the room. Aware of Falconbridge's presence to her very fingertips she kept her attention sedulously on the pages in front of her. Out of the corner of her eye she saw him peel off coat, waistcoat and linen, affording a view of a hard-muscled torso. Water splashed into the basin on the washstand. He bathed his face and hands and sluiced his neck. Willis handed him a towel and he dried himself vigorously. Once, he threw a glance her way but Sabrina's attention was apparently fixed on the book. Jacinta glared. He smiled faintly.

Then he turned and took the clean shirt offered him. Sabrina glanced up from beneath her lashes, caught a glimpse of a lean waist and narrow hips and very long legs, and looked away again. Spots of colour leapt into her face. Years spent in the wake of the army meant that she was no stranger to the sight of semi-dressed men, but this one possessed an almost sculptural beauty. Its effect was to make the room seem a lot warmer.

Unaware of the sensations he was creating, Falconbridge finished dressing. Sabrina surveyed him closely now, making no more pretence at reading. The dark coat might have been moulded to his shoulders. Waistcoat and linen were faultless. The cream-coloured breeches fitted like a second skin. She drew in a deep breath. Becoming aware of her regard he smiled faintly.

'I'm sorry to have kept you waiting.'

'Oh, no, I beg you will not regard it,' she replied. 'I have been quite entertained.'

Across the room Willis made a strange choking sound and received an icy stare from Jacinta. Falconbridge raised an eyebrow. Sabrina's cheeks went scarlet.

'With my book, I mean.'

'But of course,' he replied. 'What else?'

The innocent tone didn't deceive her for a moment. He was outrageous. Moreover, he was enjoying himself. She heard him dismiss the two servants. When they had gone, he took the volume from her hand and examined the cover.

'Lazarillo de Tormes. Does your father know?'

'Of course he knows. He lent—' She broke off, seeing the slow grin spread across his face. The gleam in the grey eyes was deeply disconcerting.

'Did he? Well, he really has attended to every part of his daughter's education.'

She wondered if he were shocked. It was, she admitted, a real possibility, for, while the concept of the picaresque novel was hardly new, this one could be read on different levels—particularly its numerous sexual metaphors.

'Do you disapprove?'

'Not at all.' He paused. 'Do you care?'

'No.' The word was out before she could stop it. She hurried on, 'I beg your pardon. I didn't mean to be rude.'

'You weren't—just beautifully frank.'

'Father always encouraged me to read widely.'

'So I gather.' He glanced again at the cover. 'And it is a wickedly good book, isn't it?'

'Oh, yes, very.'

'Wicked or good?'

His expression drew a reluctant laugh. 'Both, since you ask.'

'Good girl.'

Unsure how to take this, she eyed him quizzically. He laid the book aside and then gestured to the door.

'Shall we?'

Dinner that evening comprised local fare but it was well cooked. Sabrina was hungry, too, after their day on the road. The conversation was kept to general topics but she found her companion informed on a wide variety of subjects. It came as no surprise now. She was forced to acknowledge that none of the officers she had met in recent times had interested her half so much. He had told her something of his background but only the essentials. All in all, she thought, he volunteered very little about himself. It roused her curiosity.

'Tell me some more about your family,' she said. 'Your brother, for instance.'

The genial expression became more guarded. 'What about him?'

'You said you weren't close. May I ask why?'

His fingers tightened on the stem of his wine glass, but when he spoke his voice was perfectly level. 'We had a disagreement. It was some years ago.'

'And you've never been reconciled?'

'No.'

'How sad. What did you argue about?' The question had been innocent enough but the grey eyes hardened. Sabrina was mortified. 'Forgive me. I had no right to ask that.'

'It doesn't matter.' He paused as though inwardly

debating something. Then he said, 'It was over a woman, as it happened.'

'Ah, you both liked the same one.'

The accuracy of the observation startled him. In spite of himself he experienced a certain wry amusement. 'Yes. My brother won.'

'Was she very beautiful?'

'Very.'

'What happened?'

He swirled the remaining wine in his glass. 'She married Hugh.'

'Oh.' For a moment she was silent, uncomfortably aware of having strayed into dangerous territory. Yet having gone there, she found herself wanting to know more, to understand. 'That could not have been easy.'

He bit back a savage laugh. The understatement was huge, though she could not have known it. Did one ever truly recover from a blow like that? 'It was some years ago,' he replied, 'and one gets over disappointment. The incident belongs to the past and I am content to leave it there.'

It was a clear hint. They changed the subject after that, but the conversation had given Sabrina much to think about. For all his quiet assertion to the contrary it was evident that the lady had hurt him. Perhaps she hadn't meant to. She had clearly loved his brother more and one couldn't dictate to the human heart. Her gaze rested on the man opposite. Had his earlier experience made him wary? Was that why he had never married? It seemed increasingly likely. It was also a reaction she found quite understandable.

Falconbridge tossed back the rest of his wine and then got to his feet. 'We have another long day on the road tomorrow and it would be as well to get some rest.'

Sabrina rose, too, though rather more reluctantly, for the sleeping arrangements were etched on her consciousness. He stood back to let her precede him out of the door, and then accompanied her to the stairs. Then he paused.

'You go on ahead. I need to speak to Willis and Blakelock about arrangements for the morning.'

It was tactful and once again she was grateful. On returning to the room she found Jacinta waiting. With her help Sabrina undressed and donned her nightgown. Then she sat at the dresser while the maid unpinned her hair and brushed it out. In the looking glass Jacinta's dark eyes locked with hers.

'Do you wish me to remain here tonight?' she asked. 'As a chaperone?'

Sabrina smiled wryly. 'I assure you I am quite safe from Major Falconbridge.'

'Are you sure?'

'Why should you doubt it?'

'Because he is a man.'

'He did not create this situation. It was always possible that it would happen at some point.'

'Maybe so, but I have seen the way he looks at you when he thinks himself unobserved.'

Sabrina shook her head. 'You are mistaken. He has never shown the least regard for me, other than as a...a colleague.'

'He does not look at his other colleagues in that way.'

'I am sure there is not the least occasion for concern.'

'Best make certain. Put a pistol beneath your pillow.'

'I cannot afford to shoot the Major, Jacinta.'

'Very well, your knife then. The wound need not be mortal.'

Sabrina laughed. 'I have no intention of stabbing him either.'

'Please yourself.' The maid sniffed. 'But don't say I didn't warn you.'

She finished brushing Sabrina's hair and then, having watched her climb into bed, pulled the covers up to her chin and tucked them in tightly.

'Colonel Albermarle would not approve of this arrangement,' she told her charge severely.

'Colonel Albermarle isn't here,' replied Sabrina. 'Anyway, it's only for this one night.'

'That's what you think. I'll wager that in future there will be many inns with only one bedchamber.'

Sabrina gave an involuntary gurgle of laughter. 'And I suppose you also think that Major Falconbridge arranged it in advance, in order to have his wicked way with me.'

'Man is tinder, woman is flame and the devil is the wind. What man can resist temptation put in his way?'

'He will not be so tempted. There is too much at stake.'

'I hope you are right.'

With that sobering comment the maid departed. Retrieving Lazarillo de Tormes, Sabrina tried to occupy herself with the book but somehow it was difficult to concentrate. Jacinta's words lingered in her mind bringing with it an image of Falconbridge's lithe and powerful form. For all the maid's assertions to the contrary, Sabrina was fairly certain he wouldn't do anything foolish. Then, unaccountably, the memory of Jack Denton returned. She had trusted him, too. Involuntarily her gaze went to the trunk across the room where her pistols currently resided. Frowning, she laid aside the book and climbed out of bed.

Ten minutes later footsteps sounded outside and the door opened to admit her new room-mate. Her heart leapt. Now more than ever she was conscious of his sheer physical presence. It seemed to fill the room. He surveyed her in silence for a moment and then closed the door and locked it. She drew a deep breath.

'Everything is arranged for the morning,' he said then.

'Good.'

He crossed the room and peeled off his coat, tossing it over a chair. Sabrina feigned to study her book, comforted by the bulky mass of the pistol beneath her pillow. Under her covert gaze Falconbridge began to unfasten his neckcloth. Having done so, he pulled his shirt over his head. The sight of the powerful naked torso beneath did nothing to calm her racing heartbeat. Could she trust him? Irrationally she wondered how it would feel to be held in those strong arms. The idea was as shocking as it was unexpected. She had not considered him in that way before. She certainly could not afford to think of him in that way now. With a start she saw him cross the room and approach the bed. Her throat dried. She must have been mad to send Jacinta away, to get herself into this situation. Her free hand crept towards the pistol butt.

'May I trouble you for a spare pillow and a blanket?' he asked.

'Er, yes, of course.'

Having gathered the requisite items he retired to the divan and then glanced across at her.

'Do you want to read awhile longer or shall I blow out the candle?'

'Oh, no. I'm done.' She laid the book aside and snuggled down beneath the covers.

'Goodnight then, Sabrina.'

'Goodnight.'

He extinguished the candle and the room was plunged into gloom. She heard the divan creak beneath his weight and then the softer sound of the blanket settling around him. Her hand stole beneath the pillow and closed round the pistol butt. Its reassuring presence drew a faint smile. Then she closed her eyes, trying not to think about the man lying just feet away. It proved much harder than anticipated. She realised then that for the first time he had used her name. The familiarity should have annoyed her. It didn't. On the contrary, it had sounded a natural thing for him to do so.

For some time Falconbridge lay awake in the darkness, listening. Once or twice he heard her stir a little but then the room grew quiet. In the silence, thoughts came crowding fast. Chief among them was the semi-dressed figure in the big bed just across the room. Just for a moment he let his imagination go down that route. The response was a wave of heat in his loins as sudden as it was unexpected. He glanced across at the recumbent form and, biting back a mocking groan, turned over, mentally rejecting the temptation. For all manner of reasons she was forbidden fruit, and for both their sakes he must remember it.

When Sabrina woke the next morning it was with a sense of well-being. She stretched luxuriously, opening her eyes to the new day. The details of the room returned but a glance at the divan revealed it to be empty save for the blanket and pillow. A swift glance around the room revealed no sign of Major Falconbridge. She frowned and sat up, wondering what o'clock it might be. As yet the inn was quiet, which argued that it couldn't be too late. Throwing the covers aside she climbed out of bed and went to the window, opening it wide. The sun was just over the tops of the hills, streaking the heavens with gold and pink. All around the silent land stretched away until the rim of the hills met the sky. The quiet air smelled of wood smoke and baking bread from the kitchen.

She was so absorbed that she failed to hear the door open. Seeing the figure by the window Falconbridge paused, his breath catching in his throat. The rays of the sun turned her unbound hair to fiery gold. They also rendered her nightgown semi-transparent, outlining the curves beneath. He stood there awhile longer, unashamedly making the most of it. Then he smiled.

'Good morning.'

Sabrina spun round, heart missing a beat. Recovering herself she returned the greeting. 'You must have been up early.'

'About an hour ago.'

'You should have wakened me.'

'You looked so peaceful lying there that I didn't like to.'

The thought that he had watched her sleeping aroused a mixture of emotions, all of them disquieting. Quickly she changed the subject.

'Did you sleep well?'

'Well enough, I thank you.'

His gaze never left her, drinking in every detail from the tumbled curls to the small bare feet beneath the hem of her gown. Aided by the sunlight his imagination stripped it away and dwelt agreeably on what it found. The thoughts it engendered led to others, delightful and disturbing in equal measure. He tried to rein them in; for all sorts of reasons he couldn't afford to think of her in that way. On the other hand, it was damnably difficult not to just then.

Under that steady scrutiny Sabrina glanced down, suddenly conscious of her present state of undress and then, belatedly, the direction and power of the light. The implications hit her a second later. She darted a look at her companion but nothing could have been more innocent than the expression on that handsome face. It was enough to confirm every suspicion. The knowledge should have been mortifying but somehow it wasn't. The feeling it awoke was quite different. Striving for an appearance of casual ease she moved away from the window.

'I must dress.'

'Do you need any help?' he asked. Meeting a startled gaze he hid a smile and added, 'Would you like me to send for Jacinta?'

'Oh. Oh, yes, thank you.'

This time he did smile. 'She'll be along directly.' Then he strolled to the door. 'Breakfast will be ready when you are.'

When he had gone Sabrina let out the breath she had unconsciously been holding.

Chapter Four

During their journey that day they beguiled the time with cards. On this occasion it was piquet, a game which Sabrina enjoyed and at which she was particularly adept, as Falconbridge soon discovered.

'Is this the sign of a misspent youth?' he asked, having lost three times in succession.

'Misspent?' She smiled faintly. 'On the contrary, I had a very good teacher.'

'So I infer. Your father?'

'No, Captain Harcourt of the Light Dragoons.' Seeing his expression she hurried on, 'It was all quite respectable. He knew my father, you see, for they had had occasion to work together in Portugal and they became good friends.'

'A trusty mentor then.'

'Yes, he was.' It was quite true, as far as it went. Yet she knew she could never tell him exactly how much she owed Captain Harcourt. 'He said that knowledge of gaming was an essential aspect of any young woman's education.'

'Did he indeed?'

'Oh, yes, and he was right. His instruction has proved useful on several occasions.'

'Such as?'

'Such as the time in Lisbon, when Father and I were invited to supper and cards with the officers. One of them was a lieutenant whose honesty was highly suspect.'

'Ah, he was cheating.'

'Yes, marking cards. It took me a while to work out how he was doing it.'

'And then?'

'I played him at his own game. He lost fifty guineas that evening.' Her eyes sparkled with amusement. 'He wasn't best pleased.'

Falconbridge's lips twitched. 'I imagine he was not.'

'It served him right though.'

'Absolutely.'

Sabrina tilted her head a little and surveyed him keenly. 'Are you shocked?'

'By the revelation of a card sharp in the army? Hardly.'

'I mean by my telling you these things.'

'No, only a little surprised.'

'You think it not quite respectable?'

He smiled. 'On the contrary, I am fast coming to have the greatest respect for your skills.'

What she might have said in reply was never known, for suddenly the vehicle slowed and then men's voices were raised in challenge. The words were French. Falconbridge lowered the window and looked out.

'What is it?' she asked.

'A French patrol.'

She drew in a sharp breath. 'How many?'

'Ten—that I can see. There may be more.'

'Regulars?'

'We're about to find out.'

The carriage stopped and Sabrina heard approaching hooves and the jingle of harness. Moments later burnished cuirasses, blue jackets and high cavalry boots appeared in her line of vision. Their officer drew rein opposite the carriage window.

Falconbridge muttered an expletive under his breath. 'I think I know this man. Not his name, his face.'

Sabrina paled. 'Will he know you?'

'Let's hope not.' He glanced at his companion and murmured, 'Say as little as possible, Sabrina.'

Almost imperceptibly, she nodded. Then the French officer spoke.

'You will kindly step out of the carriage and identify yourself, Monsieur.'

With every appearance of ease Falconbridge opened the door and stepped down onto the roadway. The officer dismounted. Sabrina's hands clenched in her lap. She heard Falconbridge address the man in excellent French. On hearing his own language the officer's expression lightened visibly. For a moment or two his gaze met and held that of Falconbridge in a look that was distinctly quizzical. Then it was gone. He examined the papers that were passed to him and, apparently satisfied, handed them back.

'These are in order. You will forgive the intrusion, Monsieur le Comte.' He bowed. Then his glance went to the other passenger in the coach and lingered appreciatively. He bowed again. 'Madame.'

For the space of several heartbeats she felt the weight of that lupine stare. It stripped her and seemed to enjoy what it discovered for its owner bared his teeth in a smile. Annoyed and repelled together she lifted her chin and forced herself to meet his gaze. The rugged and moustachioed face suggested a man in his early forties, an impression reinforced by the grizzled brown hair that hung below the rim of his helmet.

'Colonel Claude Machart at your service,' he said then.

She inclined her head in token acknowledgement of the greeting while her mind dwelled regretfully on the pistols locked in her trunk.

'May I enquire whither you are bound, madame?' he continued.

'Aranjuez,' she replied.

'Aranjuez? That is some way off. May I ask your business there?'

Before she could reply Falconbridge cut in. 'A social gathering.' His tone conveyed ennui. 'One would rather not travel in these uncertain times, but on this occasion it cannot be avoided. Noblesse oblige, you understand.'

'Of course.' Machart smiled, an expression that did not reach his eyes. 'And you will be staying where?'

'At the house of Don Pedro de la Torre.'

'Then you must be attending the ball.'

Falconbridge evinced faint surprise. 'You are well informed, Colonel.'

'It is my business to be well informed, monsieur.'

'I'm sure it is.'

Machart threw him another penetrating look. 'Well, let me not detain you further. Madame, monsieur, I bid you good day and a pleasant journey.'

Falconbridge climbed back into the coach and regained his seat. As he did so the Colonel remounted and, having favoured the travellers with a nod, barked an order to his men and the patrol thundered away. Sabrina made herself relax.

'He didn't recognise you.'

'No, or we would be under arrest now.'

'Do you recall where you saw him before?'

'Yes, on the battlefield at Arroyo de Molinos last October. He was leading a detachment of cavalry.' He paused. 'My men engaged with them at close quarters. But it was many months ago and the scene chaotic. It is unlikely he would remember every face he saw that day.'

She knew the battle had resulted in a heavy defeat for the French. That would certainly have been held against them if Machart had remembered Falconbridge.

'He struck me as being an unpleasant character,' she said.

Her comment drew a faint smile. 'What makes you think so?'

'I've met enough military men to recognise the type. Let's hope we've seen the last of him.'

Falconbridge mentally echoed the sentiment. He had a good memory for faces and the ability to read those he met. For that reason he could only agree with her assessment.

Sabrina felt more than a little shaken by the incident, and suddenly Aranjuez did indeed begin to assume the quality of a lion's den. One false step would put them at the mercy of the French, of men like Machart. She shuddered inwardly, recalling what Falconbridge had told her earlier about the risks of capture and interrogation: Everyone talks by the third day. He had warned her but she had elected to come. There was no choice now but to see this through. Her father's freedom depended on it.

She was distracted from these thoughts by a strong hand closing on hers. Its clasp was reassuring, like its owner's smile. The effect was to create a sense of melting warmth deep inside her.

'Don't worry,' he said. 'Our stay in Aranjuez will be brief. Once the ball is over I shall have urgent business requiring my return.'

'That's good to hear.'

He gave her hand another gentle squeeze and then released his hold again, leaning back in his seat, surveying her quietly. The sensation of inner warmth intensified. She resisted it. He had meant only to be kind. It would be foolish to refine on something so trivial.

'I should not like to spend much more time in Colonel Machart's company.'

'No, though I believe he would not say the same of yours.'

'It means nothing. He's French so he can't help it.'

Falconbridge bit back the urge to laugh. 'How so?'

'All Frenchmen are demonstrative in that regard.'

'Are they?'

Sabrina saw the bait and refused to rise. 'So it is said.'

'And Englishmen are not demonstrative?'

'Not in the same way.'

His expression was wounded. 'What a body blow.'

'I never meant it to apply to you. I was speaking in general terms.'

'Based on your considerable experience, of course.'

'Certainly not. I never meant to suggest…' Too late she saw the expression in his eyes and knew he had been teasing her again. 'You knew that, you horror.'

'I beg your pardon.' The apology was belied by a smile. 'It was irresistible.'

Her chin came up at once. His smile widened. For a short space neither one spoke, though every fibre of her being was aware of the gaze fixed on her face. Even worse was the creeping blush she could feel rising from her neck to her cheeks.

'I wish you wouldn't look at me like that.'

'Forgive me. I was trying to be more...demonstrative.'

For a second or two she could only stare back but his smile was infectious and, unable to help it, she began to laugh.

'No you weren't. You were roasting me and enjoying it.'

The accusation left him unabashed. 'I can't deny it.'

'You are quite shameless.'

'So I've been told. I fear the habit is deeply ingrained now.'

'I am sure of it,' she retorted. 'However, I shall try not to be so easy a prey in future.'

His enjoyment increased. Better still, the apprehension he had glimpsed in her face after the encounter with Machart was gone, just as he had hoped.

'Good. I like a challenge.'

She shook her head. 'It's no use, sir. I shall not succumb. I'm wise to you now.'

'What a pity.' He sighed, eyeing her speculatively for a moment. Then, 'Now that you mention it, I think we should both be more demonstrative, don't you?' He watched the green eyes darken to emerald, their expression most attractively indignant, and waited in anticipation.

'Do you?' The tone was icy. 'And what put that thought in your mind?'

'Aranjuez. People must believe we are man and wife.'

Sabrina bit her lip. 'Oh, yes. I see.'

His expression registered concern. 'You did not think I meant anything else by it?'

'No, of course not.' Scarlet cheeks belied the words. Her heart was beating uncomfortably fast. 'I will do whatever is necessary to convince people.' She paused, eyeing him with less than perfect trust. 'What did you have in mind?'

'Oh, I don't know. The usual sort of thing: tender looks, melting smiles—a kiss or two.'

Her heart turned over. This was beyond all bounds. 'I will not kiss you, sir!'

Then she saw the familiar glint in his eye and knew he'd done it again. Furious with him and with herself she glared at him, only to see that he appeared to be choking. Her immediate response was alarm. Then she realised it was nothing of the sort; he was suppressing laughter. In reply she hurled the folded travelling rug at him.

They saw no more evidence of French troops that day, a fact for which Sabrina was devoutly thankful. However, the road became increasingly bumpy. The mud of winter had long since dried but it had left some deep ruts and although Luis did his best to avoid them, the vehicle lurched and swayed. It was well sprung but Sabrina knew she wouldn't be sorry to reach their destination that evening. It seemed that her companion's thoughts were moving along the same lines.

'Not far now,' he said.

'I'm glad to hear it. This is one of the worst stretches of road I've experienced in a long time.'

'One day someone is going to lay a good permanent surface,' he replied. 'I suspect that the last people to try were the Romans.'

She smiled. 'I'd guess no one has touched this road since then.'

'Maybe not even then.'

Before she could answer him the vehicle gave another violent lurch. Sabrina was thrown sideways, unable to save herself. She gasped as her head hit the side of the carriage. The blow was cushioned by upholstery but the impact jarred nevertheless. Then she realised they were no longer moving and that the coach was leaning at a drunken angle. Outside she could hear voices swearing in Spanish. Then a strong arm drew her upright and she was pressed against her companion. Her cheek brushed his coat. The cloth smelled faintly of spice—cedar or sandalwood perhaps. Underneath it was the scent of the man, sensual and disturbing.

'Are you all right, Sabrina?'

'Yes, I think so.'

Subjected to close scrutiny she felt the familiar warmth rising into her face. He was so close that if he bent his head their lips would touch. Almost immediately she recalled their earlier conversation and his teasing, and felt ashamed. Of course he wouldn't kiss her. The husband-and-wife act was precisely that, and anyway there was no one nearby who needed convincing. Just then the door opened and Ramon's face appeared.

'Are you hurt, *Doña* Sabrina? *Señor?*'

On hearing them answer in the negative he looked relieved.

Falconbridge straightened. 'What the devil happened?'

'A deep rut, *señor.*'

'Confound it.'

Sabrina watched him reach for the edge of the door and climb out of the vehicle. Then he turned and leaned in, holding out a hand to her. She felt the strong clasp tighten. Then it swung her up and out of the interior with what appeared to be a minimum of effort. A hard-muscled arm lifted her down beside him. It remained casually round her waist while he surveyed the damage to the coach. The offside rear wheel was sunk deep in the road surface. Behind them the chaise had also come to a halt and, leaving Jacinta in charge of the horses, his men hastened forwards to help.

'Is anyone hurt, sir?' asked Blakelock.

'Fortunately not,' Falconbridge replied. 'It's just a delay we could have done without.'

'The next town is not far off, sir.'

'Just as well. It's going to take some time to right the coach.' He glanced round. 'Luis, take charge of the horses. Ramon, give the rest of us a hand here.'

Ramon nodded. '*Si, señor.*'

Falconbridge peeled off his coat and handed it to Sabrina with a wry smile. 'Would you oblige me, ma'am?'

'Of course.' As she took the garment his hand brushed hers. The casual touch sent a shock along her skin. She tried not to stare at the lithe form revealed to such advantage by the shirt and close-fitting breeches.

Unaware of the sensations he was creating, he rolled up his sleeves. Then he turned to the others.

'All right, lads, let's get this vehicle out of here.'

Sabrina looked on, feeling unusually helpless but knowing there was nothing she could do to assist in this instance. Only sheer physical strength was going to solve the problem. Falconbridge clearly had no qualms about involving himself in the work either; she guessed that was in part why he had the respect of his men. On their first meeting he had been delivering food supplies for their benefit. She had been angry with him at the time but, seeing the situation more objectively now, decided he probably couldn't have done anything else. Of course he would put the welfare of hungry men first. The decision had inconvenienced her but it hadn't left her at risk and he knew that when he made it. She had thought him ruthless then, but now was less certain. She would have liked to learn more about his military career. It was a side to him that she knew little about and suddenly she was curious.

In the event, it took the combined efforts of all the men and the sweating horses to free the coach. Had the road been wet and muddy they might not have succeeded. As it was they were all perspiring freely by the time they had done. However, relief was short-lived. Ramon, examining the righted vehicle, shook his head.

'The accident has damaged the axle, *señor.*'

Falconbridge frowned. 'Badly?'

'See for yourself.'

He pointed to the crack in the shaft. Falconbridge saw it and gritted his teeth.

'It'll get us into town, but no farther.'

'At least the final stretch of road looks a little better,' said Ramon. 'Relatively speaking that is.'

Falconbridge nodded. 'Once we reach town I'll seek out the wheelwright.'

Sabrina heard him with a wry smile. It seemed that history was repeating itself.

Progress was slow, but they reached town with no further problems and while Falconbridge organised the

necessary repairs, Sabrina obtained rooms and a bath at
the inn. Jacinta laid out fresh clothes and then took herself off to brush out the dusty travelling dress. Sabrina
shed her hot garments and slid into the tub with a little
sigh of pleasure. It had been days since she'd had the
luxury of bathing properly. Making do was all very well,
up to a point. Years of travel had made her quite resilient
but the woman in her still enjoyed a certain amount of
pampering. Of late it had been hard to come by. It was
a delight to soap herself all over and wash away all the
perspiration and grime of the journey. It was a delight
to wear pretty dresses more often, too, or rather to have
a reason to wear them. That reason wasn't just confined
to present circumstances, as she now admitted. She bit
her lip. It would take more than a pretty frock to attract
Robert Falconbridge. Sometimes she thought he didn't
object to her company, once or twice that he found her
person pleasing, but never more than that. His heart
was his own. They might have been thrown together
for the duration of this mission, but his interest in her
went no further. Not that she wanted it to, of course.
Once bitten… It occurred to her that he, too, had known
disappointment. That was painful enough without the
added humiliation of seeing the woman he loved marry
his brother.

A door opened and she glanced across the room,
assuming Jacinta had returned. However, the outer one
remained firmly closed. Instinctively she darted a swift
look at the connecting door that led to the adjoining
bedchamber. It was open and Falconbridge stood on
the threshold. Then, taking in the scene before him, he
stopped in his tracks. Sabrina's cheeks flamed scarlet
and instinctively she crossed her arms over her breasts,
aware that her heart was thumping uncomfortably hard.

Her startled thoughts went off in a dozen directions at once, the ramifications of which sent an unexpected flood of heat through her which had nothing to do with the temperature of the bath water.

'What are you doing here? How dare you burst in like this?'

For the first time since she had met him he seemed at a loss. 'I…er…forgive me. I didn't mean to startle you. I didn't realise you would be bathing.'

'But I am, sir.'

'Yes.' He knew it sounded inane but his tongue seemed temporarily to have lost contact with his brain. His legs had, too, rooting him to the spot.

'Well?' She held the lid down on indignation. 'Was there something you wanted to say?'

He cleared his throat. 'Only to let you know that repairs are underway on the coach.'

'That's good to hear.'

'With any luck we should be able to leave tomorrow morning, albeit a little later than usual.'

She nodded, supremely conscious of having the undivided attention of that steady gaze. It was both contemplative and appraising, taking in every detail. As it did so its habitual coolness was replaced by keen appreciation and a warmer light kindled in those grey depths. Her heart thumped harder. She needed to bring this interview to a close and soon.

'Thank you for letting me know.'

It should have signalled dismissal but still he made no move to go. Did he intend to stand there all day? Along with indignation her inner demon awoke.

'I take it there were no problems then?'

He seemed to recollect himself. 'None at all. Why, did you think there would be?'

'I couldn't help wondering if someone else might have had a prior claim on the wheelwright's services.'

'Such as?'

'An army officer perhaps?'

Amusement filled his grey eyes. 'I suppose I deserved that.'

'Well, yes.'

'On that note, ma'am, I had better leave you to finish your bath in peace.'

'I'd be grateful, sir.'

The sweet smile didn't deceive him for a moment. It was also unwittingly provocative. For a moment more he indulged the fantasy of showing her just how provocative, before self-control reasserted itself. He sighed and, with a last backwards look, took himself off.

As the door shut behind him she leaned back and breathed a sigh of relief. It wasn't that she suspected him of anything untoward—his surprise on finding her thus had been genuine enough—but rather that his presence aroused untoward feelings in her. Feelings she could not afford to indulge. She had never met anyone quite like him; he was somehow larger than life. It was difficult enough being thrown together with a total stranger but when the stranger was Robert Falconbridge it lent an added dimension to the whole situation.

The sound of another door opening caused her to start, but this time it was Jacinta. For the second time Sabrina let out a sigh of relief. The water in the tub was growing cool now so she climbed out and wrapped herself in a linen towel. If the maid noticed her preoccupied air she made no comment on the matter and busied herself with hanging up the newly brushed travelling dress. Sabrina bit back a smile, thinking it was as well her companion had not returned earlier. Goodness only knew what construction she would have put on Falconbridge's presence. Possibly she might have shot him herself.

The subject of her thoughts had bespoken a bath for himself and lost no time in stripping off and sinking into the tub. He scrubbed himself vigorously, mentally rebuking himself for what had just passed. Not that he had had any idea of what he would find when he opened the door to her room. He knew he should have left right away but at the time his wits had deserted him. His behaviour had been reprehensible and he knew it, but for the life of him he couldn't regret it. The memory would remain with him for a long time. He had discovered early that Sabrina's image was not easy to banish at any time but particularly not when seen unclothed. One look at her bare shoulders and the swelling breasts partially revealed by the soapy water and all his good intentions had gone up in smoke. The knowledge was disturbing, as was the depth of his desire. Every part of him had wanted her, wanted to lift her from the bath and carry her to the bed and possess her completely.

Once again he reined in his imagination hard. They had a task ahead of them and that should be the focus of his attention. A lapse of concentration might spell disaster for them both. The consequences of being caught meant death, and he had no wish to see Sabrina led before a firing squad or delivered up to the hangman. She was his responsibility in every way. He had promised Albermarle that he would protect her; a promise he intended to keep. He sighed. She would be a test of any man's self-control but he must resist the temptation she represented. The trouble was he hadn't expected to feel like this again. After Clarissa he had believed himself immune. It was a shock to discover he had been wrong. Even so, only a fool would allow himself to fall again, and especially for a woman he hardly knew.

The following morning Sabrina rose early and went out, wanting a little time and space on her own. After what had passed between them the previous day she didn't feel equal to being shut up in a carriage with Falconbridge again until she had cleared her head. Perhaps some sketching might help to restore a degree of perspective in every sense of the word. Accordingly, she took her pad and, having informed Jacinta of her intention to visit the local shrine, the two of them set out.

A little later Falconbridge went down to the breakfast room. As Sabrina had not made an appearance yet he assumed she was still in her room. In the meantime he sent Luis round to the wheelwright's yard to check on the repair work. Within a quarter of an hour he was back. Hearing his footstep Falconbridge turned away from the window.

'Well? How are things progressing? I want to be gone from here before noon.'

'I regret that may not be possible.'

'What?'

'I went to speak with the man but he was not there.'

'Not there? Then where the hell is he?'

'It seems he was called away to a neighbouring village some five miles distant in order to mend a cartwheel for the cousin of his brother-in-law's aunt. However, he will be back this afternoon, according to his wife.'

'Back by noon!' Falconbridge's expression grew thunderous. 'The rogue promised that he would have the wheel fixed by then.'

'That is so, *señor*. However, I fear it will not be possible now.'

'Confound it, I cannot afford the delay.'

'I think it cannot be avoided.'

'We'll see about that. He cannot have taken the entire workforce with him. There must be a competent apprentice who can complete the job.'

'It is possible, I suppose.'

'Go and find out.' Then as Luis turned to leave, 'No wait. I'll come with you. Two voices may be more persuasive than one.'

He had reached the outer door before he realised that Sabrina had not yet come down. Being keen to sort out the immediate problem he left a message for her with the *patrón*. Then he and Luis set off.

The outcome of their excursion did nothing to improve his mood. Having gone to the wheelwright's premises and spoken to the man's wife, it transpired that there was only one apprentice, the son, who had gone off with his father. She assured him they would be back by noon. Having a sound understanding of the local concept of time, Falconbridge had not the least expectation of seeing the man or his son before the late afternoon. Frustration mounted, and with it, annoyance.

This was not helped when he got back to the inn and found that Sabrina was not there. He checked her room and then all the other rooms where she might conceivably be, only to draw a blank. Then he sent for the *patrón*.

'The Condesa has gone out, *señor*.'

'Gone out where?' he demanded.

'I do not know, *señor*. The lady did not honour me with her confidence.'

'Did she take her maid with her?'

The *patrón* nodded. 'She did indeed, *señor.*'

When this elicited an expression of unmistakable ire, the man added quickly, 'I will send a boy to seek for them at once. The village is not large. I am sure they will be found very soon.'

Falconbridge bit back the savage comment that would otherwise have escaped his lips. 'Never mind. I will look for the Condesa myself. If she returns in the meantime, ask her to wait for me here.'

'Certainly, *señor.*'

Gritting his teeth Falconbridge went out into the street again, looking left and right in the hope that he might see Sabrina before she had gone too far. Not that there was far to go; as the *patrón* had said, it wasn't a big place.

The end of the street brought him to a small plaza where some of the local women were fetching water from the pump. He could see no sign of Sabrina or her maid. A swift look into the few small shops proved no help either. Then at last he spied Jacinta emerging from a building across the street. He lost no time in accosting her.

'What are you doing here? Where is your mistress?'

'I came to buy fruit, *señor.*' If she had noticed his expression, her own gave no sign of it. '*Doña* Sabrina said that she wished to take the air and do some sketching.'

'Oh, did she? And you let her go off alone?'

'*Doña* Sabrina goes where she wills.'

His jaw tightened. 'Not on this trip she doesn't. Where is she?'

She nodded towards the street leading out of the plaza. 'Visiting the shrine of San Ignacio. It is not far.'

'She had no business leaving the inn and nor do you. Go back there at once.'

The tone was peremptory. Jacinta's dark eyes flashed but they swiftly veiled. 'As you wish, *señor.*'

He watched her walk away and then set off in the direction she had indicated. People glanced up as he passed but, on seeing his expression, hurried out of his way. He barely noticed their presence. All his thoughts were turned inward, focused first on finding Sabrina and then what he was going to say when he did.

In fact Jacinta had spoken the truth. The shrine was not far, and set by the edge of the road. It was little more than a stone niche containing a picture of the saint and some fresh flowers. However, Sabrina wasn't there. Falconbridge swore softly and looked swiftly about, casting in every direction. Then at last he saw her, sitting on a stone in the shade of a tree not fifty yards away. Since her attention was on the sketch pad on her lap she did not notice his arrival until his shadow fell across it.

He heard the sharp intake of breath as she looked up and saw him, and then saw her relax as she recognised him.

'Good morning. It's a fine day, is it not?' Then, as she became aware of his expression, 'Is something wrong, Major?'

'Yes, there's something wrong. What the devil do you think you're doing?'

'I beg your pardon?'

'You heard me. What are you doing here?'

The tone caused the green eyes to widen a little. 'I am sketching.'

'Don't you know better than to wander off on your own like that without even your maid in attendance?'

'Oh, Jacinta went to buy some fruit. She is not far.'

'She has returned to the inn,' he replied, 'on my instruction. I'd be much obliged if you would do the same.'

'But I do not wish to return just yet.'

'I am not offering a choice as to whether you go or not, merely the means by which you might get there.'

'I don't understand.'

'Plainly then: you may walk back or you may be carried.'

The tone had been perfectly even but it also bore a distinct shade of menace. More than anything at that moment she wanted to call his bluff, but somehow didn't quite dare.

'I will walk back, sir.'

'I thought you might.'

Sabrina gathered her things and rose to face him. 'Why are you so angry?'

'Because I am responsible for your safety. Don't you know how dangerous it is for you to be out here alone, you little fool? These hills are crawling with bandits, to say nothing of the odd French patrol.'

For the first time she felt a small twinge of guilt. 'I did not think there could be any danger so near to the village.'

'There is danger everywhere now and you would do well to remember it.' He took her arm in a firm grip and led her back towards the roadway. 'There are enough problems ahead of us without you adding to them.'

Sabrina bit her lip. 'I'm sorry. I did not mean to cause you any anxiety.'

The tone was contrite, like the accompanying look,

and his anger began to cool a little. As it did he acknowledged the first stirrings of remorse. He let go of her arm and sighed.

'I am a brute, am I not?'

She shot him a swift sideways glance. 'How truthful would you like me to be?'

His lips twitched. 'Wretched girl. You deserve that I should carry you back to the inn.'

'You really would have done that, wouldn't you?'

'Yes, and enjoyed it what's more.'

His words had the ring of perfect sincerity. However, the cold anger so conspicuous before was missing now.

'I promise I won't do it again. Go off without telling you, I mean.'

'See that you don't.'

They walked on a little way in silence. Then another thought struck her.

'Were you looking for me to tell me that the carriage is mended?'

'No, I was looking for you to tell you it is not.'

'Not?'

He explained what had happened earlier at the wheelwright's yard. As she listened she heard his unspoken frustration and understood.

'And after you had found out our journey was to be delayed, I must needs wander off so thoughtlessly.' She put a hand on his sleeve. 'Can you forgive me?'

He looked down at her in surprise but there was no mistaking the real remorse he saw in her face. And seeing it he was ashamed of his bad temper.

'In truth I should not have taken it out on you,' he said.

'You had good reason to be angry.'

He shook his head. 'Not with you. It was just anxiety when I could not find you.'

'It won't happen again.' Then, as the implications dawned, she added, 'What are we going to do now?'

'Wait till that rascally fellow returns. There's not much else we can do.'

For a wonder the wheelwright did return shortly after midday, and repairs commenced on the carriage. Ramon and Luis remained to oversee the work. It was slow and thorough but it became clear that the vehicle would not be ready until the late afternoon. At that point there would be only another four hours of daylight left.

Falconbridge sighed. 'It can't be helped. We'll use what time we have and find somewhere to stop before it goes dark.'

Blakelock nodded. 'Yes, sir.'

'It's a good thing you've got someone standing over that wheelwright, sir,' said Willis. 'He was only going to stop for a siesta.'

'What!'

'True enough, sir,' said Blakelock. 'Only then Ramon had a word and persuaded him not to. Feller didn't like it above half, but money's a powerful inducement.'

Falconbridge glared. 'So is my boot.'

'Ramon said the same, sir. Hurried things along no end.'

It was approaching four when they eventually did set off again. With only a few hours of daylight remaining Falconbridge was keen to try and make up lost ground. Fortunately the road surface was better and they were able to make reasonable speed.

'Will the delay be totally disastrous?' asked Sabrina then.

'I hope not.' Seeing her anxious expression her companion smiled. 'No, my dear, provided there are no more we should reach our destination in time.'

'I am relieved to hear it.'

'I think we must be due for some better luck.'

She nodded, truly aware now of a sense of urgency. Recent events had shaken away any feeling of complacency: so much hung on this journey. Thinking of her behaviour earlier that day she was quietly mortified. She must have seemed like an empty-headed little fool. He had been justifiably angry. No doubt in his place she would have felt the same. She was privately resolved that he should have no further cause to criticise her actions; that she would strive in every way to be the companion he needed. It came to her then that his good opinion mattered where only a few days ago it would not have. Just why that should be or how it had come about she could not have said.

Chapter Five

In fact their journey continued without further mishap or incident and, although they were half a day later than anticipated, they came at length to the house of Don Pedro de la Torre on the outskirts of Aranjuez. Barely a mile from the royal palace and standing in its own extensive grounds, it was an imposing stone building that testified to the wealth and importance of its owner. On their arrival, liveried footmen hastened forwards to open the carriage door and let down the steps. Falconbridge descended first and then extended a hand to Sabrina, a firm, reassuring grip accompanied by a smile that warmed her more thoroughly than the sunshine. Together they walked to the open doorway and into a marbled hall where their hosts awaited them.

Don Pedro was a tall, upright figure whose grey hair and beard lent him a distinguished appearance. Sabrina guessed him to be in his early fifties. His wife, *Doña* Elena, was ten years younger, a handsome woman with dark hair and eyes and an elegant figure. They greeted their guests with great courtesy and, over refreshments, enquired after their journey.

'Did you meet with any French patrols?' asked their host.

'Only one,' replied Falconbridge.

Don Pedro lifted an eyebrow. 'Then you were fortunate.'

'My thought exactly.'

'The French are everywhere. It is almost impossible to travel without encountering a patrol or a road block.'

'Fortunately we didn't encounter any difficulties.'

'Long may it continue,' replied Don Pedro. 'Apart from the French there are many renegades who take advantage of the situation to prey on travellers. I am glad you did not meet any.'

'So am I.' Falconbridge smiled. 'It is good to have arrived.'

'It is good of you to come. We are most happy to welcome you here and, of course, your beautiful wife.' Don Pedro smiled at Sabrina for a moment. She returned it, conscious of the role she was expected to play. Even so it sounded strange to hear herself referred to in that way. Just for a second she indulged the fancy. What if Falconbridge were her husband? It came as a shock to discover that the thought was not totally unwelcome.

Don Pedro threw Falconbridge a meaningful look. 'Later, when you have rested, we shall talk.'

They had been allocated a spacious apartment, beautifully furnished, with an adjoining dressing room and a balcony that overlooked the gardens to the rear. For the space of a few heartbeats they surveyed it in silence. There was, Sabrina saw, only one bed, albeit very large, but mercifully two couches as well. If need be she would appropriate one for her use. The pretence at marriage only went so far: she could not share a bed with her companion. The notion sent a frisson down her spine that had nothing to do with fear. She pulled herself up abruptly. Such a thought should never even have entered her mind yet the memory of the mishap with the coach was vivid, especially the part where Falconbridge had held her in his arms. How would it be to lie in his arms, to lie in his bed? The notion set her pulse racing. All the disgust she had experienced before was absent now, and she knew instinctively that he would treat a woman with gentleness. He was not like Denton. Falconbridge had a wicked sense of humour but he hadn't taken advantage of her. If he made any overtures to her it would only be by invitation. If she were foolish enough to do that she would lose what respect he had for her, a thought she didn't want to entertain. Aware of him now to the last fibre of her being she drew in a deep breath. Then she went to the French windows that led onto the balcony and opened them, looking out with a gasp of genuine delight.

'How beautiful!'

The garden was laid out in terraces connected by sweeping steps and a series of fountained pools that led the eye away towards a high wall where bougainvillea grew in vivid bursts of pink and magenta and purple. On either hand flowering beds lined the pathways and beyond those, to right and left, stern lines of cypress were relieved by fruit trees and blossoming shrubs.

'It's very fine, isn't it?' he said.

He was standing just behind her, his shoulder brushing hers, so close she could detect the faint scent of sandalwood from his clothing. She glanced up for a moment and then returned her attention to the view, hoping no part of her inner turmoil showed.

'A truly romantic place,' she said. 'All it lacks is moonlight.'

He smiled faintly. 'Perhaps nature will oblige while we are here. The moon is near to the full.'

'I hope so.'

'You are fond of gardens?'

'Yes, aren't you?'

'When they're like this one and there is the possibility of a moonlit stroll,' he replied. The tone was ambiguous.

She turned to look at him then, suspecting that he was teasing. However, his expression revealed no such indication. On the contrary, the grey eyes that searched hers were entirely serious. Before she could ponder the matter, he took her shoulders in a gentle clasp.

'Now we step into our new roles in earnest. Are you ready?'

'As ready as I'll ever be,' she replied, trying not to think about his closeness or the warmth of his hands through her clothing.

'Every second of our stay we are the Conde and Condesa de Ordoñez y Casal. Marianne and Antonio. Don't forget it.'

'I won't forget.'

'Good girl.' He paused. 'Joking apart, some show of affection between us will not go amiss.'

Even as he spoke she knew that, on her part at least, it would be no mere show. Just how that change had come about she couldn't have said, but something in her had altered, and on a fundamental level. With a calmness she was far from feeling she met his gaze. 'Tender looks and melting smiles, was it not?' She did not complete the original sentence.

The grey eyes gleamed. 'If you feel equal to it.'

'I shall play my part, sir.'

'I am sure you will.'

For a moment they faced each other in silence. He knew that she had meant the words and they cost him an unexpected pang. Close companionship and cooperation were essential to their mission, but he knew in that instant that he would have liked more than this necessary pretence. It wasn't just about physical attraction either, though he acknowledged it was strong. Combined with wit and intelligence it was a heady combination. Her company was more than congenial to him. With her he experienced emotions that he hadn't expected to feel again. He also knew he couldn't go there. It would be foolish and wrong. Too much was at stake for both of them. He relinquished his hold on her shoulders.

'No doubt you would like to rest awhile,' he said.

She nodded. 'It would also be good to get out of these clothes.'

'In that case I shall repair to the dressing room and leave the field to you.'

A knock at the door announced the arrival of Willis and Blakelock with the trunks. It was a welcome diversion. While they carried Falconbridge's boxes into the dressing room, Jacinta saw to the ordering of hot water and linen towels. When eventually the other servants had gone and the dressing room door was securely closed, she bustled about laying out a change of clothes for her mistress. As she did so she cast a comprehensive and disapproving look around.

'Only one bed,' she observed.

'Yes.'

'Your reputation…'

'Will be quite safe. I'll sleep on the couch over there.'

'All the same, he should marry you after this.'

'Nothing is more unlikely.'

'Would you refuse if he asked you?'

Sabrina drew in a deep breath. 'He's not going to ask me. This is a business arrangement, nothing more.'

'When a man looks at a woman in that way it is because he is thinking of a great deal more, believe me.'

'Enough, Jacinta.' The words came out with more force than she had intended and she was immediately ashamed. It was unlike her to get so rattled. 'I'm sorry. It's just tension speaking. I'll be myself again when we get out of here.'

Her companion lifted an eyebrow. 'Will you?'

'Of course. Why would I not?'

The maid clearly took it for a rhetorical question, because she made no reply. Sabrina busied herself with removing her travelling dress. In truth she was glad of the distraction for Jacinta's words had left their mark. What if Robert Falconbridge were to ask her? She gave herself a mental shaking. It was no use to think that way; theirs was just a business arrangement and she must remember it. Had she learned nothing from the past? She had been thrown together with a man who was handsome and charismatic. Although she didn't think Falconbridge was in any way like that other, if she allowed herself to fall for him it could only result in heartache.

Having removed her outer garments she bathed her hands and face. It was a delight to be rid of the dust of travel. Then she sat while the maid unpinned and brushed her hair before rearranging it into a becoming style, dressing it high so that it fell over Sabrina's shoulders in a profusion of curls. When it was done she donned the yellow gown that had been laid out for her. It suited her colouring and brought out the warm tones of her skin. The low neckline plunged into a tempting décolletage. A gold necklace and earrings completed the outfit. Looking into the mirror she surveyed her reflection in thoughtful silence.

Falconbridge emerged some time later clad in pale breeches, flawless linen and a lovat coat so expertly cut that it might have been moulded to his form. He looked across the room and opened his mouth to speak but the words dried on his lips. For a moment or two he could only stare, but his critical eye found nothing lacking. She looked every inch the golden girl. For a moment he let his gaze strip away the fabric of her gown and dwell on what lay beneath. He was aware, too, of the bed just a few feet away. In his imagination he laid her down there and made passionate love to her and tasted her passion in return. Recalling himself abruptly, he made her an elegant bow.

'If you are ready my dear, we will go down.'

She smiled. 'Quite ready.'

He offered his arm and felt the light pressure of her hand on his sleeve. It felt natural and right, as though it belonged there.

Dinner that night was a lavish meal with a dozen guests at table. The conversation flowed easily on a variety of topics. Sabrina kept up her part, occasionally glancing across the table at Falconbridge. Once, he met her eye and smiled, but otherwise seemed engrossed in what his companion was saying. She noticed that hers were not the only eyes to turn his way. Several of the ladies present evidently found him attractive, too. He stepped easily into his part, she thought, adopting the aristocratic manners that came so naturally to him. No one would question his identity. With his dark good looks, arrogant bearing and impeccable Spanish he might indeed have been the hidalgo he presented.

'Do you stay long in Aranjuez, Condesa?'

Sabrina turned to her companion, an ageing and portly gentleman who had been introduced as Señor Jorge Gonzalez, who had some government role in the capital.

'I regret not,' she replied.

'What a pity.'

'My husband does not like to be long away from home.'

'Well, in these times it is understandable. No doubt he prefers to live quietly and manage his estates.'

'Yes, indeed.'

'And you, Condesa, do you not hanker after the bright lights of the city?'

'The social whirl of Madrid holds few charms for me, *señor,*' she said. It was true as far as it went.

He snorted. 'It holds few charms for anyone since the usurper Joseph took the throne.'

'Can he hold it, do you think?'

'Not if the Spanish people have their way. He'll be sent packing and the sooner the better.'

Don Pedro glanced across the table. 'Our alliance with the English will put paid to Bonaparte's ambitions in our country.'

'The way things are going, his upstart family will soon govern most of Europe,' replied Gonzalez.

Murmurs of agreement greeted this. Sabrina looked

across at Falconbridge and met his eye again. His
expression was enigmatic. He had not taken a leading
role in the discussion that evening, seeming content to
listen for the most part. Given his guise as Ordoñez,
it was understandable. However, she knew he missed
nothing.

'The French will not long hold Spain,' said Don
Pedro. 'Already the guerrilla tactics of the partisan
forces are telling.'

Gonzalez nodded. 'Men like El Cuchillo, you mean.'

'Exactly,' his host replied. 'Hit the French and then
run. It's an effective strategy. All the same, there will
be more battles before the enemy is driven from our
soil.'

As she listened, Sabrina thought of the plans she and
her companion had come to collect and hoped that they
would provide the key to allied military success. So far
as she knew no private conference had yet taken place
between Falconbridge and their host, but it would soon
enough. Once he had the plans their real task would
begin. In the meantime, there was the ball. Part of her
was looking forward to it; in her life such events were
rare and thus the more valued, but it carried a strong
element of risk. If anyone present actually knew the
real Conde de Ordoñez. She shivered inwardly. The
penalties for spying were severe. It was a chance one
took. She had always known that.

Later, when the ladies withdrew to the drawing room,
the conversation took a different direction and Sabrina
was content to listen. Once someone asked about her
putative son, Miguel, and she made what she hoped was
a convincing reply. It occurred to her then for the first
time that it might be pleasant to have children of her

own one day. Nothing could have been further removed from the life she had been living hitherto, and yet the idea did not displease her. Of course, it would have to be with the right man. Falconbridge's face imposed itself on her memory. In one of their earlier conversations he had told her he liked children. She thought he would make a good father. That was a foolish notion of course, given what she knew of his past. Besides, he had no interest in her beyond the completion of a duty. He had told her he was married to his career. Knowing that, she was unaccountably saddened.

The gathering broke up just after eleven. Everyone knew that the following night would be a late one, for the ball would go on into the early hours, and had decided to be well rested for the event. Sabrina could see the point. In any case, the journey had been tiring and the thought of a good night's sleep was not unwelcome. Then she remembered that tonight she and Falconbridge would be sharing a room again. No one else would think anything of it. After all, were they not supposed to be man and wife? The thought sent a frisson along her skin. She had to trust him.

As she had told Jacinta not to wait up, the room was empty when she returned. Falconbridge had lingered to speak to Don Pedro and she had no idea how long he would remain. Taking advantage of his absence, she undressed and donned her nightgown before sitting down at the dressing table to unpin her hair. She was thus engaged when the door opened to admit him. For a moment he was still, looking on, before closing the door and coming farther into the room. Sabrina forced unsteady hands to continue with their task. In the glass she saw him remove his coat and slowly unfasten his neckcloth. His gaze never left her.

He heard the pins drop into the glass dish on the dressing table and watched her shake her hair loose. It fell over her shoulders in a riot of soft curls. She reached for a brush. Beneath the gentle strokes the wilful gold mass shone in the candlelight. He wanted to reach out and touch it, to run his fingers through it. Conquering the urge he tossed his coat over a chair. The neckcloth followed. He pulled off his shirt and sat down to remove his boots. Having done so, he rose and crossed the intervening space to the bed and retrieved the top cover and a pillow before retiring with them to the nearest couch.

Sabrina's hands paused at their task. 'It's my turn to sleep on the couch.'

He turned, regarding her with a raised eyebrow. 'I think not.'

'Truly, I don't mind.'

'Maybe not, but I do.'

'I should not think the worse of you.'

He smiled faintly. 'No, I believe you would not. Even so, I shall sleep here.'

The tone, though quiet, was implacable. Sabrina had come to recognise it, and also the futility of argument.

'As you will.' She paused. 'Thank you.'

'My pleasure, ma'am.'

'I doubt that somehow, but I appreciate the gesture.'

She laid aside the brush. The mirror showed him the soft swell of her breast beneath the low neckline of her nightdress. The filmy material revealed every line and curve of her body. Almost at once he felt the answering heat in his loins. He wanted her and at the same time knew beyond doubt that to follow his inclination would offend every notion of honour. She was under his protection, and to take advantage of this highly desirable situation would be to violate all trust between them. The only reason she was here was to obtain her father's freedom. She had no interest in anything else.

Drawing a deep breath he watched her cross to the bed and climb in, settling herself beneath the covers. She had shown no fear, he thought, but he guessed at some of the thoughts in her mind. He could not destroy the relationship they had built up over the past days by one ill-judged and lustful act. She deserved better from him.

Sabrina lay still as he blew out the candle and returned to his makeshift bed. Then he finished undressing and climbed in. She closed her eyes, every sense attuned to him, heart thumping in her breast. Once he had spoken about intimacy, of the need to play a part. It had occurred to her then to wonder if he would use that to take advantage and insist she play her part to the full. She knew better now. The thought of sharing Falconbridge's bed should have filled her with horror, but that was not the emotion uppermost in her mind. Horror did not cause the melting warmth at the core of her pelvis, or the sensation of painful longing in her heart. After Jack Denton's betrayal she had thought never to feel desire for a man again. Yet somehow, with no apparent effort, Robert Falconbridge had broken through her guard. It had happened so gradually that she had barely been aware of it. She could no longer deny that she was attracted to him, but it was an attraction that she didn't dare pursue.

Her companion shut his eyes, trying not to dwell on the semi-clad form just feet away from him. With a wry smile he turned his head and quietly bade her goodnight. He heard her reply in kind, and then the faint rustle of bedclothes as she turned onto her side. It was a long time before sleep claimed him.

The following morning Don Pedro solicited a private talk with his guest. For that purpose he had chosen the library. It was quiet and allowed of no possibility that the conversation might be overheard.

'You took a risk coming to Aranjuez, *señor*,' he said, 'but there was no other way of solving the problem.'

'I understand.' Falconbridge paused, eyeing his host keenly. 'But you also took a great risk.'

'In the service of my country.'

'Even so.'

'The alternative is to let the usurper, Joseph, keep the throne he has stolen.' Don Pedro's lip curled in quiet contempt. 'My post brings me into contact with influential people and sensitive information. I put it to good use when I can.'

'Your help has proved most valuable in the past. My superiors are grateful.'

'They will certainly be glad to get these.' Don Pedro turned to the bookcase and drew out a large and weighty tome. He opened it and turned the first few pages. They concealed a hollow section in which lay a flat leather wallet. He withdrew it and replaced the book on the shelf before turning back to his companion. 'This contains the most up-to-date information we have about Napoleon's troop movements, and his future plans for the war in Spain. If they can be exploited it may hasten the end of this campaign.'

Falconbridge nodded. Taking the wallet he opened it and unfolded the papers within, scanning them with a practised eye. As he did so he felt a surge of excitement. 'This is excellent. My government will be most grateful for the information. I take it these are copies?'

'Yes. It would have been too dangerous to remove the originals.'

'I shall do all in my power to ensure that Lord Wellington receives them as soon as possible.'

'Much depends on it.' Don Pedro paused. 'In the event of capture these papers must be destroyed.'

'I understand.' Falconbridge refolded the sheets and returned them to the wallet before tucking it into the inside pocket of his coat.

'If you are captured you must not be made to talk.'

'That eventuality has been considered and the contingency plan is in place.' He hoped that it would never be necessary to have recourse to the small package of pills hidden in a secret compartment of his valise. All the same, one must be prepared for every eventuality.

'Very well. Then it only remains for me to wish you luck, *señor.*' Don Pedro held out his hand. 'You and your charming companion.'

Falconbridge took the hand and clasped it warmly. 'I thank you.'

'She knows the truth, I take it?'

'Of course. It was her choice to come.'

'Then she is a very brave woman.'

'Why so, I think.' Even as he spoke the words Falconbridge knew that they were true.

'You plan to return when?'

'The day after tomorrow.'

'It is well. In the meantime, I hope you will enjoy the ball.'

They parted shortly after this and Falconbridge took himself off to the garden. *Doña* Elena had offered to show Sabrina around it that morning and he had every hope of encountering them there. For a while he wandered among the flower beds but found no sign of them until an enquiry of one of the gardeners elicited the information that the ladies were in the summerhouse.

He found it a little later, a pretty wooden pavilion painted in green and white with elaborate carved scroll-work round the doors and windows and a design of fruit and flowers along the eaves. Hearing female voices he mounted the steps and looked inside. Cushioned seats ran along the inner walls and on one of these he saw Sabrina sitting with their hostess. The latter saw him first and smiled.

'Ah, Conde Antonio. Come and join us, do.'

Sabrina followed her gaze and he saw her smile. He accepted a glass of lemonade and seated himself on a stool opposite. It gave him an ideal vantage point from which to view both ladies. *Doña* Elena was, he acknowledged, a handsome woman. However, his gaze moved on and then lingered on Sabrina, cool and pretty in her figured muslin frock. Sensing his regard she looked across and he raised his glass a little in acknowledgement. She smiled faintly and then returned her attention to what their hostess was saying. However, he found his imagination moving ahead to the ball. He had never danced with Sabrina before. They had never attended such a function together. All the usual social gatherings at which men and women met had been denied them, until now. Courtship had never been a feature of their relationship. He still knew so little about her. Yet there was so much he wanted to know. Perhaps after their mission... He sighed. First things first. Everything had gone according to plan so far but that didn't mean he could be complacent. This was occupied territory. Anything might happen. He thought of his recent conversation with Don Pedro, and then of the contingency plan he had agreed with Forbes. He hoped that Sabrina would never need to know about that. For all manner of reasons this ball might be the only one they would ever have.

The conversation turned on general topics until a servant arrived to request their hostess's presence in the house. She made her apology and left them. When she was safely out of earshot Sabrina turned to face him.

'Did you have a successful morning?'

'Very successful,' he replied.

'Then the information was all you hoped.'

'It exceeded my expectations in every way.'

'I'm glad.' She smiled. 'Now all we have to do is get it back safely.'

He returned the smile. 'There is no reason why we should not.'

'Your optimism is encouraging.'

'Do you have doubts?'

'No. I can't afford them.'

'I think neither of us can,' he replied.

'Where have you put the documents?'

'In a safe place.'

'You don't trust me.'

'Yes, I trust you, my dear, but it may be safer for you not to know.'

'I see.'

For a moment she was silent, digesting what he had said. It was another reminder of what was at stake. Falconbridge surveyed her keenly but on this occasion found her expression hard to read.

'Have I offended you?' he asked.

'No.'

He finished his lemonade and set down the glass.

'Then will you take a turn around the gardens with me?'

'If you wish.'

They left the summerhouse and strolled together through an avenue of fruit trees, the only sounds their feet on the gravel path and the droning of bees among the flowers. Sweet scents drifted into the warm air. Sabrina breathed deeply, enjoying the moment, every part of her attuned to the man at her side.

'It is pleasant to be in the fresh air again, isn't it?' he said.

'I was just thinking the same thing.' She looked about her and smiled. 'This certainly is a beautiful place. *Doña* Elena is justly proud of it.'

'I collect she has a keen interest in horticulture.'

'Yes. She was telling me earlier about the improvements she and her husband have made to the place since they came to live here.'

'A labour of many years I imagine.'

She nodded. 'And a meeting of minds. I think it must be agreeable to have shared interests like that with one's spouse.'

'I am sure it is, though I suspect it is a rare occurrence in most cases.'

'You may be right. All the same, I should like to have a garden one day.'

'Should you?'

'Yes. I think it would be restful.'

He heard her with some surprise. It was not a subject he would ever have associated with her, but then unpredictability was part of her charm. It also revealed another facet of her mind.

'Perhaps it comes from always travelling so much,' he replied.

'Perhaps it does.'

'Would you not find it dull after all your adventures?'

'Restful is not the same as dull.'

'No, I stand corrected. In truth, it is restful out here, and certainly not dull.' He smiled. 'But then I think one could never be dull in your company.'

The matter-of-fact tone saved it from being outright flattery but it caused her pulse to quicken all the same. In any case he was far from being a flatterer. It seemed most likely that he was teasing her again, but a swift look his way found nothing to substantiate the notion.

'Thank you.'

'I speak as I find.'

She made no reply to that and presently they turned down a path at right angles to their course, and came to a fountained pool where fat carp swam lazily between the lily pads. Sabrina sat down on the stone ledge and trailed her fingers in the water. Falconbridge disposed himself casually beside her.

'Have you ever visited the Moorish palaces of Andalucia?' he asked then.

'No, though I should like to.'

'They, too, have beautiful gardens, albeit on a larger scale.'

'I believe the architecture is very beautiful.'

'Yes, it is, especially in the rooms that once housed the ruler's harem. Beautiful surroundings to house beautiful women.'

'Even so, I pity those women. It must have been an unenviable lot.'

'I imagine that boredom was the biggest enemy.'

'Yes, to have nothing to do all day but think of one's appearance must be dull indeed.'

He grinned. 'And yet there are many women in the first ranks of society who seem to do little else.'

'You speak knowledgeably.'

'I have some small experience of the breed.'

'You sound as though you did not approve.'

'A fair face and fine clothes are no substitutes for an informed mind,' he replied. 'Ideally the three should go together, but rarely do.'

'You have exacting standards.'

'Is that a fault then?'

'By no means, but I think it may be hard to find many ladies who meet the criteria.'

'Precious few, and for that reason their price is above rubies.'

She laughed. 'Then make sure you are not as Othello's base Indian.'

'An injunction I shall heed most carefully, I assure you. A man would be foolish indeed to throw away such a gem.'

The tone was light, almost bantering, but for a moment was belied by the expression in his eyes.

'The same criteria could be used to judge men,' she replied, 'for a handsome face and an elegant coat may conceal a complete fool.'

He grinned. 'True. Do I take it then that intelligence is an important consideration in your evaluation of men?'

'Oh, yes. What woman would want to spend her life with a fool?'

'Many do, my dear, especially where the fool is rich and titled.'

'Then I would guess that they never find true happiness.'

'Happiness takes many forms. It's a question of what the individual is prepared to settle for.'

'That is a mercenary outlook.'

'So it is, and commoner than you might think.'

'But surely it cannot be agreeable to marry where there is no real esteem, no love?' She smiled wryly. 'Does that make me sound very naive?'

'On the contrary, my dear. It makes you sound very wise.'

'Well, that makes a change at least.'

'I have never heard you say anything that was not sensible, except of course when you agreed to come on this trip with me.'

'That was not sensible,' she agreed. 'All the same, I'm glad I did.'

'So am I.'

'You are generous. I know the prospect did not please you at first.'

'It still doesn't—in that way. But the man must be hard to please who did not enjoy your company.'

The words were accompanied by a look that was hard to interpret, but which had the effect of summoning a tinge of warmer colour to her face. It also left her unsure how to respond. She could not tell him that his company was the most agreeable of any man's she had ever met, or that his presence caused her heart to leap. To do so would be disastrous. Such a declaration would be perceived as an invitation to greater intimacy. His regard was not lightly given and it pleased her to think that she had it, albeit in some small measure. She would not do anything to forfeit that.

They walked together back to the house and later rejoined the others for a light luncheon. It was a convivial gathering and, since good manners decreed that they must keep up their part in the general conversation, she had no opportunity for further speech with him then. It was only afterwards when the company went their separate ways for the siesta that they found themselves alone once more.

In the privacy of their chamber he seemed larger than life somehow, as if his presence filled the space.

'We have a late night ahead of us,' he said then, 'and a long journey afterwards. It would be a good idea to get some rest now.'

She nodded. The siesta was a Spanish tradition that she had come to value. 'Yes, you're right, of course.'

'Do you want me to call Jacinta?' he asked.

'No, there is no need.' She took off her shoes and then perched on the edge of the bed while he closed the window shutters and the louvered outer doors to the balcony. Through the dim light she saw him remove his coat and neckcloth and draw off his boots. Knowing she would rest more comfortably if she removed her gown, she reached up, fumbling with the buttons, but they were stiff and resisted her efforts. For a little while he watched in quiet amusement. Then he drew her gently upright.

'Turn around.'

Somewhat hesitantly she obeyed, hoping he wouldn't notice her inner confusion. This closeness had another dimension now; setting her pulse racing, filling her entire being with shameful longing. She felt him lift her hair aside. Steady, competent hands unfastened the gown and gently pushed the fabric over her shoulders. His hands brushed her skin, a touch that sent a tremor the length of her body. She drew in a deep breath, fighting temptation. How easy it would be to let this go further, to let him finish what he had begun and undress her completely, to feel the touch of his hands on her naked flesh. The thought created a sensation of melting warmth in the region of her loins. She darted a glance at the bed. At once the warmth translated to her neck and face. If he knew, if he even suspected...

It seemed he did not for he stepped away then, leaving her to remove the dress, and retired to the couch. Out of the corner of her eyes she saw him stretch out. Those precious seconds gave her time to regain a little more composure. She struggled out of the gown and tossed it over a chair. Then she, too, lay down to rest.

For a little while neither one spoke, but the silence was companionable rather than tense. Then she turned her head and looked across the intervening space.

'What will you do when the war is over?'

'Return to England, I imagine,' he replied. 'And you?'

'The same.' She smiled reflectively. 'Though I think it would seem strange after all this time. Rather like a foreign country.'

He thought it an apt analogy. Going back would be like returning to a past life. Except that one could never go back. The trouble was, while time and people moved on, the reminders lingered.

'Do you have a house in England?' she continued.

'Yes.'

'Will it not seem dull to live there after this?'

He grinned. 'Perhaps.'

'My aunt wanted me to go and live with her in Reading, but I refused. I know she meant it kindly but it would have been unbearable.'

'I can understand that.'

'She would try to find me a husband, too. I'm sure of it.'

'You dislike the idea?'

'Marriage sounds dull to me, but perhaps it depends upon one's choice of partner.'

'I'm sure it does.'

'Being married to your career you have the ideal partner, do you not?'

'Well, at least my career won't leave me at the altar.'

For a moment she was silent, unsure she had heard him aright. Falconbridge felt his jaw tighten. He hadn't meant to speak of it but somehow the words had come out anyway. Perhaps it didn't matter now.

'Is that what happened?'

'Yes.' He drew in a deep breath. 'Clarissa was very beautiful—the most ravishing débutante of the year. Every man in London was wild about her. I was no exception. I could scarce believe my luck when she accepted my offer of marriage. Our families favoured the match and so a date was set.' He paused. 'The church was packed with our friends and relations; it was one of the most splendid marriages of the season. Or rather, it should have been. However, when it came to the key question, Clarissa refused to go through with it.'

Sabrina felt intense sympathy for him. While she had heard of brides getting cold feet she had never, until then, known of one who had jilted her fiancé at the ceremony.

'She informed me that she couldn't marry me because she loved another,' he continued. 'With that she fled the church.'

'Good heavens!' His companion stared at him, appalled. 'What did you do?'

'For a little while, nothing. I just wanted the earth to open up and swallow me. Then somehow I got outside; I needed some air, needed to clear my head, try to think... and that's when I saw them. They were standing together by the lych gate, Clarissa in my brother's arms.'

'Your brother?'

'Yes, Hugh, whom I loved; the person I had always looked up to most; the one with whom I had shared so many adventures, the person I had trusted above all others.' He gave a hollow laugh. 'It was Hugh to whom I had first confided my love for Clarissa. Once we were engaged, of course, she and my brother met far more often than they had erewhile. They soon became good friends but, being a gullible fool, it never occurred to me that it was anything other than innocent. At some point she must have realised Hugh's interest was more than brotherly affection and seized her chance.'

Sabrina was genuinely shocked. 'How could she do that? How could any woman?'

'Hugh was the heir to an earldom. I was only the younger son.' He grimaced. 'I realise now that Clarissa never really loved me, but I was too besotted to see it.'

'What did you do...when you discovered the truth?'

'At first I wanted to kill them. They knew it, too; saw it in my face, for both of them were ghastly pale. But...' he let out a long breath '...what would have been the point? When I saw their fear all I felt was contempt, and in the end I just walked away.'

'And then?'

'The scandal was enormous. I had no wish to remain in England to be an object of pity or ridicule so, with my father's help, I purchased a commission in the army. It was a good decision. I discovered that I had an aptitude for the work and enjoyed its challenges. I made some good friends along the way, too.'

'Have you never been back to England since?'

'No, though I corresponded with my father and sister at regular intervals,' he replied. 'When my father died, he left me a handsome competence and one of the smaller country seats. I half-expected that Hugh would challenge the will but he never has.'

'He has that much honour then,' said Sabrina.

'Perhaps his conscience prevented it. Who knows?'

'His conscience must prick him dreadfully. He deserves that it should.'

'Well, it's in the past now.'

'All the same, it must have been very difficult for you.'

His lips twisted in a wry smile at the enormity of the understatement. 'At the time.'

'And now?'

'Not now.'

'You no longer love her?'

'No.' It was true, he thought. Anger and pain had diminished, too. If only memory were so easily vanquished.

'How long ago?'

'Three years.'

'Have you forgiven her?'

He hadn't been expecting that, and the question gave him a sharp mental jolt. The answer, when it came, was no less jarring. His companion was remarkably astute for one so young. No one else had ever dared to probe so far and would have got short shrift if they had tried. This was different, more like speaking to a confidante, even though he had known her for so short a time. Her manner was quite artless and strangely hard to resist.

Somehow it invited him to speak of things so long kept hidden; to open up a dark place to the light of day.

'No,' he replied. 'Such duplicity as hers is hard to forgive.'

'Yes, it is.' She hesitated. 'And your brother?'

'Nor him. I never shall.' Now that it was revealed, he thought the dark place looked as ugly as an unhealed wound.

'But if you do not, how can you put it behind you and move on?'

'I have moved on.'

'Have you?'

The answer to that one should have been secure—having thrown himself into his career he had put the past behind him, hadn't he? A sudden and unexpected tension in the region of his solar plexus revealed it wasn't as far behind as he would have liked. The ramifications were disturbing on many different levels.

When he didn't reply, Sabrina didn't press him. The conversation, so innocently begun, had led to places she had never anticipated, and she had no wish to trespass there. Nevertheless, she could not regret that he had told her; it made a lot of things much clearer. For the first time she glimpsed the depth of his hurt and the reason for his anger. After such an experience he would find it difficult to forgive or to trust again. Instead of a loving, supportive marriage it was his career that now provided the stable framework of his life. She didn't care to think of what might happen if he lost that, too.

A swift sideways glance revealed that his eyes were closed. She knew he wasn't asleep but the hint was sufficient. She smiled ruefully. It was none of her business and if he did not speak of it again, she would not.

Chapter Six

When Sabrina woke in the late afternoon her companion was gone. She heard the muted sound of male voices coming from the dressing room and assumed that he was closeted with Willis, no doubt getting ready for the ball. She rose at once and summoned Jacinta. Then she bathed and began the lengthy toilette so necessary for her participation that evening.

When at last it was completed she surveyed her reflection in the glass. Her hair, dressed high on her head, was entwined with a rope of pearls. Another strand decorated her neck and matching pearls hung from her ears. The white satin ball gown, with its daring décolleté, was overlaid with spangled gauze that shimmered with every movement. Satin slippers and long gloves completed the ensemble. The effect was pleasing and she smiled at herself in the mirror. Jacinta smiled, too.

'You look beautiful. Far too good for him.'

Sabrina didn't pretend to misunderstand. 'He will not be paying any attention to me.'

'Oh, is he dead then? I hadn't heard.'

A gurgle of laughter greeted this. 'Of course he isn't dead. I meant he will have other things on his mind.'

'Not when he sees you in that dress, he won't.'

The words caused Sabrina's heart to leap. Falconbridge's opinion should not have mattered one iota but she knew full well that it did. The knowledge added to her feeling of nervous anticipation. It had been many months since last she had attended a ball of any kind, and even then it had not been so splendid a function as this promised to be. Neither had she had so handsome and charismatic an escort. She realised that she was looking forward to dancing with him. It would be the first time. It might very well be the last. The realisation brought with it a sharp pang.

He had long since emerged from the dressing room and taken himself off leaving the field clear for Sabrina. Clearly he had some idea of how long it took a lady to ready herself for such an occasion, and she appreciated the consideration. She could only hope that he would be appreciative of the effort made on his behalf.

She had not long to wait for the answer. He returned a little later to see if she was ready to accompany him. He took two steps into the room and then stopped in his tracks as his heart performed a sudden and wildly erratic manoeuvre. He had thought that her beauty could not be improved on but he had been wrong. His gaze drank in every detail and found no fault.

'You look gorgeous,' he said, though to his ears it sounded lame. If he knew anything about it, every other man in the room this evening was going to be rampant with envy. The notion was most gratifying. However, if they thought to do any more than look they were going to be disappointed. Tonight at least, she was his.

Sabrina smiled. 'Thank you.'

He crossed the room and took her hand, raising it to his lips. Then he smiled. It warmed the grey eyes and lit his face.

'All set, my dear?'

'All set.'

'Then let us join the fray.'

He retained his hold on her hand and led her to the door. Sabrina drew in a deep breath, partly in trepidation at what might lie ahead and partly because he was near. As always, his slightest touch set her senses alight. It was as well he did not know it.

'Incidentally,' he said as they descended the stairs together, 'don't give anyone else the first dance. I intend to claim a husband's privilege.'

Her heart missed a beat, but she kept the tone light. 'As you wish, sir.'

'It is exactly what I wish. In fact, I feel extraordinarily possessive.'

Her heart skipped another beat. 'Do you?'

His gaze lingered a moment on the décolletage of her gown. 'The sight of you in that dress is enough to heat the blood of a saint.'

'But you are no saint.'

'It hasn't taken you long to realise that.'

'Oh, I realised it the first time we met, sir.'

'Jade.'

She smiled, her expression both unrepentant and irresistible, and he wished very much that they had been alone. For the first time in years he found himself prey to a lot of unexpectedly erotic thoughts. Unfortunately, from his point of view at least, they reached the bottom of the stairs and their hosts were waiting to greet them.

Already the guests were gathering and Sabrina's gaze took in several French uniforms among the elegant crowd. She glanced up at Falconbridge and felt him squeeze her hand. Then they went in together. Happily, the first people they encountered were other house guests already known to them: Gonzalez and Don Fernando Muñoz, with his twin brother, Cristóbal. The latter were in their early thirties but, although not ill-favoured, showed signs of over-indulgence at table in their thickening waistlines. Their short stature did nothing in mitigation of the fault, but their manners were easy and pleasant.

Don Fernando made Sabrina an elegant bow, his gaze taking in every detail of her appearance and warming as a result. She returned a polite greeting and, while Falconbridge spoke to Don Cristóbal, glanced across the room. As she did so her gaze fell on the small group of French officers she had noticed before.

'Some of your countrymen, Condesa,' said Don Fernando.

'Yes,' replied Sabrina. 'I confess I am surprised to see them here.'

'It does not pay to offend the ruling elite, as our host is well aware.'

'No, I suppose not.'

'You do not approve of their presence?'

Sabrina contrived a casual shrug. 'It is not for me to say whom our host should invite to his house. Besides, I take little interest in politics.'

'Of course not. It isn't a subject that should concern a lady. It is far too tedious.'

Sabrina tried for a vapid expression. 'I confess it is. Antonio tries to explain it to me, but I'm afraid I just can't grasp it at all.'

'A woman shouldn't trouble her pretty little head over such matters.'

'There are so many more interesting things to talk about, are there not?'

'My view exactly,' he replied.

Seeing her chance she seized it. 'What an elegant gown that lady is wearing. I really must try to discover the name of her dressmaker. Of course, she may not wish to divulge it. Perhaps you would introduce us, Don Fernando.'

He professed himself most willing to oblige, and to point out other guests whom she did not know. Sabrina adopted a look of rapt interest. Having diverted him to safer ground she didn't want him to quit it.

In the event, he had no chance because the music started and then Falconbridge was beside her again.

'I believe this dance is mine,' he said.

She breathed a silent sigh of relief and allowed him to lead her away. His expression suggested private amusement.

'What?' she asked.

'Nothing to trouble your pretty little head over, my dear,' he replied.

For answer he received an eloquent look and enjoyed it enormously.

'Eavesdropping is a bad habit,' she said.

'I know but sometimes it's irresistible.'

They walked out onto the floor and waited as the first set formed up around them. Then the music struck up. Moving through the figures, he had leisure to observe that his partner danced well. He could detect no hint of awkwardness in her movements. He was aware, too, that other eyes watched them. It was inevitable, he thought. Men would always watch a woman like Sabrina. While one part of him deplored the attention they were attracting, another part relished their envy.

'Where did you learn to dance like that?' he asked. 'You must have had a good teacher.'

'The best. Captain Harcourt was most insistent on that.'

He frowned, experiencing a stab of something remarkably like jealousy, and determining to know more, but the next manoeuvre divided them briefly. When they came together again he fixed her with a gimlet stare.

'Captain Harcourt again? What had he to do with it, pray?'

The expression in the green eyes was the epitome of innocence. 'Why, he asked his wife to teach me.'

Falconbridge bit back a laugh, knowing he'd been set up. For the second time that evening he wished they were alone. It would have pleased him very much to exact a fitting retribution. For just a moment he indulged that delicious thought.

'My compliments to the lady,' he replied.

'I'm sure she'd be delighted to know of your approval.'

For a moment her gaze met his again and, involuntarily, they both smiled. The next figure separated them again and he waited for her return.

'Your relationship with the Harcourts seems to have been highly educational.'

'Oh, it was, sir.' She could never tell him why.

'I am sorry not to have made their acquaintance.'

'I think you would have liked them. Father did.'

For a moment he saw a shadow cross her face. Then it was gone. He guessed that the mention of her father brought back the memory of his present predicament. He squeezed her hand gently.

'Don't worry. We shall see your father safe.'

His expression was so patently sincere that it brought a lump to her throat. Once, she would never have thought this man capable of kindness or warmth, and yet she had come to learn that he possessed both.

When the dance ended he led her from the floor where they were joined a moment later by Elena.

'Condesa, there is someone I'd like you to meet.'

Sabrina forced a smile. 'Of course.'

She would have liked to stay with Falconbridge but it was impossible. Good manners decreed that she must go. He smiled at her.

'I'll see you later, my dear.'

Elena led her across the room to another group and performed the necessary introductions. To her intense relief everyone seemed to accept her at face value. The Condesa de Ordoñez y Casal was admitted to their ranks with welcoming smiles. Their conversation turned on general topics to which she listened with apparent interest. Across the room she could see her erstwhile companion engaged in conversation with a small group of grandees. The ladies in the group seemed to hang upon his every word, admiration writ large in their eyes. Admiration and desire. Once, she heard him laugh in response to something that was said. The sound caused an unfamiliar pang. Before she could analyse it a familiar voice jolted her back.

'Condesa, what a pleasure to see you again.'

Sabrina turned round and felt her stomach somersault as she recognised Colonel Machart, now resplendent in full dress uniform. His lupine gaze swept her in a comprehensive look and glinted appreciatively. Then he bowed.

'May I say that you are looking even lovelier this evening?'

Recovering quickly she made a polite curtsy. 'You are all kindness, sir.'

'I would have the honour of the next dance.'

It was the last thing she would have wished for. Unfortunately there was nothing to be done save consent with as good a grace as possible. He led her out and they joined the other couples on the floor. Machart danced with practised ease but the watchful gaze made her feel apprehensive. It rested often on her bare shoulders and bosom. In it she read admiration and lust and something else that instinctively put her on her guard.

When the dance was over she hoped to slip away, but her partner was not so easy to get rid of.

'Come, don't deprive me of your company so soon. It is not often that I have the pleasure of talking to a Frenchwoman, or one so lovely.'

'You flatter me, Colonel.' She smiled. 'However, my parents left France when I was very young. I regret to say that I have no memory of it.'

'That is a pity.'

'I have always thought so.'

'And they came from?'

'The Languedoc.'

'I also.' He bared his teeth in a smile. 'May I ask your family's name?'

'De Courcy.'

'I know it. An old and respected lineage,' he replied. 'Not that I claim acquaintance, unfortunately.'

His look grew warmer. Sabrina redirected the conversation.

'I have been told that the Languedoc region is very beautiful.'

'Indeed it is. There is nowhere to compare with it.' He glanced across the room towards the group that contained Falconbridge. 'You should persuade your husband to take you there.'

'My husband travels rarely, preferring to live quietly on his estates,' she replied.

'What a shame that you live so retired.'

'Not at all. I have no taste for city life either, Colonel.'

'So lovely a lady should not be buried in the country. It is not generous of your husband to deprive the rest of us of your company.' He paused, casting another look towards Falconbridge. 'Not that I blame him for wishing to keep you to himself.'

'I have no complaint to make.'

'No, that is on my side.' His gaze returned to the front of her gown. Feeling increasingly uncomfortable, Sabrina wanted nothing more than to escape. However, it seemed her companion still wasn't ready to let her go.

'Do you know, when we met on the road I had the strangest feeling that I had met your husband somewhere before.'

Her stomach wallowed. It took every ounce of self-control she possessed to face him. 'Really?'

'Yes. I rarely forget a face.'

'Perhaps it was someone who looked like my husband.'

'Perhaps, but just now the recollection eludes me.' He paused and grinned. 'However, I know that we have met once before, Condesa. Indeed I could never forget it.'

'Nor I,' she replied, with perfect sincerity.

'I should like to know you better,' he went on. 'Do you stay long in Aranjuez?'

Her skin crawled beneath that speculative gaze. 'No,

sir. My husband does not like to be away from home too long.'

'Then I must use the available time.' He bowed. 'I shall hope to dance with you again later, Condesa.'

He possessed himself of her hand and raised it to his lips. Feeling the heat of that unwelcome embrace, Sabrina was thankful to be wearing gloves. However, she didn't dare let anything of her inner thought show. This man was a predator if ever she had met one, and he would be quick to sense fear. All the same, she wanted nothing more than to be rid of him.

Across the room Falconbridge watched. Then he turned and murmured something to Elena. Their hostess smiled and left him, making her way casually through the crowd with a smile here and a few words there, until she reached Sabrina's side.

'Forgive me, Condesa, but there is someone who particularly desires to make your acquaintance.'

Sabrina regarded her arrival with real gratitude. 'Of course. Please excuse us, Colonel.'

He bowed again. Sabrina walked away, aware of his gaze burning into her back. Her companion eyed her shrewdly.

'A little of his company goes a long way, does it not?'

'Yes. Your rescue is most timely.'

'Your husband thought it might be.'

Instinctively Sabrina looked over her shoulder towards the far side of the room. Falconbridge was still with the same group, apparently listening with interest to what was being said. However, as though sensing her regard, he looked up briefly and she saw him smile before returning his attention to the speaker. Though it was a fleeting expression it warmed her all the same, like a protective cloak.

'Machart has a certain reputation,' Elena continued.

'I can well believe it.'

'Not just with the ladies either.' Elena lowered her voice. 'There are tales about his military conduct which are not particularly pleasant. Of course, they may have been exaggerated.'

Somehow Sabrina doubted it but kept her own counsel. A few moments later she was admitted to a different group of people. Another casual glance across the room a few minutes later revealed that the French Colonel was engaged in conversation with another gentleman, a short, slight individual of middle years. The lined face with its pointed features and sharp eyes reminded her vaguely of a rodent. Both of them were looking in her direction. Her stomach knotted. Was anything wrong? Had they suspected something? She turned away, telling herself not to be foolish. It probably meant nothing. Machart would know many of those present this evening.

Don Cristóbal was standing nearby so she enquired whether he knew the identity of the man with Machart.

'That is Jean Laroche,' he replied. 'He works for the French intelligence service.'

The knot tightened in her stomach. 'What is he doing here do you suppose?'

'Keeping an ear to the ground, I imagine. He attends all the important social functions.'

She nodded and managed a smile. If that were the case there was no reason to suppose that his presence here had any significance beyond that. All the same, the combination of Laroche and Machart was disquieting.

Her hand was solicited for several dances and that

precluded the need for conversation, or kept it to a minimum. After that she went in search of refreshment. The rooms were very warm now despite the fact that the windows along its length were open. A glass of fruit punch would be most welcome.

'A glittering occasion, is it not?'

Her heart leapt and she turned to see Falconbridge at her shoulder. 'Yes, I think that everyone who is anyone is probably here tonight.'

He put a hand under her elbow and drew her gently aside. 'I noticed you speaking to the Colonel earlier.'

She nodded. 'Yes, and I was never more glad to be rescued.'

'I thought you might be.'

'How right you were. I don't care for him at all.'

'No, an unpleasant character all round I gather.'

'He told me that he is sure he knows you.'

'Damn,' he muttered. 'The man's no fool. He'll remember eventually.'

Sabrina paled. 'What do we do now?'

'Act as though nothing were wrong. We have to get through the rest of the evening without attracting attention.' He squeezed her arm gently. 'Tomorrow we'll be on our way.'

'I hope we may.' She paused. 'Has Don Pedro mentioned a man called Jean Laroche?'

'Yes. He pointed the gentleman out earlier.'

'Do you think Laroche's presence here is significant?'

'I think not. I understand he likes to be present at social functions such as this.' As he saw her anxious expression, his face cleared and he smiled. 'As we are here and must remain awhile longer, will you honour me with another dance?'

She returned the smile. 'Of course.'

They returned to the ballroom for the next two measures, and Sabrina forgot about Machart and the other guests thronging the room. Her attention was solely for her present partner, the touch of his hand, his smile, the warmth in his gaze. When he looked at her like that all else became unimportant and she abandoned herself to the music and the moment, content just to be in his company, to be near him.

When at length the second dance ended, she expected that he would return her to Elena or one of the other ladies, but he did not.

'It is hot in here. Would you like some fresh air?'

'Yes, very much.'

'Come then.'

He placed a hand casually under her elbow, steering her towards one of the open doors that led onto the terrace. After the heavy atmosphere of the ballroom the night air was blessedly sweet and cool and scented with jasmine. Overhead the moon rose among a million brilliant stars and silvered the canopies of the trees. Somewhere among the branches a nightingale sang, the pure liquid notes travelling on the still air. Unwilling to break the spell she remained silent. This night might be the only one she would ever spend with him thus. Tomorrow they must leave, must get those secret papers to Wellington. After that... She bit her lip. Would the end of the mission be the end of the relationship?

'A penny for them.'

His voice drew her back. 'I was thinking about the future. Of what might happen.'

'Are you afraid?' he asked.

'Yes, a little.' It was true, she thought, but not for the reasons he supposed.

'Don't be. All will be well.'

'Will it?'

Something in the tone touched him and he smiled gently. 'Of course. I will do all in my power to ensure it.'

He lifted her hand to his lips. The imprint of his kiss seemed to scorch her skin. She made no attempt to withdraw from his hold for it seemed that her hand belonged there. Heart pounding, she turned towards him, waiting, trying to read his expression. Suddenly he tensed and his fingers tightened on hers.

'Don't look round,' he murmured. 'Keep looking at me.'

'What is it?'

'Machart is watching us from the doorway yonder.'

'Why would he?'

'Perhaps he was hoping to get you alone.' Falconbridge smiled. 'I think we should show him how futile his hope is.'

'How?'

He released his hold on her hand but only to slide an arm round her waist and draw her against him. His lips brushed hers, tentatively at first, then more assertively. Liquid warmth flooded her body's core and she swayed against him, her mouth opening beneath his. The kiss grew deeper, more intimate, inflaming her senses, demanding her response. She had no need to pretend now, nor cared any longer who was watching. All that mattered was the two of them and the moonlight and the moment.

He took the kiss at leisure, every part of him wanting her, in no hurry to end it. This had nothing to do with Machart any more; he kissed her now because he wanted to, because it was what he'd wanted to do from the first.

Heart hammering in his breast he drew back a little and looked into her face, trying to read her expression.

'I beg your pardon,' he said. 'I confess I got carried away, but then I had not expected to enjoy it so much.'

Sabrina hid hurt behind a smile. So it had just been an act then. She pulled herself up at that thought. It wasn't as if he hadn't warned her, was it? Tender looks, melting smiles—a kiss or two. How could she have guessed he would be so very accomplished an actor? Her throat tightened, but she swallowed the lump threatening to form there and glanced towards the open doorway. Machart was gone.

'Our companion got the hint,' she said. 'We must have given a convincing performance.'

Falconbridge surveyed her keenly. It hadn't been a performance and they both knew it. What he had felt could not be feigned. Nor had he imagined the spark that had ignited between them. It had been all too real. And that, he acknowledged, was the danger now. A danger she had recognised perhaps, and was seeking to avert? She was right. They could not afford distraction. Resisting the desire to take her in his arms again, he merely nodded.

'As you say, my dear.' He held out a hand. 'I think perhaps we should go back now.'

'Yes.'

She placed her fingers in his and allowed him to lead her back to the ballroom. They did not speak and she was glad of it. Her lips still burned from his kiss, her body remembered the delicious sensation of being held in his arms. She swallowed hard. At all costs she must try and put the incident behind her, forget it had ever happened. She did not deceive herself that it would be easy.

He danced with her again when they returned and then relinquished her to another partner. She performed the steps mechanically now, fixing a smile on her face. Her gaze searched the room but found no sign of Machart. That was a relief at least.

It wasn't until the company sat down to supper that she saw him again, though at the far end of the room. He glanced her way but, much to her relief, made no attempt to approach her.

'May I?'

A tall figure appeared in her line of vision and she looked up to see Falconbridge. She saw him smile and returned it, feeling the answering leap in her heart.

'Of course.'

He took the seat beside her. Now it seemed only natural and right that he should, as though he belonged there. She could not envisage any other man in his place. With an effort she reminded herself that all this was an act performed for the benefit of others, and yet how beautiful the illusion was, and how seductive. No matter what happened later she would remember tonight as long as she lived.

Throughout supper, conversation flowed lightly and easily and she was content to let others do most of the talking. Once again the other ladies present made no secret of their interest in the handsome Conde Antonio, laughing and flirting, seeking his attention. Once or twice she intercepted looks of envy from among their ranks. Outwardly Sabrina ignored them, but she was woman enough to enjoy their response as well, albeit privately. All her senses were attuned to the man beside her, drinking in each detail from the clean lines of the profile at present turned towards her, the easy smile as he responded to the words of a lady opposite, even to the way he held his fork. He seemed perfectly relaxed, quite at home in this company as though he had been there all his life. Of course, she reflected, he had, or its English equivalent anyway. Accustomed to move in the first ranks of the *ton,* he would be at home anywhere.

'May I pour you a little more wine?'

She realised that he was speaking to her. 'Oh, yes, thank you.'

He refilled the glass. 'The chicken is particularly good. Have you tried it?'

'I…er, no.'

'Allow me to fetch you some.'

He retired briefly to the buffet and returned with another plate.

Having tasted a little of the chicken, she nodded. 'You are right. Quite delicious.'

He smiled. 'Much better than some of the fare you have been served of late.'

'It is not the same thing at all.'

'I know it isn't.'

'I meant that you are not comparing like with like and, therefore, the criticism is perhaps a little unfair.'

'Perhaps.' He leaned back in his chair and surveyed her keenly. 'A bit like comparing cheap wine to champagne.'

'Yes, something like that.' Acutely conscious of his scrutiny, she took a sip from her glass with what she hoped looked like casual ease. 'Of course, a true connoisseur would never make that mistake.'

His lips twitched. 'No, indeed, as he could never mistake plainness for beauty.'

'Do you consider yourself a connoisseur of such things?'

'I was not, until recently.' He let his gaze travel from her face to her neck and throat and thence to the décolleté of her gown where it lingered quite unashamedly. 'Now the case is quite altered.'

Her colour fluctuated delightfully. 'Now you are being deliberately provoking.'

He grinned. 'That's right. Is it working?'

She returned him a most eloquent look and then laughed reluctantly. 'You know perfectly well that it is.'

'Excellent. I should have been disappointed else.'

The words brought her back to earth with a jolt. This light flirtation was all part of the act and she would do well to remember it. For all manner of reasons she could not let this man get under her skin. This meant no more to him than a passing amusement. In his world such things were the norm and only a complete gudgeon would read more into it. The knowledge rallied her.

'I should hate to disappoint. Therefore, I shall humour you, sir.'

Hr laughed softly, enjoying her. 'Will you humour me in everything?'

'Certainly not, for then you would grow complacent.'

'Where you are concerned, my dear, I would never be so foolish.'

'I admit that foolishness it not a trait I associate with you.'

'I'm pleased to hear it.' He paused. 'What traits do you associate with me?'

She surveyed him coolly. 'Commitment to duty, attention to detail, thoroughness, a certain degree of ruthlessness and, withal, a touch of arrogance.'

His expression did not change, though for a brief instant the grey eyes were veiled. 'You are honest.'

'I must speak as I find.'

When he thought back to the occasion of their first meeting he could understand why she would consider him ruthless and arrogant. All the same her words stung a little.

'Have I not redeemed myself in any way?' he asked.

'You are quite beyond redemption, sir.' The smile robbed the remark of malice but he was not entirely sure it had been mere banter. It should not have mattered and yet he knew it did. He could not have said exactly how it had come about, but suddenly her opinion of him mattered a great deal.

When supper was over he rose and, taking her hand, led her out of the room. She had expected that they would part then and go their ways for a while, but he retained his hold on her hand. It was gentle but it would not be resisted. He drew her round to face him.

'Dance with me again.'

'Is that a command?'

The grey eyes glinted. 'Most assuredly it is and, as I am your husband, madam, you are sworn to obey.'

Her chin came up at once and he had the pleasure of seeing a rosy flush mount from her throat to her cheeks. He saw it was on the tip of her tongue to deliver a pithy set down, and waited for it. Instead she smiled sweetly.

'How I could I refuse such a charming invitation?' His enjoyment increased and she saw it. Lowering her voice she added, 'Do you have any idea how odious you can be?'

'Of course, for you told me yourself. Arrogant and ruthless I think you said.'

'Yes, an assessment only too accurately borne out now.'

'But then I did warn you at the outset that I should not brook disobedience.'

'Why, I would never dream of it, sir.'

'Liar. You are contemplating it now, but I promise you it will not be tolerated.'

The tone was disturbingly ambiguous, like the look in his eyes, and suddenly she felt as a swimmer must who inadvertently steps off a shallow ledge into deep water. She should have been afraid but the feeling was more akin to excitement. Unable to think of a reply she tried to focus on the dance but it wasn't easy when every fibre of her being was focused on him.

He kept her with him for another measure and then led her from the floor. After that, they mingled awhile with the other guests. Sabrina cast a surreptitious look around for Machart but did not see him, and for that was devoutly thankful.

As the hour grew later the company began to thin out and as the carriages arrived at the door Falconbridge said their goodnights and steered Sabrina away.

'You look tired, my dear.'

'I confess I am a little.'

'There's time for a few hours' sleep before we leave.'

She glanced at the clock in the hall. The hands indicated half past two. 'Are we leaving today?'

'We are.'

'Is it really necessary?'

'I believe it is.'

He took hold of her elbow and guided her up the stairs and along the passage to their chamber. The room was empty.

'I told Jacinta not to wait up,' she said.

Closing the door behind them, he nodded. 'I can perform the offices of a maid if need be.'

'I can manage.'

'As you will.'

He crossed to the far side of the room and began to undress. Inevitably, he achieved it more quickly and then retired to the couch. Then he lay for a while, watching her complete her own preparations for bed. Conscious of that steady regard, Sabrina did not linger over the matter, shedding her clothing as quickly as possible, save only for the chemise beneath. Then, having removed her jewellery, she seated herself before the glass and unpinned her hair, shaking it loose over her shoulders. She brushed it vigorously, feeling it leap beneath the strokes. When it was done she blew out the candle and bade her companion goodnight before sliding into bed. She heard him reply and then the faint creaking of the couch as he turned onto his side. She smiled in the darkness and then yawned. Snuggling beneath the covers she closed her eyes and in minutes was asleep.

Across the room, her companion lay awake rather longer, his mind replaying the events of the evening. He had not imagined the spark that had kindled between them, nor was he imagining the attraction he felt now. Given the least encouragement he would have followed his inclination and taken her to bed. Fortunately, she had too much sense to let things get out of hand. She had shown herself to be more than capable of holding him at arm's length, and of doing it with wit and charm. He permitted himself a wry smile. Far from putting him off, it had served only to fuel enjoyment and desire. It was his fault, of course; she had been in no way to blame for what had happened. Yet if he had known the consequences then, would he have avoided that kiss? The answer returned in an instant; he would not have missed it for the world. He knew he was never going to forget it either. As long as he lived he would remember how it felt to hold her in his arms. How could he have imagined that what had begun as a simple ruse would rebound upon him so spectacularly?

Chapter Seven

Sabrina slept soundly and dreamlessly, worn out by the combination of a long journey and the late hour. Ordinarily a ball would have meant a long lie abed the following day to recover. However, it seemed like only minutes, before she was gently shaken awake by a hand on her shoulder. She muttered something and turned over, but the hand was insistent.

'Come, my dear, it's time to move.'

Vaguely recognising the voice, she groaned and opened one eye. 'It can't be.'

'I'm afraid it is.'

'But I've only just gone to bed.'

'Never mind, you can sleep in the coach.'

This time, both eyes opened and focused resentfully on the familiar figure beside her. 'What o'clock is it?'

'Seven, or thereabouts.'

'Seven! We didn't retire till three.'

'I know and I'm sorry, but we cannot afford the luxury of lying abed.'

'Have you no mercy?'

For answer, a ruthless hand drew back the covers. Equally ruthless arms lifted her bodily out and dumped her on her feet. 'Get dressed. We need to be gone. It isn't safe to remain.'

The words penetrated the fog in her brain. 'What is it? Not Machart?'

'Not yet, but there's every chance his memory will return. I want to be long gone before it does.'

Sabrina nodded, coming to at last. 'Yes, of course.' Then she looked more closely at her companion.

Falconbridge was fully dressed and alert and looked as fresh as a man who had had eight hours' sleep, not four. His arm was still around her waist. She could feel the warmth of his hand through the filmy fabric of her nightgown. The memory of what had happened the previous evening returned with force. She couldn't afford any kind of romantic illusions. This man was married to his career. All that could ever happen between them would be a brief affair. The knowledge brought her back to reality.

Disengaging herself gently, she crossed to the washstand and sluiced cold water over her face. The shock woke her completely. She fumbled for a towel. A glance over it revealed the coolly appraising stare that swept her from head to toe. Only then was she fully aware of her own dishevelled appearance and scanty attire. She met his gaze with a level stare.

'If you would excuse me, I need to dress.'

'Of course. I'll see you downstairs.'

'I'll be ready in a quarter of an hour.'

He smiled faintly, his expression revealing deep scepticism about the proposed time scale. 'I'm ever optimistic.' She threw him a withering glance. It bounced off. He crossed to the door. 'As soon as may be, my dear.'

* * *

In fact, he was pleasantly surprised when Sabrina joined him some twenty minutes later. His critical gaze could find no fault with her appearance either. She was, he thought, a rare woman.

While the last of the boxes were carried down they took leave of their host.

'If anyone asks for us, tell them urgent business called me home,' said Falconbridge.

'I will, though it will be hours yet before anyone in this house will be stirring.' Don Pedro held out his hand. 'In the meantime, I pray you may have a safe and uneventful journey.'

'Amen to that.' Falconbridge shook his hand warmly. 'And thank you, sir. For everything.'

'*Vaya con Dios.*'

Sabrina raised her hand in farewell as the carriage drew away. Then she leaned back in her seat and breathed a sigh of relief.

'We did it.'

Falconbridge shook his head. 'We're not out of the woods yet, my dear. I'll want a lot more distance between us and Aranjuez before I'll dare to hope so.'

'With any luck Machart and company will be sound asleep at this moment. We'll be long gone by the time he wakes.'

'I pray you're right.'

He did not labour the point but she knew him well enough to know that he had doubts on the matter. In consequence, she kept an eye on the countryside through which they passed, half-expecting to encounter a French patrol. However, they met none. By then fatigue was making its presence felt and Sabrina slipped into a doze.

* * *

She had no idea how long she slept but when she came to again the sun was much higher. Her companion smiled.

'Feeling better?'

'Yes, I thank you.' She glanced out of the window. 'We're making good progress.'

'So far.'

'You expect pursuit?'

'Not expect, no, but it remains a possibility. Thus, it behoves us not to tarry.'

'At least this time we are going in the right direction, away from the lion's den.'

'The lion's territory is large and his reach is long,' he replied.

Sabrina looked out of the window again but could see nothing to occasion any alarm at present. She leaned back in her seat regarding her companion steadily for a few moments. The handsome face gave nothing away.

'This is all familiar to you, is it not? The risk, I mean, and the adventure.'

'Every soldier encounters risk at some point. It just comes in different guises. We do what the job demands.'

'Do you enjoy it?'

'It has its moments,' he replied. 'All the same, I shall be glad when this task is satisfactorily completed.'

It occurred to her that the end of the mission meant the end of their brief relationship. The knowledge cast a cloud. Somehow, in a matter of days, she had grown so accustomed to his presence that it was hard to imagine life without it. There could be no denying that what she felt for him was more than mere liking for an agreeable companion, but neither was it infatuation. Her feelings were quite different. This man's absence was going to leave a gap that could not easily be filled, if ever.

He saw the shadow cross her face and mistook the reason for it. 'Don't worry. I am sure that you will see your father soon.'

'God willing.' She paused. 'And you will return to regular duty for a while.'

'Yes, unless Major Forbes has found another task for me to perform.'

Her heart thumped. If he were sent on such another mission she might never see him again. 'Do you think it likely?'

'Where Forbes is concerned, anything could happen.'

'But surely if you are promoted to Lieutenant Colonel you will outrank him.'

Falconbridge laughed. 'What a very pleasing thought.'

'Yes, although I suppose he would still have the ear of General Ward.'

'And of Wellington.'

'A fearful trinity,' she observed.

'It is an apt description.' He paused, eyeing her keenly. 'And you, my dear, what will you do once your father is freed?'

Sabrina shook her head. 'In truth I hadn't thought beyond that moment, but I suppose we will go on as we did before. Perhaps Forbes will find another mission for me, too.'

His expression became more serious. 'Indeed I hope he will not.'

'Why so?'

'I would not see you exploited in this way again.'

She smiled wryly. 'He exploited my feelings, but that is all. I could have refused.'

'No, you could not,' he replied. 'You are too loyal and too brave.'

She felt a start of surprise for there had been nothing in his voice or look to suggest he was anything but sincere. It stirred a strange emotion in her breast.

'Not so brave. It was a calculated risk.'

'All the same, very few young women would have agreed, I think.' He paused. 'Forbes is a scoundrel if he ever subjects you to such a risk again.'

'I shall exercise due care.'

'I pray you will. I would not have you come to harm, my dear.'

Again the sincerity in his tone was unmistakable and her heart beat faster in response. 'Nor I you,' she replied. 'But I'm sure you will not heed my advice and ignore Major Forbes.'

He returned her smile. 'He's a hard man to ignore.'

'He has a certain way with him, does he not?'

'That's putting it tactfully. He's a devious rogue with a smooth tongue and considerable skill in manipulating people.'

'Exploitation of others is part of the job. The intelligence service could scarcely operate without it.'

'Its dealings are usually with those inured to its ways or hardened by long experience,' he replied. 'You are neither.'

'Yet it was my choice to be involved. I just hope it proves to be worth all the effort.'

'I really believe it will.'

They had lapsed into silence after this and did not speak again until the carriage stopped half an hour later. It was a welcome respite and Sabrina was relieved to get down and stretch her legs. She was hungry, too, and readily agreed to the light luncheon that Falcon-bridge suggested. However, a few words with the *patrón* revealed a limited menu.

'He says that today he has *fabada*.'

Sabrina grinned. 'Well, I suppose that narrows the choice.'

'What choice?'

'Do you want it or not?'

He laughed. 'I happen to like *fabada,* but can you eat it?'

'I have no objection, provided it is well-cooked.'

Indeed it proved to be and they helped themselves to a huge tureen full of the delicious fava bean and pork stew. It was accompanied with bread and a jug of the local wine. Sabrina ate hungrily.

Her companion smiled. 'I never met a woman so easily pleased by such simple fare.'

'Simple does not mean bad,' she replied. 'When one is hungry most food seems delicious.' Then, eyeing him askance, 'Or do you imply that my palate is unrefined?'

He seemed taken aback. 'By no means. I meant it as a compliment.' Then he saw the mischievous sparkle in her eyes. 'As you well knew, you rogue.'

She grinned. The thought occurred to him that he would miss her company when this was over. Some-how it had grown on him, and in lots of unexpected ways. If she had flirted or tried to attach him he would have found it easy to resist, but this innocent charm was harder to overcome. Just then he wasn't even sure he wanted to.

Before either of them could say more they were interrupted by the sudden appearance of Corporal Blakelock.

'Beg pardon, sir, but there's a group of riders heading this way. I spied 'em with the glass from the top of yonder knoll a few minutes ago.'

Falconbridge was on his feet in a moment. 'How far?'

'A couple of miles off, I reckon, sir.'

'How many?'

'Hard to say from the dust they were kicking up, but I'd guess at least fifteen. Could be more.'

'French?'

'Very likely, sir.'

Sabrina looked at Falconbridge. 'Machart?'

'Probably, but we're not going to stay around long enough to be sure.'

'We can't outrun them with the carriage.'

'No. We'll have to ride.' He turned back to Blakelock. 'Get the carriage and chaise out of sight and have the horses saddled at once. We leave as soon as may be.'

'Aye, sir.'

When the other departed on his errand, Falconbridge looked at Sabrina. 'Have you suitable clothes for riding?'

'Of course.'

'Then I suggest you change as fast as you can.' He headed for the door. 'I'll see you outside shortly.'

She needed no second bidding. Calling for Jacinta she issued swift instructions. Within minutes the necessary box was brought indoors and, after withdrawing to a private chamber, the two women stripped off their travelling dresses and pulled on breeches, boots and jackets.

'You will need this.' Jacinta handed Sabrina her sword and, while her mistress buckled it on, returned for the case that held her pistols. 'Primed and loaded,' she observed.

'Good.' Sabrina thrust one into her waistband and gave her companion the other, before sliding a slim blade into her boot.

Jacinta picked up a wicked-looking dagger and fastened the sheath to her belt. Finally she took out two cloaks. 'It gets cold in the hills at night.'

Hastily shoving their discarded clothing back in the box they took a final glance around. Sabrina glanced at her companion.

'Let's go.'

By the time they rejoined the others, the horses were saddled and ready. Blakelock had returned to the knoll behind the inn to watch the progress of the advancing force, and he returned at a run.

'They're about a mile away, sir, but if they've been pushing their horses hard it gives us an advantage.'

'Then let's make the most of it,' said Falconbridge.

He saw Sabrina and Jacinta mounted and swung himself into the saddle of a rangy chestnut gelding. Then the whole party set off. For a while no one spoke. The pace was too swift anyway to admit of conversation and everyone was anxious to put as much space as possible between themselves and pursuit. At some instinctive level Sabrina knew their pursuer was Machart, and also knew what the consequences of capture would mean. In another part of her was determination not to let that happen, and she settled down to ride.

Having followed the road for another three miles or so they turned off and headed away across country towards the hills. With Ramon as their guide they followed little frequented tracks and sheep paths, using rocks and trees for cover.

'It won't take the Frenchman long to work out what we've done,' said Falconbridge, 'but while he does we'll be moving well ahead of him.'

Sabrina regarded him steadily. 'He strikes me as the sort who does not give up easily.'

'You may well be right. We'll know soon enough.'

They rode until dusk and made camp on a wooded hillside. Even though there was no immediate sign of pursuit, Falconbridge wouldn't allow a fire so they ate cold rations brought from the inn: bread and cheese and a little cured ham. Sabrina ate her portion in thoughtful silence, listening intently. The only sounds were of crickets and the muted murmur of male conversation, occasionally punctuated by the stamp of a horse's hoof on dry earth. It was cooler now and the air sweet with pine and wild herbs. Above her, the first stars shone in the deepening blue. It brought back memories of the times she had camped like this with her father and, unbidden, a lump formed in her throat.

'Are you all right?'

A familiar voice brought her back to the present. 'Oh, yes. Thank you.'

Falconbridge regarded her quizzically for a moment and then seated himself on a convenient rock nearby. 'I regret the basic nature of the accommodation,' he went on. 'It's not what I had planned.'

'I've slept in worse, on some of Father's expeditions.' She grimaced. 'I recall one inn where the beds were so flea-ridden that we had to sleep in our cloaks on the floor.'

'You miss him, don't you?'

'Very much.'

'These last months must have been lonely.'

'Not as lonely as they would have been without Jacinta and Ramon and Luis. They have been very kind to me.'

'It speaks of the regard in which they hold you and your father.'

'I just hope he will rejoin us soon.'

The tone was wistful and in that moment he glimpsed the vulnerability that she tried so hard to conceal. Although she undoubtedly knew how to use them, the sword and pistols were merely part of the disguise designed to keep unwanted attention at bay, like the outwardly confident manner she assumed. At times it slipped a little, as now. The effect was to touch him more deeply than he had ever thought possible. Suddenly he found himself wanting to know more, to understand what drove so lovely a young woman to lead such a demanding and often comfortless life. She would not be out of place in London society; indeed, few of the young women there could hold a candle to her.

Aloud he said, 'I'm sure he will. And he will be very proud when he learns of the part you played in obtaining his freedom.'

'He hasn't got it yet. First we have to shake Machart off the scent.'

'Yes, but I believe it can be done.'

'I hope so. I should not like to fall into his clutches.'

'I'll try by every means to prevent it.'

'I know you will.'

The tone was soft but something about it and the accompanying look caused his heart to beat a little faster. Could a man be mistaken about such a look? He had been mistaken once before. Yet here was no Clarissa. Nothing in Sabrina's manner had ever struck him as underhand or devious—unconventional perhaps, but not treacherous. She was a free spirit but, as he had observed before, loyal and brave and, of course, very lovely. Imagination transported him back to a moon-lit terrace and the touch of her lips on his. What had been intended as a mere subterfuge had turned into a moment of heart-stopping delight. The spark that had been kindled had not been extinguished and he knew it, but to repeat the experience would be to take advantage of her youth and inexperience. He was responsible for her welfare. He had made a promise to Albermarle and, he now realised, a promise to himself as well. He smiled and squeezed her shoulder gently.

'Best try to get some rest, Sabrina. We have a long, hard ride ahead of us tomorrow.'

He made his own rude bed close by and, laying his sword beside him, stretched out. Soon she could hear the soft, even tenor of his breathing. Only a few feet separated them. She could still feel the comforting pressure of his hand. He had used her name, too, with an easy familiarity that bore in it not a shade of offence. It sounded so right on his lips. How easy it would be to encourage him, to invite his kiss, to let him lead her aside and lie with him beneath the pines and share his warmth; share his passion. The thought ought to have been displeasing but it was not. She drew her cloak closer and shut her eyes, mentally rebuking herself. She could not afford to think of him in that way. To do so would lead only to heartache.

The night passed uneventfully and at first light they set out again, keen to use every available hour of day-light to put distance between themselves and pursuit. The pace was slower than Falconbridge would have liked but the trail was narrow and rocky and, in places, steep. Sometimes they had to dismount and walk.

At any other time Sabrina would have admired the scenery more; the peaks of the cordillera, the wooded slopes, the lakes and creeks combined to form a landscape that was spectacular. Once, she glimpsed ibex, and once, an eagle soaring on the warm air currents. Small lizards basked on sunlit rocks and the trees were full of birds. However, she found herself listening not for their songs but for the sound of hoofbeats that would indicate pursuit. She had no fear of their getting lost; Ramon knew this country well and she trusted him to guide them. It was the knowledge of how far they were from help that created the tension she now felt. Rests were few and short and always one of the men was on lookout. Even if they only walked, Falconbridge kept the group moving forwards.

'We'll make better speed when we're through the mountains,' he said, reining his horse alongside. He did not add barring brigands and accidents, but he didn't need to. Sabrina had travelled enough to know the risks. Just then, though, her attention was on the man beside her. The apparently casual ease with which he rode and controlled his mount was the mark of the true horseman. She guessed that he had been taught to ride almost as soon as he could walk.

Becoming aware of her quiet scrutiny, he shot her a sideways glance. 'I'd like to ask if I pass the test,' he said, 'but I'm rather afraid of the answer.'

'Test?'

'Yes. It's not often I am the subject of such close observation.'

'I beg your pardon.' She paused. 'And, yes, you did pass—with flying colours.'

One dark brow lifted a little. 'Now I am intrigued. Dare I enquire as to the nature of the test I have passed?'

'I was just thinking that you ride very well.'

'I'm flattered.'

'Not at all.'

'Of course, I should know that by now,' he replied. 'And, since you are also sparing with your praise, I shall take your remark as a compliment and treasure it. I know I may have to live on it for some time.'

The sober expression that accompanied these words did not deceive her in the least. 'I cannot imagine any words of mine being taken to heart by you.'

'Can you not?'

'No, for you are proof against praise or censure.'

'I dispute that. No man can consider himself beyond praise or censure, and to do so would argue a considerable degree of conceit.' He hesitated. 'Is your opinion of me really so low?'

'No, for I find that it has improved upon better acquaintance.'

He bit back the laughter that threatened. 'I am relieved to hear it, truly. I should not like to think I had sunk lower in your estimation since our first meeting.'

'That would scarcely have been possible, sir.'

This time he could not prevent the laughter from escaping, even as he inwardly acknowledged the hit. 'Wretched girl! I shall take consolation from your praise of my riding skills.'

'It's my belief that you learned from an early age and were taught by someone who knew what he was about.'

'Yes, an old groom by the name of Jackson. I never met a man who knew more about horses, and he was good with us boys, too.'

'You and your brother tried his patience a few times I take it.'

'I think we'd have tried the patience of a saint when we were young. Lord knows we got into enough scrapes.'

'You were fond of your brother back then?'

'Yes. We were very close as boys. Hugh was the person I looked up to most.'

'That must have made the rift between you much worse.'

'Yes.' It was an understatement, he thought. The discovery that his adored older brother had feet of clay had proved a shattering experience.

'I'm so sorry,' she replied. 'I never had brothers or sisters; at least none who survived past infancy. I always thought it would be pleasant to have a sister—someone to laugh with and to confide in.'

He heard the underlying wistfulness in her tone and glimpsed the loneliness she must have felt at times. Having a caring father was surely a blessing, but a young woman without a mother or older sister to turn to for guidance was at a distinct disadvantage.

'There must have been occasions when you would have welcomed some female company and support.'

'Yes, there were.' For an instant Jack Denton flashed into her mind. 'I am sure I would have made fewer mistakes if I'd had that help.'

'I cannot imagine you making very many mistakes,' he replied. 'You have too much common sense.'

'Yes, now, but I was not always nineteen years old.' She bit her lip. 'Experience is a good teacher but sometimes a painful one, is it not?'

He eyed her curiously, wondering what she was alluding to, but knew better than to force a confidence. If she wanted to tell him she would do it of her own volition.

'Yes, it is,' he agreed, 'but it makes us wiser.'

'And warier.'

'Yes.'

It was true. Experience had certainly made him warier, but what had prompted her to say that? His curiosity mounted. What had happened in the past to make her say that now? And wary of what? Or whom? Was it that earlier experience that had made her so adept at keeping him at a distance? For the first time it occurred to him that there had been another man in her past. Yet why should there not have been other admirers? Other men had eyes, too. From what she had said it did not seem as if the affair had been entirely happy, but it had clearly left its mark. Was she still in love with him? The notion jarred.

Before he could follow it up, Willis' voice broke in and claimed their attention.

'Beg pardon, sir, but my horse is going lame. He's favouring his near foreleg.'

Falconbridge gritted his teeth and signalled a halt. Then he and Willis dismounted and the latter bent to examine the site of the suspected injury.

'There's a lot of heat in the tendon, sir, and some swelling. It's a sprain, I reckon. Probably take a week to mend.'

Falconbridge also ran a hand down the leg and his fingers verified the words. 'Unfortunately, you're quite right. Unsaddle the beast and turn it loose. You'll have to ride double with Blakelock.'

It was far from ideal, but they were left with no choice now. However, it was going to slow their progress and everyone knew it.

Chapter Eight

It was later that same afternoon when they paused to rest the horses that they first caught sight of their pursuers. The wooded defile they had followed earlier had led into a wider valley. Ramon had climbed to the top of a rocky outcrop, scanning the countryside with a keen eye. Suddenly he became very still, all his attention focused on the spyglass. Then he lowered the instrument and hurried down to rejoin the others.

'Riders coming, *señor*.'

Falconbridge swore softly. 'They stick to the trail like leeches.'

'I think they have a tracker with them,' replied Ramon. 'A man named Valdez.'

'How can you be certain?'

'I'm not certain, but Valdez rides a dun-coloured horse and there's a dun leading the way down there.' He handed Falconbridge the glass. 'See for yourself, *señor*.'

He trained the glass on the line of horsemen strung out along the trail. It took only moments to verify what Ramon had said. 'How do you know this Valdez?'

'Anyone who knows this region has heard of the man. He has a reputation for hunting and tracking that is second to none.'

Luis regarded him quizzically. 'Then, if it is he, we are in trouble, I think.'

'Believe it. He will not give up until he has his quarry.'

'But why would he help the French? It is not patriotic.'

'For some men gold outweighs all else.' Ramon looked at Falconbridge. 'I think we should not linger, *señor*.'

The other nodded. Then he snapped the glass shut and stowed it in his saddlebag. 'Mount up everybody. We're leaving.'

They rode fast now, pushing the horses harder. From time to time Sabrina looked over her shoulder half-expecting to see their pursuers, but they were not yet in clear view. Occasionally they were forced to stop to let Willis get up behind Ramon or Luis, and thus relieve Blakelock's mount. She knew they couldn't afford to lose another horse.

When they halted briefly Ramon put an ear to the ground. 'Nothing yet, but they won't be far behind.'

'Then we ride,' said Falconbridge.

Sabrina urged her horse on, trying not to heed her aching muscles. She wondered what would happen when eventually they were forced to stop. If it came to a confrontation they would be outnumbered. Suddenly, death or capture was more than a vague possibility. For the first time since their mission began she felt the prickling of fear. Resolutely, she pushed the thought aside, unwilling to dwell on it until she had to.

They rode on until the sun was low on the horizon,

and made camp beneath a tall ridge. Having tended to the horses' needs they ate cold rations, for again it was not prudent to light a fire. Falconbridge organised guard duties so that there would always be someone on watch. Sabrina looked out from their vantage point over the quiet land, blue in the gathering dusk. She could detect no sign of life or movement. Common sense dictated that even their pursuers had to rest at some point, but gradually they would make up the ground until they caught their quarry. She shivered inwardly.

A shadow fell across her and she looked up quickly to see Falconbridge standing there. Not for anything would she let him see her fear and therefore summoned a smile. He returned it.

'You looked to be deep in thought. Am I intruding?'

'By no means.'

'Then may I join you awhile?'

'Of course.'

He sat down beside her and for a moment or two said nothing. Aware of him to her fingertips, she knew this was to be no casual conversation.

'There is something on your mind.'

He met her gaze and smiled faintly. 'Am I so transparent?'

'No, but under the circumstances it seems likely.'

He nodded. 'I cannot pretend to be unconcerned by our present situation.'

'You think that Machart and company will overtake us.'

'I fear so. If we had not lost a horse we might have outrun them, but as it is…'

'Then it will come to a fight.'

'Quite likely.' He paused. 'Do you remember the

conversation we had in the garden the day you accepted Ward's offer?'

'Yes.' How could she forget, when every detail was etched on her memory? 'You think that what we discussed then is about to happen, don't you?'

'It is a possibility only. Anything might happen, but it is as well to be prepared for every eventuality.'

The grey eyes were cool, almost sombre now. For a few seconds more they held hers; then he reached into a small pocket inside the waistband of his breeches and withdrew a small package, about an inch square. It looked like a piece of oilcloth.

'I want you to have this.'

'What is it?'

'A last resort.' He paused. 'I had hoped it would never be necessary to mention it, but as things stand I can do no other.'

Sabrina's brow wrinkled. 'I don't understand.'

'It's poison, swift and deadly. In extremis, it offers a way out.'

For a moment she was quite still, staring at the package in his hand. The implication sent a chill along her spine like the touch of iced velvet. Now, the truth of their earlier conversation was forcibly borne upon her. *If you are captured, death is the best you can hope for. Before that there is always interrogation.*

'I may not always be able to protect you, Sabrina.'

'I see.' Suddenly she did see, and with awful clarity.

'It is a precaution only,' he continued, 'but it would please me to know that you had this with you.'

For a moment, Machart's lupine stare imposed itself on her imagination. It was horribly vivid and her mind recoiled. Wordlessly, she nodded and took the package, slipping it into a small inner pocket of her jacket.

Falconbridge watched it safely stowed. He had wondered what her reaction would be. She was so young and, just then, seemed so very vulnerable. If only he and his men had been involved he might have regarded their situation with greater *sang-froid*. What he felt now was fear, not for himself but for her, and the maid, too. He knew only too well what men like Machart were capable of, and the knowledge filled him with silent fury. The thought of any man doing them hurt was an affront. The idea of any man laying violent hands on Sabrina was past bearing.

'I wish with all my heart that you had not come on this mission,' he said, 'but in truth I have enjoyed your company.'

Rather shyly she said, 'And I yours.'

'In spite of my conspicuous lack of gallantry?'

'I have not found you ungallant. Well, perhaps once,' she amended, 'but I understand the reason for it now.'

He surveyed her closely. 'Does that mean I might entertain the hope of forgiveness?'

Under that penetrating gaze she reddened a little. 'I bear you no grudge.'

'I am glad, for of all people I should least desire your enmity.'

'I feel none.'

The words caused his heart to beat faster. Unable to help himself he leaned closer, glimpsing in her face what he had unconsciously hoped to see and what she could not hide. For a moment they remained thus, before his lips brushed hers. He felt the familiar spark leap between them, igniting desire. Then his arms were round her shoulders drawing her closer.

She knew she should resist and, equally, knew she did not wish to. Every part of her wanted this, wanted to be in his arms, to taste his mouth on hers, to breathe the scent of him. It felt so right. Surely this could be no act on his part. Yet he had not mentioned any emotion stronger than liking. It would be anathema to have him think her an easy conquest, to forfeit all respect. She never wanted to see him look at her as Jack Denton had once looked at her. His good opinion mattered too much. He mattered too much. That knowledge was enough to make her pull gently away from him.

'Forgive me, I...'

'What is it, Sabrina?'

She shook her head, unable to find the words to explain. She had half expected him to be angry, but instead he took her hand in his and squeezed it gently.

'You need not be afraid of me.'

'I know.' That was true, she thought. It was not him she feared.

'Nor will I ever seek more than you wish to give.'

Her stomach lurched and she lowered her gaze from his, lest he should read the dismay his words had caused. He wanted her, but not in the way she had hoped. If she encouraged him it would lead only to a furtive and illicit coupling, a brief affair that would mean nothing to him beyond the pleasure of the moment, but which she knew would break her heart. Better to lose him than to let that happen.

'I cannot give you what you want, Robert.'

Her use of his name thrilled through him even while his mind assimilated the rest of what she had said. Was this hesitation urged by love of another man? His throat tightened.

'Forgive me, I did not mean...'

'The act is unnecessary. Machart is not watching now.'

Suddenly there was tension in every line of his body. The grey eyes burned into hers. 'An act? Is that what you think?'

'What else should I think?'

She tried to disengage her hand but his grip tightened. 'I'll not deny that I kissed you first as an intended ruse, but it took only seconds to know that it was no ruse, that Machart was merely an excuse.' He paused. 'This time it needed no excuse. I kissed you because I wanted to and because I hoped you felt the same. Was I wrong?'

'I would be lying if I said so.'

'Then you fear I am not to be trusted. Is that it?' When she did not answer his jaw tightened. 'Well, I suppose I cannot blame you.'

'It's not that exactly.'

'Then what?'

'I…it's hard to explain.'

He was almost certain now that it involved another man but he needed to be sure. 'Will you not try?'

She took a deep breath. What would be his reaction if she told him the truth? Would the truth disgust him? There was more than one way to lose a man's regard, such as him finding out that she had once been taken for a slut by a fellow officer.

He saw her hesitation. In the gathering dusk her face looked pale, the expression in her eyes almost fearful. Again he was reminded forcibly of her youth and her vulnerability and he regretted his earlier surge of anger.

'Sabrina?'

The tone was soft and coaxing, the hand on hers

warm and strong. If she succumbed, she was lost. She took another deep breath.

'I'm sorry, but I cannot. Not now.'

'I see.' He gave her hand a last gentle squeeze and then released his hold. 'Perhaps you are right. Some things are better left unsaid, are they not?'

'Yes.'

'I can only apologise for my behaviour and assure you that it will not be repeated.'

He made her a polite bow and withdrew. As she watched him walk away, a cold weight settled in the pit of her stomach. The last vestiges of sunset splintered through the water in her eyes. She had lost him, but at least she had not lost his respect.

Falconbridge took the first watch that night, wanting time apart from his companions. He found a suitable vantage point among the rocks and settled down to wait, his gaze searching the darkening trail. However, the evening was quiet save for the usual chirring of the insect population, and the occasional murmur of conversation from his men. As he watched, he tried not to let his mind dwell on the recent scene with Sabrina, but it kept returning unbidden. He blamed himself for what had happened, for letting what had been a business arrangement get so out of hand. Her private life was none of his business. Once again she had pulled things back from the brink. He grimaced. At his age he ought to know better. It was just that as soon as she was near, all his good intentions vanished like smoke in the wind. The knowledge made him angry. Had they not got enough problems without his complicating things further?

'I shall conquer this,' he muttered, 'for both our sakes.'

* * *

The night passed uneventfully and at first light they saddled the horses and moved on. Now they made better progress but, although the open terrain offered that advantage, it also made them more vulnerable, since they could no longer conceal their presence. Falconbridge was keenly aware of that fact. Before they stopped for the night they needed to find a location that was at least defensible. During the ride that morning he made no attempt to single out Sabrina or to engage her in private speech, though his manner towards her was courteous and correct in every way.

She followed his lead in this. It should have been a relief but the feeling it engendered was quite different. This polite stranger was nothing like the man she had come to know, and she felt the loss keenly. However, pride forbade the utterance of those sentiments she felt in her heart.

Jacinta, riding alongside, cast surreptitious glances her way from time to time, but did not comment. When she spoke it was of general topics only, though the expression in her dark eyes was more knowing.

Only when they had paused for a brief rest at midday and Sabrina only picked at her portion of food did she allude to the subject at all.

'You must eat to keep up your strength.'

'I'm just not hungry.'

'I think it is not the quality of the food which causes this loss of appetite.' She glanced to where Falconbridge sat talking to the men.

Sabrina followed her glance briefly and then looked away. 'No, I guess it's anxiety about our situation.'

Jacinta nodded. 'There is much to be anxious about, but that is not it either.'

Her companion sighed. It was pointless to deny there was anything wrong; Jacinta had known her too long for that. 'You're right, but I can't talk about it.'

'Time to talk may be running out. Perhaps you should speak while you can and,' she continued, ignoring Sabrina's attempt to interrupt, 'I don't mean to me.'

'There's nothing to speak about.'

'No?'

'No.'

'If you say so,' replied Jacinta. 'After all, you best know your own heart, do you not?'

With that she resumed eating. Her companion shot her a sideways look but Jacinta's gaze was fixed on the distant view. Sabrina sighed. Just then she was afraid to acknowledge what was in her own heart. She stared at the portion of stale bread in her hand. The other woman was right about that at least; she did need to eat. With a determined effort she bit off a lump and began to chew.

Soon after this, the party set off again. Sabrina mentally girded herself for the effort. The long hours in the saddle and the swift pace were tiring. Every muscle ached and flesh grew sore. She thought fondly of a hot bath and a soft bed but knew they were a fantasy, many days' ride away. If they could not outrun the men who followed them she might never be afforded such luxuries again. It was a sobering thought and helped focus her mind on the task in hand.

In the mid-afternoon, as they walked to let the animals breathe awhile, Falconbridge called a brief halt so that he might find a vantage point from which to use the spyglass. What he saw did not please him. He made no attempt to disguise the truth from the others. In any case, his expression would have been enough to tell them.

'They're gaining,' he said.

'We cannot outrun them, sir,' said Blakelock. 'Not when we're a horse down and the rest almost spent.'

'No. We need to find somewhere to take cover.' He did not add, *and to make a last stand*, but it was understood.

For this purpose they selected a knoll which, though set back some way from the road, permitted a clear view and afforded some large rocks which would give cover under fire. It also precluded the possibility of the enemy sneaking up on them unawares. They made their camp and secured the horses before setting a watch. The men had rifles and ammunition which, Sabrina knew, would at least give them a chance. It all depended on how many pursuers there were.

Falconbridge used the remaining daylight to study the oncoming force. Eventually he was able to give an accurate estimate of their numbers.

'Twenty,' he said, passing the glass to Blakelock.

The other confirmed it with a nod. 'That's the size of it, sir.'

He did not comment on the fact that their own party numbered only seven, or that two of the number were women.

'We may be able to hold 'em off for a while, sir, but not for too long.'

'No,' replied Falconbridge, 'but perhaps for long enough.'

He returned and summoned the others. Then he told them the situation. They heard him in stony silence.

'I cannot disguise from you the fact that capture is highly likely,' he said then.

'We can give a good account of ourselves first though, eh?' said Luis.

'We can do better than that.'

'How so?'

Falconbridge reached for the inner pocket of his coat and drew out the slim leather wallet that resided there. 'Whatever happens, these must get to Wellington.'

Jacinta looked from them to him. 'And what are they, *señor?*'

'The documents that I went to Aranjuez to collect. They contain sensitive military information that could change the whole course of the war.' He paused. 'There is no possibility that all of us can get away, but one man might be able to. The rest will have to stay and keep the French occupied for as long as we can to cover his escape.' He looked directly at Ramon. 'Only you have the local knowledge that might enable you to succeed.'

Ramon stared back. 'What you say is true, but how do you know I can be trusted with this? We have known each other only a short time.'

'Miss Huntley trusts you. That's good enough for me.'

Hearing these words, Sabrina felt her heart give a peculiar lurch and she threw Falconbridge a swift glance. However, his attention remained on Ramon.

'Will you do it?'

'I have a duty here, *señor,* and that is to protect *Doña* Sabrina.'

'That's right, and that's why she and Jacinta must go with you. The rest of us will hold off pursuit as long as we can to buy you time.'

Sabrina shook her head. 'We cannot ride as fast as Ramon could alone and we would only slow him down. We must remain and take our chances here.'

'I applaud your courage, my dear, but—'

Sabrina shook her head. 'There is no time to argue, Robert. Ramon must go. Those plans must be delivered or this whole mission will have failed.'

Ramon met her eye. 'I promised your father.'

'And I know what my father would say if he were here now.'

Hearing her reply, Falconbridge felt his heart swell with pride and pleasure. She had so much courage and spirit. Most of the women he had ever met would have been weeping wrecks by now. He would have spoken then, but Jacinta was before him.

'*Doña* Sabrina is right. You have to go, Ramon.'

'*Sí,*' said Luis. 'Only you have a chance of success.'

Ramon's dark eyes burned. 'A chance to save myself and leave my friends to die, you would say?'

'No, *amigo mio,* it is a chance to help drive the French from Spain. That is something worth dying for.'

'We knew the risks when we came,' said Sabrina. 'Don't let all this count for nothing.'

The silence that followed her words was deep. Ramon looked round but saw in every face the same resolution.

'I will carry the documents to safety, but I will not leave you to die.'

Falconbridge frowned. 'I don't follow.'

'You are right when you say I have local knowledge, *señor,* but it is not confined merely to the geography of this region. I know its people, too.' He glanced back down the trail. 'People like Valdez, for example—and also El Cuchillo.'

They stared at him in slack-jawed astonishment for all present knew the name of the guerrilla leader.

'You know El Cuchillo?' said Luis.

'Our paths have crossed before.'

'You never told me this.'

'You never asked.'

'That is not the point.'

Blakelock frowned. 'What has El Cuchillo got to do with anything?'

'His camp is in these hills, and not so far from here, either,' replied Ramon. 'If I can find it I may be able to bring reinforcements.'

'Why would he help us?'

'He has helped the British before.'

Falconbridge nodded. 'That's true, but even if you found him and he agreed to come, time is not on our side.'

'Then the sooner I leave the better.'

'Agreed. But do nothing to jeopardise the safety of those papers.'

'I give you my word.'

They watched Ramon stow the leather wallet inside his jacket. Jacinta prepared some rations in a small bundle and then they went with him to the horses. He mounted and raised a hand in salute.

'*Hasta luego.*'

Sabrina summoned a smile. She thought that the chances of them meeting again were remote, in this life anyway, but it served no purpose to say so. Instead she watched in silence as he turned the horse's head and rode away.

'I pray he may succeed,' murmured Falconbridge.

The sound of that voice jolted her from her thoughts. For the first time it sounded less than completely confident, and in that moment she glimpsed the strain he must be under, being answerable for their safety and for the success of this mission. He had always seemed so self-assured and so impervious to doubt or fear. It was oddly touching to discover that he was as human as the rest of them underneath that cool exterior.

'If anyone can do it, I think it is he,' she replied.

'You have great faith in him.'

'He has never let me down yet. Whatever happens, he will ensure the plans get to Lord Wellington, somehow.'

'Then this mission will not have been in vain.'

'I know it will not.' Her eyes met his. 'In the meantime, we must do as Luis says and give a good account of ourselves.'

'You have never done anything else.'

The words were quietly spoken but the tone was unmistakably genuine, like the look in his eyes. A look that caused her heart to beat faster. A look that must be resisted at all costs. Besides, she had doubts of her own which she needed to voice.

'If…when…Ramon delivers those papers to Wellington, will my father still be freed? Even if I do not return, I mean?'

'When the papers are delivered, the mission will have succeeded. The agreement will be honoured.'

He saw her smile then, a sad and wistful smile that tore at his heart. Just then he would have given anything to have her safe, to have her a thousand miles from here in some haven where nothing could harm her again.

'I am glad,' she replied, 'and all this will have been worthwhile.'

The words reminded him with force about why she had come on this mission in the first place. Her decision had had nothing to do with him per se, though when they were thrown together, she seemed to find his company agreeable enough. It was he who had overstepped the mark, and she who tried to keep their relationship within professional bounds. He had no right to make things harder than they already were.

He smiled. 'All may yet be well.'

'Yes.' She hoped, rather than believed, it to be true.

Chapter Nine

The French force came into view in the early evening. They were riding slowly, no doubt having pushed their horses before. From her position on the knoll Sabrina could see the blue uniforms and distinctive grey shakos. At their head was a rider on a dun horse.

'The man, Valdez,' said Luis, and spat into the dust.

Blakelock smiled grimly, lining the distant figure in his sights. 'Shall I blow his brains out, sir?'

'No, he is mine,' replied Luis.

'Don't fire yet,' said Falconbridge. 'Let them get closer.'

Sabrina glanced at Jacinta and received a faint answering smile. She wished they, too, had rifles. Pistols were only of real use at closer range. Once they were discharged would there be time to reload before the enemy reached the top of the hill? After that it would be hand-to-hand fighting. Her stomach knotted. The encounter with brigands she and her father had once experienced was vivid still in memory, and there had been far fewer of them. Brigands were bad enough. Trained soldiers were another matter entirely. Even if Falconbridge and the other men could pick off some of the French contingent, they would still be badly outnumbered.

She turned again to Jacinta. 'I'm so sorry to have got you into this.'

'It was the French who got us into this, not you, *Doña Sabrina*.'

'It's true,' said Luis. 'We were involved from the moment they invaded our country. We will make them bear the consequences.'

Sabrina looked down the hillside and saw that the troop had halted. The figure on the dun horse was riding ahead alone at a slow walk, his attention on the ground immediately in front of him.

'The bastard's looking for sign,' muttered Blakelock.

Willis nodded. 'Aye, and it'll not take him long to work out what's happened.'

Luis bared his teeth in a feral smile. 'Good. It means I shoot him all the sooner. That will teach the scum to betray his countrymen.'

A few minutes later the dun horse stopped and its rider looked directly up at the knoll. Then he turned back and rejoined his companions. Evidently words were spoken, and they saw him point towards their place of concealment. The troop dismounted. Leaving their horses they began to fan out, moving slowly forwards towards the slope.

'Here they come,' said Falconbridge. 'Get ready.'

Sabrina's heart hammered in her breast and in spite of the heat she felt cold sweat start along her skin. Just feet away Blakelock's finger squeezed the trigger. There followed a loud report and a French trooper cried out and fell. Almost simultaneously a second shot rang out and the tracker dropped like a stone.

Luis smiled with grim satisfaction. *'Bueno!'*

Blakelock threw him a sideways glance. 'Not bad shooting—for a Spaniard of course.'

'Keep watching, Englishman. I'll show you how it's done.'

Seeing two of their number go down, the rest of the French force dived for cover among the rocks. Moments later they began to return fire. Luis darted a glance at the two women.

'You must stay down.'

'Thank you for that,' replied Jacinta. 'The thought would not otherwise have occurred to us.'

He returned her a pointed look but had no time to reply because, just then, the answering fire intensified. Lead shot whined around them. The higher ground afforded the defenders an advantage and two more French soldiers fell. Then some of their comrades advanced, dodging among the rocks and bushes, while the rest gave covering fire.

Falconbridge looked across at Sabrina. 'Are you all right?'

'Yes.'

'Good girl.'

His smile gave her fresh courage and she returned it. 'I was never in a battle before.'

'When you shoot, aim for the widest part of the man's body. Make each shot count.'

'I will.'

He nodded and then turned his attention back to the task in hand. They needed to lower the odds before the French reached their position and they were reduced to hand-to-hand combat. He tried not to think about what would happen then; tried not to think about Sabrina and Jacinta run through by French sabres, and his men slain.

Soldiers accepted the risks of warfare, but women were another matter. He knew he would defend them to the death, but would that be enough? Lining up his target he squeezed off another shot. A man yelled, clutching his arm. Falconbridge smiled grimly and reloaded.

Sabrina crouched behind a rock, pistol drawn. With pounding heart she risked a peek round the edge of the sheltering stone and saw blue-coated figures only fifty yards away. Soon they would be overrun. Her jaw tightened. This was no time for cowardice. If she went down, it would be fighting. Glancing at her companions, she knew there was no company she would rather die in.

A blue-coat rose up from behind a rock. Without thinking she lifted the pistol, aimed and fired. The man cried out and pitched backwards. Hurriedly, she reached for ball and powder to reload. Beside her Jacinta loosed off a shot of her own. Somewhere nearby a man cursed. Around them the air thickened with smoke and the acrid scent of powder. They heard Willis swear and clutch his sleeve. Blood welled through his fingers. Sabrina shoved the pistol in her belt and dropped into a crouching run, reaching him a few moments later.

'How bad is it?'

'Just a crease, ma'am,' he said between gritted teeth.

'Hold still. I'll bind it for you.'

She improvised a bandage from a handkerchief and neckcloth and tied it firmly. He smiled his thanks. Then retrieving his rifle, he reloaded. A blue-coated figure loomed above their crouching figures. Sabrina saw the shadow and looked up in horrified surprise. Her throat dried. She had a fleeting impression of the raised sword before a shot rang out and the man slumped. She spun round to see the smoking rifle in Falconbridge's hands, and swallowed hard, her gaze meeting his for a moment. The expression in his eyes sent a shiver through her; it was utterly uncompromising, the look of a man who would kill to defend his own. She stammered out her thanks and saw him nod.

'My pleasure.'

Out of the corner of her eye she saw a blur of movement and turned in horror to see that the vanguard of the French force had reached the top of the knoll. Falconbridge followed her gaze and his jaw tightened. Letting fall the rifle he drew his sword and launched himself into the attack, fighting now for all he held dear. He felt the blade connect with flesh; heard a cry and saw his opponent slump. Moments later another took his place. Again Falconbridge was on the offensive, keeping up the momentum, not giving his enemy even a moment to pause, using every means at his disposal to win. Finesse had no part in this; it was fierce and dirty with fists and boots supplementing steel.

Just a few feet away Sabrina drew her own blade and prepared to meet the nearest foe. The Frenchman's face registered surprise and then amusement as he took in the nature of his opponent. The hesitation cost him dear as the edge of her sword slashed his arm. Blood bloomed through the torn fabric. For a split second he stared at the wound in outrage and disbelief. Then his expression hardened and he pressed forward his attack. She fought as well as she knew how but determined resistance wasn't enough. Superior skill and strength forced her into retreat, step by step, until her back slammed against stone. Trapped against a boulder with no room to manoeuvre she knew she was lost. The Frenchman smiled. Sickened she watched him raise the blade for the *coup de grâce*.

And then, before her terrified gaze, her opponent checked, his face a mask of astonishment. The sabre dropped from his fingers and his legs buckled. Jacinta tugged her sword point from between his ribs. For a moment her gaze met Sabrina's and the dark eyes glowed with inner fire. Then she smiled.

Sabrina found her voice. 'Thank you.'

'*De nada.*'

Before she could say more, an armed figure rose up behind her. Sabrina yelled a warning. Jacinta spun round, but not quickly enough to avoid the swinging rifle. The butt connected with the side of her head and felled her instantly. The assailant stepped across the prone body towards Sabrina. Too late he saw the mouth of the pistol pointing at him. There was a sharp report and he fell, clutching a hole in his chest. However, Sabrina's attention was no longer on him.

'Jacinta!'

In a moment she was kneeling beside her companion, desperately trying to rouse her. A bloody gash and a lump testified to the site of the injury. Jacinta groaned. Sabrina felt relief flood back. She wasn't dead, only stunned. Her frantic gaze cast about for something to staunch the wound with. Then, without warning, she was seized from behind. Strong hands drew her upright. She fought them, kicking and struggling to free herself but the grip was like steel, pinning her arms behind her back and holding them like a vice. Casting a wild look around, she saw with sinking heart that the knoll was overrun and the fighting all but over. Blakelock and Luis were now held at gunpoint. Only Willis and Falconbridge were still engaged in combat but, hopelessly outnumbered, they were driven to stand at bay against a high rock. Then she heard a voice.

'Throw down your weapons. Further resistance is useless.'

She saw Falconbridge hesitate and for one dreadful moment thought he was going to refuse. Then he glanced around, taking in the whole scene, and nodded to Willis.

'Do as he says.'

The two men let fall their swords. As they did so the speaker advanced and a French officer strode into her line of vision. With him went the last vestige of hope and her stomach churned as she recognised Machart. For a moment he, too, cast a comprehensive look around. Then his gaze returned to Falconbridge.

'I was hoping we'd meet again, Monsieur le Comte. Though I think that is not the name by which you were known on the occasion of our first meeting.' He paused. 'Arroyo de Molinos, was it not?'

Falconbridge returned the gaze with a cool and insolent stare. 'I have no idea what you're talking about.'

'Come now. I admit my memory was faulty at first but I never forget a face,' the other went on. 'You have put me to a deal of trouble, monsieur, but I feel certain the effort will be repaid in due course.' He turned his attention towards Sabrina, his gaze taking in every detail of her altered appearance. His face registered sardonic amusement, though the smile stopped well short of his eyes. 'It is a pleasure to see you again, madame. I look forward to renewing our acquaintance.'

Her stomach wallowed. She fought it, knowing this man would be very quick to sense fear. With a supreme effort she forced herself to meet his gaze and to remain silent. She would not bandy words with him.

He gestured to his men. 'Bind the prisoners and fetch their horses.'

'You are out of your jurisdiction here,' said Falconbridge, 'and have no authority to detain us.'

Machart appeared untroubled. 'I believe I have the authority to apprehend a group of English spies. Of course, if I am mistaken I shall apologise, but I do not think I am mistaken.'

'Where are you taking us?'

'To Castillo San Angel, where we shall discuss the matter of identities.'

Sabrina darted a glance at Falconbridge but his expression was impassive and he remained still while they bound his wrists. Then her attention was reclaimed by rough hands binding her own. She made a token gesture of resistance but it was useless. When tested the cords yield not a whit. A few minutes later she and the others were manhandled down the slope and forced to mount their horses. It was then that she realised Jacinta wasn't with them. Had they left her for dead? Then she remembered what happened to the wounded after a battle, and fear congealed to a lump in her stomach. Perhaps the French had believed her already dead. If Jacinta had been conscious she would have had enough sense to remain quite still. How bad was her injury? There were predators in the mountains other than the human sort. Could she survive out here alone, at least long enough to make it to the nearest village perhaps? If so, there might be hope for her. She was brave and resourceful. If anyone would survive it would be her. At least she was not a prisoner and there was some comfort in that.

The cavalcade set off and her attention refocused on staying in the saddle. The pace was swift and conversation impossible. Besides, Falconbridge was in front of her. Suddenly her fear was all for him. *Everyone talks by the third day.* She was certain now that Machart would use every means at his disposal to find out what he wanted to know. She had never heard of Castillo San Angel but it bode ill for her and her companions. Where was it exactly?

They had not long to wait and find out, for in the early evening they came to a small castle, perhaps once the seat of a minor nobleman. Sabrina eyed it uneasily. It seemed to be quite old, judging from the state of the perimeter wall, and an attempt had been made to repair the worst areas of crumbling masonry. The stout timbers of the gate were faded and cracked. As they rode through she could see weeds growing among the stones in the courtyard and the buildings had an air of dilapidation. The place must have been commandeered for use as a military base, she decided. Certainly it held an uncomfortably large number of French troops.

Sabrina and her companions were dragged from the saddle and taken through an archway, along a wide inner corridor and down a flight of stone steps. They found themselves in an underground vault lit by torches. Although it now doubled as a prison, it had originally been intended solely for storage. The dim light revealed barrels and sacks and coils of rope. It was distinctly cool down here, the air musty. Several doors led off the main chamber. Their captors unlocked one of these and she and Falconbridge were shoved into the room beyond; the others taken to the adjoining chamber. Machart paused on the threshold. Then he spoke to his men.

'Untie their bonds.'

He watched as the order was obeyed. Then he smiled

faintly. 'You see, I am not so unfeeling as to separate a husband and wife. Enjoy each other's company while you can.'

With that, he and his men withdrew and the door slammed shut behind them. A key turned in the lock. At the sound, Sabrina shivered inwardly. From the passage outside she heard men's voices and then the sound of retreating footsteps. Automatically she massaged her bruised wrists. Falconbridge frowned.

'Are you all right, Sabrina? Have they hurt you?'

'No, I'm unharmed.'

'Hardly that,' he replied, looking round. 'I'm so sorry that I have brought you to this.'

She shook her head. 'It isn't your fault.'

'Who else should bear the blame but I?'

'You tried to dissuade me from coming along, but I insisted.'

'I should have moved heaven and earth to prevent it.'

'It would have made no difference.'

He returned a wry smile. 'No, I suppose it wouldn't, at that.'

She glanced around. The room was bare save for a small stool and a rough wooden cot on which lay a sacking mattress filled with straw. It was covered by a dirty blanket. A bucket in one corner served as a privy. A small, barred window set high in the wall was the only source of light. She guessed it corresponded roughly with ground level outside. The only exit was the door, three inches of iron-studded oak.

'They did not bring Jacinta,' she said.

Falconbridge frowned and immediately felt a twinge of guilt. In all the confusion he had not noticed the maid's absence.

'She was hit on the head with a rifle butt,' Sabrina continued. 'I was trying to ascertain the damage when we were overrun.'

'It may be just a concussion. If so, she will be recovered soon enough.'

'I pray she will be able to reach help—a village perhaps—though I don't know how far that might be.'

'By my estimation we were about ten miles from Burgohondo, but it's entirely possible she might find a small farmstead en route.' He paused. 'Jacinta strikes me as being resourceful. If anyone could survive it would be she.'

'She is resourceful, and brave, too.'

'She is not alone in that,' he replied. 'I saw you fight back there.'

'Not too well. Had it not been for you and Jacinta I'd have been run through.' She hesitated. 'I have not thanked you properly for saving my life.'

'I beg you will not mention it.'

'How can I not when I owe you so much?'

'You owe me nothing. Comrades look out for each other.' The words were accompanied by a faint smile. They were also meant to absolve her of obligation and keep their relationship on a professional footing. He was right to do it, she thought, but her dominant emotion was one of sadness.

She nodded. 'Yes, of course.'

For a moment he scrutinised her in silence. 'You must be exhausted, Sabrina. Why don't you try to get some rest?'

'What about you?'

'I'm not tired yet,' he lied. 'Besides, after the time we've spent on horseback it will be good to stand for a while.'

She moved across to the pallet, eyeing it with distaste. The mattress smelt musty and she tried not to think about how old it was or how many other occupants the cot might have had. She stretched out and let her aching muscles relax a little. Beneath veiling lashes she saw Falconbridge move away to the door, glancing out through the narrow metal lattice, apparently deep in thought. Once, she might have found this close confinement intimidating, but now his presence was a comfort. She had not been deceived by his earlier protestations; he, too, must be tired yet he had given up the cot to her use. His manner now could not have been more different from the one she had seen at first. It revealed a gentleness that she would never have suspected then.

Unbidden, Machart's face returned and with it, his words. *Enjoy each other's company while you can.* She shivered, trying not to think of the implication behind that, or what the morrow might bring. Now more than ever she was glad that Jacinta was free, and Ramon, too. At least the plans were safe and well out of Machart's grasp, and at the end of it all her father would be delivered from imprisonment. Not a total failure then, she thought.

Falconbridge remained where he was for some time, trying to order his thoughts. He was under no illusions about what lay ahead for him and his men if Machart discovered the truth. Spies were shot. It was a risk one took and while he might regret that matters had not turned out better, he could not be so philosophical where Sabrina was concerned. He could try to appeal to his captor's sense of honour and ask that she be set free, but suspected that Machart's notion of honour was not the same as his own. He could plead her youth and innocence if it would do any good.

He glanced at the cot. She lay quite still, eyes closed, her breathing soft and regular. She had never once reproached him for their predicament or shown any fear. His admiration and his regard had grown proportionately. She was indeed the rarest of women. He would have liked to know her better; to court her as a young woman should be courted. It was too late for that now, but he would no longer try to deny the depth of feeling she inspired in him; a feeling he had never expected to experience again.

He sighed and crossed quietly to the sleeping figure. Reaching for the blanket, he opened it out and laid it over her. Although it was only a meagre covering, it was better than nothing, for the air was cool down here. Then he sat down on the stool and watched her sleep. Her face looked very peaceful, the expression untroubled as though she had not a care in the world. He knew that face so well now, every line and curve. Its beauty haunted his dreams. Clarissa had been beautiful, but her beauty was of a different kind. Sabrina's owed nothing to artifice of any sort. She would be lovely when she was fifty—if she lived so long. His jaw tightened. If by some miracle they got out of this with a whole skin he would make it his mission to ensure nothing harmed her again.

At some point he must have dozed because he came to with a start. His neck and limbs felt stiff. It was darker now and the only light a faint ruddy glow through the lattice from the torch-lit corridor outside. He got to his feet and straightened slowly, wincing as his muscles protested. A glance at the bed revealed that Sabrina was sleeping still, though more restlessly now, huddled beneath the thin blanket. He reached out and touched her hand lightly. The skin was cold. He saw her shiver, and roll onto her side, drawing the cover closer. As he saw it, he knew there was one useful service he could perform.

He lay down beside her and curled his body protectively around hers, holding her close, sharing his warmth. She stirred a little but did not wake. He dropped a kiss on her hair and closed his eyes, trying not to think that this might be all they would ever have. However, as the shivering stopped and her warmth returned, the thought persisted. He would have liked to seize the moment and explore in intimate detail every curve of the body pressed so close to his; to know her in every sense of the word. There was a spark; it would not take much to fan it to a flame. If he did, would she perhaps surrender in the name of some brief, dubious comfort? He sighed. Even if honour had not forbidden it, he cared too much ever to take such blatant advantage.

He slept soon after, weary after the exertions of the day, and woke in the early dawn. Grey light was filtering through the bars in the high window. He glanced at his companion but she was still dead to the world. He smiled faintly. Unwilling to wake her yet, he drew the coverlet a little higher and remained where he was. In truth he did not want this brief intimacy to end. Despite the primitive surroundings it felt good to lie here quietly thus, to hold her in his arms again.

She began to rouse a little later, surfacing from deep sleep to a comfortable doze, and turned instinctively towards the source of the warmth. He gently kissed her parted lips. She smiled and her mouth yielded to his. The kiss grew deep and lingering. With a supreme and heart-thumping effort of will he drew back. Sabrina opened her eyes and looked into his face.

He smiled. 'Good morning.'

She stretched lazily and returned the greeting.

'I won't ask if you slept well for I know that you did,' he continued.

She was suddenly very still and he saw the green eyes widen as the nature of their situation became truly apparent. 'Robert! What…?'

'Have no fear. I merely wanted to keep you warm.'

'Keep me warm?'

'You were shivering last night so I took the liberty of sharing some body heat.' He paused. 'Besides, I was tired, too, and there is but one bed.'

'You mean that you…that we…you were here all night?'

'That's right.'

She knew then that she had not dreamed his kiss. The realisation sent a deeper warmth to the core of her being. This sudden enforced intimacy should have been shocking and repellent but it wasn't. Instead it felt comforting; somehow it felt right and good. It wasn't only that either: his presence took the edge off her fear, rather than adding to it.

Misinterpreting her silence he added, 'It was about shared bodily warmth, Sabrina, nothing more.'

Hearing the gentleness in his voice she felt a lump form in her throat. If he were dishonourable he could have taken full advantage of the situation. He was bigger and stronger and even if she had fought, he'd have over-powered her without undue trouble, secure in the knowl-edge that even if she had screamed for help no one would have come to her aid.

'I know,' she replied.

It wasn't what he had been expecting. 'Then you do not suspect a more sinister motive?'

'No.'

She made to sit up but his arm checked her. 'Stay awhile. It's early yet.'

She lay quite still, heart thumping, every fibre of her body aware of him. Feeling the tension in her stillness he regarded her quizzically.

'What are you afraid of?'

'Nothing.'

'Not so. Will you not tell me?'

How to tell him it was not him she feared but her own desires? If he only knew how close to the surface they lay...

'Sabrina?'

Suddenly the handsome face was closer to her own, his gaze searching. His lips were dangerously close now. If he kissed her she would not be able to help herself and he would take it as an invitation. The thought of what would inevitably follow turned her loins to fire. How easy it would be to surrender, to give in and let desire take its course. And if she did, what then? If they ever got out of this alive, how would he regard her after? In his eyes, she would be no better than a whore. She could hear the echo of Denton's voice: *Come...you know you want it. We have all afternoon...make the most of it.* Desire was replaced by flooding shame. There could only be one end to surrender now and she knew full well what it meant. Experience was the best teacher. The thought of Robert Falconbridge regarding her in those terms was unbearable. To hide her confusion she turned her head aside. Mistaking the reason for it, he drew back a little.

'It's all right, my dear. You don't have to say anything.'

He stroked the hair off her face. 'Go back to sleep for a while.'

She turned onto her side and felt his body curve round hers once more. Closing her eyes, she let herself relax, pushing aside all thoughts of the future, content just to be in the moment. And so he held her while she drowsed and let his arms provide at least the illusion of security.

Some time later they were roused by the sound of voices and heavy footfalls in the passageway without. Falconbridge was on his feet in an instant, listening intently. Sabrina came to stand beside him, her face pale.

'They have come for us.'

'Come for me,' he replied.

'Oh, Robert, I'm so afraid.'

He squeezed her arm. 'If you are questioned, my dear, you must stick to your story.'

She nodded. 'I will.'

'If Machart finds the slightest discrepancy in what we say he will exploit it. For all our sakes we must continue to sing from the same hymn sheet.'

'I understand.'

The footsteps stopped outside the door and a key turned in the lock. The door swung open to reveal four French soldiers. Two of them seized hold of Falconbridge.

'What do you want?' he demanded.

They made no answer save to bind his wrists.

Sabrina started forwards. 'What are you doing? Where are you taking him?'

The questions still elicited no response. They merely hustled their prisoner from the room and locked the door behind them. Sabrina rushed to the lattice and peered out, craning her neck to watch the retreating figures until they disappeared from view. Then, weak-kneed, she leaned against the wood and prayed quietly.

Falconbridge had known what to expect, but the pain still took him by surprise. Wrists bound, he crouched on the stone floor, gasping, waiting for the next kick from the booted feet in his line of vision. Every breath brought sharp protest from his bruised ribs. Blood trickled from the cut on his lip. His face throbbed from repeated blows. Rough hands hauled him to his feet so he could see his interrogator.

'I'll ask you again. Who are you?' Machart's voice reached him through the haze.

'I've already told you.' He gasped as a fist connected with his solar plexus.

'And I told you, I never forget a face. You were at Arroyo de Molinos.'

Falconbridge gritted his teeth. 'Someone who looked like me perhaps.'

'You play me for a fool, monsieur, and that is most unwise.' Machart nodded to the guards. Several more blows thudded into the prisoner's midriff, doubling him over. 'Tell me the truth and spare yourself more pain. What were you doing at Aranjuez?'

'You know. You were there.'

'What is your relationship with De la Torre?'

'He is my cousin.'

Machart's lip curled. 'Do you know I don't believe you?'

A heavy fist smashed into Falconbridge's jaw. He felt warm blood trickle from the resulting cut.

'No, I think you are a spy,' the Frenchman continued.

'I think your reason for visiting Aranjuez was something other than a social obligation, and I mean to find out what.'

The reply was an insolent stare. It drew down on the prisoner several more hard blows. He bit back the cry of pain that rose to his lips unbidden. This was just the softening-up process. Machart hadn't really got started yet. When he did, Falconbridge wondered how long he could hold out.

'Perhaps a flogging would help to loosen his tongue,' said a voice from across the room.

Falconbridge registered the rodent face of Jean Laroche. As soon as he had set eyes on the intelligence chief he knew his presence here meant serious trouble. Did they already suspect De la Torre of subterfuge? Had they been keeping an eye on him anyway? Or was this interrogation merely because Machart's memory had returned? He hoped for De la Torre's sake it was the latter.

'Not yet,' replied Machart. 'I have a better idea.'

'What?'

'We'll ask the woman.'

Cold dread congealed in Falconbridge's gut. 'Leave her alone. She's done nothing wrong and she can't tell you any more than I can.'

Machart regarded him speculatively for a moment. 'We shall ascertain that soon enough.' He looked beyond the prisoner to the guards. 'Bring her here.'

Chapter Ten

Sabrina heard boots on stone in the outer passageway and got to her feet, hoping it was Falconbridge returning. Her heart leapt as the key turned in the lock. However, it wasn't her companion who entered the cell. Seeing the two guards she lifted her chin, eyeing them with distaste.

'What do you want?'

'Someone desires a word with you, madam,' replied the first.

Her heart sank but there was no possibility of refusal. They took hold of her arms and escorted her out of the cell and back towards the stairs. She took a deep breath, resisting panic. It was happening, the thing she had subconsciously been dreading. From somewhere she dredged up the remains of courage, praying it would not be she who broke under questioning and so betrayed her companions.

She was taken along another corridor and brought at length to a wooden door. The guards knocked and a familiar voice bade them enter. The hairs on the back of her neck stood up. Then she was drawn across the threshold to be confronted by Machart and Laroche.

'Ah, Condesa, what a pleasure.'

Machart's greeting went unheeded. All her attention was on Falconbridge, her shocked gaze taking in the details of his battered face.

'What have you done to him?'

'Nothing much—yet,' replied Machart.

The pleasant tone sent a shiver through her. Unwilling to let him see her fear she faced him, forcing herself to meet his eye.

'By what right do you hold us here? By what right have you assaulted my husband?' It surprised her how naturally that word had tripped from her tongue.

'By the authority of His Majesty King Joseph. Your husband is an English spy.'

'That is nonsense.'

'Is it? We shall see.'

She darted a swift look at Falconbridge and met his steady gaze. In that instant she understood her own heart. If this was the end of the road she would die with him, and gladly, too. He would have no cause to be ashamed of her at the last.

'I have brought you here to help clarify a few points that have eluded us so far,' Machart continued.

He moved closer, his predatory gaze lingering a moment on her face. One hand stroked her cheek. Sabrina jerked her head aside. Machart bared his teeth in a smile.

Falconbridge glared at him. 'Leave her alone.'

'If you wish us to leave her alone you will tell us what we want to know,' said Laroche. 'It would be a pity to spoil such beauty.'

'You cowardly scum.' The defiant tone gave no hint of the sick dread that gripped him now.

'Oh, I don't think it will be necessary to go to such extremes,' said Machart. 'I believe I know what will work just as well, and will be infinitely more enjoyable.' He turned to the guards. 'Tie him to that chair.'

Falconbridge struggled but it was a token resistance only. Two minutes later he was securely bound. The sick feeling in his gut intensified but his fear was not for himself.

Laroche frowned. 'What do you intend?'

'To discover the truth,' replied Machart. 'If you will permit me some time alone with madam, I believe we shall arrive at it very soon.'

'As you will.' Laroche rose from his seat. 'Just don't take too long.'

'Not long at all, I assure you.' Machart glanced at the guards and jerked his head towards the door. 'Get out.'

When they and Laroche had left, he turned back to Sabrina. 'Now, madam, you are going to help me discover what I wish to know.'

'I will never lift a finger to help you.'

'On the contrary, I think you will be invaluable.' He glanced at the bound figure across the room. 'And you will do everything I demand.'

Falconbridge fought the restraining cords but they held fast. 'If you harm her, you filth, I'll kill you.'

'It seems to me that you are not in a position to make threats,' replied the Frenchman. 'Besides, it is not my intention to harm the lady.'

Sabrina gave him a cold stare, though her heart was thumping in her breast. 'Then what do you intend, Colonel?'

'I've been looking forward to renewing our acquaintance, madam. I intend us to forge a more intimate bond.'

Her jaw tightened as the import of the words became clear. 'Never.'

Machart seized hold of her waist and dragged her up against him, bringing his mouth down hard on hers. Taken by surprise, sickened and half-stifled by fetid breath, she struggled hard. It availed her nothing. He took the kiss at leisure before allowing her to come up for air. Furious she struck out at him, the slap ringing loud in the quiet room.

'Let go of me, you oaf!'

The response was a chilling smile. Without warning a large hand shot out and closed on her throat. She gasped, her hands clawing, trying to break his hold, but he held her easily. Through the drumming blood in her ears she heard Falconbridge's shouted protest; then the Frenchman's face was thrust towards her own.

'Looking forward to renewing the acquaintance and intending to make the most of it,' he continued.

His hold never slackened as he forced her backwards across the room to the desk. With his free arm he swept everything from its surface, scattering documents, sending paperweight, blotter and pens flying. Then he forced Sabrina down, pinning her against the wood with his weight.

'Soon now your husband will tell me everything I wish to know.'

Across the room, Falconbridge fought his bonds, unaware of the blood that trickled over his wrists. 'Let her go, you blackguard.'

'After going to such trouble to find her again? I think not.' Machart released his grip on her throat and reached for the fastenings of her breeches. Gasping for breath Sabrina tried to rise. A slap across the cheek sent her reeling back. Then he resumed, accomplishing the task with little trouble. 'No, I have other plans entirely.'

Sabrina felt her clothing loosen and then coarse hands sliding beneath her shirt to her breasts. She tried to scream but her bruised throat permitted only a faint croak. Frantic hands clawed at the face looming over hers. He slapped her again. Moments later her wrists were imprisoned and clamped to the desk. Then his mouth closed over hers, hot and hard, forcing her jaw open, his tongue thrusting in. She could feel his erection against her thigh. Sick with horror she writhed beneath him.

Machart released her mouth and looked into her face. 'Believe me, madam, when I've finished you will not think of your husband's embraces again, I promise you.'

'No!' Sabrina thrashed. 'Please, no! Let go of me!'

'Let go?' His smile mocked her. 'Later perhaps, but first your husband is going to watch while I take you.'

Falconbridge's grey eyes locked with the Frenchman's for a moment. 'You cur! You filthy little cur!'

'Jealous, monsieur? You should be. Watch and you will learn.' He leaned closer and spoke to Sabrina. 'You are about to discover what it is that you've been missing.' He paused. 'Don't you want me to tell you?' Leaning forwards he murmured words for her ear alone. Their effect was to make her struggle harder. Seeing her desperation increase, he smiled. 'I'm going to give you the time of your life.'

Suddenly four years rolled away. Machart's face blurred and dissolved until all she could see was Jack Denton's leer, hear his mocking tone as he held her down: *Like it rough, do you? Well, by God, Jack's your man.* The memory brought welling fury and disgust that overrode fear. Her current persecutor was strong, too, but she knew she would rather die than submit.

Machart reached for the fastenings of his own clothing. She felt him shove her thighs apart. In desperation she brought her knees up, hand groping along the top of her boot, seeking the blade concealed there. He misinterpreted the movement and smiled.

'Not so reluctant after all then? Be assured, *ma chère,* you'll get what you want.'

Sabrina stifled a sob, her fingers scrabbling against leather. Machart fumbled for the last buttons on his breeches. They held. She heard him curse softly, saw him look away, intent on the task. It was enough. She darted a glance towards her boot and located what she sought. Her fingers closed round the hilt of the knife. The last buttons released their hold and Machart leaned forwards, his weight crushing her against the desk. Sabrina took a deep breath and drew the blade, bringing the point up under his ribs in one swift movement and driving it in as hard as she could. Flesh proved more resistant than she had imagined. For a few seconds he froze an expression of sheer astonishment on his face as he took in the knife.

'You bitch!'

With a sharp indrawn breath he pulled it out and clapped a hand to his side.

Feeling the warm blood on his palm he glanced down and his expression became murderous. Then he lunged for her. She rolled to evade the groping hand and tumbled over the edge of the desk to land sprawling on the floor amid the strewn stationery. Her fingertips brushed something small and solid, a glass paperweight. She grabbed it just before Machart's fist seized her jacket and hauled her upright. Swinging round, Sabrina struck out. The paperweight caught him across the side of the head and sent him staggering backwards. He lost his balance and fell, hitting the floor with a heavy thud, and then lay still. Trembling with revulsion she stared at the silent form, unable to believe what she had done. Then her horrified gaze turned to the other occupant of the room. His eyes spoke of pity and anger and pride.

'Oh, my dear, brave girl.'

The words were softly spoken and they recalled another man in another place, another witness to her humiliation. She had been much younger then but all her former sense of shame and fear returned. For a moment she thought she might be sick. With shaking hands she hurriedly reordered her clothing, appalled to the depths of her soul that he of all men should have observed the scene, and wanting nothing so much as for the earth to open up and swallow her whole.

'Sabrina, can you find the knife?'

She took a deep breath and looked about distractedly. The blade lay just feet away beside the desk. With a grimace of distaste, she bent and retrieved it. Moments later Falconbridge was free.

'Good girl.'

He staggered to his feet, stifling a gasp. Instinctively she reached out to steady him. Then his arms were round her, warm, protective, holding her close. For a while her body shook with reaction. Unable to speak she drew in long sobbing breaths, her face white. Its deathly pallor shocked him to the core.

'My dearest girl. I'm so sorry. So very sorry.'

At last she found her voice. 'I think I've killed him,

Robert.' She ought to have been glad but the feeling engendered was one of sick horror.

'If you have, no man deserved it more.' He drew in a sharp breath, dreading to ask the next question. 'Sabrina, did he…?'

'No.'

His throat tightened and he knew a moment of relief more intense than any in his life before. Silently, he thanked God. 'I never saw anything so brave as you this day.'

Tears flowed down her face unbidden. 'I did not feel brave, only frightened.'

'That is scarce to be wondered at.' He held her gently at arm's length. 'Let us not waste the chance you have won for us.'

Suddenly the wider peril impinged upon her thoughts once more. 'What are we going to do, Robert?'

'Get out of here,' he replied.

She looked at his cut and swollen face. 'You're injured. They must have hurt you terribly.'

'I've known worse.'

He released his hold and crossed the room. His bruised ribs protested as he bent to retrieve the Frenchman's sword. Then he hurriedly checked the drawers in the desk. One side proved quite useless, the other revealed a pistol which he lost no time in appropriating.

'Machart dismissed the guards but the chances are they haven't gone far,' he said. 'We need to take care of them first. Then we can set our companions free.'

'Tell me what I must do.'

'Take this.' He handed her the pistol. 'If you need to use it, shoot to kill.'

Her stomach wallowed at the thought, but she nodded. Quietly, he opened the door and glanced out. The corridor was empty of other human presences. Clearly the guards had taken Machart at his word. Sabrina's heart thumped and with every step she expected to hear a shouted challenge. However, none came. Not until they reached the stairs leading to the underground vault did they see any sign of life, one man on duty. Falconbridge ducked back out sight.

'Can you distract his attention while I come up behind him?'

Dumbly, she nodded assent. Shaking her hair loose over her shoulders she opened the front of her shirt to reveal the upper curves of her breasts. Then, assuming what she hoped was a provocative stance she summoned all her courage and strolled forwards. The guard turned, regarding her with astonishment; then he reached for his musket, levelling it at her.

'Who goes there?'

She surveyed him coolly, praying her voice would not shake. 'I am the Condesa de Ordoñez y Casal.'

'The Condesa is Colonel Machart's prisoner.'

'No,' she replied. 'As from now, his mistress.' Seeing him hesitate she forced a smile. 'The Colonel really knows how to appreciate a woman, doesn't he?'

Seeing her dishevelled appearance the guard returned a knowing grin and opened his mouth to reply. The words were never uttered because the hilt of a sword dealt him a blow to the head and felled him in an instant. Falconbridge surveyed the still form and then looked at his companion.

'Wonderful girl! Get his musket and powder horn. We'll need them.'

While she obeyed, he retrieved the bunch of keys from the man's belt. Then he and Sabrina hurried down the steps to the cells. A minute later the door was unlocked and their companions were free. His men beamed.

'Good to see you, sir.'

'Aye, that it is, sir.'

Falconbridge nodded. 'It's good to see you, too, and you, Luis.'

As they emerged from their prison and got a proper look at Falconbridge, the men frowned.

'The filthy scum gave you a rough time, sir,' said Blakelock.

'I'll live,' he replied.

Luis caught sight of his companion and smiled. '*Doña* Sabrina! Are you all right? We heard them take you away earlier.'

'Quite all right, Luis.'

'I am truly glad to hear it.'

Falconbridge tossed the musket to Willis and gave Blakelock the sword. 'Here. It's a start, but we're going to need more than these if we're to have a hope of getting out of here.'

Sabrina met his eye. 'What are you going to do?'

'Go back along the corridor and check those other rooms. It's a risk but there's no other choice.' He paused. 'In the meantime, we'll take one of those coils of rope.'

Luis hastened to obey, selecting the most suitable and slinging it round his chest like a bandolier. Then they retraced their steps. Leaving Sabrina and Luis at the entrance to the passageway the other three moved quietly forwards. With thumping heart she watched as Willis put his ear against a door, listening. He opened it and glanced in. No shouts or challenges resulted but he shook his head. Further along Blakelock grinned. She heard him hiss to the others. Then all three vanished into the room, to emerge a short time later with swords and muskets.

Luis grinned and moments later he, too, was armed. *'Estupendo!* Now we go over the wall, eh?'

Falconbridge nodded. 'That's the general idea, and preferably before anyone finds Machart or that guard.'

The junction of the passageway revealed the door that led onto the courtyard. Falconbridge looked around the corner and mentally cursed as he counted at least a dozen soldiers there. He ducked back quickly.

'No go. Let's try the other way.'

They fled down the passage towards the archway at the end. From there it was no more than twenty yards to the wall. A crumbling flight of steps led to a small lookout platform on what remained of the rampart. It was currently empty. Falconbridge looked swiftly left and right and, having ascertained the coast was clear, jerked his head towards the steps.

'Up there. It's our only chance.'

They ran for the wall and began to climb. The steps were in a parlous state, some only a few inches wide, the rest having crumbled away. Nor was there any kind of handrail and the fall, though it wasn't high enough to kill, would likely result in a broken limb. Luis went first, testing each step gingerly. Beneath his weight the ancient stonework broke away in places sending down small showers of rubble. However, he reached the platform unscathed. Quickly, he slid the coil of rope off his shoulder and tied one end to a stone merlon. Then he turned and signalled to the others. Willis went next, and then Blakelock, disappearing over the edge of the drop. Falconbridge turned to Sabrina and smiled.

'Ready?'

She nodded and began to climb, trying not to look

down and to concentrate on where she was putting her feet. She reached the platform a short time later, closely followed by Falconbridge. He squeezed her arm.

'Your turn now.'

Before she could reply, they heard shouting in the distance.

'At a guess they've found Machart,' he said. 'Hurry, Sabrina.'

She needed no second bidding. Unheeding of rough stone or the rope burning the palms of her hands, she slid swiftly down to where the others waited. A short time later he joined them, and together they ran for the cover of rock and scrub, trying to put as much distance as possible between themselves and the walls of the castillo. Without horses though, the chances of success were small and everyone knew it.

'It won't take them long to find out how we escaped,' said Falconbridge. 'We can expect mounted pursuit fairly soon, I think.'

Sabrina shivered inwardly. If they were recaptured, they would die this time, but perhaps not quickly. The French would want revenge for their slain. She thought of the pills Falconbridge had given her and was glad. Better a swift end thus, than a protracted one at the hands of their enemies.

They ran hard until at length they were forced to slow down to catch their breath. Even then the Castillo was still only about a mile away. Not far enough. Sabrina pressed a hand to her aching side, forcing herself on. Falconbridge kept pace beside her, his smile lending her strength. She knew he must be in pain himself from the beating at the hands of Machart's guards, but he made no mention of it. To judge from the bruising on his face it must have been hard for him even to smile. If he could keep going, so could she.

Eventually they paused, taking shelter behind a group of scattered rocks. Luis flung himself down, ear to the ground, listening intently. Then he frowned.

'Many horses coming, though some way off yet.'

Falconbridge gritted his teeth against the pain in his ribs. 'We can't outrun them. Take cover. We'll have to make a stand here.'

They knew it wasn't going to be much of a stand, given the limited weapons and ammunition available. Their defiance would be counted by minutes, not hours. Nevertheless, it was the only option now. Surrender would likely not delay the inevitable outcome by very much. They took cover and waited for the appearance of the enemy. Sabrina crouched behind a large rock, resting her cheek against the rough surface. There could be no doubt now that she would not see her father again. She had gambled and lost. The long-dreamed-of reunion would never happen. He would be grieved by her loss but at least he would be free to continue his work for the war effort. She glanced at the man beside her and smiled faintly. If they had only met under other circumstances things might have been different. There might have been time to get to know each other better, time for talking and laughing, time in which to relax and to be herself. Unfortunately, time was the one thing they didn't have.

'I'm truly sorry things have turned out like this,' he said. 'I'd planned it all rather differently.'

'What was it the poet said about the best-laid plans?'

'Best-laid? Under other circumstances I'd want to laugh.'

She hesitated, and then took courage in both hands. 'I wish we had met under other circumstances.'

His gaze held hers. 'Yes, so do I, and yet I would not have missed knowing you. In truth, I have never met a braver woman.'

His words brought an inner glow of pleasure. At least she had not lost his regard. Since they had little time left, and since there might never be another opportunity, she needed to say what was on her mind. 'I would not have missed knowing you, either.'

'I thank you. It is a compliment I have done little to deserve.'

'Not so. You saved my life.'

'Only to fail you when it mattered most.' His lips curled in self-disgust. 'When I think of you in the clutches of that lecherous brute, it sickens me to my stomach. Yet I could do nothing. Nothing.'

'It was not your fault, Robert.'

'Yes, it was. I should have insisted you ride on with Ramon. Instead, I as good as delivered you to Machart.'

'Machart was a sadistic beast, but he is unlikely to trouble us any more.'

'And I thank God for it. To be tortured is one thing, but to be forced to watch while he… No civilised man could countenance it. I was not afraid until that moment.' He reached out and took her hand in a warm clasp before raising it to his lips. 'I honour your spirit and your courage.'

The words, so sincerely spoken, brought a deeper glow of pleasure. She made no attempt to disengage herself from his hold. It did not repel her. Rather, its warmth and strength were comforting, like his nearness now. 'There are men who consider themselves civilised in every way who do not baulk at it.'

He regarded her intently. 'You say that with some authority.'

'With authority enough.'

Curiosity mounted. There was so much he wanted to know and so little time left them. However, before he could speak, Blakelock's voice interjected.

'Here they come, sir.'

Falconbridge followed his gaze into the middle distance and saw the oncoming soldiers. His heart sank. Even from here it was possible to make out their blue uniform jackets and grey shakos. He relinquished his hold on Sabrina's hand and lifted the musket, aware of bruised muscles protesting.

'Let them come then. We'll account for as many as we can.'

She threw a sideways glance his way and nodded. 'Yes, we will.' Then, hoping her hand would not shake, she drew the pistol from her belt.

Chapter Eleven

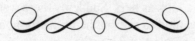

Falconbridge grimaced, mentally counting the number of the oncoming force. With sinking heart he reached twenty. This was going to be a fight to the death. Knowing what to expect at the hands of the enemy there was no point in contemplating surrender. Better a quick ending here. He glanced at the faces around him and saw the same resolution in each one. A man could feel proud to die in such company. His gaze rested a moment on Sabrina. As though she sensed his regard she turned her head and met his gaze with a smile. He returned it, albeit crookedly, and his admiration increased. Truly, she was the rarest of women: the woman he would defend to the death. Setting his jaw he lined the first oncoming soldier in his sights. Alongside him his companions did the same.

As the shots rang out and three of the French vanguard fell, the others drew rein, and for a few moments there was shouting and confusion. Then a command rang out and the rest of the force drew their sabres. Falconbridge heard the order to charge and cursed softly.

Men on the ground were no match for cavalry. This was going to be a slaughter pure and simple.

Another volley of shots brought down three more of the French, but it did not slow their advance. The thunder of hooves grew louder. Sunlight glinted on naked blades. With no time to reload, Falconbridge thrust Sabrina behind him.

'Behind that rock. Stay down.'

'If I am to die then I'll go down fighting with you.'

His throat tightened. A man could not be mistaken about such a look as hers. Suddenly there were so many things he wanted to say, but had time for none of them. Instead, he nodded. 'So be it.'

Heart thumping, she watched him draw the sword at his side, knowing they had no chance now. Soon the sabres would cut them down. If not... Her fingers felt for the small package inside her jacket and felt its reassuring presence. She would never be a prisoner of the French again.

More shots rang out and on the warm air she heard the sound of galloping hoofs. It could only mean reinforcements. She swallowed hard. There came more shots and then shouts and cries of pain. At any moment the vanguard would be upon them. For the space of several heartbeats she waited. Then, slowly, she became aware that the impetus of the French charge was lost, and those riders remaining had veered off, turning their attention another way. Her bewildered gaze took in the large host of roughly-dressed horsemen that was bearing down on them. She was not alone in her astonishment.

Luis looked round at his companions. '*Que pasa?*'

'Your guess is as good as mine,' replied Willis.

Sabrina stared at the newcomers. 'Wait, aren't those redcoats among them?'

Willis narrowed his eyes, looking intently in the direction she had indicated. 'By heaven, you're right, ma'am.'

'But what are redcoats doing among those others?'

Falconbridge grinned, ignoring the pain in his cut lip. 'I think Ramon found help after all.'

For a moment or two the implication was lost and she could only stare in disbelief at the oncoming horde. Then she experienced a sudden surge of hope so intense it was almost painful. Turning she met his eye. What she read there caused her heart to leap.

'You mean we're not going to die after all?'

'We're certainly going to die,' he replied, 'but not today I think.'

Tearing her gaze away, she watched with bated breath as the opposing forces met amid shouts and the clash of arms. There followed a short spell of fierce hand-to-hand fighting as the desperate French tried to stave off the unexpected assault, but, hopelessly outnumbered, they were cut down one by one. Soon the area was littered with the fallen, the scene confused by riderless horses. Then, as the last of the enemy fell, the battlefield grew quiet.

Sabrina heard voices in Spanish and saw a few figures dismount, moving among the fallen. Those French still living were swiftly dispatched. She drew a deep breath, fighting the churning sensation in her stomach. Then she became aware of mounted figures moving towards them. The first was a British officer. For a moment he and Falconbridge surveyed each other in silence.

Falconbridge smiled wryly. 'I'm glad to see you, Tony.'

'And I to see you,' the other replied.

'Your arrival was most timely.'

'So I see.' The officer paused, looking at Sabrina. 'Will you not introduce me to this lady?'

'Forgive me. I have the honour to present Miss Huntley, my companion on this mission. Miss Huntley, Major Lord Anthony Brudenell.'

'We are much obliged to you, Major,' she replied.

Brudenell's blue gaze swept her from head to foot and then he smiled. 'I wish I could take the credit, ma'am, but that rightly belongs to El Cuchillo and his men.'

Sabrina's gaze went to the horseman who had reined in alongside. Like most people she had heard of the guerrilla leader, for his reputation preceded him. Her imagination had supplied a figure from high romance, something very different from the person before her now. He was perhaps in his early forties, and she guessed of average height. Like most Spaniards he was dark. The swarthy, bearded face was not handsome, but it was arresting, the left side being marred by deep scars across the cheek and brow. Piercing black eyes took in every detail of her appearance but gave nothing away. He favoured her with a slight inclination of the head, then turned to the man beside her.

'I am glad we arrived in time, Major.'

'You are not alone in that, *señor,*' replied Falconbridge. 'In truth, I thought it was all up with us.'

The conversation continued but Sabrina's attention was arrested by a familiar figure that had appeared from the group, ranged behind the guerrilla leader. Then her heart leapt.

'Jacinta?'

'*Doña* Sabrina!'

The two women embraced. Sabrina's voice caught on a sob. 'How glad I am to see you.'

'And I you.'

'I prayed you would live.'

'I received a concussion only,' replied Jacinta. 'It gave me a headache for a while, that is all.'

'Thank God.'

'Amen to that.'

'But how came you to be with El Cuchillo and Major Brudenell?'

'By good fortune only. It seems that when Ramon located the guerilla hideout, Major Brudenell was already there on business of his own. When he heard the name of Falconbridge he brought assistance as fast as he could. They found me near the place where we fought with Machart's men. I heard the French mention Castillo San Angel before they took you away. That is how our friends knew where to come.'

'Where is Ramon now?'

'Taking those papers to Lord Wellington. As soon as he knew aid was on its way to you, he set off.'

As the pieces of the story fell into place they brought about a feeling of relief so intense that Sabrina found herself trembling. Never in a thousand years could she have hoped that matters might have so happy a conclusion.

'I am sorry to interrupt,' said a voice behind them, 'but it would be as well not to linger here.' They turned to see Major Brudenell. 'I will have my men bring you a horse, ma'am.'

'I'm much obliged, sir.'

'At least that won't be hard to arrange,' replied Jacinta as he walked away. 'There are enough loose ones hereabouts.'

'True enough.'

'I will go and see that he provides something suitable.'

As Jacinta set off in Brudenell's wake, Sabrina experienced a moment of surprise. Then she saw Falconbridge approaching and understood the reason for the sudden departure.

'Can you bear the thought of another long ride?' he asked.

Sabrina smiled. 'If it takes us away from here I find I can bear the thought very well.' She surveyed him critically. 'But I think it is you who will find it hard going. Those cuts and bruises need attention.'

'Presently,' he replied.

'Do you fear my ministrations?'

'By no means, but Brudenell is right. We shouldn't linger here.' He grinned. 'When we make camp I'll submit willingly to your attentions.'

'I intend to hold you to that.'

'Indeed I hope so, ma'am.'

It was hard to know what to make of that and Sabrina decided it was safer not to pursue the matter. There was no time, in any case, for Brudenell's men returned with mounts. She swung into the saddle of a cavalry horse and watched her companions mount, too. Then the entire cavalcade set off.

They made camp that night in the hills. Sabrina took the opportunity to fetch clean water and cloths, and asked Luis to find out if any of the company had any medicinal salves or embrocation. The enquiry proved positive, for some time later he returned with a small pot which he presented to her triumphantly.

'Salve,' he said, 'and most efficacious for bruising.'

She sniffed the contents and wrinkled her nose. 'How do you know it's efficacious?'

'Does it not smell terrible?'

'Yes.'

'That proves it. The worse the smell, the better is the ointment, eh?' Seeing her dubious expression he added, 'Trust me in this.'

'Of course.'

He threw her a beaming smile and took himself off. Sabrina watched him go and shook her head.

'Trust him in what?' asked a familiar voice.

She turned to see Falconbridge and grinned. 'In matters medical.' Putting down the cloths and bowl of water on a nearby rock, she bade him be seated. He obeyed without argument.

'I would trust Luis at my back in a fight any day of the week,' he observed, 'but I had no idea he was an expert in medicine, too.'

'I think it self-styled expertise.'

'Ah.'

She dipped a cloth and began very gently to bathe the cuts and bruises on his face. They looked painful, but so far as she could tell the damage was superficial. That anyone should have hurt him in that way brought a surge of anger. For men to fight each other in combat was one thing, to torture and maim quite another. Her hand moved to the cut on his lip and she saw him wince.

'I'm sorry. I didn't mean to hurt you.'

'No matter. Besides, if it hadn't been for you, things would have been much worse.' He paused. 'When you dealt with Machart you saved both our lives.'

She shuddered visibly. 'He is…was…an evil man.'

'Yes. I could almost wish the brute here again just so that I could have the pleasure of killing him for certain.'

'If he is dead then I hope he's in the hottest part of hell.'

Her quiet vehemence took him by surprise and he eyed her speculatively. 'I imagine that is his likely destination, and no man could deserve it more.'

Sabrina said nothing, merely dipped the cloth again and continued her ministrations. In spite of his injuries her touch was causing unexpectedly pleasurable sensations along his skin. Now that she was so close to him he could smell the scent of leather and horses on her clothing, but beneath it the scent of the woman. It was subtle and arousing. The last time he had been this close was when he had shared the cot with her in the cell back at Castillo San Angel. It had been a brief enough interlude but one he knew he would remember all his days. If she had given him any encouragement he would have taken it further, but she had not. Neither would she now, in all likelihood, for what woman could respect a man who had let her down so badly? He had gathered from previous conversations that something had happened in the past to make her exceedingly wary of giving her affections. His failure to protect her in her time of greatest need would only have reinforced that tendency.

Becoming aware of his regard, Sabrina kept her attention on her work. Having bathed his face, she laid down the cloth and reached for the pot of salve. Then, very lightly, she applied a little to the bruised areas of skin, taking care to avoid the open cuts. Falconbridge wrinkled his nose.

'What on earth is that stuff?'

'Goodness knows. Luis assures me it's good for bruises.'

'Good for embalming, too, from the smell of it.'

Sabrina grinned. 'Perhaps it has a two-fold purpose. I must ask him.'

'It might be better not to know.'

She completed her task and then paused. 'Take off your jacket.'

'Why?'

'I want to check the bruising on your ribs.'

His initial reaction was to say it wasn't necessary but just as quickly he decided against it. He didn't want to lose her company or to end this unforced intimacy.

'Would you mind helping me with this?'

'Of course.'

She stepped in closer and gently eased the coat off his shoulders. Falconbridge winced again, and with perfect sincerity. The blows he had received earlier were now very painful. The other events of the day hadn't helped either. Sabrina eyed him closely, wondering at the extent of the hidden damage.

'Pull up your shirt.'

Gingerly he obeyed and heard her gasp. Glancing down he saw that his ribs were a mass of ugly red-and-black bruises.

'Dear God, Robert, you should have said something sooner! These must be agony.'

He smiled wryly. 'I've felt better.'

'Let me put some of this on for you.'

'I suppose it can't do any harm.'

'Luis says that a strong smell means an effective treatment.'

'In that case I should be as right as rain by tomorrow, unless the French sniff me out first.'

She returned the smile and then set to work again, gently smoothing the salve onto the bruised areas of his back. She was careful, trying by all means not to hurt him, but once or twice she heard a sharp intake of breath. It occurred to her to wonder then just what he had endured before she had been brought onto the scene. Looking at the damage caused by that beating, she was even less sorry for the injuries she had inflicted on Machart.

Gradually, she worked round to the front again, kneeling beside him now to ensure that no bruises were left untreated, applying the salve with light, deft touches along the muscles of his stomach and waist. Once, not so long ago, it would have been unthinkable to touch him or any man so intimately. Yet now it seemed quite natural and right. She could feel his leg warm against her side but the closeness did not repel her. On the contrary, what she felt now was melting warmth in the region of her pelvis. She drew in a deep breath of her own and finished the task.

He let the shirt fall. 'Thank you.'

'You're welcome.'

He tucked the fabric carefully into his breeches and then reached for his coat.

'May I importune you this one last time?' he asked.

'One last time?' She tilted her head to one side, regarding him thoughtfully. 'Really? Or was that just a figure of speech?'

He smiled. 'It probably was.'

She took the coat from him, gently easing the garment onto his arms and then drew it up over his shoulders. He got to his feet and turned to face her. For the space of several heartbeats neither one of them spoke. He wanted so much to kiss her but after what had happened he feared that such attentions must be unwelcome. Instead, he reached for her hand and raised it to his lips.

'Thank you.'

'You have no need to thank me.'

'I think I do.' His expression grew serious. 'That is twice you've come to my aid today. I should hate it to become a habit.'

'Should you?'

'This reversal of roles is deucedly uncomfortable, I find.'

She nodded sympathetically but there was a familiar gleam in her eyes. 'It must be, especially with so much bruised flesh.'

'Wretch! I was serious.'

'I know, but it is no use repining over what cannot be altered, Robert.'

'True, but I hope one day to make it up to you somehow.'

'It really doesn't matter.'

'Yes, it does. It matters a great deal.'

'Ah, bruised pride.' She saw him stiffen slightly and went on, 'I recognise it, you see, since my own has taken a heavy battering, too.'

'Of course, forgive me. What happened today has hurt both of us, in different ways.'

'Some hurts go deep, do they not?' She sighed. 'As deep as years.'

He regarded her intently now. 'What hurts, Sabrina?'

She bit her lip, hesitating, wanting to tell him but fearing to, as well, dreading his reaction.

'It seems to me that we have been here before,' he said. 'Will you not tell me what it is that so troubles you?'

She made no immediate reply and for a moment he thought she would refuse. Then she drew in a shuddering breath and nodded.

'What happened with Machart…it happened to me once before.'

He stared at her, appalled. Whatever else, he had not expected that. 'Oh, my dear girl.'

'Today brought it all back, every last sordid detail.'

'I'm so sorry. You don't have to tell me, Sabrina.'

'Yes, I do. I wanted to before but the time wasn't right.' She turned to face him. 'Will you hear me?'

'You know I will.'

'You may think ill of me afterwards.'

He smiled gently. 'May not I be the judge of that?'

Resuming his seat on the rock he gestured for her to join him. So they sat together and she told him about Jack Denton, of the way they had met, of their stolen moments together and her growing infatuation with him.

'…and then one afternoon we went out riding to see some cave paintings that he said he'd found by chance, while out on patrol.' She paused. 'I was a little apprehensive; we were alone and the place remote, but he was…persuasive. Of course, when we reached the cave there were no paintings.'

Falconbridge was very still. 'And then?'

'I discovered how badly mistaken I had been in his character. He…he tried to kiss me…' The memory had lost none of its power to chill. The kiss he took then was unlike those first chaste salutes. Hot, searing, demanding, it shocked her, like the tongue thrusting into her mouth and the crude hand exploring her breasts. When she tried to pull away his hold only tightened. 'I tried to get away but he threw me down on the floor of the cave…tore my clothing.'

An expression of disgust crossed Falconbridge's face. She quailed before it, but knew she had come too far to go back now.

'I tried to fight him but he was too strong. I begged him to stop.' In her mind she could still hear his reply.

'Come now, you little tease. You've led me on for weeks. You know you want it as much as I.'

Furious and frightened, she fought Denton in earnest, biting, yelling, kicking. If anything it seemed to inflame him further.

'You can't get away, my sweet, so don't think it. Besides, when I'm done, you'll be begging for more.' He smiled. 'We have the whole afternoon before us and I mean to make the most of it.'

Panicking, she struggled harder, feeling his greedy mouth fasten on her breasts. She twisted in revulsion, got a hand free, clawed at his face. He caught her wrists and pinned them. His smile chilled her.

'Like it rough, do you? Well, by God, Jack's your man.'

His free hand shoved her skirts round her thighs and then unfastened his breeches. Terrified now, she screamed. His knee thrust her thighs apart...

Sabrina took another deep breath to steady herself. 'Just when I was certain that...that all was lost, a hand reached out and dragged him away. It was Captain Harcourt.'

'Harcourt?' The name registered at once and Falconbridge was aware of other pieces of the puzzle dropping into place.

'Yes, it seems he had noticed Denton's attentions to me and, knowing the man's reputation, had kept an eye on him. When he saw us ride off together, he followed.'

Her companion's gaze hardened. 'A fortunate circumstance.'

She nodded miserably. 'He hit Denton several times

before pushing him up against the rear wall of the cave with a sword at his throat. I don't recall everything he said, but I heard him utter the promise of death if Denton ever came near me again or disclosed a word of what had passed. Denton swore to keep silence so the Captain let him go.'

'Did he?' The tone was icy. 'And what of you?'

'He carried me back to his horse and took me home. He was very kind and uttered no word of reproach or blame, but all his gentleness could not dispel the searing sense of shame and humiliation that I felt.' She drew in a ragged breath. 'He took a back route to town, riding by little-frequented streets to minimise the chances of meeting anyone we knew. When we reached his lodgings he gave me into the care of his wife. She tended me and mended my garments as best she could. When I was calmer and reasonably presentable, they took me home.'

'Your father's reaction I can well imagine.'

'He never knew.'

'What!'

'Mercifully, he was elsewhere when we returned and I never told him what had happened. Nor did the Harcourts, at my insistence. Had we done so, he would certainly have called Denton out. Lord Wellington had expressly forbidden duelling among his officers, so even if he were not killed or injured, the affair would have put paid to my father's career. I could not bear to think that such ill fortune might befall him on account of my folly.'

'I see.'

'At first, I thought the whole sordid affair was over but it seems that, one evening, when Captain Denton was in his cups, he revealed something of it to two of his fellow officers. It was enough to lead to speculation and rumour. Captain Harcourt learned of it in the officers' mess and nipped the conversation in the bud. However, enough damage had been done by then to have an impact.' She swallowed hard. 'Nothing was ever said directly but there were covert looks and sly smiles from some of Denton's acquaintance. Ladies who had been friendly before now grew cool or, in one or two cases, shunned me completely, and invitations to their houses ceased. Had it not been for the kindness of the Harcourts, I would have been lost. Being of excellent social standing and also generally popular, their continued friendship and public refusal to give credence to rumour did much to aid my cause.'

'You seem to have been fortunate in your friends.'

'I did not know how fortunate until then,' she replied. 'After that, my relationship with the Harcourts became much closer. They took on the role of guardians, particularly in my father's absence, and saw to it that I came to no more harm.'

'And Captain Denton?'

'He was killed by the French in an ambush a few months later.'

Falconbridge's face was expressionless, save for the cold anger that burned in his eyes. 'How old were you when all this happened?'

'Fifteen.'

'Good God!'

'It is not a pretty story, is it?'

'Hardly.'

Her heart sank as she looked at his expression. He was sickened all right. Perhaps it had been a mistake to tell him, to be so totally frank. Perhaps she had lost his regard by doing so.

'The blackguard should have been whipped at the cart tail,' he went on. 'What man worthy of the name takes such advantage of a young girl?'

'I was very foolish.'

'Weren't we all when we were fifteen? In any case, foolishness is not a crime. Cold-blooded seduction of a minor most certainly is.'

'Then you do not blame me for what happened?'

'Good heavens, no. Why would I?'

'I was afraid you would think me light.'

His jaw tightened. 'I have never thought such a thing of you. Nor would I ever think it.' He paused. 'Is that what you believed when I kissed you before?' Seeing she remained silent, his brow creased. 'It was, wasn't it?'

'I couldn't be sure. I'm sorry. I see now that it was foolish.'

'I hope you do.'

'I was so afraid of what you would think.'

'Does my opinion matter so much then?'

'Yes, it does.'

'Then be assured that I hold you in the highest regard and always will.'

Part of her was glad, another part saddened. High regard was valuable but it was not the same as love; nor was it enough. Yet what man would want to marry a woman with such a history, even if it was not all her fault?

Before either of them could say more, a redcoated figure appeared in their line of vision. He stopped a few feet away and saluted.

'Beg pardon, sir, but Major Brudenell asks if you would be good enough to attend him.'

Falconbridge cursed mentally. Aloud he said, 'Very well. Tell him I'll come presently.'

'Yes, sir.'

The soldier departed. Falconbridge looked at Sabrina. 'Forgive me. I must find out what Brudenell wants.'

'Of course.'

'We will speak again later.'

She watched him walk away and thought sadly that there could be little more to say on the subject. He had assured her of his regard and she had believed him, but he had not spoken of anything deeper than regard. For her to admit to her own feelings, while being unsure of his, was impossible. It did not pay to wear one's heart on one's sleeve. To make a fool of herself again after her previous experience would be foolish beyond permission. Better they remain as friends instead.

Falconbridge listened with close attention as Brudenell outlined his plans for their collective return to Ciudad Rodrigo.

'For it will be safer if we return as a group. El Cuchillo's men will guarantee us safe passage out of the Gredos, of course, but there is still some way to go before we can consider ourselves in friendly territory.'

Falconbridge nodded. 'You're right, and I accept the offer.'

'Good.'

'Miss Huntley has been exposed to enough danger already. I would spare her any further risk, in so far as I may.'

'She is a courageous young woman.'

'The bravest I ever met.'

Brudenell did not miss the tone in which it was said, or the accompanying expression on his friend's face.

'She is also very attractive.'

'Yes, she is.'

'Some fellows have all the luck when it comes to assignments.'

Falconbridge met his gaze. 'My brief association with Miss Huntley has been a privilege.'

'I should say so. If I'd known beforehand, I'd have asked Ward to swap our roles. Then I could have spent three weeks in close proximity to a pretty girl.'

'Damn it, Tony.' The grey eyes turned steely. 'What exactly are you implying?'

'Nothing at all.' With a sense of shock Brudenell saw the glacial expression. 'My dear fellow, I was joking.'

'I don't much care for the joke. Nor will I suffer Miss Huntley's name to be used in such a way.'

'Good God, Robert. You cannot seriously think I meant anything by it? If so, then I apologise.'

For a moment Falconbridge remained quite still, his gaze locked on the other man. Then, suddenly, the tension left him.

'Apology accepted.' He made a vague gesture with his hand. 'I beg you will forgive my ill humour. It has been a trying day.'

'Forget it.'

'It's just that Miss Huntley is a most esteemed… colleague.'

'Of course she is, my dear chap.'

Falconbridge managed a wry smile. 'Well then, I'll relieve you of my tiresome company. A good night's sleep will no doubt cure my foul temper.'

Having bidden his companion farewell, Brudenell followed the departing figure with his eyes. Then he whistled softly.

'I think it's going to take more than sleep to cure what's wrong with you, my friend.'

Having left Brudenell, Falconbridge walked apart a little way, needing time to think. Finally he found a tall pine and eased himself down onto the dry grass beneath. Annoyed with himself for what had taken place just now, he admitted that his response had been an overreaction. Of course his friend had never meant to slight Sabrina. It was just that following so close on the heels of her confidence to him, he had been instinctively protective. She was vulnerable in so many ways, and so strong in others. It was part of her considerable charm. She had told him that she valued his good opinion, an admission that caused both surprise and delight. Then he told himself not to attach undue significance to that remark. It meant only that she had come to value him as a colleague. He smiled in self-deprecation. A colleague? When he'd seen her in Machart's clutches he'd realised she meant a lot more than that, but he'd been powerless to help her. So far from acting the hero, it had been he who had needed rescuing. It was hardly the stuff of romance. Yet it seemed to him that their adventures together had forged a friendship between them at least, for she had trusted him with her confidence. Her tale made a lot of things much clearer and he could only look on his earlier behaviour with regret. Though well intentioned, he realised it had not done him any favours.

Chapter Twelve

Sabrina ate with Jacinta that evening and then retired early. Sleeping under the stars was not a new experience and she made the best of it, using the cavalry saddle as a pillow and the attached blanket roll for warmth. Although she was tired, sleep proved elusive, for her thoughts kept crowding in. Soon now their mission would be over and, God willing, her father restored to her. That day could not come too soon. But what of Robert Falconbridge? Would she see him again afterwards, or were their lives destined only to touch briefly?

No answer to this presented itself and eventually she fell into a fitful doze, only to wake in the early hours feeling chilled and stiff. Once when she had been cold, a man had warmed her, but that had been in a special set of circumstances that would never be repeated. A lump formed in her throat. How much she would have given just then to feel his arms around her. Mentally she gave herself a shake. It wasn't going to happen. To her horror she felt a tear slide down her cheek and hurriedly dashed it away. Then, pulling the blanket higher, she turned over.

* * *

It was dawn when Jacinta woke her with a cup of coffee. Gratefully she accepted the offering, feeling the warmth carve a path to her stomach. Jacinta joined her, eyeing her critically.

'Did you sleep well, *Doña* Sabrina?'

'Yes, very well, thank you.'

'Neither did I.'

Sabrina threw her a swift sideways glance, and then smiled ruefully. 'Is it that obvious?'

'Dark shadows under the eyes give away the game, no?'

'The ground is very hard when one has become used to a bed.'

'So it is.'

'To say nothing of hours spent in the saddle.'

'That, too, is guaranteed to make the muscles stiff.' Jacinta took another sip of her coffee. 'Or a beating like the one Major Falconbridge received.'

Sabrina lowered her gaze. 'Yes. The bruising was very bad.'

'Machart?'

'He.'

'*Puerco!*'

'That is an insult to pigs.'

'Luis said it was you who killed the swine.'

'I do not know if he is dead, only that I injured him.'

'A good thing if he were dead. The world would be well rid of such a one.' Jacinta paused. 'May I ask how you hurt the brute?'

'With a sharp knife between the ribs.'

'*Así?* You make me proud.'

'It was not about pride; it was about survival.'

Briefly she summarised what had occurred. As she spoke, her companion's face paled.

'If I had not stabbed him he would have raped me and killed us both afterwards,' said Sabrina. 'I had no choice. Even so, it is no easy thing to live with the knowledge that one may have killed a man.'

'Yet you shot men before.'

'I know, but it's different somehow. A gun lends distance to the act; a knife brings one horribly close.' She shook her head. 'I'm not explaining it very well.'

'You need feel no guilt over this matter. Be thankful you had the chance to be avenged.' Jacinta's dark eyes glittered. 'I was not so happy.'

Sabrina frowned. 'When your village was destroyed, you mean?'

'The French soldiers looted it first. They killed all the men, even the very old and the sick. After that they rounded up the women, my mother and sisters among them. They were taken to a barn where the soldiers took it in turns to rape them.'

'Oh, Jacinta, no.'

'Oh, yes. When they had finished, they closed up the doors after them so that none could escape. Then they set the barn alight and burned it to the ground, along with every house in the village.' Her companion paused. 'The only reason I didn't die with the rest was because my mother had sent me out earlier on an errand. I was on my way back, but when I saw the soldiers I hid in a ditch until they went away. By then, all my family were dead and our home gone. I didn't know what to do or where to go, but I knew I could not stay, so I set off for the hills. A week later your father found me. I was half-dead from lack of food. If it had not been for his intervention, I would have perished.'

'Dear Lord.'

Sabrina's throat tightened as she struggled with the enormity of it. Never until now had she known the full story of Jacinta's past. Having being told she could only stare at her in horror. Jacinta met her gaze and held it.

'The soldiers who did those things were led by a man just like Machart,' she went on. 'You need feel no guilt for his death. Only remember what he would have done if you had not thrust that blade between his ribs.'

Sabrina shivered inwardly. 'When I agreed to come on this mission I knew the risks, but they seemed unreal somehow, as though they could never happen to me. I cannot believe I could have been so naive.'

'And yet, these things will make you stronger.'

'I hope so. As I hope all this will achieve my father's freedom.'

'I pray for it, too. He is among the best of men.'

'Yes, he is.'

'And Major Falconbridge?'

'I did not think so when first we met. Now…yes, I believe he is.'

'Good. Then he is worthy of you.'

'You mistake—our relationship is not of that kind. We are merely friends.'

Jacinta lifted one dark brow. 'If you say so.'

'I do say so.'

'If you repeat it often enough, you may come to believe it, but it won't alter the truth.'

'And what is that?'

'Do you need me to tell you?'

Sabrina sighed. It was impossible to feign anything with Jacinta. 'No, but I cannot reveal my feelings until I know his.'

'They are written all over him.'

'Are they?'

'Ha! The man is transparent.'

Before the remark could be explored further, Luis hove into view. He greeted both women and then informed them that the column was due to move out.

'El Cuchillo's men like to make use of the cooler hours,' he explained.

'Do they come with us then?' asked Jacinta.

'Until the far edge of the sierra. There is safety in numbers, eh?'

'I expect there is, even though the numbers be comprised of bandits.'

'Never look a gift horse in the eye.'

'Mouth,' amended Jacinta. 'Never look a gift horse in the mouth.'

Luis frowned. 'That is nonsense. How can one look a horse in the mouth? It cannot be done.'

Jacinta muttered something under her breath. Sabrina grinned and got to her feet.

'Frankly, I'm not looking forward to seeing any part of a horse today, but needs must.' She glanced at Jacinta. 'Come on, let's pack our things and saddle up.'

Luis nodded and took his leave. They watched him walk away and then set to. It didn't take long to roll up the blankets and stow the mugs in the saddlebag. Then, hefting saddles and bridles, they walked to the picket line where the horses were tethered. It took a relatively short time to tack up and mount. Sabrina stifled a groan as her aching muscles protested. Jacinta read her expression correctly.

'Are you ready for another delightful ride through the mountains, *Doña* Sabrina?'

'I can hardly wait.'

In fact, the pace was slow and easy, for which she was

grateful. Moreover, now that she was in the centre of so large a company, the fear of a surprise attack receded. She estimated that El Cuchillo's force numbered at least fifty. They were rough, silent men who rarely spoke and whose expressions gave nothing away. Occasionally she intercepted the odd glance towards Jacinta and herself, but that was all. Never by word or deed were they shown the least discourtesy. Every man there was armed to the teeth and all looked as though they could kill without a qualm. It was reassuring to know that they were allies, and she was glad of their protection. No French patrol was going to take them on, assuming any such were in the vicinity. It left her at leisure to admire the mountain scenery and to think.

She saw little of Falconbridge that morning, for he was riding at the head of the column with El Cuchillo and Major Brudenell. She missed his company and their lively conversations and thought that it was impossible to be bored in his presence. It also occurred to her that life was going to seem very dull without it when all this was over. Perhaps they might meet sometimes, until the army moved on. At a guess, Wellington would try to take Salamanca; the city was of great strategic importance. That implied another battle to drive the French back. She bit her lip, unwilling to think of the implications. Captain Harcourt had once told her that a man's luck could only hold so long. The idea of anything happening to Falconbridge was deeply unsettling. She thought she could bear his absence as long as he was alive and well somewhere in the world.

The column halted at midday by the edge of a wide creek. After the horses were watered and tethered, the men broke out provisions. While they were thus occupied, Sabrina made a necessary trip into the under-growth and then strolled down to the water's edge to bathe her hands and face. The sun was hot now, and the water wonderfully refreshing. Had she been alone she'd have been strongly tempted to strip off and bathe. Unfortunately, that wasn't an option just then.

She was so engrossed in thought that she failed to hear the quiet footsteps approaching until a man's shadow fell across her. She turned with a start and then felt her heart give a little leap as she recognised him.

'Forgive me. I didn't mean to startle you.'

'Not your fault. I was miles away.'

'So I gather.'

She eyed him critically. The cuts on his face and lip had scabbed over but the bruises were livid, particularly the one around his right eye. He noted the scrutiny and sighed.

'I look like a pirate, don't I?'

'Not quite so bad. You must still be very sore.'

'Somewhat,' he admitted, 'though I have to say that salve you applied did help considerably.'

'I'm glad to hear it. I would hate to think you had undergone the treatment for nothing.'

'Far from it.' He held up a small cloth bundle. 'Are you hungry? I've got some provisions here. We could share them if you wish.'

Feigning a calm she was far from feeling, she smiled acceptance, so they sat together by the water and she watched as he unfastened the cloth and examined the contents.

'Hmm. Half a loaf, at least two days old; a chunk of chorizo, possibly rancid; an onion and a wedge of dry cheese.'

'A veritable feast,' she replied.

He smiled ruefully. 'I regret that I cannot offer you something better.'

'It doesn't matter.'

'What shall we essay first?'

'Some bread and cheese?'

He took out a pocket knife and sawed into the loaf. Several minutes later he was still only halfway through it. 'Maybe I should use a sabre instead.'

Sabrina smiled. 'Better not. It might dull the edge.'

He persevered and finally succeeded in dividing the bread, handing her a portion before setting to work on the cheese. This proved marginally easier. He sniffed the chorizo.

'It seems all right. Will you chance it and have some?'

'Why not?'

'We won't go into that.'

She laughed and suddenly he found himself staring. Yet she seemed quite unaware of the effect she was having. Making a conscious effort to get a grip on himself he turned his attention to the food.

Of necessity they ate in silence for a while, the loaf demanding serious effort. Eventually Sabrina dunked her portion in the creek to soften it a little. He watched her quizzically.

'Better?'

'It doesn't do a great deal for the texture,' she admitted, 'but it tastes all right.'

'That's good enough for me,' he replied, and immediately followed suit. Having done so, he tried the bread again and rolled his eyes in mock appreciation. 'Absolutely divine.'

'And to think you once told me I was easily pleased.'

For answer he held up the onion. 'Can I tempt you?'

Sabrina shook her head. 'I draw the line there.'

'I think you may be right.' He discarded it and regarded her with another rueful smile. 'This must rank as the worst meal I have ever offered you.'

'By far the worst,' she agreed.

'Will you allow me to make amends and treat you to a better one when we return?'

Her heart gave another peculiar little lurch. 'I'd like that.'

'Then I promise that you shall be wined and dined in style.'

'With a fresh loaf?'

His grey eyes glinted with amusement. 'Loaf and cheese. I guarantee it.'

'I look forward to it, sir.'

'And I,' he replied. 'Besides, after all the dire culinary experiences you have been forced to endure, it is the least I can do.'

'Only one dire culinary experience to date.'

'You are generous.'

He reflected that it was true. Never once had she complained about the fare or indeed any of the trying conditions on this trip. She was truly a gem among women.

Keenly aware of that penetrating gaze, she wondered at the thoughts behind. If he had meant the invitation, then she would see him again after they got back. The thought made her happy and anxious together. Was it a token gesture, an acknowledgement of services rendered on their mission? Or was it because he genuinely wanted her company? How much she hoped it was the latter, that they might truly remain good friends. Then another, more pressing, thought occurred to her.

'You have invited me to dine but I shall have nothing to wear.'

'Really? What a delicious prospect.'

She gave him an accusing look. 'My dresses are in the trunk that we left back at that inn.'

'The landlord has instructions to send them on with the carriage when an appropriate driver can be found. The man will be well paid for his trouble.'

'You seem to think of everything.'

'I do my best. Of course, this being Spain, it may take a little time for the carriage to arrive, but you will get your things eventually.'

'That is a relief.'

'In truth I feel slightly disappointed, given the alternative.'

Sabrina grabbed the food cloth and flung it at him. It landed against his chest in a shower of crumbs. Much to her chagrin she heard him laugh.

'You are not to feel disappointed,' she admonished.

'Oh, good. Does that mean my hopes will be met?'

She glared at him. 'It does not, you dreadful man!'

The expression of contrition which followed was belied by the expression in his eyes. For a moment or two Sabrina regarded him with outrage. Then her sense of humour got the better of her and she began to laugh, albeit ruefully.

'I should be proof against this by now.'

'But I'm so glad that you are not.'

'Does it amuse you to tease me then?'

'What do you think?' he replied.

'I fear it does.'

'Only because I know I can expect the like in return. I have not been disappointed yet.'

Sabrina eyed him askance. 'How am I to take that?'

'As a compliment, my dear.' He paused, his expression suddenly serious. 'Very much so.'

Under the intensity of that look the blood mounted to her neck and face. Before she could think of a suitable reply the men around them began to stir. Noting it, Falconbridge sighed.

'I think that is a hint.'

'I'm afraid so.'

'It would be so much more pleasant to stay here for the rest of the afternoon.'

'Yes, but I fear that is not an option.'

'Come then.' He got to his feet with a stifled groan, and then held out a hand. 'Allow me.'

She took the offered hand and felt his fingers close round hers, drawing her easily to her feet. The touch sent a familiar charge along her skin. He retained his hold a little longer, relinquishing it with apparent reluctance. Then they made their way back to the horses.

He untied her horse's reins and held the bridle while she mounted. Then he retrieved his own horse. She expected him then to return to his place at the head of the line but he did not, reining his mount alongside hers.

'How do you find your cavalry charger?' he asked.

'A very willing beast, though quite a change from my usual mounts.'

'I imagine it is a change for him, too, since he has to carry only half the usual weight.'

'I had not thought of it like that.'

'No, but I'm sure he has.'

She laughed and patted the bay's neck. 'He will be back in service soon enough I have no doubt. The army always needs good horses.'

'True—and when those horses have been taken from the French they are the more highly prized.'

They lapsed into silence after this, but it was companionable, rather than awkward and she knew there was no company she would rather have. It felt so right to be with him. Once she had thought never to feel that about any man again and yet, in a short space of time, her feelings had changed so completely that she hardly recognised herself.

From time to time as they rode he pointed things out: a pair of eagles in flight above a distant peak; a small snake basking on a stone or brown trout finning lazily in the shallows of the stream.

'You have an eye for detail,' she said.

'It's useful in this line of work.'

'Have you always had it?'

'I grew up in the country. Perhaps that affects the way one sees things.'

'I am sure it does.'

'My brother and I always seemed to have a gun in one hand and a fishing rod in the other.'

'You had similar tastes.'

'Very similar tastes.'

Realising the implication she reddened. 'I beg your pardon. I didn't mean…'

'I know you didn't. Pray, do not be concerned.' He paused. 'Yes, Hugh and I were alike in many ways.'

'You were close?'

'Very close—then.'

Though the tone was perfectly even she sensed the

hurt beneath. It was dangerous ground and, having no wish to alienate him, she sought to change the subject.

'It's all right,' he replied. 'You need not fear to offend my sensibilities. I am equal to hearing my brother's name spoken.' Even as he said the words he knew them for truth, and that a shift had occurred somehow without his even being aware of it. 'I think I have you to thank for that.'

'I'm not sure I understand.'

'It was you who first made me face the things I had kept hidden for so long.'

'It was unintentionally done. I had no wish to pry.'

'I know. That is why I spoke of it.' He paused. 'Perhaps it was overdue.'

Sabrina remained silent, not wanting to interrupt him now, knowing just how hard it was to reveal the secrets of the past.

'You once asked me if I had forgiven my brother for what he did,' he continued. 'The thought has stayed with me ever since. The answer is the same: I still cannot forgive or forget, but I think it is time to draw a line under the affair.'

'I'm glad. The past should not be allowed to blight the future.'

He shot her a penetrating look. 'No, it should not, though I fear that too often it does.'

She nodded, accepting the veracity of that remark. Was she not a prime example? 'My father once said that it is not misfortune that shapes us, but how we respond to misfortune.'

'He was right. Either we go under or we become stronger.'

Recalling her recent conversation with Jacinta, Sabrina felt the words resonate strongly. 'I cannot imagine the circumstances that would drive you under.'

'Everyone has their breaking point. I am no different in that respect.'

'Everyone talks by the third day?'

'Exactly.' He smiled faintly. 'In any case, there are many kinds of hurt and even the strongest of us are not immune.'

'I think that time helps us put things in perspective.'

'Time helps,' he agreed. 'But it is thanks to you that I have been able to put things in perspective.'

'To me?'

'You made me face up to the past, to voice the feelings I had buried for so long. Once they were out I had no choice but to confront them. I cannot pretend it was comfortable, but it was necessary.'

'It is not easy to face down our demons.'

'No, it isn't, but past demons shrink before present evils.' He paused. 'When I was forced to watch while Machart assaulted you…it was the worst hour of my entire life. Nothing could compare to the horror of that.' The grey eyes met and held her own. 'I could not bear to see you hurt or demeaned in that way…in any way. I'd give my life to prevent it.'

She stared at him in complete astonishment, trying to gather her scattered wits. Never in a thousand years would she have expected to hear such words from him. Somehow she found her voice. 'I think that is the nicest compliment I have ever been paid.'

'You deserve only the highest of compliments.' He smiled wryly. 'And a decent dinner, of course.'

Chapter Thirteen

The conversation remained with her long afterwards and its effect was to leave a warm glow inside. Though she would not allow herself to refine too much upon it, nothing could diminish the pleasure of knowing she had his esteem.

As their journey progressed there were fewer opportunities for private speech, and though she was often in his company it was invariably in the presence of others. One of them was Major Brudenell for whom she had formed a real liking. Quite apart from the fact that he had been instrumental in saving her and her companions from the French, he had easy, unaffected manners and was invariably pleasant company. It was not hard to see why he and Falconbridge were friends as well as colleagues.

'We've been through a fair few campaigns together,' he confided one evening as they sat around the fire. 'He's a good fellow to have at your back in a fight.'

'Yes, he is,' she agreed.

He regarded her in momentary surprise. 'Of course, you would know that.'

'He has demonstrated as much on several occasions.'

'I own I did not think he would ever permit a woman to accompany him on a mission,' he said. 'No offence meant, of course.'

'None taken,' she replied. 'Major Falconbridge did not wish me to come, but he was given no choice.'

'I see.'

'In fact he did everything he could to dissuade me.'

He smiled. 'Quite unsuccessfully it seems.'

'He did his best.'

'He is known to be most assertive on occasion.'

'Oh, he was. All the same it did no good.'

'Marvellous. I wish I'd seen it. It's not often anyone bests him thus.'

They both laughed. Neither of them noticed Falconbridge, who had just returned from inspecting the picket line. He paused on the edge of the ring of firelight, surveying the scene. The two were sitting close, as old friends might, clearly enjoying each other's company. As he looked on he experienced a stab of emotion uncommonly like jealousy. It took him aback and almost at once he felt ashamed. His friend had never shown anything other than gentlemanly courtesy towards Sabrina. Nor was he a womaniser. He had a wife back in England to boot. There was not the least occasion to be jealous. Taking a deep breath he stepped forward into the ring of firelight and joined the group who were gathered there.

Brudenell glanced up and, seeing who it was, smiled. 'Ah, Robert. Miss Huntley and I were just talking about you.'

Falconbridge helped himself to a mug of coffee. 'Indeed?'

'Nothing damning, of course.'

'I'm relieved to hear it.'

'It seems the lady holds you in high regard.'

Falconbridge felt his heart skip a beat. Schooling his expression he surveyed the two of them calmly. 'I am honoured.'

'Yes, you are. Miss Huntley tells me you have demonstrated your worth many times.'

His face reddened and he was glad of the flickering shadows around them. 'The lady is generous.'

'Not so,' she replied. 'I spoke only the truth.'

For a moment she met his gaze across the fire. Was that a depth of warmth he glimpsed there, or was it merely the reflected glow of the flames? Before he could respond, Brudenell leapt in.

'There you are, straight from the lady's own lips.' He turned to Sabrina. 'I am in total agreement, ma'am. He's a good fellow to have with you in a tight spot.'

Falconbridge's hand clenched round the coffee mug. 'Brudenell, you talk too much. It's a bad habit.'

Far from being disturbed by the intelligence, his friend only laughed. Falconbridge glowered quietly, privately wondering if there wasn't a badger sett nearby that he could stuff him into. After that he'd very much have liked to take Sabrina aside for private discussion. No, he amended, not discussion. What he would have liked to do was take her in his arms, to repeat the heart-stopping delight he had experienced once before. Unfortunately, the circumstances were not conducive to it. The best he could do was to change the subject as soon as possible.

The conversation moved seamlessly on to other topics, interspersed at intervals with good-humoured jesting. It passed the evening agreeably until it was time to turn in. For a long time afterwards Falconbridge lay awake, looking at the stars, and feeling strangely happy. His mind returned to what Brudenell had told him earlier. The lady holds you in high regard. The words had been spoken in a bantering tone but their import meant far more than that. His friend could not know how cheering their effect had been, or how they gave him hope.

Their party remained with El Cuchillo's men until they came at last to the western edge of the Sierra de Gredos. There the guerrilla leader reined in and gestured towards the plain below.

'This is where we part, my friends. Follow the path yonder and it will bring you safely down. From there it should be but a few days' ride to Ciudad Rodrigo.'

Falconbridge nodded. 'And you?'

'We have other fish to fry.'

'Then I wish you God speed.' He held out his hand and the other man took it in a firm clasp. 'And I thank you again for your most timely assistance. It will not be forgotten, I assure you.'

A ghost of a smile played around El Cuchillo's lips. 'Allies must help each other. Besides, it is no hardship for us to harry the French, believe me.'

'Wellington shall hear of your part in the matter.'

'And we shall make good use of the guns he has supplied.'

'I imagine you will.'

El Cuchillo nodded. Then he touched his hat. '*Vaya con Dios.*'

With that the Spanish force rode away, heading back along the trail that led into the hills. For a little while Falconbridge watched them go. Then he turned his horse and led the descent to the plain. They reached it without incident. The pace was swifter then and they made good progress, though keeping a sharp look-out for any sign of French troops. However, they encountered none.

'With any luck we really shall be back in Ciudad Rodrigo in a few days,' he said, bringing his horse alongside Sabrina's mount.

'I pray we will meet Ramon there.'

'And I.'

She shot him a sideways glance. 'You do not doubt him?'

'Not in the least, but, in spite of his local knowledge and survival skill, he has had to make a perilous journey alone.'

'A calculated risk, surely? If you had any serious doubts on the matter you would not have given him the plans.'

He smiled. 'Quite right. All the same I try never to count chickens before the eggs are hatched.'

'I can see the sense in that. Nevertheless, you must have had faith.'

'I did. For that matter I still do.'

'But you take the precaution of keeping your fingers crossed as well.'

'Right now, my dear, everything is crossed.' He threw her a penetrating look. 'You must be looking forward to the end of this journey.'

'I confess I am. Even so, I shall never forget it.'

'Nor I.'

'It has had its moments.'

'Moments that I think neither of us will forget,' he replied.

Something in his tone caused her pulse to beat a little quicker, though when she looked at him his expression was impossible to read. She could only hope he, too, had taken some positive things from their time together.

'Some I would rather forget,' she admitted, 'but by no means all.'

There followed a small hesitation. Then he said, 'What will you choose to remember?'

'The night of the ball.' It was out before she had time to think of all its implications and what construction he might place on the remark. As these things belatedly occurred to her she felt suddenly much warmer. Striving for casualness, she added, 'And you?'

'There are many things I will remember,' he said. 'The ball not least.'

In an instant she was back in a moonlit garden with his arms around her and his lips on hers. Of course, that had been a ruse to deceive Machart, but the moment would stay with her always. Was her companion thinking of that, too? Had it meant anything to him? He made no direct reference to it so she must assume that it had not. In any case, it was dangerous ground. She managed a smile.

'I think there will be little opportunity for dancing for a while.'

'Opportunities can be created,' he replied.

'Yes.'

'We must seize those that come our way.'

She drew another deep breath, knowing full well that if there was ever another opportunity to dance with him she would seize it. The force of the realisation shocked her. Did he feel the same, or was he speaking in general, rather than specific terms? Again there was no way of knowing.

'I shall make every effort to do so.'

He smiled. 'I shall remind you of that, in the event that such an opportunity arises.'

Just then another horse drew alongside and he looked round to see Blakelock.

'Beg pardon, sir, but Major Brudenell asks if he might have a word.'

Falconbridge quashed a desire to tell Blakelock and Brudenell to go to blazes, and nodded instead. 'Certainly.' Then he turned back to Sabrina. 'Will you excuse me, ma'am?'

'Of course.'

With real regret she watched him trot on ahead, and presently he and his colleague were engaged in private conversation.

Afterwards she found herself thinking of the future with mixed feelings: on the one hand, it would be wonderful to bathe and change into feminine garments and sleep in a bed again; on the other, she would see less of Falconbridge. He had intimated that he would like to see her again, but she knew it could not be often. His duties would command his attention and he would have little time to think of anything else. Gradually, the immediacy of their adventure would fade, though perhaps he might remember it from time to time and recall her with affection. In the meantime there was every chance that her father would be freed. Her spirits lifted at the prospect. He was the reason she had come on this mission and his safety mattered more than foolish dreams of romance.

When they stopped to rest the horses a little later she was joined by Major Brudenell. It seemed that his thoughts had been turning on similar lines to her own.

'No doubt you will be glad to get back to civilisation, ma'am.'

'Yes, indeed.'

'This rough living gets wearisome after a while, even for soldiers. It must be doubly so for a lady.'

'I am not unused to rough living, sir, for I have accompanied my father on numerous expeditions into the back of beyond. All the same, some creature comforts will be most welcome.'

'I'm sure. As I am sure that you must be longing to see your father again.' He paused. 'Major Falconbridge outlined the circumstances to me.'

'Ramon is the key to my father's release now.'

'Ah, yes, Ramon. A most persuasive gentleman as I recall.'

'He can be.'

'He rode into El Cuchillo's lair as if he owned the place. There must have been at least twenty muskets pointing his way, and he didn't turn a hair.'

'I wish I had been there to see it.'

He shook his head. 'I felt trepidation enough riding in there, and I'd been invited.'

'Well, I'm glad El Cuchillo didn't have him shot or I wouldn't be here either.' She paused. 'I understand that is due as much to your good offices as Ramon's intervention. All the same, I'm surprised the guerilla agreed to help us. We must have seemed expendable in his eyes.'

'I got the impression that he didn't have much choice—something about him returning a favour.'

Sabrina grew thoughtful, recalling an earlier conversation in which Ramon had admitted to knowing the guerrilla leader. He had not explained the connection and neither she nor her companions would have dreamed of prying. Now it appeared that the connection was more than one of casual acquaintance.

'I don't know the details,' Brudenell continued, 'but it appeared to be about a matter of honour.'

'Indeed?'

'Yes. Then, when Ramon told me the name of the officer leading the mission, I added my voice.'

'I'm glad you did.'

'To be honest I don't think it made any difference. I'm sure El Cuchillo had already decided by then.'

It was intriguing, though it brought her no nearer to an answer. Only Ramon could clarify matters there. Perhaps when she returned he would tell her.

'The strange thing was that once El Cuchillo had said he would help, your friend got on his horse and rode off in the opposite direction. Said he had urgent business elsewhere. Didn't even wait to see if the chap would keep his word.'

'Ramon must have known he would.'

'Evidently. I thought then that he must have had a very good reason for leaving.'

'He did.'

'Major Falconbridge has since apprised me of the facts.'

'Had it not been of the gravest importance, Ramon would not have left. I can only pray he has reached his destination unscathed.'

'I have every confidence he has, ma'am. Who would dare to try and stop such a man?'

Sabrina could only hope he was right.

She was still thinking about it when Falconbridge joined her later.

'Most interesting,' he said after she had summarised

what Brudenell had told her. 'Your friend Ramon is a
dark horse.'

'Maybe so, but I'd trust him with my life.'

'You already have, and he has proved himself worthy
of your regard.'

She nodded. 'Do you think he has got those plans to
Lord Wellington by now?'

'I sincerely hope so.'

'I little thought events would turn out this way. I had
visions of a triumphant return in which you handed over
the papers to the great man himself, while Ward and
Forbes looked on in open-mouthed admiration.'

He laughed out loud. 'I must say I like the sound of
that. Unfortunately, things rarely do turn out exactly
as we imagine. The important thing is that Wellington
does get those papers.'

She hesitated. 'How soon do you think it might be
before my father is released?'

Looking into her face just then Falconbridge was
touched by its earnest expression. 'If Ward has any
notion of honour it will be very soon.' He squeezed her
shoulder gently. 'I will do all in my power to ensure that
it is so.'

His touch and his kindly expression warmed her.
'Thank you.' She paused. 'Will there be a ceremony
for your promotion to Lieutenant Colonel?'

He choked off a laugh. 'About as much ceremony as
it takes to hand over the paperwork and tell me to clear
off and get on with it.'

'Oh. I thought it would be more elaborate than
that.'

'A forlorn hope, my dear. Of course, on the day I'm
given a Field Marshal's baton they may well organise a
parade.'

'You'd be able to command one then.'

'So I should.' He grinned. 'I'm very flattered that you think I might attain such high rank.'

'I think you would make an excellent Field Marshal.'

'Have a care, lest you turn my head.'

'You would not let your head be turned by me or anyone else.'

'Oh, you turn heads, my dear, I assure you.'

She flushed faintly. 'Hardly—not dressed like this at any rate.'

'It would make no difference if you wore sackcloth. Not that I advocate any such thing, you understand.'

'I'm relieved to hear it. Mine is not a penitential nature.'

His eyes gleamed. 'So I've noticed.'

'Sackcloth is not part of my plans, even if I do not get my trunks back.'

'What would you do then?'

'Then I should be forced to wear breeches and boots henceforth.'

'What a dreadful notion. I shall spare no effort to see that your gowns are returned to you with all haste.'

'I would be most grateful.'

He raised one eyebrow. 'How grateful exactly?'

'It is most improper of you to ask, you horrid man.'

Falconbridge laughed softly. Was there ever such a girl?

It was a thought that stayed with him when the journey resumed a short time later. Their earlier conversations had led him to hope that his company would not be unwelcome to her in future. It gladdened his heart. Once he had thought never to experience that feeling again. If he had ever considered the notion of a more settled life it had always been in the dim and distant future when the war was over. It had involved the pursuits of a country gentleman and was far removed from any thought of romance. Now, in a few short weeks, all those notions had been turned on their heads. The thought of losing Sabrina's company was unpalatable because he knew how devilishly dull life would be without it. For all its perils he had enjoyed their shared adventures. A sage in ancient times once said that journeys cause men to reveal their true characters. The saying held good for women, too. Despite the short duration of their acquaintance he realised he knew Sabrina better than he had ever known Clarissa. Guile and duplicity were as far from her nature as the earth was from the stars. Events had tested her severely and she had not been found wanting. Falconbridge smiled in self-mockery. He had once proclaimed that he was married to his career; now he realised that his career wasn't enough.

'Penny for 'em,' said Brudenell, coming alongside.

Falconbridge started. 'Oh, er, I was just thinking about our return to Ciudad Rodrigo.'

'I'm looking forward to it myself,' admitted the other. 'This saddle is making life damned tedious.'

'Getting sore, eh?'

'Let's just say I'd give a great deal for a hot tub.' Brudenell lifted his sleeve and sniffed at it, wrinkling his nose in distaste. 'I'm starting to smell like a dead ferret.'

Falconbridge glanced ruefully at his own travel-stained garments. He couldn't recall the last time he'd bathed. 'Make that two dead ferrets.'

'These adventures are all very well, but I'm beginning to think a spell of routine duties would suit me nicely.'

'I suppose there's something to be said for routine.'

'Aye,' replied Brudenell, 'hot water, clean linen and a soft bed to start with.'

'The hallmarks of civilised living.'

'Not forgetting feminine company, of course.'

His friend smiled faintly. 'At least I have not lacked for that.'

'No, you lucky dog. It was a cruel fate that rewarded you with the company of the delightful Miss Huntley, and me with El Cuchillo.'

'Cruel indeed.'

'It's worse than that. For reasons that I cannot fathom, the lady likes you.'

Falconbridge felt his face redden. 'I fear I have done little enough to deserve it.'

'Not what she says, old boy. Of course, I tried to put her on her guard and tell her what an undeserving brute you are, but she was having none of it.'

It drew a deprecating grin. 'Unkind, Tony. You might have put in a good word for me.'

'What, and seen myself quite cut out?' Brudenell sighed. 'Not that it did me any good. She is oddly impervious to my charm.'

'So she should be. You're a married man.'

'That isn't the point.'

'Isn't it? I rather thought it was significant.'

His companion returned the grin. 'You're a hard man, Robert.'

'Hard? I have it on good authority that I'm quite odious.'

'Good Lord. Who dared to say that to your face?'

'Miss Huntley.'

Brudenell chuckled softly. 'Did she, by God?'

'Oh, yes, and a lot more besides.'

'Really? What more?'

'If you think I'm going to tell you that, Tony, you're delusional.'

Far from dismaying his friend, it served only to fuel his enjoyment. 'How I should have loved to be a fly on the wall.'

Falconbridge regarded him with a jaundiced eye. 'I have no doubt you would.'

'Offensive, was it?'

'Deeply.'

'Wounding?'

'Most hurtful.'

'Bruised your pride?'

'It may never recover.'

'Splendid.' Brudenell beamed. 'I take it you'll be seeing her again when we get back then?'

'I wouldn't miss it for the world.'

Chapter Fourteen

Three days later they surmounted a hill and saw the Agueda River below. Beside it lay Ciudad Rodrigo. Sabrina smiled, letting her eye travel from the big gun batteries on the Great Teson opposite the town, to the familiar details of its fortress and churches and ancient stone bridge. Somewhere down there was her godfather and, she hoped, Ramon. Perhaps soon her father, too.

'There were times when I thought we would not live to see this place again,' said Jacinta.

Sabrina nodded. 'And I. It seems strangely like coming home.' She paused. 'I don't know why I should feel that when my acquaintance with the place is so slight.'

'Home is where we happen to be, no?'

'True—in our case anyway.'

'Besides, it is people who make places significant.'

'Yes, you're right.'

For the first time it occurred to Sabrina that it might be pleasant to put down roots and have a permanent home. Involuntarily her gaze flicked towards

Falconbridge. Then she pulled herself up sharply. She could have no expectations there; he was married to his career and would go wherever the army decided to send him. Today, Ciudad Rodrigo, next week, Salamanca perhaps. She thought that anywhere would seem like home if he were there, and everywhere empty without him.

As they rode slowly towards the town she could not help comparing it with the first occasion. Then she had been trying to forget Robert Falconbridge. Now she knew she never would.

'Damned glad to see the old place again,' said Brudenell.

'Yes. There were moments when I thought we might not,' replied Falconbridge.

It was so precisely an echo of what Jacinta had said that Sabrina looked up quickly. He met her gaze and smiled. 'At least now I can look your godfather in the face—and keep my liver intact.'

'What has your liver got to do with it?' she asked.

'A private matter, between gentlemen.'

'Oh.' She had an idea he was teasing her again, though his expression did not suggest it. 'Well, I'm glad to learn your vital organs are safe.'

He bit back a laugh. 'It's a relief to me, too.'

The cavalcade clattered over the bridge and through the gates, following the road to the Castillo. They dismounted in the courtyard and Brudenell sent a runner to announce their arrival. Then he looked at his companions.

'Well, I suppose we'd better go and give an account of ourselves to Ward.'

'I suppose we had.' Falconbridge turned to Sabrina. 'Are you equal to it, my dear?'

'Certainly.'

'Good girl.'

Before there was a chance for further speech they heard the sound of footsteps behind them. They turned to see Colonel Albermarle. Sabrina's face lit in a smile. Then she was enveloped in a hearty hug.

'My dear girl, how glad I am to see you.'

'And I to see you, sir.'

'I have thought of you constantly since the day you left.' He held her at arm's length. 'Are you well?'

'Quite well.'

'I was expecting your return by coach, not on horseback. Was there some mishap?'

'Circumstances forced us to leave the coach behind,' she explained.

'Indeed. Well, you can tell me the details later over dinner.'

'Of course.'

Albermarle's gaze went from her to the rest of the group and came to rest on Falconbridge. 'You got her back safe, Major. I'm obliged.'

'Precious few thanks are due to me, sir. The credit rightly belongs to Miss Huntley herself.'

Albermarle saw the glance that passed between the two of them and knew there was more to the matter than he was being told. However, he decided that this was not the right time to probe.

'Am I to take it that your mission was successful?'

Sabrina bit her lip. 'Yes and no.'

'I'm not sure I follow you, my dear.'

'Godfather, have you not spoken to Ramon?'

Albermarle frowned. 'Ramon? No, how should I? He is with you.'

The others exchanged looks of consternation. Sabrina heard Falconbridge swear under his breath.

'Am I to understand that Ramon has not returned, sir?' he asked.

'No, he has not, or not to my knowledge.'

Suddenly all the elation of the past few minutes leached away. It was replaced by sudden deep unease as the implications began to dawn.

'Nothing would have kept Ramon from coming here, save for some misfortune,' said Sabrina. 'Perhaps his horse went lame.'

Falconbridge frowned. 'Perhaps. I just pray it is only that.'

Thinking of the possible dangers their companion might have encountered, she felt her stomach knot. Was Ramon lying dead or injured as a result of an encounter with a French patrol? A glance at Luis and Jacinta revealed that the possibility had occurred to them as well. Willis and Blakelock frowned.

'If his horse went lame it may have taken some time to find another, depending on where it happened,' said Albermarle. 'In which case he'll turn up in the next few days, I expect. He is an able man. I'm sure you need not fear for his safety.'

'It isn't just a matter of his safety, sir,' replied Falconbridge.

'What do you mean?'

'Ramon has the plans we brought back from Aranjuez.'

'You mean you entrusted the documents to this man?'

'That is correct, sir. I would not have done it, save under the most extreme of circumstances.'

Albermarle shook his head. 'This is unfortunate indeed. No doubt you acted for the best but—'

'He could not have done anything else, sir,' said Sabrina.

For a moment her gaze met Falconbridge's and she saw him smile faintly. Then he turned back to Albermarle.

'I take full responsibility for the decision,' he replied. 'It seemed the only choice at the time. I had hoped that Ramon would have returned by now. Unfortunately nothing can be done until he does, or we find out what happened to him.'

'You realise that General Ward will have to be apprised of the circumstances.'

'Of course.'

His expression gave nothing away, but Blakelock's and Willis's did, and Sabrina began to feel deeply uneasy in her turn. Surely they did not think that Ward would somehow blame Falconbridge for this mishap? Then she realised that that was exactly what they did think.

'Well, we'd better go in.' Albermarle shot a glance at his goddaughter. 'No doubt you will want to retire to your lodgings and rest after your journey, my dear.'

'I'll rest later,' she replied. 'Right now I have to go along to this debriefing.'

Luis nodded. 'Maybe we should all go, *Doña* Sabrina. It may be that Major Falconbridge will require corroboration of his report to General Ward.'

The others murmured their agreement. Albermarle looked round in surprise.

'Surely there is no need for all of you to attend?'

'I think there is every need, sir,' replied Sabrina.

He saw the resolution on every face and then shrugged. 'If you insist.'

'We do insist.'

Thus they set off together across the courtyard. As they did so, Falconbridge fell into step with her.

'Thank you,' he murmured.

'For nothing.'

'Not nothing, I think.'

'They cannot blame you for this, Robert.'

'I let vital papers pass out of my hands.'

'You had no choice.'

He vouchsafed no reply, forbearing to say that this was the army and that his superiors tended to see things their way.

They arrived outside Ward's office a short time later. Albermarle spoke to the adjutant on duty and they were shown straight in. Looking round, Sabrina could not but remember the last time she had been here, a reluctant participant in a military scheme. It was no more than three weeks ago, yet how very different her feelings were now.

Ward looked up in surprise as the group walked in. However, he made no remark on the matter and merely rose from his chair.

'Ah, Major Falconbridge and Miss Huntley. Returned safe and sound.' He paused. 'Well, man? Did you obtain the papers?'

'Yes, sir.'

'Where are they?'

'I no longer have them, sir.'

Ward's brows drew together. 'I think you'd better explain.'

Falconbridge summarised events, omitting nothing and exaggerating nothing.

Ward heard him out without interruption but his

expression was wintry. 'So the documents are now in the possession of this man, Ramon?'

'That is correct, sir.'

'A partisan, I believe.'

'Yes, sir.'

'What do we know about him?'

'I believe him to be honest and reliable.'

'I didn't ask what you believe, Major. I asked what is known,' replied Ward. 'The documents in his possession are worth a great deal of money in more than one quarter.'

Sabrina, who had been following the conversation closely, stared at him in disbelief. It was followed immediately by a surge of anger. Beside her Jacinta and Luis stiffened visibly. Suddenly events were taking a turn she could never have envisaged. Even so, she couldn't let the imputation pass unchallenged. Striving to control her voice, she spoke up.

'Ramon is both honest and loyal, sir. He would never do such a thing."

Ward glanced at her. 'Men will do all manner of things for money, Miss Huntley.'

'If he is not here now it is because something happened to prevent it,' she replied.

'Let us hope you are right, ma'am.'

Her face paled but Ward had turned his attention back to Falconbridge.

'The decision to let the documents out of your keeping amounts to a dereliction of duty, Major.'

Falconbridge's jaw tightened. 'Had I not done so, the French would have found them when we were captured. I gave them to the one person who had a realistic chance of getting away and delivering them safely.'

'What Major Falconbridge says it true,' said Sabrina.

'And every member of our party here will attest to it, General.'

Ward surveyed her coolly. 'Be that as it may, the documents are still missing. Of course, your friend Ramon may yet deliver them.'

'If he can, he will,' she replied.

'Again, let us hope you are right, ma'am,' he replied. 'So much hangs on it, does it not?'

The implication of the words was not lost on her and she was suddenly sickened. If Ramon did not come, all their efforts would have been for nothing. Her father would not be freed. Beside her she heard a faint hiss of indrawn breath and glanced at Jacinta. The woman's face was a mask of cold fury, an outward expression of Sabrina's own sentiments.

'Major Falconbridge, you will return to your quarters and stay there. I shall want to talk to you again later. Lord Wellington will require a full report of course.'

'Yes, sir.'

Ward favoured Sabrina with another chilly smile. 'Your servant, Miss Huntley.'

It was dismissal and there was nothing they could do about it. They trooped out of the office and into the corridor. Sabrina turned to face Falconbridge.

'I'm so sorry, Robert.'

'Thank you for what you said back there.'

'It was the least I could do. I wanted to hit the old buzzard for implying those things.'

He gave her a wry smile. 'It is perhaps as well that you did not.'

'Yes, I suppose it is, though it would have served him right.'

Albermarle shook his head. 'Damnable situation

all round, but I cannot blame you for what happened, Major.'

'Thank you, sir.'

The Colonel turned to his goddaughter. 'Will you walk back to your lodgings, my dear?'

'Presently, sir.'

'Then I'll leave you for the time.' He nodded to Falconbridge. 'Let's just hope your man, Ramon, turns up.'

With that Albermarle walked away. For a little space they watched him go. Then Falconbridge looked at Sabrina. 'I had hoped to call on you after you had rested, but I fear that may not be possible for a while.'

Her heart skipped a beat. He did want to see her after all. 'Then I shall have to be patient.'

'I fear you will.' He sighed. 'It's a devil of a mess.'

'But not of your making.'

'You are generous. The consequences for you may be harsh indeed.'

'You must not think that way. Ramon will come. I know he will.'

'I pray he will. The thought of all your efforts being for nothing appals me.'

'I am not the only one who stands to lose something. Your promotion—'

'Is unimportant, compared with your father's freedom.'

The words brought a lump to her throat. 'It may yet be well.'

He hoped with all his heart that she was right.

After they parted Sabrina rejoined Jacinta and Luis and walked back to her lodgings. How different it all was from the way she had imagined it. Her vision of their triumphant return had been a fantasy indeed. When they reached the door, Luis paused.

'I must leave you here, *Doña* Sabrina. Jacinta will look after you for the time being.'

'Where are you going?'

'To find out what has happened to Ramon.'

'He could be anywhere, Luis.'

'Then I must discover where that is.'

'Will you not eat first and rest a little?'

He smiled, revealing strong, white teeth. 'The sooner I leave, the sooner I shall find him.'

Jacinta frowned. 'How do you know you will succeed?'

'I will find him. Everyone must be somewhere, you see.' He paused. 'Besides, Ramon is my friend and I did not much care for the slurs of General Ward.'

'None of us cared for them,' said Sabrina. 'When Ramon returns he can shove them back down the General's throat.'

'Exactly so.'

'He may also wish to consider where he'd like to shove General Ward's secret papers when next they meet,' replied Jacinta.

Sabrina choked back indecorous laughter.

Luis grinned. 'I will suggest it to him. In the meantime, I must find a fresh horse.'

'When you get one, come back. I will have some provisions ready for you,' said Jacinta.

'*Muchas gracias. Hasta entonces.*'

With that he bowed and left them.

Some time later, in the privacy of her room, Sabrina stripped off her travel-stained garments and climbed into a hot tub. She sank into the water with a sigh of real pleasure. It seemed so long since she had bathed properly or worn clean clothes. She scrubbed herself vigorously and washed her hair before leaning back to relax and let the heat unknot her aching muscles. The water was cooling before she felt ready to climb out. Having dried herself off she donned one of her older gowns, a rose-pink muslin that had remained behind in the wardrobe. When her hair was dry she brushed it out and tied it back with a ribbon.

A close scrutiny in the mirror revealed that her appearance was at least acceptable, although her face and neck were lightly tanned from the time spent in the open air. The effect was not entirely displeasing though, for the colour enhanced her hair and eyes. Some hand cream would help restore the softness lost through outdoor living. As she began to massage the cream in she realised she was still wearing the wedding ring that Falconbridge had given her when they set out for Aran-juez. She had grown so accustomed to its presence it had almost become part of her hand. It cost her a real pang to remove it, but to do anything else was totally inappropriate. She laid it carefully in the small jewel box on the dresser and closed the lid. That part of the adventure was really over.

Satisfied that she was presentable again, she went downstairs in search of something to eat. She was met by Jacinta, also bathed now and dressed in clean garments.

'I will make you a tortilla,' she said. 'It will keep the wolf from the door until dinner.'

'Make enough for yourself, as well,' replied Sabrina. 'You must also be hungry by now.'

Jacinta nodded. 'It will be good to have some fresh food again, no?'

'Yes, it will.'

'And bread that is not the consistency of brick.'

Sabrina smiled sadly, recalling the meal she had shared with Falconbridge when they had sat by the creek together. The rations had been scanty and poor but his conversation had not. Just being in his company was sufficient compensation for stale bread and cheese. Would they ever have the dinner together that he had promised her? Circumstances seemed to be ranged against it. General Ward had made no secret of his displeasure. If Ramon did not return… She didn't want to think about the consequences of that, for Falconbridge or for her father.

Almost as if she knew her thoughts, Jacinta met her gaze. 'If anyone can find Ramon now, it is Luis.'

'I hope you are right.'

'One does not suffer a friend to be insulted. You spoke up for Ramon before General Ward. Now Luis will do his part.'

'Ramon is my friend, too,' replied Sabrina. 'My father also holds him in the highest regard. He would have been deeply angered had he been there today.'

'Yes, I believe he would. For his sake, too, Luis will find Ramon.'

Later, when they had eaten, Sabrina went out into the garden, wanting some fresh air and some space in which to think. Without making any conscious choice she followed the path to the stone bench she had sat on with Robert Falconbridge the last time she had been out here. He had tried every means to dissuade her from accompanying him on the mission. Every detail was etched on her memory. Even then she had been aware of him, his sheer physical presence, his look, his touch.

She could never have thought then that one glorious moonlit evening he would take her in his arms and steal her heart.

She was so rapt in thought that she failed to hear the footsteps on the path until the visitor was close. She caught sight of a red uniform jacket and her heart leapt. Then she realised with a stab of disappointment that the newcomer was a total stranger. He bowed and smiled.

'I have been charged to deliver this letter, ma'am. Compliments of Major Falconbridge.'

Her heart gave another lurch. 'Thank you for your trouble, sir.'

'No trouble at all, ma'am.'

When he had gone she sank back onto the stone seat and broke open the wafer with a trembling hand. The missive contained one sentence only: *Since a Field Marshal's baton appears to be out of reach for the present, I comfort myself with the slender hope that you might consent to dine with a humble Major, as soon as he can arrange it. F.* Sabrina read it and felt laughter bubble up in her throat. He had meant it then. Suddenly all her earlier gloom lifted. All might yet be well. Having re-read the note half a dozen times, she carefully refolded it and tucked it safely inside the bodice of her gown. Then she went indoors to find pen and paper.

Some time later an orderly arrived at the officers' quarters. 'A note for Major Falconbridge,' he announced. 'Arrived just now, sir.'

Brudenell gestured across the room. 'The Major is yonder.'

Falconbridge took the letter and dismissed the man. Then he studied the direction. The handwriting was unfamiliar but it was unquestionably feminine in nature.

Hope leapt. Taking a deep breath he opened it, eagerly scanning the contents. It contained just one sentence: *Whilst the loss of a baton is deeply regrettable, the notion of dining with a lower-ranking officer is, on balance, to be preferred.* There was no signature but it needed none, and his face lit with a grin.

'Good news?' inquired Brudenell.

'Very good news.'

'It's about time.'

'Yes, it is.'

Refolding the paper, Falconbridge stowed it carefully inside his breast pocket. It was about time, he thought; time to draw a line under the past and get on with his life. At least now he knew what he wanted the future to be.

His thoughts were interrupted by the arrival of an adjutant summoning him to Lord Wellington's head-quarters in the Palacio de los Castro. He exchanged glances with Brudenell and then nodded.

'I shall come directly.'

When the adjutant had departed, his friend frowned. 'What does the old man want now?'

'To hear my report, I imagine. Unless of course he wishes to tell me himself that Ramon has returned with the papers.'

'That would solve a few problems, would it not?'

'Aye, it would.'

'You did the best you could, Robert. Damned bad luck his getting delayed like that.'

'It's a pity Ward doesn't see it in the same light.'

'No, well, he wasn't surrounded by hostile French troops wanting to carve him into slivers, was he?'

'Even so…' Falconbridge moved to the door '…I

made an error of judgement. The trouble is that others besides myself will be made to pay for it.'

When he arrived at Wellington's door a short time later it was to see Ward and Forbes there as well. His heart sank. Schooling his face to a neutral expression he halted in front of the desk.

'You wished to see me, sir?'

Wellington looked up from the letter he had been writing and leaned back in his chair, surveying his visitor coolly. The stern lines of his face gave nothing away but the piercing eyes missed nothing. Under their fixed scrutiny his visitor felt the knot in his gut tighten.

'Damned bad business, Falconbridge.'

'Yes, sir.'

Ward nodded and interjected, 'You should not have let those papers out of your hands.'

'I believed I had no choice, sir, with capture imminent.'

'You should have brought the documents yourself.'

'That would have meant leaving my companions to die, sir.'

'All soldiers know the risks of war.'

'Miss Huntley is not a soldier.'

'No, but she also knew the risks.'

Falconbridge's eyes became steel grey. 'Not a good enough reason, in my opinion, for leaving her to the mercy of the French.'

Ward glared and made to reply but Wellington was before him. 'The situation was an unenviable one and I have no doubt you did what you thought right, Major. Nevertheless, the fact remains that a third party now has in his possession the most sensitive of information.'

'Information that our man in Madrid went to great lengths to obtain,' said Forbes.

'I believe that Ramon will deliver it if he can,' replied Falconbridge.

Ward snorted. The sound drew a swift quelling glance from Wellington but just as quickly his attention returned to Falconbridge.

'You appear to have great faith in this man.'

'I do, sir, and so does Miss Huntley. Ramon was a good friend of her father's.'

'Well, we'll see soon enough whether your faith is justified.'

'Touching the matter of John Huntley, sir...'

'Well?'

'His freedom was the condition that caused Miss Huntley to agree to go on the mission in the first place. She has performed her part in exemplary fashion, sir, and kept her side of the bargain.'

'But you did not return with the papers you went for,' said Ward.

'That is not her fault. It is mine, and she should not be punished for it.'

Wellington lifted one eyebrow a little. 'I should have thought there was no question of her being penalised in any way. Major Forbes, have not negotiations already begun for the release of prisoners?'

'They have, sir.'

'John Huntley among them?'

'Yes, sir.'

'Good. You will keep me informed of how things progress.'

Falconbridge breathed a silent sigh of relief. At least that much might be salvaged from the affair. Before he could pursue the thought any further he became aware that Wellington was addressing him again.

'For the rest we can only wait and hope. In the meantime, in the absence of information, I must try and outguess the French. You may return to your duties, Major Falconbridge.'

Being thus dismissed he walked back to his quarters with the words ringing in his ears. Waiting and hoping were indeed the only options available to him just then, on the career front anyway. On a personal level, he felt a different kind of hope. Sabrina's face drifted into his mind and he recalled a promise he had made. That at least was a matter he could do something about.

Chapter Fifteen

The following morning Sabrina received a courteous letter from Major Falconbridge inviting her to dine with him and Brudenell that evening. Her face lit with a smile as she read the invitation. He had kept his promise, and done it with tact and sensitivity. The occasion coincided with ladies' night in the officers' mess. Moreover, as Colonel Albermarle was also invited to join the party, she would have a highly respectable escort. For all sorts of reasons it promised to be an enjoyable occasion and she lost no time in returning a note of acceptance.

However, it threw up another difficulty. Her boxes still had not been returned to her and the choice of gowns remaining in her wardrobe was slim. In the end she selected one of her newer muslin frocks. The gown was fashioned in a simple but becoming style and, when combined with a silken shawl, a fetching hairstyle, a necklace and earrings and a pair of long gloves, the effect was of simple understated elegance.

Heads turned as she and Colonel Albermarle made their entrance, and Falconbridge felt the first stirrings of pride that she was to be his guest that evening. Beside him, Brudenell was following her progress, too.

'My word, Robert, but she's a beauty.'

'That she is.'

'What on earth does she see in you?'

'Lord knows.'

They moved forward to meet their guests. For a moment Falconbridge took her hand, letting his gaze travel the length of her. Then he smiled.

'You look wonderful.'

'Thank you.'

He felt another surge of pride, fully aware of the covert looks coming their way, and knowing every man there would like to be in his shoes. In consequence, he forgot that he had retained her hand far longer than was necessary or correct.

Beside him Albermarle coughed. 'Well, then, shall we sit down?'

Sabrina smiled and took her place beside their host. The meal was excellent, a real treat after the Spartan rations they had endured in the latter days of their journey. A tasty vegetable soup was removed with trout, cooked *à la plancha,* and then a sirloin of beef, chicken in a lemon sauce and a game pie. Dessert was a light and frothy syllabub, with fruit and sweetmeats.

The conversation flowed easily throughout. As ever, Falconbridge and Brudenell were excellent company, being well informed on a variety of topics, and often witty. Many times Sabrina found herself laughing at the tales of their past exploits. These, she had no doubt, had been carefully censored and were thus totally unexceptionable, but always hilarious. Albermarle, too, relaxed and became expansive, keeping up his part in the conversation. Aware of having the company and undivided attention of three distinguished men, Sabrina found herself positively enjoying the covert and envious looks that came her way from some of the other ladies present. It occurred to her then that both Brudenell and Robert were very handsome in their different ways. Even so, she had eyes for only one.

Becoming aware of her attention Falconbridge smiled and, seeing that the other two were temporarily engaged in discussion, seized his chance. 'You look thoughtful, ma'am.'

'I was thinking,' she admitted.

He lowered his voice a little. 'About what?'

'I shall not tell you for fear you should grow conceited.'

He grinned. 'Now I am intrigued.'

'Good.'

'Vixen.'

Sabrina laughed. It might have been the candlelight or the wine or the sparkle in her eyes, or all three, but again he found himself staring and felt a sudden rush of heat to his groin.

'If we were alone, my girl, I should compel you to speak.'

'Do you think so?'

'Do you think I would not?'

The tone and the accompanying look sent a delicious shiver the length of her body. Suddenly she wished very much that they were alone together, somewhere out in the back of beyond; that she was in his arms again and yielding to that tender compulsion. Startled by the tenor of her thoughts she lowered her gaze, afraid that he might read too accurately what lay behind.

Fortunately their attention was recalled by Albermarle who had directed a question to Falconbridge.

Gathering his wits he made some reply but it wasn't easy while his thoughts were all on the woman beside him.

For the remainder of the evening there was no further opportunity for private speech until the time came for her and Albermarle to leave.

'Thank you,' she said. 'It has been a wonderful evening. And it was a truly delicious meal.'

He raised her hand to his lips. 'I keep my promises.'

'So you do.' She smiled. 'And most handsomely, too.'

Resisting the urge to take her in his arms, he contented himself with a bow. 'It was my pleasure.'

'Capital evening, Major,' said Albermarle. 'First rate.'

'I'm glad you enjoyed it, sir.'

'Hope to return the favour one day soon.'

'I'll look forward to it, sir.'

With real regret he watched his guests depart, following their progress until they were out of sight.

For a while Sabrina and her godfather walked in companionable silence. Then he cast a shrewd glance her way.

'I'd say that young man has taken quite a fancy to you, my dear.'

Her cheeks reddened and she was glad of the concealing darkness. 'Would you?'

'Couldn't keep his eyes off you all evening. Not that it's to be wondered at. You're a devilish pretty girl.'

'Thank you, sir.'

He hesitated and then said casually, 'I think you're not indifferent to him either.'

She bit her lip. 'I like him very well.'

'Thought so. I confess it surprised me at first. I'd a notion you didn't care for him at one time.'

'No, I didn't, but my knowing him better has improved my opinion of him.'

'I see.' He paused. 'Good sort of fellow, Falconbridge.'

'Yes, he is.'

Albermarle made no reply but merely smiled to himself.

Sabrina did not see or hear from Falconbridge for several days after that and guessed that his duties kept him fully occupied. Then one morning he came to call.

'I regret that Wellington has assigned me to another mission. I shall be going out of town for a while.'

Sabrina's heart sank. This was the very thing she had been dreading. Although she had known it must come at some point she had not thought it would be so soon. Somehow she summoned a smile, trying not to let her disappointment show.

'Will you be gone long?'

'A week or so, I believe.'

'I see.'

'I deeply regret the necessity, but my orders are to leave at once.' He looked down into her face. 'However, I wanted to see you first.'

'I am so glad that you did.' She hesitated, hating to ask but needing to know the answer. 'Is it going to be dangerous, this mission of yours?'

'Would that matter to you?'

'You know it would.'

'On this occasion I think there is likely to be little danger.'

'May I ask where you are going?'

'I am not at liberty to say what it is at present.'

'Forgive me, it was a tactless question.'

He shook his head. 'No, just a natural one. When I return, everything will be made clear.'

'A mystery then.' She laid a hand on his sleeve. 'I beg you will be careful. You have trouble enough at present without adding injury to the list.'

'I promise to heed the advice.'

'I wish I were going with you. I hate the thought of sitting here and doing nothing.'

'You have already done far more than could ever have been expected of you. Besides, you will want to wait for news of Ramon.'

'Yes,' she replied. 'We have heard nothing from Luis since he left.'

'I fear the task will be like looking for a needle in a haystack.'

'He felt he had to do it anyway,' she replied. 'General Ward's comments went deep.'

'Yes, they did.'

She met his gaze and held it. 'If Ramon does not return, will things go ill for you, Robert?'

'I cannot deny that matters are a touch awkward at present, but all may yet be well.'

'If it had not been for me and Jacinta you would have brought those documents back yourself. Your men would have provided a diversion to cover your escape, and they would all have done it as a matter of duty. But you would not leave two women behind to be captured while you left the scene.'

'Nor would any man worthy of the name.' He took her shoulders in a gentle clasp. 'You should not feel guilty on that account.'

'I cannot help it.'

'I took the decision and I stand by it. Do you really think I could have left you there?'

The warmth of his hands and the gentleness of his tone brought a lump to her throat. 'You should have, but I am glad you did not. In consequence, all of Lord Wellington's plans are thrown awry.'

He smiled. 'I think you overstate the case a little. This is a setback, no more.'

'Now you will not get your promotion.'

'It doesn't matter. There will be other opportunities. What matters to me is your safety and well-being.'

'And yours to me.'

His heart beat a little quicker but before he could reply they heard booted feet in the hall. Then Corporal Blakelock appeared at the door. 'Beg pardon, Major, but it's time.'

'Very well. I'm coming.' Falconbridge smiled ruefully at Sabrina. 'There is so much I want to say to you and no time now to do it in, but I'll be back, I promise you.'

She managed to return his smile. 'I'll hold you to that.'

He pressed his lips to her hand, and then left her to join the waiting men. Sabrina watched until they were out of sight and only the warm imprint of his kiss remained.

The days following his departure seemed long and dull. Nor could she settle to anything. Reading, sewing and sketch pad were abandoned in succession. Every time she heard a horse in the street or a footstep in the hall her heart leapt. She knew it could not be him, but lived in the hope that it might be Luis or Ramon or both, and each time the hope was dashed. Then her thoughts would turn back to Falconbridge, wondering where he was and what he was doing at that moment. She had known she was going to miss him, but now his absence left a void that nothing could fill. Moreover, she missed action, the sense of having something important to do.

Needing to make herself useful, she accompanied Jacinta to the market each day and explored the local shops to see what they might have to offer in the way of dress fabric. Her trunks had not yet arrived and there was no absolute certainty of their doing so. In consequence, her wardrobe was drastically reduced, and she needed to furnish herself with some new gowns. The choice proved to be limited but she found two lengths of figured muslin cloth and some thread, with matching ribbon for trim. At least sewing new gowns would provide a worthwhile occupation.

'Perhaps you will have them ready by the time Major Falconbridge returns,' said Jacinta.

'Yes, perhaps,' she replied.

Seeing her downcast expression the other woman continued, 'You need not worry for him. He will come back. That one is like a cat; he has nine lives.'

Sabrina made no reply. This parting, though not wholly unexpected, had come sooner than she had anticipated. Being separated from him was like losing a part of her. It caused a lowering of the spirits quite unlike her usual buoyant self. Her abstracted air had not passed unnoticed in other quarters. Colonel Albermarle, with whom she was dining that evening, was sufficiently concerned to enquire.

'Is something wrong, my dear?'

Unable to open her heart just then, she sought refuge in a partial truth. 'It's only that so many days have passed without news of Ramon or Luis. I really thought they might have returned by now.'

It had been his thought also but he did not say so. 'If they have not there will be a good reason for it.' He regarded her shrewdly. 'It is an anticlimax, isn't it, coming back to routine after such an adventure?'

'I confess it is.'

'Look, I have to ride out to the Great Teson tomorrow morning. Why don't you come with me?'

Sabrina brightened a little. 'I'd like that.'

They went out early, and once on horseback again Sabrina felt her spirits revive. The morning air was sweet and cool and the company congenial. As they rode towards the hilltop batteries, Albermarle pointed out the repairs and improvements underway. Even at this hour the place was a hive of activity. Seeing so many redcoats she began automatically to seek for one in particular, even though her mind told her he couldn't possibly be there. Then she told herself sternly not to be such an idiot.

They returned to the house just before ten to see two horses outside, one a particularly poor specimen. Since she didn't recognise either, Sabrina assumed it must be someone seeking Albermarle.

'Possibly, my dear,' he said. 'I left word where I would be if needed, though I don't know anyone who owns such a nag as that chestnut. Never saw such an ancient, sway-backed, spavined, cow-hocked bag of bones in my life.'

The comment was not unjustified. The horse looked as though it might have walked straight out of the pages of a Cervantes novel.

'Perhaps it belongs to one of the traders hereabouts,' she suggested. 'I'll ask Jacinta.'

The two of them dismounted and went in together. They had no sooner entered the hallway than they saw the maid speaking animatedly to two men in dirty and travel-stained clothes. Seeing the newcomers she looked up, smiling. Then the men turned around. Sabrina's heart leapt.

'Ramon! Luis! How glad I am to see you.'

'Did I not tell you I would find him?' said Luis.

'I knew if anyone could, it would be you.' Sabrina turned to Ramon, examining him critically. 'Are you injured? Have you been unwell? We have been so concerned.'

He smiled ruefully. 'I am well, *Doña* Sabrina, I thank you.'

'Glad to hear it,' said Albermarle, 'but where the devil have you been, man?'

'I regret the tardiness of my return, Colonel, but it could not be avoided.' He looked at Sabrina. 'The day after I left you, my horse put its foot in a hole and broke its leg. I had to shoot it. Then I walked for three days more before I came to a farmstead where I could obtain another beast. Unfortunately, I had no money and it took all my powers of persuasion to make the man part with it. Even then I had to swear a sacred oath to return with payment.'

'It must be some horse.'

'Oh, it is.'

Light dawned. 'Not that ghastly old crock I saw outside?'

'The very same.'

Albermarle snorted. 'The rogue should rather have

paid you for taking it off his hands. It's a miracle you got here at all.'

'At times I did wonder if it would not have been quicker to walk.'

Luis grinned. 'When I met him he was not twenty miles from town, carrying the horse.' Then, seeing their expressions of incredulity, he added, 'All right, I admit I exaggerate a little bit. He was not carrying it just then.'

Jacinta threw him a quelling glance and Albermarle turned back to Ramon.

'Have you got the papers, man?' he demanded.

'I have them safe, Colonel.'

The collective sigh of relief was audible.

'Luis told me that my delay has meant trouble for Major Falconbridge,' Ramon went on, 'and for that I am truly sorry.'

'The matter must be rectified at once,' said Albermarle.

Luis nodded. 'By taking the papers to General Ward, no?'

'Ward be damned. Take 'em straight to Wellington.'

Afterwards, it was as though a load had been lifted from Sabrina's shoulders. The only cloud over her pleasure was that she couldn't let Falconbridge know straight away. A pleasant diversion arrived some three days later in the form of the previously abandoned coach, and with it her missing boxes. Having given the driver a handsome tip, she lost no time in having these carried upstairs. Then she and Jacinta spent an hour unpacking. Initially Sabrina had wondered what condition her things might be in, but, apart from a little creasing, the garments seemed to be untouched by the recent adventure.

It came as a relief. Although she did not want for funds, they would not have stretched to the replacement of almost her entire wardrobe.

Jacinta gathered an armful of dresses. 'I will take these for pressing. They will soon be as good as…'

The words were drowned by loud knocking on the door. Then they heard Luis's voice.

'*Doña* Sabrina, you must come!'

Her stomach lurched. Immediately her thoughts went to Robert. Had something happened to him? Was he injured? Captured? Dead? Dear God, not dead. She hurried to the door and threw it open.

'What is it? What's happened, Luis?'

'He is back!'

She let out a long breath. 'Thank heaven. Is he all right?'

'A little tired perhaps, and thinner of course, but otherwise all right.'

She stared at him. 'Thinner?'

'*Si,* but it is to be expected. Probably he has had a little fever. It is not unknown.'

Sabrina paled. 'A fever?'

Jacinta stepped forwards and glared at Luis. 'Who has a fever, you fool?'

He looked affronted. 'I did not say that anyone had a fever. I only said he might have had one, being thin as he is.'

'Why should Major Falconbridge be thin?'

'Not Major Falconbridge, woman.'

'*Idiota!* Who then?'

'Why, Señor Huntley of course. Who else?'

Sabrina went pale and red by turns. 'My father? My father is back?'

Luis nodded. 'That is what I have been telling you.'

He had no time for more because Sabrina was out of the room and running along the passage to the head of the stairs. She paused there a moment, her gaze searching the hallway below. Several men were waiting there. Among them was a man of middle years with greying brown hair. His face was pale and gaunt, the blue eyes tired. Though of upright carriage he was dusty and travel-stained and indisputably thinner, but she would have known him anywhere.

'Father.'

At the sound of her voice the blue eyes brightened and a tremulous smile formed on his lips. Sabrina raced down the stairs and across the hall. Moments later his arms were round her.

'Oh, my dearest child, how I have dreamed of this moment.'

'And I also.' Her breath caught on a sob. 'I thought I might never see you again. I feared you would never be freed.'

'I might not have been but for you. Major Falconbridge has told me what you did to obtain my release.'

She looked round and saw him just a few feet away and suddenly a lump formed in her throat. 'This was your mission. This is why you went out of town.'

'Yes,' he replied. 'It was General Ward who charged me with the office, but he had his orders from the very top.'

'Lord Wellington?'

'Apparently so. When he received word that the return of the English prisoners was imminent, he sent me to oversee the handover and to ensure your father's safe return. I did not tell you because I wanted it to be a surprise.'

'The very best of surprises. Thank you. Thank you from the bottom of my heart.'

'No thanks are necessary. It was my privilege.'

Sabrina didn't know whether to laugh or cry and ended by doing both. He smiled gently.

'You and your father must have a great deal to say to one another, so I'll leave you for the time being.'

Unable to speak, she nodded, dashing tears from her eyes with a shaking hand. Her father put an arm about her shoulders and then looked at his deliverer.

'Thank you, Major, for all that you have done. I am most grateful.'

'An honour and a pleasure, sir.' He bowed. 'Your servant, Miss Huntley.'

With that he turned and left them. Sabrina stared at the empty doorway, her heart full.

Falconbridge's mind was also agreeably preoccupied: Sabrina's joy on being reunited with her father had given him a very real glow of pleasure. That he had been able to contribute to her happiness in some small way, gladdened him immeasurably.

On leaving them he had delivered his report to Wellington, informing him that the exchange of prisoners had taken place without a hitch. It was then that he learned of Ramon's return and the safe delivery of the military plans. For a moment or two he wasn't sure he'd heard correctly. When his brain did assimilate the information, his overriding feeling was one of enormous relief. His lordship had no difficulty reading the expression.

'You did well, Major Falconbridge. The information was every bit as valuable as I'd hoped.'

'I am glad of it, sir.'

'It would appear that your faith in that fellow Ramon was quite justified.'

'I never doubted him, sir.'

'The feeling would seem to be mutual.'

'Sir?'

'May I say that you have inspired an extraordinary degree of loyalty among your confederates on the Aranjuez mission. Quite apart from a detailed explanation about why he was delayed so long, the chap was also quite tediously emphatic that what occurred was none of your fault.'

'Was he, sir?'

'Damn it, man, with a dozen like him we needn't have besieged Badajoz at all; we could have talked our way in.'

Falconbridge's lips twitched. 'I'm grateful for his support, sir.'

The hawk-like gaze held his. 'Then perhaps you should go and tell him that yourself.'

'I mean to, sir.'

'Good. Do it soon, would you? Then perhaps I might be left alone to get on with the organisation of this campaign.'

Falconbridge left the room, aware that he was grinning quite inanely but unable to help it. He would have gone directly to speak with Sabrina but tact forbade it. She and her father needed time together.

Thus it was another two days before he presented himself at her door. It was opened by Jacinta who informed him that her mistress was in the garden.

'It's all right,' he said as she made to accompany him, 'I know the way.'

He walked through the salon and let himself out

through the open French window, pausing a moment on the pathway among the brightly coloured beds. He saw her sitting on a stone bench by the fountain, apparently absorbed in a book. The sound of the water covered his footsteps until he was close. He paused, drinking in the details, realising that imagination had fallen well short of reality. The dusty and dishevelled companion of his travels was far removed from the feminine vision before him now. She was wearing a pretty pink gown that he had never seen before. It showed off to advantage the curve of a figure whose perfection he had glimpsed more intimately on other occasions. The golden curls were arranged in a knot on the crown of her head, and trailed artlessly over her neck and shoulders.

As if sensing that quiet scrutiny she looked up and saw him. Her cheeks paled, then flooded with warm colour. The book slid unheeded from her lap.

'Robert.' She rose to greet him, holding out her hands. 'How glad I am that you have returned.'

He lost no time in possessing himself of the offering, holding her fingers in a familiar warm clasp as he returned her smile. Then he enquired after her father.

'I hope he is in better health.'

'He is much improved having had good food and plenty of rest. Of course, there is still some way to go yet, but I am sure that it will not be long before he is fully restored.'

'Indeed I am happy to hear it.'

'I cannot thank you enough for bringing him back to me.'

'It was but a trifling service to escort him the last few miles home.'

'Not trifling to me,' she replied. 'You cannot know what it meant.'

'And I must thank Ramon. Lord Wellington told me of his return.'

'Is it not wonderful? I cannot tell you how it felt to see him come back safe, and with the documents intact.'

He smiled. 'I think I can imagine it.'

'He went straight to see Lord Wellington and put the matter right. He felt it was the least he could do in view of his tardy arrival.'

'His lordship informed me that Ramon spoke most eloquently on my behalf.'

'I am quite sure he did.' She was suddenly aware that he was still holding her hands. She really ought to free herself.

He drew her to the bench and sat down beside her. 'I have wanted so much to speak with you,' he went on. 'I have missed your company these last two days.'

Her heart began to beat much faster. 'Have you?'

'More than I can say.' He hesitated. 'If I dared to, I would hope that you have also missed me, just a little.'

She smiled, regarding him askance. 'Are you fishing for compliments?'

'Absolutely. Is there any chance I might get one?'

'No chance at all. Though I did miss you—a little.'

His eyes gleamed. 'Only that?'

'In truth, rather more than that.'

For the space of several heartbeats his gaze searched her face. Then he did release her hands, but only in order to take her in his arms. The precipice yawned at her feet but now it induced no desire to draw back. Sabrina closed her eyes and leapt, relaxing against him, surrendering to the embrace, wanting this. Her entire being delighted in his nearness and in the familiar scents of leather and cedar, and the warmth of his lips on hers.

Their touch engendered more erotic thoughts and blood became fire. Her mouth opened beneath his, soft and yielding inviting total possession. He tightened his hold and the kiss became deliciously intimate, but now there was no fear or revulsion, only a deep-seated feeling of belonging.

Eventually he released her and drew back a little, looking down into her face.

'How many times I have wanted to do that.'

'Have you?'

'Ever since the night of the ball.'

A small pulse leapt in her throat. 'Then it wasn't just a ruse?'

'A ruse?' His brows drew together for a moment. 'It may have begun that way, until I actually held you in my arms and kissed you. Then I realised that my feelings had grown deeper than even I had suspected.' He sighed. 'I had no expectation of their being returned, of course. You had made it clear that our relationship was to remain on solely professional lines.'

'I was afraid that if I did not you would think…'

'What?' he prompted gently.

'That you would think of me as Jack Denton once did. I could not bear to see you look at me like that.'

'My dearest girl, I would never look at you that way. You are most precious to me.' He drew her to his breast, pressing his lips to her hair. 'I think I did not know how precious until I saw you in Machart's clutches. The thought of any man doing you harm is intolerable. If I had my way you would never be harmed again.'

'Nor would I see harm come to you,' she replied.

'I imagine that was not always the case.'

'True. The first time I met you I confess I could cheerfully have wrung your neck.'

'Ah.' He pulled back enough to look into her eyes. 'And now?'

'I have no wish to, even though this behaviour can hardly be described as professional.'

'I'm afraid it's about to become even less so.'

Without warning Sabrina was tipped back into the crook of his arm and for a while after that speech was impossible. When next he looked into her face all suggestion of laughter was gone.

'In case I'm not making this plain enough, I love you to distraction and can think of nothing else.'

The green eyes danced. 'That is shockingly unprofessional, sir, but I must tell you that the feeling is mutual.'

His heart performed a dangerously original exercise. 'It's clearly hopeless so there's only one thing to be done.'

'What do you suggest?'

'Marry me.'

The words brought a sudden surge of joy so intense that for a moment it eradicated all else. Sabrina reached up and brought his face down towards hers for a long, lingering kiss. Then she drew back a little in her turn. 'In case I'm not making this plain enough, the answer is yes.'

He grinned. 'Would you do that again, please, for the sake of clarity?'

The matter was clarified several times more before they came up for air.

'I would like us to be married as soon as possible,' he said then, 'but I know that there are other considerations.' He paused, choosing his next words with care. 'Perhaps you want time to get used to the idea of marriage. We have known each other only a short while.'

'How long does it take to know your own heart?' she replied.

'I think I did not know mine until I met you.'

'We have learned more about each other in those weeks than most people discover in years.'

'Then you would not object to our marrying sooner rather than later?'

'I want to be your wife, Robert. It cannot come soon enough for me.'

'Nor for me, either.' He gave her a wry smile. 'I gave you a wedding ring once before, and with precious little ceremony as I recall.'

'I still have it.'

'I'll give you a much finer one, set with diamonds perhaps.'

'If you don't mind, I'd like it to be the original. It has more significance to me than any diamonds ever could.'

'Are you sure, Sabrina?'

'Quite sure.'

'So be it.' He rose, bringing her gently with him. 'May I speak to your father?'

She nodded. 'It will doubtless come as a shock to him.'

'Then we will allow him some time to get used to the idea.' He grinned. 'A little time, that is.'

Chapter Sixteen

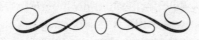

The wedding was to be a simple ceremony performed by the chaplain before a small number of witnesses. Falconbridge arrived early with Brudenell, but found it impossible to sit still and wait. Instead, he paced slowly the length of the hallway outside the chapel to try to dissipate the knot of tension in his gut. He heard the clock strike the hour but there was still no sign of his bride. The knot in his gut tightened. Was it all going to happen again? He shut his eyes and took a deep breath, telling himself not to be a fool. Brudenell eyed him shrewdly.

'She'll be here, Robert.'

He forced a smile. 'Yes, of course.'

'It's a bride's privilege to be late on her wedding day.'

'I know.'

'Then stop wearing out those stones and let us go in.'

He nodded and they walked up the aisle to take their places. Around them the assembled guests smiled, but he saw only a blur of faces. His throat was dry. With an assumption of calm he was far from feeling he took his place with his friend. As he stood there he found himself praying silently.

It seemed an age that he remained there thus, but in reality only a minute or two, before they heard a noise behind them, gasps and murmuring voices. Both men glanced round and then remained thus, staring.

'By heaven and all the saints,' murmured Brudenell. 'You lucky...'

Falconbridge hardly heard him and could not have replied anyway, for he had no breath to do it. For a moment he was quite still, his gaze taking in every detail of the woman who walked towards him, leaning lightly on her father's arm. She was exquisite, every detail perfect from the long-sleeved gown of white satin and lace, to the pearls adorning her ears and throat and the silk flowers nestling among her gold curls, to the small bouquet of red roses that she was carrying. His heart swelled with love and pride. Then, gathering his wits again, he stepped forwards to meet her.

From among the assembled guests Wellington surveyed the proceedings with a keen eye. 'Damned handsome couple, what?'

Beside him Albermarle nodded. 'Indeed they are, my lord.'

'Good man, Falconbridge.'

'Oh, unquestionably, my lord. I've always thought so.'

The ceremony was simple and short, a brief exchange of vows and the placing of the gold ring to bind them together as man and wife. Sabrina stole a look at the man who was now her husband and received an answering smile.

The chaplain smiled, too. 'You may kiss the bride.'

Robert Falconbridge drew his wife close and for a moment looked down into her face. His heartbeat accelerated as he read the answer in her eyes. Then he bent his head and brought his mouth down on hers in a tender and lingering embrace.

Sabrina closed her eyes. For a moment she felt light-headed, dislocated from reality. Yet the warmth of his hands was real enough, like the scent of leather and cedar wood from his uniform and the pressure of his lips on hers. Her blood tingled and, deep within, a flame kindled in her body's core. Its glow remained even after he had drawn back. In shy confusion she became aware of voices raised in congratulation and good wishes. Then his hand closed around hers and squeezed it gently.

'Come, Mrs Falconbridge.'

Colonel Albermarle had arranged for the wedding breakfast to be held in a private room adjoining the officers' mess where they were joined by a larger group of friends and colleagues. Carried along on a wave of happiness Sabrina was yet keenly aware of the goodwill emanating from those gathered around them. Many were Falconbridge's colleagues who had managed to arrange a few hours off duty and who thronged around to wish him well. Over his bride they were positively foolish, and she found herself the recipient of numerous compliments and gallantries.

Her husband smiled and, seeing he had no chance of claiming her for a while, turned his attention to Ramon who, with Luis and Jacinta, had been watching the proceedings with approbation. All three offered their congratulations. Luis blinked away a tear.

'You must forgive me. I always cry at weddings.'

'It is true,' said Jacinta. 'He does.'

Falconbridge grinned. 'It is a tradition, I believe.' Then, seeing his chance, he turned to Ramon. 'There is something I would like to ask, if I may.'

The other man nodded. 'You can ask.'

'How did you persuade El Cuchillo to help us?'

For a moment Ramon was silent. Then he smiled faintly. 'I called in a favour.'

'I see. You've known him some time, I collect.'

'We go back a long way, he and I. We grew up in the same village.'

'Ah, you were old friends then.'

'We were never friends. I might even say we detested each other. Certainly we had numerous fights when we were boys. By the time we were young men we each had a healthy respect for the other.' Ramon paused. 'Then, one day, his family's house caught fire, trapping his mother and sister within. I had been working nearby and saw the smoke. When I went to investigate I heard the screams, so I broke in and managed to help them to safety.'

'And so you and he became friends in the end, eh?' said Luis.

Ramon smiled ruefully. 'No, we were never that exactly. All the same, he saw the rescue as divine inter-vention and believed himself obligated to me as a result. He went to the church and swore a sacred oath before the altar that one day he would repay the debt.'

Luis frowned. 'How long ago was that?'

'Twenty years.'

'His memory is long.'

'So is mine.'

'How could you be sure that he would keep his word?' asked Luis.

Jacinta met his eye with a level stare. 'Time does

not affect a sacred promise. To break it would dishon-
our himself and his family, and imperil his immortal
soul.'

'That is so,' replied Ramon. 'But, more than all of
that, El Cuchillo hates the French as much as he loves
a fight. He would never pass up such an opportunity.'

Falconbridge laughed. 'Whatever his motivation, I
am glad of it, believe me.'

Watching the little group from across the room,
Sabrina smiled. In that moment it truly felt as if all her
family were gathered again at last. It seemed, too, that
happiness was infectious. All around her, laughter and
banter flowed like wine. Even her father was smiling
and doing his best to look cheerful, though she knew
that inwardly he felt sad, too.

'You need not worry for me,' she said. 'Truly I have
married the best of men.'

He squeezed her hand. 'I could not have parted with
you had I not thought so, my dear.'

As soon as Sabrina had expressed her wish to marry,
he had lost no time in speaking with Albermarle to find
out all he could about his prospective son-in-law. The
conversation had proved to be reassuring, rather than
otherwise, and he had taken comfort from it. Sabrina's obvious happiness and her new husband's evident
love and pride did much now to alleviate any lingering
doubts.

For his part Falconbridge had taken as much time
as he could to get to know his wife's father and, when
they did speak, to be as open and honest as possible. It
had done him no disservice. Nor did he find John Huntley's company in any way irksome. Both men were well
travelled and well read and thus had enough common
ground to be able to converse with ease. Though he yet

detected some faint reserve in Huntley's manner, he had every hope of their becoming the best of friends.

Colonel Albermarle waited for his moment and, seeing it, lost no time in taking Falconbridge aside to wish him happiness. The two shook hands heartily.

'I thank you for your good wishes.'

'Look after her, my boy.'

'I intend to, sir.'

'And be sure to make her happy.'

'I promise to do my best.'

Albermarle's eyes glinted. 'You'd better.'

'I know.' Falconbridge smiled wryly. 'I am also much attached to my liver and shall not give you any reason to try to remove it, sir.'

The older man beamed. 'I think we understand each other very well.'

'I believe we do.'

The meal progressed in an atmosphere of conviviality. Later there were speeches and numerous toasts were drunk to the bride and groom. Then, somewhat unexpectedly, Lord Wellington got to his feet. As the conversation faded he turned to the newly-weds.

'I shall not repeat what others have said before, although I share their sentiments unreservedly. It merely remains for me to give you this.' He drew a heavy, sealed pack of official papers from the pocket of his coat and handed it to the groom. Then, as the latter stared at it and him in silent bemusement, he added, 'Congratulations, Lieutenant Colonel Falconbridge.'

For a moment there was silence before the import dawned and the room erupted with cheers. Gathering his wits, the recipient got to his feet and shook the proffered hand. 'I really don't know what to say, my lord, except to thank you.'

Wellington raised an eyebrow. 'You may wish you hadn't when we make our push for Salamanca.' For a moment the hawk-like gaze rested on the other man. 'In the interim, you will want to be with your lovely wife. Take three days' leave. That's an order.'

'Yes, my lord.'

Sabrina who had been following every word felt only swelling joy. Three days! Never would she have foreseen anything like this. It was a gesture as generous as it was unexpected. Before she had time to do more than add her thanks, her husband gathered her in his arms and bestowed on her a resounding kiss. She smiled up at him, eyes shining.

'Congratulations, Robert. I'm so proud of you.'

'I could not have done it without you.'

'I keep thinking I shall wake in a moment, and find all this a dream.'

'No dream, my love, but the start of our life together.'

'A wonderful start,' she replied. 'I little thought to be as happy as I am now.'

'I want you to be happy, Sabrina. I will try by every means to make you so.'

She stood on tiptoe and kissed him softly on the lips. Suddenly he found himself longing for the time when they would be alone. The touch of her hand in his, the scent of her perfume, the warmth of her smile went to his head like wine.

Sabrina saw the intent expression and regarded him quizzically. 'You seem rather pensive.'

He grinned. 'You're right. Indeed, I could get locked up for the thoughts in my mind at this moment.'

Her eyes danced. 'Not more unprofessional thoughts?'

'Shockingly so.'

The implications set every sense alight and the knowledge that she would share his bed this night added spice to what had been the happiest of days.

In fact it was not until much later that they returned to the house. Her father had retired long since and the place was quiet. At last they reached the sanctuary of her room and locked the door behind them. Then he took her in his arms for a long and lingering kiss.

'I've wanted to do that all day,' he said then. 'Amongst other things.'

The green eyes expressed apparently innocent interest. 'Oh? What other things?'

Never taking his eyes from her face, he shrugged off his jacket and tossed it over a chair. It was followed by his neckcloth and shirt. At the sight of the hard-muscled torso beneath, her breathing quickened. He moved towards her. Then, turning her gently, he reached for the buttons of her gown and unfastened them. With slow care he slid the fabric over her shoulders and drew off her gown, laying it aside before returning to her petticoat. He unfastened that, too, sending it the way of the gown. With the same unhurried care he removed the pins that held her hair and let it fall, shaking it loose and sliding his fingers through its silken length.

She saw him bend his head and felt his lips on the hollow of her shoulder, travelling thence to her neck and throat and then the lobe of her ear, nibbling gently and sending a delicious shiver the length of her body. He drew her closer for another kiss, his free hand brushing her breast, gently teasing the nipple. She shivered again but not with fear, drawing him close, her hands exploring the muscles of his back, breathing his scent, tasting his mouth on hers.

She could feel his arousal but now there was no fear or disgust, only desire and an answering heat in her loins. She felt him lift the hem of her chemise and then the warmth of his fingers on her thighs and buttocks, stroking, caressing, raising sensations of delight that she had not known existed. He moved to the place between her thighs, drawing a finger slowly through the slippery wetness it encountered there. He heard her gasp, continued stroking, teasing, feeling the shudder through her body and his own hardening response.

An arm slid around her waist and another under her knees, lifting her with consummate ease and carrying her to the bed. He removed the rest of his clothing and came to join her, resuming what he had begun, restraining his passion to increase hers. Very gently he drew the chemise upwards, letting his gaze drink in the details.

'You are so beautiful.'

A rosy flush bloomed along her skin. He pulled the garment higher and she moved to accommodate him, so that he could remove it altogether. The immediacy of her nakedness against his both thrilled and shocked her as the length of his body pressed against hers. His hands resumed their caresses, gentle, sure and infinitely disturbing. With thumping heart she felt him part her thighs, and slowly he entered her. It hurt and she experienced a moment of panic, fighting him. With infinite patience he brought her back, stroking her gently, whispering reassurance. Then the moment was past and he pushed deeper until she had the length of him. She felt him move then, slowly at first but gradually with stronger and more powerful strokes. The movement sent a series of shivers through her body's core. Instinctively she raised her knees, closing her legs around him, moving with him, surrendering completely to the mounting fire in her blood.

He felt her shudder but held back, controlling the urge that would give rein to lust, knowing he must do nothing that would frighten or disgust; tonight she would know only pleasure at his hands, and the desire for more. For a moment or two he was still, holding her there, making her wait. He felt her writhe beneath him, panting, her fingers clutching his arms, her eyes darkened to emerald now as she yielded to her own passion. Slowly he resumed, rocking gently against her, stroking internally, hearing her sharp intake of breath. He continued until another, deeper shudder shook her body; then another and another. He bit back a groan, thrusting into her, letting the rhythm build. He heard her cry out, felt her nails rake his back as she arched against him. And then restraint was gone and power surged in the sudden hot rush of release. He cried out, experiencing a sensation of delight so fierce he thought it might stop his heart. For a little while he remained inside her, not wanting to let this go. Then, breathing hard, he lowered himself onto his forearms, brushing sweat from his forehead, and slowly withdrew to collapse beside her.

Sabrina lay still, her mind oblivious to everything except joy. She had wanted this but had never imagined how marvellous it might be, for nothing in this experience had borne any resemblance to what had gone before. Deliciously sated, she closed her eyes and smiled.

'That was wonderful.'

'Yes, it was,' he replied. 'And it will become more wonderful still.'

It was the truth. Having wanted her from the first he

had expected to enjoy this, but had never anticipated the intensity of the joy he would feel.

She turned her head and smiled. 'More unprofessional thoughts?'

'Quite disgracefully so.'

Far from alarming her, the words gave rise only to a sense of pleasurable anticipation. This love-making was so different from anything she could have dreamed. Sated and drowsy she snuggled closer and closed her eyes, letting herself drift. She was vaguely aware of a light kiss on her shoulder and smiled faintly, slipping into a blissful doze.

For some time he lay awake, watching her sleep, his gaze taking in each loved detail of her face and the soft rise and fall of her breathing. As he did so the last shadows of the past dissolved and vanished. What took their place was a soft, warm radiance that filled his heart and soul with hope. Life had given back far more than had ever been lost. He smiled; what he had won was treasure beyond counting and he would guard it with his life, for without it his own meant nothing. Taking care not to waken her, he curled his body around Sabrina and held her close. Thus embracing his future, he, too, slept.

* * * * *